# All's Fair in Love and War

## Also by Virginia Heath

**THE MERRIWELL SISTERS**
*Never Fall for Your Fiancée*
*Never Rescue a Rogue*
*Never Wager with a Wallflower*

*The Discerning Gentleman's Guide*
*Redeeming the Reclusive Earl*
*Miss Bradshaw's Bought Betrothal*
*The Scoundrel's Bartered Bride*
*Her Enemy at the Altar*
*His Mistletoe Wager*
*That Despicable Rogue*

**THE WILD WARRINERS SERIES**
*A Warriner to Protect Her*

*A Warriner to Rescue Her*
*A Warriner to Tempt Her*
*A Warriner to Seduce Her*

**THE KING'S ELITE SERIES**
*The Mysterious Lord Millcroft*
*The Uncompromising Lord Flint*
*The Disgraceful Lord Gray*
*The Determined Lord Hadleigh*

**THE TALK OF THE BEAU MONDE**
*The Viscount's Unconventional Lady*
*The Marquess Next Door*
*How Not to Chaperone a Lady*

# All's Fair in Love and War

*A Novel*

**VIRGINIA HEATH**

ST. MARTIN'S GRIFFIN
NEW YORK

First published in the United States by St. Martin's Griffin, an imprint of St. Martin's Publishing Group

ALL'S FAIR IN LOVE AND WAR. Copyright © 2024 by Susan Merritt. All rights reserved. Printed in the United States of America. For information, address St. Martin's Publishing Group, 120 Broadway, New York, NY 10271.

www.stmartins.com

Designed by Gabriel Guma

Library of Congress Cataloging-in-Publication Data

Names: Heath, Virginia, 1968– author.
Title: All's fair in love and war : a novel / Virginia Heath.
Other titles: All is fair in love and war
Description: First edition. | New York : St. Martin's Griffin, 2024. | Series:
    Miss Prentice's protegees ; 1
Identifiers: LCCN 2023057979 | ISBN 9781250896070 (trade paperback) |
    ISBN 9781250896087 (ebook)
Subjects: LCSH: Governesses—Fiction. | LCGFT: Romance fiction. | Novels.
Classification: LCC PR6108.E1753 A79 2024 | DDC 823/.92—dc23/eng/20240104
LC record available at https://lccn.loc.gov/2023057979

Our books may be purchased in bulk for promotional, educational, or business use. Please contact your local bookseller or the Macmillan Corporate and Premium Sales Department at 1-800-221-7945, extension 5442, or by email at MacmillanSpecialMarkets@macmillan.com.

First Edition: 2024

10  9  8  7  6  5  4  3  2  1

For Greg

Because I needed to write a hero who was 90% free spirit and 10% no compromise, just like you, lol x

*England expects every man will do his duty. . . .*

—Vice Admiral Horatio Nelson

## Chapter
# ONE

⚜

*G*eorgie stared up at the strange building while her stepfather's latest dour housekeeper supervised the unloading of her things from the back of the hackney.

It didn't look like a school.

A school would surely be more imposing than this neat white townhouse on the unfashionable outskirts of Mayfair. At least, unfashionable was what the driver had claimed it was when they had swapped conveyances from the Ipswich post an hour ago, although the area still looked very smart to her. Certainly smarter than she was used to, at any rate.

"Well, what are you waiting for, girl?" The housekeeper waved her forward. "Knock on the door and go in! I haven't got all day."

Georgie put her foot on the first step, then paused, anxious. "Are you sure we have the right address?" Only this cheerful four-story residence, with its shiny black railings, pristine lace curtains, and sparkling windows did not seem to be the sort of place her miserly stepfather would send her to. But then again, her being sent away to school in the first place had been grossly out of character for him too because the colonel did not believe in the education of girls, so this was all as bizarre as it was sudden. His housekeeper clearly agreed that something odd was afoot as she pulled the folded piece of paper from her reticule to check, then glanced up at the nearby street sign to be sure.

"Number three Half Moon Street is what it says here, so this is definitely it." Even so, the older woman still searched for a plaque of some sort and frowned when she found nothing. "This is your home now."

Was it?

The colonel had neglected to mention that when he had informed her she was going off to learn how to be a governess so that she could earn her own living one day. It wasn't as if Georgie was his, after all, so she could hardly expect him to be responsible for her in perpetuity.

"Will I be going back to Ipswich to visit for Christmas, at least?" Not that she really had a connection with anyone, bar a few of the friendly servants in his latest house, thanks to the nomadic life they lived due to his always more important military career. Nor was there any love lost between her and the man her mother had been forced to marry after she had been left a penniless widow, but still . . . Having all her flimsy ties cut with the place that was currently "home" was beyond daunting.

"You'll have to take that up with the colonel. My only instructions were to ensure that you got here in one piece."

The coachman placed Georgie's trunk on the pavement beside her with a sympathetic smile. "I'm sure it'll all be all right, miss." His wink did little to reassure her. "This is Mayfair after all, so how bad could it be?"

No sooner had he tipped his hat than the housekeeper had already turned back to the hackney, ready to climb inside.

A wave of panic hit her. "Aren't you staying with me for a bit?" Georgie had loathed the housekeeper for the entire two months she had known her, but right now, she wanted to cling to something familiar for as long as she could before she was cast adrift into the unknown again. This time completely alone.

"I've got to get back." There wasn't an ounce of compassion on the woman's pinched face. "I've got the colonel's house to run, so I don't have the time to mollycoddle you." She curled her lip in disgust in the exact same manner as the colonel always did whenever he deigned to glance her way. "You're not a child anymore, Miss Georgina. You turned sixteen today, it's long past time you grew up."

With that heartfelt happy birthday, the door slammed shut and the carriage lurched away.

Left by herself on an alien pavement, with not a single soul in the world who cared one jot about her, Georgie had the sudden urge to weep. In case she did, she sat on the tatty old trunk filled with all her hastily packed belongings and sucked in a calming breath.

She hadn't had a soul who had cared in six years, so that was nothing new, and this *was* vibrant Mayfair, after all, and not a joyless army barracks, so how bad could it be?

For good measure, she clutched her mother's locket as if her life depended upon it. Usually, despite having only fading memories of her mama, the dented gold pendant soothed her, but today, even that precious talisman wasn't working. She was too scared. Too confused by where she was and what lay ahead to find any comfort. Three days ago, before he had unexpectedly shipped her off, all the colonel had barked was that he was finally getting shot of her, which hardly filled her with any hope that her miserable lot in life was about to improve—even if this *was* Mayfair.

A big, fat tear drizzled over her cheek, and she let it fall. It felt like a final act of rebellion as the colonel had never had time for tears. The only emotions he made time for were disdain, disappointment, disinterest, or his customary outright disgust whenever she dared to open her mouth. She had concluded long ago that, seeing as any word she uttered, no matter how innocuous, seemed to infuriate him, she might as well be hung for a sheep as a lamb, so she had made sure each word counted. Defiant pride and rebellion were the only weapons she had in her pathetic arsenal, so she had honed both to cause the maximum impact. She had assumed that was how things would be until she reached her majority and had lofty plans of making a rousing, vitriolic speech before she flounced out of his oppressive house on the day she turned one and twenty. However, had she known that her recent outspokenness and tendency to poke fun at his pomposity would have ended with her swift banishment, she might have curbed her tongue and her redhead's temper.

Might have.

Even now, in enforced exile on this faraway pavement, she had to scoff at the preposterousness of that ludicrous thought. Curbing her tongue for that humorless, granite-hearted despot would have felt too much like surrender, and it would be a cold day in hell before she ever allowed that to happen. She didn't only hate him for herself—but for the complete disregard he had treated her dear mama with too, so good riddance to him! Good riddance to his frigid, disagreeable character and his latest soulless household and all his stupid, pointless rules! If the colonel was glad to finally be shot of her, she was gladder to be shot of him. In fact, if she ever saw him again, it would be too soon!

She steeled her shoulders and swiped the second tear away before she remembered that she was crying to spite him, and then decided that she would howl like a baby right this second, simply because she could. And she would have, too, if the shiny blue front door to the supposed school hadn't opened to reveal three beaming female faces, which were all about the same age as hers.

"You wouldn't happen to be Georgina Rowe by any chance, would you?" A pretty blonde was the first to bound down the steps.

She nodded. "I am—but I prefer Georgie to Georgina." Her stepfather had hated that nickname with a vengeance and had forbidden anyone to use it after her mama had passed, so it felt good to resurrect it. A fresh start for . . . whatever this was.

"I'm Lottie." The blonde grabbed her hand and shook it firmly, as if they were two robust gentlemen rather than two young ladies. "Well, it's Charlotte really, but *Charlotte* is much too formal and proper and I'm not quite ready to behave like a young lady yet."

"By that, she means that she doesn't know *how* to behave like a young lady because she has grown up in a house full of men and would still be wearing the beloved breeches she turned up in if Miss Prentice would let her get away with it." A brunette stepped forward and held out her hand. It was covered in ink stains. "I'm Portia." Her handshake was exactly like a young lady's should be, but as she let go, she winced at the navy ink all over her fingers and shrugged. "I am in the midst of writing a treatise reiterating everything Mary Wollstonecraft argued in *A Vindication of the Rights of Woman*, as I find it staggering that over two decades have passed and still nobody has thought to reform Parliament."

"She's our resident bluestocking." The other, slightly darker brunette pushed between her friends to shake Georgie's hand too. "And I'm Kitty—the resident disaster."

"Because she daydreams all of the time," said Lottie with a roll of her eyes. "That is how she spotted you out here during our first deportment class. She was gazing out of the window rather than at the tutor. She seems to do that a lot. I've only known her two days and I swear she's spent half of them wool-gathering."

"Are you new too, then?" Somehow that made Georgie feel better.

"We all are." Lottie gestured to the other two. "We four make up half of the new cohort of first-years." She included Georgie in the next sweeping gesture, and that made her feel better still. Part of something when she hadn't been anything but alone in forever. "We all arrived on Saturday, but Miss Prentice told us to leave a quarter of the wardrobe free for you, as you'd be coming later."

"You drew the short straw, I'm afraid, as you have to share a room with us for the next few years—or most especially, me. I shall apologize in advance as I am bound to drive you all to distraction." Kitty smiled and pointed to the windows on the third of the four stories. "That's our room right there. It's a bit of a tight squeeze with all the beds, but at least we get a good view of all the comings and goings of Mayfair and Piccadilly." She jerked her thumb in the direction of that busy thoroughfare, which was within spitting distance, and pulled a joyfully scandalized face, unaware the thought of staying in the same room for the next few years sounded like absolute heaven to Georgie. Thanks to the colonel, she had been forced to uproot and move every few months since the age of five. "It all seems to go on in Piccadilly."

"We should move you in before Miss Prentice returns." Lottie threaded her arm through hers. "She was expecting you tonight and will be most upset that she wasn't here to greet you personally—but she will be thrilled that you are here for afternoon tea. Afternoon tea is apparently sacrosanct here at this school and happens on the dot of three every day. Cook puts sultanas in the scones." Her new friend sighed as if she could taste them. "Miss Prentice insists upon it, as she is of the humble opinion that a plain scone is too dry. Now that I've tasted one stuffed with sultanas, I concur."

None of that sounded bad at all to Georgie. If anything, things definitely seemed to be looking up. She would have a permanent bed—apparently at least for the next few years—and seemed to have friends already. Three of them! All while being spared the depressing and oppressing sight of the colonel!

Kitty and Portia grabbed the handles of her trunk and led the way up the four neat steps to the house, leaving Georgie to follow, arm in arm with the lovely Lottie.

"Who is Miss Prentice?"

The three girls stopped on the threshold and blinked at her as if she had gone mad before Kitty answered, wafting her arms around the neat hallway. "Why, she is the proprietor and sole benefactor of this school. I'd have thought that you would have known that, seeing as she personally handpicked you to receive one of her coveted scholarships."

That was more news to Georgie. "She . . . picked me?"

"Of course she did," said Portia as she and Kitty dragged her trunk upstairs. "Miss Prentice's protégés-in-training are always handpicked, that is what makes them so special, so you should feel very honored to be one of us."

"That is Miss Prentice." Lottie paused on the stair before a portrait of a kindly faced woman with a profusion of silver curls. "She was an exceptional governess in her day, then in later years, went on to be a lady's companion and did such a good job of it that the old lady she worked for left her this house and all of her money. So obviously she set up a school to pass on her wisdom. By the time you leave here as a full-fledged protégé, Georgie, she'll have equipped you with all the skills you need to earn your own decent living. Everyone who is anyone knows that a protégé of Miss Prentice can command twice the salary of any of the other governesses, ladies' companions, or secretaries out there. Once we graduate, the world will be our oyster as we shall be the crème de la crème and highly sought after—just as she was. But that's because we are taught the Four *D*'s and all those other girls won't be *in the know*." She winked and patted the side of her nose. "It is the secret of Miss Prentice's unique success."

Lottie smiled at Georgie's baffled face and pulled herself upright to mimic the commanding air of what Georgie assumed was the mysterious Miss Prentice. "The Four *D*'s are the cornerstones of this school's proud ethos and every girl who leaves here epitomizes them to her very core—duty"—she counted them off on her fingers—"decorum, diligence, and discretion at all times." Her new friend giggled. "Although I have absolutely no idea why Miss Prentice handpicked me, as I currently possess none of those proper attributes."

Neither did Georgie, who was now more confused than ever by this strange, but seemingly fortuitous, turn. "But how could she handpick me when I've never heard of her, let alone met her?"

Portia shrugged. "So far, that remains one of life's great mysteries. I was stunned when my letter arrived out of the blue a few months ago. We all were, weren't we, girls?"

As they all nodded, Kitty took up the tale.

"All we know is that Miss Prentice is selective about who she teaches. Scholarships to this school come via her exclusive invitation only, and absolutely all her protégés have two distinct things in common." She held up her arm and pointed to it as if that held all the answers. "We all have blue blood lurking somewhere in our impoverished veins but possess none of the dowries or prospects or connections that usually go with it . . ."

*Chapter*
# TWO

꧁ ꧂

MISS PRENTICE'S SCHOOL FOR YOUNG LADIES, MAY 1820 . . .

*T*think it is time to face facts." Miss Prentice glanced at the latest rejection letter lying on her desk with a pained expression. "Interviews are not your forte, Georgina."

Unfortunately, that was a statement Georgie could not argue with. Eighteen months after graduating as a fully-fledged protégé, thirty-three interviews, and thirty-three similarly depressing rejections, it was looking increasingly likely that she would never secure a position as a governess anywhere decent. Or anywhere at all for that matter, as the current curt but cruel missive on her beloved mentor's desk was testament. The Steadman family weren't particularly good *ton* and didn't even reside in London, but desperate times had called for desperate measures, so Miss P had put her forward for the job in the hope that they wouldn't be too picky.

While that was humiliation enough, the uppity Lady Steadman hadn't tried to be polite in her rejection either. Instead, she had stated plainly that she hadn't given Georgie the job, not because there was a better candidate who had pipped her to the post, but because "regrettably, and despite her glowing references from the school, Miss Georgina Rowe had too much to say for herself and did not pass muster at all." The *at all* had been underlined.

Twice.

"What on earth did you say to upset this family?" It was clear Miss P's legendary patience was wearing thin.

"I am not entirely sure . . ." Which was a lie because Georgie had felt the palpable and frigid change in the wind the moment Lady Steadman had brought up the touchy subject of discipline early in the interview. "I very definitely did try to bite my tongue, exactly as you cautioned."

Two wily blue eyes locked with hers. "You tried."

"I most definitely did. I tried really hard to curb my regrettable and rash inbred tendency to speak my mind." The eyes were relentless now, boring into her soul to get to the whole, unvarnished truth. "I genuinely tried my best this time." Which she had—right up until the moment that she hadn't and the real Georgie had spoken.

But the most galling thing was that she had been working hard on suppressing that rebellious aspect of her character because there really wasn't a need for it now that the sanctimonious colonel and all his ludicrous rules were very much in her past. Georgie hadn't seen hide nor hair of her stepfather since the day he had dispatched her to Miss Prentice's, and she had no reason to rebel. Here, within these calming walls, were reason and affability. Voices were rarely raised because they did not need to be, and everyone treated everyone else with respect, no matter their age. Yet still, Georgie could not tolerate unfairness. She abhorred injustice, ignorant stupidity, and pointless rules. The slightest whiff of any of that and, as her friend Lottie was so fond of saying, she instantly turned into Joan of Arc. Fully armed and ready to march into battle.

"*Tried* implies that you tried—then failed." When Miss P glared, it was too potent a weapon to ignore. Georgie instantly began to wither beneath it until she could stand it no more.

"All right . . . we had a minor disagreement about the phrase 'spare the rod and spoil the child.'" An overused quote of the colonel's, usually before he threw something at her, which never failed to raise her hackles.

"Not again." Miss P's palm slapped her forehead before she huffed out a sigh of resignation. "How many times must we have this same conversation, Georgina? How many times do I have to tell you that vocalizing your principles aloud and acting upon them quietly in the background are two entirely different things? When the simple truth is a family hire a governess to keep their offspring from being underfoot and frankly do not care what methods that governess employs to keep the little dears quiet while she does it."

She could feel herself bristling again in zealous rebellion, because "children should be seen but never heard" was another one of the unimaginative colonel's lecturing mantras and yet another old adage she fundamentally disagreed with. Children should be both seen *and* heard. Listened to. Engaged with. Their rampant curiosity about everything nurtured and encouraged. Fed with all the answers and then emboldened to ask all the questions, even those that had no answers yet. Because, if history had taught the world anything, it was that independent thought was something to be celebrated, not oppressed.

Where would civilization be if some unique thinker hadn't invented the wheel? Or spread forbidden knowledge to the masses via the printing press? Or the brave souls through the ages who had drawn a line in the sand and stood up to the rampaging tyrants intent on taking what wasn't theirs? They would still be oppressed serfs living in the Middle Ages! Independent thinking and progress went hand in hand and . . .

Georgie almost groaned aloud as she wrestled St. Joan back into her box so that she could temper her answer. "Respect always commands more discipline than the rod ever could, and makes for a much better and more sustainable environment for learning." Georgie believed that to her core. "You have never been one for draconian punishments or rule by fear either, so I know you agree with me, Miss P. At least on the fundamentals." Even after seven years, Georgie still chafed against the rigid stricture of the Four *D*'s. Decorum and discretion, especially, had never come easy to her. "I politely tried to explain my ethos to Lady Steadman but—"

Her mentor stopped her with a lackluster raised palm. "An untried and untested governess has no right to claim an *ethos*, Georgina. Until you have put it into practice outside of these walls, and reaped the rewards of it, it is still a *theory*. An unproven one at that. That it is an ethos that I also happen to subscribe to is by the by in this instance. I have a reputation as a successful educator with decades of experience, and you do not. Not yet at least, and you will never achieve that reputation unless you actually get a job doing it, dearest."

"So I must pretend that I shall beat my charges within an inch of their lives if they dare to put a foot wrong to placate their disinterested parents? Pretend that I subscribe to all those silly old doctrines and archaic, nonsensical customs during an interview simply to get hired? Lie to a potential employer's face from the outset? Be disingenuous and dishonest?"

Miss P glanced skyward as if seeking strength from the heavens. "There is an ocean of difference between lying and tactful diplomacy, dear. When Lady Steadman suggested that you should not spare the rod or spoil the child, you could have nodded and said that you firmly believe that good discipline forms the foundation of a good education—because it does and you wouldn't be lying. No child will learn anything if they are allowed to run riot or swing from the chandeliers. Whether you use the rod to keep them in check or your yet-untested ethos will make no difference so long as the children learn. And so long as the chandeliers remain unswung on, and all appears on the surface to be running precisely as they envisage it, their parents are unlikely to ever set one foot into the nursery, so how you intend to run that is a moot point. Once you have their confidence, the nursery shall be your kingdom to rule over as you see fit. That has always been the way of things."

"Just because something has always been done a certain way does not necessarily mean that way is right." She believed that to her core too. How on earth could one embrace all the potential possibilities if one plowed the same old furrow day after day? Obviously, there should be rules and boundaries—but surely they, too, should have the capacity to bend and change according to circumstances. Change was always four-fifths for the better, especially when the march of progress was relentless.

"Of course it doesn't. However, the purpose of an interview is to make those parents see you as *employable*, Georgina. Taking issue with them during it is never going to get you the job—as this is proof." She picked up the letter and waved it. "You are an excellent teacher. The best I have ever trained—canny, adaptable, unflappable, intuitive, imaginative, and always top of every class. You possess that rare and unique talent of getting the best out of your students. That is a gift. A miraculous gift that I envy because I was not blessed with it. With your talent, you should have your pick of positions. Employers should be beating a path to your door, begging you to deign to work for them and weave your phenomenal magic on their children, yet you are the only one of my protégés who has never been offered a single position. In the decade since this school was founded, thirty-three consecutive rejections is a record, young lady, and not one that you should be proud of."

Miss Prentice had her there. If anything, Georgie was mortified by her abysmal record. Since she had technically graduated almost two summers ago, she had watched all her classmates secure positions and leave the school for better things. Her best friends, Lottie, Portia, and Kitty, had all been employed within weeks of their graduation. Lottie and Kitty had even been dismissed from their posts in the last eighteen months—in Kitty's case, repeatedly—and they still managed to quickly find reemployment simply because they were protégés.

Georgie had been forced to watch all the protégés from the year below her do the same. Soon she would watch the next cohort flap their wings and flee the nest and, if Lady Steadman's assessment was correct, she'd be left behind again because she did not pass muster at all. Which all rather suggested the fault for Georgie's persistent lack of employment lay squarely at her door. Or, more precisely, at her outspoken flapping jaws.

"I will get the next job, Miss P, I promise." She had to, because she couldn't impose on Miss P's charity forever despite her mentor never once telling her that she felt imposed upon. She also had to start her own life. Find her own place to belong. Not romance and family, of course, because impoverished governesses rarely left the station they had been forced into and hardly ever married, so she never tortured herself with those unattainable dreams, like her friend Kitty did. But there were other routes to happiness and fulfillment;

nurturing other people's children to be the best version of themselves
was hers. If only she was given the chance. "Even if it means biting
my wayward tongue so hard I snap it off."

The older woman smiled kindly across her desk as she rang
the bell for tea. "We can always live in hope, dear, can't we? In the
meantime, you might as well make yourself useful by taking today's
geography class."

---

*D*espite leaving for the Admiralty at the crack of dawn, it was
close to midnight by the time Harry's carriage dropped him
back home in Hanover Square. But it couldn't be helped. Not when
he had work coming out of his ears and not enough hours in the day
to do it all. The current bane of his life and the root of his growing
dissatisfaction with it, if one ignored keeping each of His Majesty's
ships stocked with enough supplies to keep them sailing, was the
HMS *Boadicea*.

Construction of the one-hundred-and-twenty-gun first-rate ship
of the line was running behind schedule. Grossly behind schedule.
It should have set sail on its training maneuvers two months ago,
and they had been postponed twice. If the shipbuilders continued to
drag their feet and they were postponed for a third time, he'd have no
choice but to visit the dockyard in Plymouth himself to give the lazy
landlubbers a swift kick up the backside.

Just the thought of heading back to Devon made him shudder.

Oh, how he loathed that place! It was filled with nothing but bad
memories, which he much preferred to forget, and his biggest humiliating mistake, which he couldn't. Every time he heard fresh news of
the bloody *Boadicea*, the specter of Plymouth loomed on the horizon
to taunt him, and it never failed to sour his mood.

He wouldn't have to think of any of those memories at all if it weren't for the bloody *Boadicea*. Those work-shy shipwrights had shilly-shallied long enough that if that troublesome ship wasn't leading the fleet by summer, he might well be the one to bring back keelhauling! A nice dunk in the Channel might encourage those slothful slackers to step lively. They'd had four years, for pity's sake, which was surely enough to build a whole flotilla of gunships? When he became admiral of the fleet, those who did not do an honest day's work for an honest day's pay would have no place in *his* navy.

But as the great military philosopher Sun Tzu said, victory comes from finding opportunities in problems, and that was Harry's particular skill. That was what the Admiralty paid him handsomely for and would soon, if he continued to impress them, promote him handsomely for too. Where others saw only the insurmountable, he always found a way around, even if he had to resort to blasting his way through! Or venturing to blasted Plymouth and the hornet's nest that awaited him there!

Annoyed, he bounded up his steps and then had to stand there because nobody came to open the front door. Harry was forced to hammer on the door until Polly, the young scullery maid, finally let him in.

"Begging your pardon, Captain, sir. I was tidying the drawing room and did not hear you." She bobbed an apologetic curtsy as he stalked inside, then stopped dead again at the haphazard mountain of mismatched luggage littering his hallway.

Instantly, his shoulders slumped because there was only one person on the planet capable of making this much mess—and that was his only sibling, Flora. The sheer size of the pile also suggested she wasn't alone.

God help him.

As a harried Simpkins finally made an appearance on the landing, his butler's tight, ever-so-slightly beaten expression confirmed his suspicion.

"Please tell me this is just a fleeting visit, Simpkins, as I'm still not fully over the last." When he had, once again, found a million excuses not to venture back to Devon at all last year, Flora and her chaotic brood had stayed for two weeks at Christmas, and it had, for want of a better phrase, been pure, unmitigated torture. Harry loved his older sister. Adored her, in fact, because Lady Flora Pendleton was as sharp as a tack, had a heart of pure gold, and a sparkling personality that lit up a room. Unfortunately, along with those admirable traits, she was also as undisciplined and disorganized as their bohemian artistic parents had been, and he could only ever cope with that amount of chaos nowadays in small doses.

Exceedingly small doses.

"Lord and Lady Pendleton are bound for Egypt until July, Captain, as his lordship's latest quest is to find the source of the Nile."

"Hallelujah! Somebody has to, so it might as well be him." Harry didn't give two figs where the Nile started, or where it ended for that matter either, but he was over the moon that an expedition to the land of the pharaohs guaranteed him several months of blessed peace from his family's unexpected and frequent invasions. Flora on her own was a nightmare. When you added her nomadic, scatterbrained, academic husband and her three practically feral children into the mix, that nightmare always turned into all-out Armageddon. The children, in particular, ran him ragged. Probably because the little Machiavellis knew that all they had to do was stare up at him with their wide, soulful eyes and he was basically putty in their manipulative, grubby little hands. They had made him read them so many stories over Christmas his voice had been hoarse for weeks afterward, and his left knee was still a trifle stiff from all the crawling around on the floor they made him do when he had stupidly allowed them to climb on his back so they could ride him like a bloody horse.

An irony which wasn't lost on him.

He'd slept on the cold, hard floor under the desk in his office at the Admiralty for two nights over New Year's simply to get some peace. "When do they leave?"

"I am afraid they have already left, Captain Kincaid. Your sister waited all morning to say her goodbyes to you, but had to leave several hours ago as her ship departs Tilbury on the dawn tide."

Harry stared at the scruffy pile of luggage in resignation.

How typical of Flora to leave for an ocean voyage without her baggage.

"Fetch someone with a large cart and pay the fellow whatever he needs to drive this lot overnight to Tilbury." He checked his left pocket watch and did some quick calculations in his head. Assuming high tide was in around four hours, and they could find a cart quickly—and the wind was behind it, the road was good, and they all prayed for a miracle—it might just get there in time. "Although knowing my sister, she'll pass it on the road when she realizes she left everything here, and we'll be stuck with her for days while she waits for the next ship to leave because she'll have missed the first."

Because of course she would.

That was Flighty Flora all over, and yet she would still find the wherewithal to laugh about it. His big sister found humor in every single catastrophe she created, whereas he would be having palpitations if he ever failed to make a sailing. Not because the Royal Navy did not take kindly to one of its most trusted officers going absent without leave—the top brass would have his guts for garters if he ever contemplated that again—but because he personally could not cope with tardiness in any way, shape, or form. Where the rest of his family would be late for their own funerals, and thanks to a rogue April blizzard, his father had been, Harry would have to arrive at least two hours early. Probably even six, just to be certain, as time had a habit of filling itself and his was always all accounted for.

That was precisely why he always carried two pocket watches with him wherever he went. Just in case one stopped ticking and he momentarily lost track of the time and missed doing something important. As Nelson had so aptly once said, time was everything and five minutes could make the difference between victory and defeat.

Or words to that effect.

It wasn't so much the exact words of the great military minds of the past that enthused him so, it was more the sentiment, and old Horatio's were on the nail regarding time.

He sincerely doubted Flora, like their mother before her, had one working clock in her anarchic home on the Devonshire coast, or even owned a clock at all, for that matter. If she did, she wouldn't be able to wind the blasted thing because she'd have lost the key, and any and every subsequent replacement. He and Flora had always been chalk and cheese despite the scant and unseemly nine months of difference in their ages.

It never ceased to amaze him that two children who came out of the same womb in such quick succession could be so different. Harry had always been an ordered, neat, and logical individual exactly like their grandfather, the admiral, had been, whereas Flora and her offspring were as different to that as it was humanly possible to be. She was all the worst bits of their mother and father combined. Scatterbrained, impulsive, and bohemian. With no respect for rules, routines, time, or boundaries.

No wonder the poor maid hadn't heard him when he had arrived. If the Pendletons had been in his shipshape drawing room for so much as ten minutes, it would be a miracle if it wasn't a scene of total and utter carnage.

He was too blasted busy to deal with all that malarkey now. He barely had time for dinner, let alone uninvited, unruly houseguests.

Uncharitably, he immediately contemplated how much it would cost to charter a vessel at Tilbury to take her to Egypt to save him the inconvenience of hosting them for a single night. Probably an arm and a leg, but it would be worth it. For the sake of his blasted sanity alone, it would be worth mortgaging this house if he had to, simply to be shot of her . . .

Something about Simpkins's agitated manner set a distant alarm bell ringing. His normally unflappable butler had a distinctly odd look about him. A look of foreboding which Harry had never witnessed before in the decade he had known him. They had sailed the seven seas together, for pity's sake, so he knew all of Simpkins's expressions well, and this new one made him panic. "What do you know that I don't?"

"Your sister *has* her luggage, sir, and so does her husband. This . . ." He wagged a nervous finger in the direction of the baggage heap. ". . . belongs to your nieces and nephews who, I was reliably informed by a most insistent Lady Pendleton, will be staying with their favorite uncle for the duration of her trip abroad."

"I'm sorry?" That raised every single one of Harry's battle-honed hackles. Surely he hadn't heard Simpkins right?

"Did you not get the urgent express I sent this morning stating as much, sir? The one where I asked you how you wished me to proceed?"

"Do I look like I know what the blazes you are talking about,

Simpkins!" Although now that he came to think upon it, there had been an urgent express, he now remembered. An express his clerk had brought to him the second it had arrived, and instead of opening it, as he patently should have, he had put it to one side. In his job, there were always expresses and most of them were storms in teacups which sorted themselves out before he needed to intervene, so Harry had ignored it. Had intended to read it in a free moment. Except there hadn't been any free moments thanks to the bloody work-shy layabouts who were supposed to be building the bloody *Boadicea* and all the other insurmountable problems the Admiralty kept sending his way. When he became admiral of the fleet, he would ensure there were at least ten men employed to do his job. Harry was spread too thin and stocking all those ships should not have rested on the shoulders of just one man!

Simpkins wrung his hands and began to pace, and that was yet another new and worrying behavior Harry had never witnessed before. Even under heavy American bombardment at the ill-considered and ill-fated Battle of Baltimore when he had been an exasperated lieutenant on the verge of mutiny and his butler had been the ship's quartermaster. "It was all in the message, Captain. I assumed you would come home to deal with it the second you received my missive as there really was nothing I could do to dissuade her. Lady Pendleton not only outranks me; she was resolute. She did not think it was prudent to drag them all over Africa at this time of year, especially with malaria so rife and with all the crocodiles, so she has left her children with you, sir."

"What!" It was a bloody miracle the top of Harry's head didn't explode with the volcanic fury of his anger. "Suddenly, after thirty-one years of possessing absolutely no common sense whatsoever, my sister has the gall to become *prudent*?" He began to stomp in outrage.

"What was she thinking?" Before Simpkins answered that, he stayed him with an abrupt raised palm. "She wasn't thinking, was she? Because Flora doesn't bloody well think! At least not rationally." One of these days, he was actually going to kill her. "I have a job, Simpkins! A career! People depend on me at the Admiralty, and I have a promotion to secure!" One which was long overdue but well earned. "I don't have time to look after her blasted children until blasted August!" No matter how much he loved the little monsters. Being a doting uncle whenever he saw them was one thing. Being left with them all alone, quite another.

"I said as much sir, but she said that she was due an adventure."

"Well, I suppose that makes this gross inconvenience all right, then!" His sarcasm came out high-pitched because blasted Flora and her bloody adventures had always been the bane of his life.

As children, she had insisted on dragging him on them too. Which was why he knew what it felt like to be trapped in a pitch-black cave overnight while the tide lapped at his toes. Why he had fallen thirty feet out of the oak tree she had insisted they build a treehouse in and had broken his arm. Why he had lost both his eyebrows during a failed alchemy experiment to turn a lump of pilfered lead pipe into gold. "I shall drop everything, let down everyone who depends on me, simply because my irresponsible sister is due another adventure! Does she not know that it is my job to feed the blasted fleet?"

"I did mention your enormous responsibilities, sir, but Lady Pendleton was confident that if anybody could juggle so many things in her absence, it would be you. She also thought the experience would be good for you." His butler instinctively backed away, in case Harry threw something in temper, to tell him the next bit. "*Practice*, she called it. To encourage you to get back in the saddle." Simpkins winced in apology because they both knew that hideous topic was totally out of bounds—to everyone, apparently, except blasted Flora. "Seeing as it has been four and a half years since your last fateful gallop . . ."

Before his head actually exploded in outrage under the fresh assault of those bad memories, the maid chose that moment to leave the drawing room. Much like him, she appeared to be at her wit's end. "I still can't get the jam out of the Persian rug, Mr. Simpkins. I've tried everything we have, but it's going to take more than soap to get that black currant off. But I did manage to scrub it out of the curtains."

"Which idiot gave them jam and allowed them to take it into *my* drawing room?" Harry stared first at the maid and then at Simpkins. "And please tell me that somebody is currently in the drawing room with the little vandals."

"In the absence of any alternative orders, I took it upon myself to put the children to bed, sir. Just before you arrived home. After the long journey here, they were exhausted and after several hours of trying to keep the unruly scallywags entertained, so was I." Simpkins squared his shoulders, a most stubborn glint in his eye. "If you had read my missive, the black currant could have been avoided and your sister would have been sent away with a flea in her ear *and* her children. Instead, she is already on board her ship and her children are now our problem until she returns in the summer."

"Over my dead . . ." The plaintive howl of what sounded like a wolf coming from the direction of the kitchen cut him short, and this time both Simpkins and the maid cringed as it continued unabated. "What the hell is that?"

"That would be Norbert, sir. The Pendletons' new dog."

"She's left me with a bloody puppy too!" If the reminder that he hadn't so much as fallen off the saddle as been kicked off it four and a half years ago hadn't been incendiary enough, then this was the last straw. Harry stalked down the hallway toward the howling as his butler scurried behind.

"Actually, sir, Norbert isn't . . ." Harry flung open the kitchen door and something gray, shaggy, and as big as a cow almost knocked him over in its haste to get out. "A puppy."

The hound's nails clattered across the parquet at speed, skidded at the staircase, then bounded up it in search of his owners, howling all the way.

As Harry gaped open-mouthed, the butler shook his weary head, all the fight in him gone. "Her ladyship said Norbert doesn't like to be left alone, mustn't be fed chicken as it makes him gaseous, and told me to tell you that he will need a decent walk at least twice a day somewhere with trees, as he will refuse to do his business otherwise."

"She has gone too far this time!" The understatement of the century. Harry's fury was so incandescent his fists clenched, but instead of unleashing it unfairly on Simpkins, he snapped open one of his pocket watches, then snapped his fingers. Time was tight, but he was a man on a mission with only one hope left.

"Have the carriage and a cart readied and put this pile of rubbish on it quick sharp, then go wrestle that devil-dog in behind it!" In the absence of his sister's neck to wring, he kicked a battered trunk. It had been packed so badly, the latch popped, and his two nieces' dresses exploded onto his mirror-polished floor alongside a battered cricket bat. "I'll fetch the children! I don't care what bloody time it is or how exhausted they are, their *favorite uncle* is driving the uncivilized, black currant–covered little rascals and their wolf to Tilbury and giving them all back to his infuriating bloody sister himself!"

Chapter
# THREE

꧁꧂

here is a gentleman in my office in urgent need of a governess." Miss P grabbed Georgie's hand and practically dragged her out of the lesson she was teaching. "*Urgent. Need.*" Excitement danced in her wily blue eyes. "I've told him I have somebody he can interview straightaway!"

"What?" Prospective employers did not usually visit the school without an appointment. Furthermore, the hiring of governesses was usually done by the lady of the house, so a man here who wasn't either delivering or fixing something was a rarity indeed. "What is a gentleman doing here?"

Miss P tugged her into the empty dining room, then frowned as she began to fuss with Georgie's hair, which was doubtless doing its own thing wildly—as usual. "His name is Captain Henry Kincaid, grandson of the famous Admiral Augustus Gaunt, no less."

"I've never heard of either of them."

Miss P rolled her eyes. "Admiral Gaunt was the commander in chief of the Channel Fleet for over a decade." When that was met with Georgie's blank expression, she rolled her eyes again. "He basically spent his entire life saving us from the threat of a French invasion, dearest, back when I was your age and none of us dared trust the French as far as we could throw them, thanks to all their guillotines and revolutionary ideas. A very important man at the Admiralty in his day, and now his grandson seems to be following suit as he is apparently very high up in the Admiralty too. So high up they cannot possibly spare him. He needs a temporary governess to look after his sister's children who have unexpectedly been left with him. Lord Bishop from the War Office personally recommended our school; hence he is here. *Here* and quite obviously desperate." She gave up trying to rectify the calamity of Georgie's hair to neaten Georgie's dress instead, then centered her locket before holding her out at arm's length. "This is your chance to finally prove yourself, Georgina! Serendipity! I can feel it in my bones."

"But I'm not prepared for an interview. I haven't planned a thing to say . . ."

"I know. Isn't that marvelous?" Miss P yanked her back into the hallway toward her office. "Even better, it gives me a perfectly valid reason to be in the interview with you to keep your wayward tongue in check."

"Well, I—"

Miss P cut her off with a finger to the lips as they stopped dead outside her closed door. "Speak only when spoken to, but do not be a church mouse either. You are a *protégé*, so sit up straight and look him in the eye. Be confident—but humbly so. An expert in your field but not a know-it-all. Keep your questions to a minimum and your opinions to yourself. Better still, ask no questions, as you are bound to ask the wrong one."

"Perhaps it would be easier if I played mute!" What she had meant as outraged sarcasm, Miss P gave considered thought.

"Oh yes! That is a much better idea. Silence is golden, after all, and the less you say, the less chance there is of you saying the wrong thing. And for pity's sake, just this once, try to remember what we stand for." Her finger wagged in time with each of her next words. "Duty. Decorum. Diligence. Discretion. In your case, let us also add *diplomacy* too." The finger prodded Georgie just above her straight-ened locket. "Before you open that big, outspoken mouth of yours, look to me first. Follow my lead. And for goodness' sake, curb your redhead's fiery temper and bite your wayward tongue!" With that, she flung open the door and sailed in, smiling regally as if she owned the place, which, to be fair to Miss P, she did.

"Captain Kincaid, thank you so much for waiting." The captain was seated with his back to her, but that rear view alone was impres-sive. He positively dwarfed the chair and when he politely stood, she realized why. He was well over six feet and she had never seen such an immaculate coat tailored so perfectly to a torso. Atop the broad shoulders that filled it was a dark head, which turned slowly to reveal a face that could well have been chiseled out of marble by Michel-angelo, such was its symmetry. His gaze swept her up and down in one fast, fluid motion before he blinked rapidly, clearly disappointed at what he saw. "Allow me to introduce you to Miss Georgina Rowe."

He quickly masked his obvious surprise at her horrid carrot-colored hair and woeful lack of height. "Miss Rowe." He bowed with all the precise elegance one would expect from a military man, his deep brown eyes never once leaving hers as he did so. They were intelligent eyes. Overly serious. Perhaps even judgmental. Assessing her so thoroughly she felt exposed beneath the intensity of his gaze. "Thank you for agreeing to see me at such short notice."

Georgie bobbed a self-conscious curtsy that annoyed her be-cause she wasn't usually a shy or nervy person. Yet for some reason before him, she was suddenly both. Maybe because his stiff, unyielding military bearing was too familiar. Anything that reminded her of the colonel always unsettled her. Was this captain another colonel? Possibly—her gut told her probably—but she would be gracious and give him the benefit of the doubt. It would not be fair to make a snap judgment simply because the man in front of her had the right to wear a uniform. Although he was commanding enough not to need one to impress.

"It was no trouble at all, Captain Kincaid." That said, there seemed little point in not concluding that when he did wear it, he would wear his uniform very well. He was the sort of man whose outstanding appearance was guaranteed to turn a lady's head. Thankfully, Georgie had never been that shallow.

She wasn't blind, though, so she obviously noticed all of Captain Kincaid's overt, masculine charms, but as she had grown up around handsome men in uniforms and had lived beneath the roof of one who only lived for his, she was quite immune to shiny brass buttons and ceremonial trim. Besides, after the colonel, hell would have to freeze over before her discerning head would ever turn for a military man!

"Shall we sit?" As he had already been assigned the chair opposite the desk, Miss P grabbed the spare chair she kept in the corner for Georgie and positioned it directly next to her own. In front of it was a tray containing her best Sèvres tea set. "Georgina—will you pour for us all while the good captain here explains his unique predicament?"

As that was clearly a test to show the captain how adept she was at the correct social niceties, Georgie did her best to summon her inner duchess while she prepared three cups. All the while keeping one eye on him and her own gaze as serene and competent as she could make it.

"Indeed . . ." He waited for both ladies to sit before he did, then settled back into the chair with the quiet confidence of one used to being in charge. Big hands loosely clasped in his lap. One ridiculously long, booted leg crossed over the other. The fabric of his perfectly tailored buff breeches pulled taut over thighs that were clearly no stranger to exercise. "As I have already explained to Miss Prentice . . ." He said that as if he was a little put out at having to repeat himself and then waved away the offer of sugar in his tea when Georgie held up the tongs, as if sugar was a silly frippery he had no time for. Both things were so reminiscent of the colonel she had to suppress her rebellious scowl.

"Due to entirely unforeseen circumstances, my two nieces and nephew are currently staying with me while their parents are abroad. As they are gone to *Egypt* . . ." Maybe it was Georgie's imagination, but she was certain his jaw clenched slightly at that. "I do not expect them to return for at least three months. Maybe longer." She hadn't imagined it because it clenched again. Exactly like the colonel's used to when his ordered life was inconvenienced. "As I am a busy man, I urgently need the services of a good governess to take care of them in their mother's absence. I certainly cannot spare the time as the Admiralty takes all of it."

While Georgie decided her snap judgment of this pompous officer had been entirely accurate, Miss P nodded at him in sympathy. "You have come to the right place, Captain Kincaid, although usually at this time of the year, all my girls would be gone. I would not normally consider allowing anyone to borrow dear Georgina here from me under any circumstances—she is invaluable, you see. Practically my right-hand. But as this position is only temporary, I *might* be persuaded to make an exception."

As Georgie handed him his tea, Captain Kincaid leaned forward slightly, and she noticed that he appeared to be sporting the chains of two pocket watches, one on either side of his sedate but obviously expensive cream silk waistcoat. She was on the cusp of asking him why that was when Miss P kicked her under the table as a timely reminder that she wasn't supposed to ask any questions.

"Why don't you tell us a little about the children, Captain?" Miss Prentice smiled as if butter would not melt in her mouth.

"Well . . . um . . . they are . . . um . . ." Clearly, he knew nothing about them if his rapidly blinking eyes were any gauge, as that question flummoxed him.

How typical of a puffed-up, self-important military man to be so oblivious of everything beyond his duty to king and country. And, of course, himself.

"Perhaps start with their names and ages—assuming that you know them." That flippant comment earned her another nudge under the table from Miss P.

"Yes . . . of course." He shuffled in his seat momentarily. "Felix—my nephew—is the eldest. He is ten and likes insects and cricket in that order." Bizarrely, the corners of the captain's mouth curved upward slightly. Almost as if he actually possessed some human feelings.

"I know it is unconventional for a boy to be educated by a governess, Georgina, as they usually go away to school." Miss P interrupted to pat Georgie's arm. "But under the unique circumstances, I have assured the good captain here that you are quite capable of providing a suitable curriculum for him as well as for the girls." Then she smiled at him. "Pray continue, sir. You were telling us about the children."

"Yes . . . well . . . Marianne is nine and fancies herself both an opera singer and a ballerina." The lips miraculously curved some more and drat him, the smile suited him. "Then the youngest, little Grace, is five and has so much energy she doesn't quite know what to do with it all." The wistful smile made him seem almost . . . tolerable, despite making him more annoyingly handsome. "Beyond bump into the furniture. Usually at speed. Fortunately, her bones appear to be made of rubber, so she hasn't broken one yet." As if he suddenly realized he was smiling, he sipped his tea to kill it stone dead. "Thank goodness."

"They sound delightful." Miss P said exactly what Georgie was thinking. Or at least part of what she was thinking because half her thoughts were still contemplating what Captain Kincaid's smiles meant.

That he could smile at all was, in all fairness, a massive point in his favor, as the colonel hadn't possessed any smiling muscles at all.

"They are." His half smile wavered until he nailed it back in place—making Georgie wonder if he were being entirely honest. "Of course they are. They are perhaps a tad boisterous at times . . ." Then, there was a touch of panic in his eyes. "But I am sure they are nothing that someone of the experience of Miss Rowe here cannot handle. Miss Prentice assured me that all governesses from this school are masters in the art of disciplining the unruly and are sticklers for running an ordered ship."

Before Georgie could respond, her mentor's foot came down on hers in warning. "Miss Rowe will be the undisputed mistress of her classroom, Captain, so you'll have nothing to worry about on that score. She is an excellent teacher. One of the best I have ever had the pleasure of nurturing. Your nieces and nephew will thrive under her tutelage."

"Splendid . . . *splendid*." His eyes darted to hers again—no doubt taking in her diminutive but depressingly sturdy stature and vivid, rebellious hair—and didn't look convinced. She would have opened her mouth to reassure him that she was far mightier than she looked and nobody should be daft enough to judge a book by its unpleasant orange cover, but Miss Prentice's slipper was still pressing down on her instep to remind her that she was supposedly mute. "Not that I have a classroom, or even a nursery for that matter, as I've never had any use for either. But of course I have the space for both if she needs them, and I shall equip them with whatever Miss Rowe sees fit."

Georgie felt Miss P stiffen. "Is there a Mrs. Kincaid, Captain?"

"No." When he saw the older woman's eyes widen, he caught on quickly that his bachelor status was a potential fly in the ointment. "But I have a cook—Mrs. Rigby—who lives in. As does Polly, the maid, so Miss Rowe will not be the only female residing in the house. Plus Marianne and Grace, of course. Not that two little girls really should be considered chaperones, but . . ." Uncomfortable, he lifted his cup again rather than glance Georgie's way in case even a glance would label him as a despoiler in Miss P's eyes. "I can assure you everything in my house is above board. I am an officer and a gentleman, madam, as anyone who knows me will attest." He took a sip of his beverage with the casual, commanding air of someone who was obviously beyond reproach, then almost choked on it at the older woman's next question.

"Is there a lock on her bedchamber door? For if there isn't, I will have to insist on the immediate installation of a sturdy one to which only Miss Rowe has the key."

"There isn't, madam, but obviously I will honor your request, as that is only proper." He now seemed so mortified by the implication Georgie almost felt sorry for him. Especially as she sincerely doubted that a man who looked like him had to resort to barging his way into short, uninspiring, freckle-faced, ginger-haired governesses' bedchambers to slake his urges. Not when some of the scandalous ladies of the *ton* were probably queuing outside his already. A tall, dark, handsome, and wealthy man, especially one who had the right to wear regimentals, would probably have to beat them off with a stick. "However, I feel that I must also reiterate that as an officer and a gentleman, Miss Prentice, I take both of those responsibilities with the utmost seriousness. And always have. As Nelson himself once said, one cannot be a good officer without being a gentleman."

Miss P pressed on her instep again before Georgie blurted out that the philandering Nelson was hardly the best example of gentlemanliness to quote from. "I am exceedingly pleased to hear that, Captain." As much as she minded biting her tongue, it was impressive to watch her mentor in action. Somehow, she had managed to flip this situation on its head and had turned him into the interviewee. Without skipping a beat, Miss P changed the awkward subject. "It goes without saying that you would want the children to be taught a broad curriculum that embraces the essentials as well as the arts and sciences. Miss Rowe has a particular specialism in the sciences. She is also rather musical and can teach your nieces piano if you have one."

"I'm afraid I don't." By his frown, he was now contemplating buying one of those, too, if it would help, but Miss P waved it away.

"Do you have any particular topics you would wish to see on her curriculum?"

"Er . . . apart from some much-needed decorum and discipline, not really." There was a long silence which her mentor made no attempt to fill, and the foot at the end of his crossed leg began to bounce. "I should probably mention that the children have a . . . dog." He stared straight at Georgie and there was that slight glint of panic again. "You are not afraid of dogs, are you, Miss Rowe? Only he is quite attached to the children and prefers not to be parted from them."

"She adores all of God's furry creatures, Captain Kincaid, so the addition of a faithful hound will hardly faze her."

Georgie nodded, and he exhaled with relief until the upright naval officer returned again with a vengeance. He stood, no doubt intentionally to regain the upper hand. "Splendid. When can you start, Miss Rowe?"

The foot over hers pressed down harder as Miss P nonchalantly sipped her tea. "I think we should discuss terms first, Captain, before *I* decide if Miss Rowe can be spared. One of my protégés doesn't come cheap and one of Miss Rowe's caliber comes at a premium—especially for a temporary position. There is a lot of upheaval involved, after all, for both this school and her."

He pulled himself up to his impressive full height, which seemed to add several inches to his already looming presence, the ferocity in his gaze so intense Georgie felt it everywhere.

"Whatever the going rate is for someone with such impeccable and impressive credentials, I will *double* it if Miss Rowe can move in by Wednesday."

"Will she get *every* Saturday afternoon off and alternate Sundays too?"

He did not bat an eyelid. "Yes, and I'll even pay her for them."

"Then congratulations, Captain Kincaid. Miss Rowe would be delighted to accept."

Just like that, and after barely uttering any words at all, she was finally employed. But instead of experiencing relief or even joy at that miracle, all Georgie felt was off-kilter.

*Chapter*
# FOUR

❧

*H*is house was an oasis of uneasy and unsustainable calm as Harry welcomed his new governess into it. He knew that blissful state of affairs was doomed to be short, so he was eager to dispense with his part in today's proceedings as quickly as possible. Before all hell broke loose again the second Simpkins returned with the mad Norbert, Harry wanted to be seated astride his horse and halfway to the Admiralty, blessedly unburdened by the unwelcome additional responsibility blasted Flora had saddled him with.

It was undoubtedly the coward's way out that labeled him the worst sort of uncle, and yet, as much as he adored the destructive little monsters and was starting to loathe the Admiralty, he was entirely at peace with it.

The last few days had been chaotic torture. Their lack of routine, responsibility, and structure was so reminiscent of his own shambolic childhood, before the admiral had rescued him and taught him the meaning of discipline, that he fully expected his roof to leak at any moment and the debt collectors to knock at his door to make the nightmare complete. Worrying about those things was ludicrous, he knew, as he had his roof thoroughly checked every September and he did not owe a single soul a shilling because, unlike his father and because of all his grandfather's strict but practical tutoring, Harry never spent beyond his means and paid every bill promptly.

His mother, on the other hand, might well have been the admiral's daughter, but she hadn't spent her formative years being brought up by him. Instead, thanks to his wife's rapid, tempestuous affair with a free-spirited and scandalous artist ten years her junior, she had been brought up in hedonistic and decadent disorder. Then had chosen to fall head over heels with a man much the same. Between her and his poet father, it was a wonder they ever managed to buy a house. That they managed to own it for the fourteen years it took for Harry to be able to earn his own wages to keep those debt collectors at bay was a blasted miracle. Twice, his mild-mannered papa had been taken away in irons to debtors' prison before Harry had turned ten. He had lost count of how many debt collectors hammered on their door over the years and how many times he had to suffer the public shame of watching more of the family's belongings get carted away. A decade and a half on and those old wounds were still deep. Deep enough that he had awoken twice this week in a cold sweat, convinced that he had traveled back in time and the bailiff was about to remove all the family silver.

"Welcome to Hanover Square, Miss Rowe."

"Thank you, Captain Kincaid. I am delighted to be here." The polite smile she offered was more reserved than delighted. Wary, measured, and assessing as she took it all in. He supposed he couldn't blame her for that. Not when she really had no comprehension— yet—of the battle she had agreed to fight. With some luck and a good wind, this small and seemingly humorless woman was everything the

lauded Miss Prentice had claimed she was and would swiftly implement the structure, routine, and discipline the children desperately
needed. Harry loved his sister as much as he loved her feral offspring,
but knew she wasn't the best role model for them if they were going to
succeed in the world as he had. Having them foisted upon him might
well be a huge inconvenience, but at least he could gift them with the
tools to help them learn some self-control.

He took a surreptitious glance at his new governess and almost
sighed aloud.

If one ignored her much-too-pretty face, overtly feminine figure,
and the striking hair that constantly drew his gaze—three things
that had, worryingly, taken his breath away the first time he had
set eyes upon her—Miss Rowe did not look commanding enough to
be able to control the little savages for more than five minutes, let
alone teach them any self-control. Frankly, it would take Joan of Arc
and the better part of her crusading army to defeat his indefatigable
nieces and nephew into civilized compliance.

They had certainly defeated him these past few days.

There was just too much of Flora in them, and by default, far too
much of his parents. Scatterbrained, undisciplined unruliness was
as ingrained in the Kincaids' blood as the spots were on a leopard's
coat, and those spots never changed. But he was hopeful some of it
could be trained out of them, at least in the short term. Enough that
he could survive this ordeal with most of his hair and sanity intact
until his blasted sister reclaimed them and his life returned to its
usual even, albeit overworked, keel.

Which all rather hinged on the success of the unimposing yet
strangely compelling woman standing before him.

God help them both.

"I have made arrangements for Mrs. Rigsby, my cook, to take

you under her wing this morning and show you around." Keen to get going while the going was good, Harry ushered her along the quiet hallway with a sweep of his arm as the groom dragged the first of her three enormous trunks upstairs. "The children have been told to expect their lessons to begin after luncheon today, so you have until then to settle in. I thought it only fair to ease you in gently." As Simpkins had quite rightly pointed out, they currently needed Miss Rowe more than she needed them, so it wasn't in Harry's best interests to scare her with the unvarnished, ugly truth straightaway. It would be harder for her to run screaming for the hills if she were unpacked and in the thick of it. "However, I personally wanted to show you the teaching space I have organized. I hope the preparations I have made meet your particular expectations—despite the short notice."

While still as reluctant to speak as she had been in her interview, Miss Rowe had been quite verbose in her subsequent letter to him in which she listed all the extensive paraphernalia she required to teach his unruly charges what she called "a broad and stimulating curriculum." Some he understood and approved of—dictionaries, atlases, and abacuses all made perfect sense. Some he sort of understood, as even the most diligent students needed some respite from the necessary rigors of mathematics and good penmanship. Therefore, he had been more than happy to purchase the paints and the easels and the long list of fanciful books filled with children's rhymes she had specified. Diversions he assumed she would use to fill the lesson-free Saturday mornings and church-free Sunday afternoons.

What she planned to do with all the magnifying glasses, scissors, string, ribbons, buttons, and colored feathers, he had no clue, but had purchased them anyway in case the absence of feathers caused an immediate change of heart that left him governess-less. Despite all his many, many, *many* reservations about the diminutive redhead beside him being up to the job he had been press-ganged into giving her, the alternative was terrifying. Four failed days of coping with them himself and he was already exhausted, and poor Simpkins could barely stand, he had been run so ragged.

"This is your classroom." He flung open the morning room door, quietly proud of the transformation he had achieved in such a short space of time.

Where he had once read his newspapers while he watched the sun rise over his beloved garden, was now a school room that even Eton would be proud of. Three sturdy desks sat where his comfortable Chesterfield had been, all strategically turned to face the wall so that his easily distracted relatives would not be waylaid from their studies by any birds or buzzing insects beyond the French doors.

That wall, which had once displayed a whimsical Gainsborough he had inherited from his un-whimsical grandfather, now housed a substantial chalkboard. Above that, of course, was a clock. As futile as it likely was, Harry had wanted a timepiece front and center in hopes that Miss Rowe could instill upon the little savages, in their disorganized mama's absence, the importance of time. Their inability to do anything, beyond spread carnage, in a timely manner since they had arrived had him pulling his hair out. Every single task they did apparently took them at least twice as long as what he deemed necessary to do it in. Even a simple stroll around the perimeter of St. James's Park—which usually took him a mere seven-and-twenty minutes at his usual brisk pace—had taken them all an hour and a half yesterday. Granted, a significant chunk of that was the stupid dog's fault—but still. Norbert's regrettable incident with the pie seller aside, the children had turned dithering and dallying into an art form.

Harry had been a spent force by the time he had wrangled them all back to the house thirty minutes late for supper. Slightly traumatized too by the ordeal, truth be told. Again, much of that was down to Norbert. Like their exasperating mother, Felix, Marianne, and Grace marched to their own drum irrespective of the reassuring, steady beat that the rest of the world dictated. That absence of haste, of purpose, or of any need for any rational, forward momentum, combined with their atrocious lack of self-discipline, made it easier to herd cats in fog than it did to shepherd three Pendletons on a simple lap of the park.

Everything about them was such a shambles that Harry genuinely dreaded to think what sort of adults they would turn into without this timely Flora-less intervention. Thankfully, before he had turned irreversibly into a shambolic Kincaid himself, the admiral had intervened when Harry had been around Felix's age. His grandfather had then instilled within him all the morals which had been so deficient in his parents and put him on a path of meaning and purpose in the navy. Thanks to the admiral's heavy guiding hand, Harry was the man he was, and if there was one silver lining to Flora's latest debacle, it was that he now had a chance to return that favor. He would use his guiding hand and solid, sensible principles on the children in the hope that he might be able to save his nieces and nephew from becoming full-blown shambolic Kincaids too.

With that in mind, as encouragement, he had taken the liberty of noting some pertinent times down the side of the blackboard to remind them that a happy, ordered life required a schedule. Their first lesson would start each day at nine sharp. They would be granted a short break of ten minutes at eleven, then work diligently till one when Mrs. Rigby would serve their luncheon. Then, suitably rested and replenished, the little miscreants would work solidly from two till five to maximize all the best hours of the day.

Then with any luck, and if Sun Tzu was right and the line between disorder and order did indeed lie in the logistics, the miniature hurricanes would be too tired from a day of hard educational yards to wreak too much havoc in the two hours they had left before their bedtime.

That was the planned course he had charted, and he had everything crossed that everyone would follow it.

He glanced at Miss Rowe again, hoping that she did indeed possess the spine of steel she would need for the voyage ahead and all his justifiable misgivings about her were unfounded. However, rather than being hugely impressed at his efforts to build her a classroom from scratch in mere days, he sensed she was unimpressed. Unimpressed enough that he felt an explanation for his reasoning was in order in the hope he could prize some gratitude from her flattened lips.

"Obviously, I faced the desks away from all distractions of outside." He gestured to the French doors. "However, please feel free to cover all this glass with paper if you feel it needs to be done. Or draw the curtains if you prefer."

A perfectly sensible suggestion which elicited a wrinkle of her pretty, freckled nose. "Wouldn't both of those things make the room a bit dingy, Captain? Darkness is hardly conducive to learning."

"No. I suppose it isn't." He could tell she already thought him a clueless idiot, at least where education was concerned. She was right, of course, as his own education had been as ramshackle and piecemeal as the rest of his childhood had been until the navy saved him, but it still made him feel foolish and pathetically eager to correct that assumption. "Perhaps a screen is the answer to stop their limited attention from wandering?"

She went to speak, then bit her lip while she nodded with polite insincerity. It drew his eyes to that plump, pink flesh and that in turn

made him supremely aware of his own lips—which was most disconcerting.

"I am sure we will manage well enough as things are." She bit
her lip again as if she wanted to say more but had decided against it.

"Er . . . um . . ." Harry wrenched his gaze from her mouth,
shocked that he had allowed his mind to be waylaid by it. "Luncheon
will be served at one sharp and the children's supper promptly at five.
Mrs. Rigsby will apprise you of the staff's mealtimes, as what goes on
in the galley is nothing to do with me."

Both Simpkins and Mrs. Rigsby would mutiny if he ever inter-
fered downstairs again and, after he had offered one suggestion too
many, he was banned from the kitchen if his formidable cook was
in it. It was, with the benefit of hindsight, a solution that benefited
them both. Mrs. Rigsby made the most delicious meals and kept tidy
accounts, and in return, whatever happened downstairs were, by and
large, blessed things he did not have to worry about.

Harry was all about delegating if he could entrust the person to
do the job properly. Unfortunately, experience had taught him that
most people needed managing. He hoped that Miss Rowe wasn't one
of them.

"Noted," said Miss Rowe, not noting anything down at all. "One
and five. Sharp."

"You will find all the equipment you requested in those boxes."
The numbered stack lived out of the way in a corner to keep the deck
clear. He pointed to the labels affixed to the sides of each, wondering
what it was about her that made him all flustered when he hadn't
found much to like about her so far beyond her seductive appearance,
and he certainly did not want to like her like *that*!

"For convenience and expediency's sake, I've listed what is inside of each." He had modeled the inventory on a ship's manifest, all

alphabetical and complete with a grid to keep an accurate tally of what needed replacing when things inevitably perished. "That way you can count everything out and count it all back in again." If the abacuses lasted a week in the clumsy hands of his sister's offspring, it would be a blasted miracle.

Her gaze scanned his comprehensive tally but still gave nothing away, making Harry feel once again that he was the one being judged, exactly as he had in Miss Prentice's study. Miss Rowe had watched him then like a specimen under a microscope. With open curiosity and yet still with complete and somewhat superior indifference. As if from that one meeting alone he had been weighed, measured, and found wanting.

It had been most unsettling at the time, and it still galled that he had handled that whole interview wrong. In his panic, mere hours after he had watched his blasted sister's ship sail toward the horizon, too late to stop her, he had been so desperate to secure a governess to handle the mess Flora had left him with that he had allowed himself to be—frankly—bullied. As a result, instead of putting Miss Rowe through her paces to ensure she was the right candidate for the job, it had been he who had to jump through hoops. Leaving him now in two minds as to whether he had been either blindsided or hoodwinked.

Aside from all Miss Prentice's gushing claims about her *indispensable* protégé, which he had no way of substantiating because he had been too befuddled by that meeting to insist upon further references, Harry knew nothing about the woman beside him. Nothing beyond the fact that she was punctual—a definite point in her favor—barely reached his shoulders, was too damn attractive for her own good, and was as sparing with her words as she was with her praise.

"Does this all meet with your satisfaction, Miss Rowe?" He was going to pry some acknowledgment for his efforts out of her distracting, pursed lips if it killed him.

"It is very ordered." He could not read any reaction at all in her very green eyes as she ran her fingertip over the neat pile of new books lining the bookshelf. A bookshelf Harry had personally dragged in from his study at close to midnight last night so that she had somewhere to store everything neatly. "Almost military in its precision."

Finally, she had noticed something he had done well! "I applied the same logic to this layout as I do on board a ship, Miss Rowe."

"A place for everything and everything in its place."

"Precisely." He smiled and when she failed to smile back, felt compelled to defend the process of his sound logic further. "Chaos only wastes time." Thanks to the unmitigated chaos of the last four days, he had wasted so much of it that it would likely take another week to just catch his tail. He had never been so behind in his work. For the children, it turned out, ate all his time for breakfast. And luncheon. And dinner. In fact, this ordered classroom had barely come about in the nick of time because it had taken him and Simpkins until close to one this morning to achieve, as it had been a particularly trying day.

The worst day of the four so far, and that was saying something when the previous three had been unbearable.

After a full day at the Admiralty, he had relieved a frazzled Simpkins of sentry duty as soon he had rushed home so that his second-in-command could have well-earned rest from herding the Pendleton brood, eat some dinner, and doubtless cry in a corner. Stupidly, Harry had thought it might be a good idea to take the lot of them out for a bracing walk to allow Norbert to do his business because the stubborn mutt refused to do it in the garden. Harry had hoped, fruitlessly it turned out, that the exercise would be all it took to get the disorderly brood in the mood for bed. Two birds, as it were, and one stone.

In theory, it had been a sound plan.

In practice, it turned out, not so much. Largely because he had foolishly failed to factor in Norbert's talent for sniffing out food or the brute strength he could unleash to get to it. Therefore, when the mutt's sensitive nostrils had caught a whiff of the unsuspecting pie seller, he had almost yanked Harry's arm out of its socket as he dragged him in hot pursuit of the pastries.

What had happened next was not an ordeal he was proud of, as he had been forced to purchase the dog three steak-and-kidney puddings before Norbert would release the pie man from the end of the alleyway he had pinned him to. Then had learned the hard way that it wasn't just chicken that disagreed with the beast's bowels.

In a place where bowels had no place—Norbert had used the only trees available to empty them—the two potted, miniature conifers flanking his imperious neighbor Lady Flatman's pristine doorstep.

The mere memory of the incident made him shudder.

The memory of Lady Flatman's understandably explosive reaction to the violation made him shudder some more before he remembered to paste a more appropriate expression back on his face.

Miss Rowe gave him an odd look but didn't comment, thank goodness, sparing him from having to explain to her the depravity he had been forced to endure. Instead, she moved to the three identical pencil pots, frowning at the three rulers lined up together exactly one inch apart beside the similarly arranged compasses and notebooks.

"I see no sign of chaos here, Captain." Somehow, she managed to ensure even that compliment sounded like an insult, making him wonder why she so obviously didn't like him when he had bent over backward to cater to her every whim. Then wonder why he cared about her opinions at all when he was the one paying her wages!

"Discipline is the soul of an army, Miss Rowe." Was that Nelson or Wellington? He was so aggrieved he couldn't remember.

"Perhaps so—but we must also be mindful that these are children and *not* soldiers." Her smile was insincere. "But obviously I will bear your sentiments in mind." Which he took as tantamount to her telling him he was an idiot because she knew better.

He considered countering, then decided against it. As Sun Tzu so sensibly said, the most prudent know when to fight and when not to fight, and he had more important things to do today than wasting time correcting his prickly new governess.

As Miss Rowe scrutinized the rest of his handiwork, he surreptitiously scrutinized her to see if he could gauge some more of her apparent *superior* measure. He had always, with just one notable exception, been a good judge of character. But so far, she baffled him. If she was the irreplaceable educational paragon Miss Prentice had promised, he saw no sign of it. However, her eyes, which were everywhere, hinted that she possessed an inquisitive and clever brain. The plain, sensible dress and unfussy bun suggested she was the sort to brook no nonsense, but she lacked the gravitas necessary, in his humble opinion, to enforce it.

If he, with all his years of experience managing men, could not make those children behave without pathetically resorting to bribery, he feared for her sanity. Toss her petiteness and the exuberant Norbert into the mix, and he feared for her safety too. For all her bold, direct stares when she did deign to speak to him, and all the subtle ways she found to look down her dainty, upturned nose at him, she still seemed ill-equipped to rise to the challenge his irrepressible family presented.

That cold dose of pragmatism forced him to reevaluate the situation at speed, as was his way, only this time that unique skill of identifying a problem long before it happened gave him no satisfaction. If he was right about her, the children would eat her alive and there wasn't much he could do about it beyond watch them spit out the bones.

If he was lucky, he estimated he had a week before she quit and left screaming in surrender. Thanks to Miss Prentice's clever manipulation of his dire situation, Harry had done something he hadn't done in years. He had hired the wrong person to do the job. Miss Rowe was a mistake. A small, snooty, and costly one. But one he had no choice but to live with.

He could not dismiss her. Not yet at least. No matter what the grounds or provocation. Beggars could not be choosers and he was a desperate man, so no matter how ineffectual she proved to be or how unsuitable or unpleasant, he had to keep her for as long as he could.

However, as was also his way when he sensed storm clouds gathering, his problem-solving mind was already planning a contingency. He made a mental note to tell Simpkins to start sourcing her first replacement immediately. To line them up like cannon balls in readiness for the bloody, senseless conflict ahead. Forewarned was forearmed, after all, and poor Miss Rowe was destined to be the first of many who would fall before blasted Flora returned—that was the sad fact—so he would need to be nimble, resourceful, and think well ahead to mitigate for all the inconvenience. All the things he excelled at. Cold comfort after he had allowed himself such high hopes.

To cover his disappointment, he continued with his tour. "I had this clock installed yesterday." He pointed to it, proud that he had still had the wherewithal to think about purchasing a special clock for the classroom at all when she had forgotten to request one. Further proof, if proof were needed, that he was always at his best during a crisis. Even when he was positively drowning in crises right, left, and center.

Instead of thanking him profusely for correcting her oversight, she gave another curt nod of acknowledgment. "A clock will be useful." And just like that, she dismissed it to take in the blackboard. Her eyes widened slightly at his neatly chalked timetable written down the side of it before she turned to him, emotionless, her finger flicking to his two watch chains. "I see that you are a stickler for time, Captain."

"*Tempus fugit*, Miss Rowe." Out of habit, or perhaps because he had just used one of the admiral's favorite sayings, he touched the pocket that held the watch his grandfather had always worn. "Time flies—unless you keep a firm hold upon it and, like Wellington, I much prefer to do the business of the day in the day."

"I see you are also a fan of misquoting the military men of yore." Her emotive nose wrinkled again in a way that showed she disapproved more of him misquoting Wellington than she did of the duke himself. "Nelson last week. Wellington today."

"It would be foolish not to stand on the shoulders of giants, Miss Rowe." As he had no clue who to attribute that quote to, he shrugged. "And I like to read . . . when I have the time." Her gaze followed his fingers going unconsciously to one of his pocket watches before it wandered back to his precise timetable for the day, making him feel as though he was out of step, pedantic, crusty, and old.

So very old.

"I assume I can tweak this classroom to *my* satisfaction, Captain?"

Was it his imagination, or did even the word *captain* sound begrudging? As if his sixteen years serving king and country were a mark against him. "But of course." Although why she would want to change anything when absolutely everything she needed was no further away than three paces, he didn't understand. "This is your bridge, Miss Rowe, and the helm is yours." Heaven help them all, for this voyage had more of the stench of doom about it than his frustrating stint on the *Baltimore*.

But Harry would look on the bright side.

At least her presence here in the short term would give him and his staff some respite from the relentless chore of keeping the children and their outsized dog entertained. It would also give him some limited peace of mind that they were all safe while he did his wretched duty at the Admiralty even if he still had to keep a close eye on her, so he would be thankful for small mercies, no matter how brief. Or small. And talking of small . . . Of their own accord, his eyes wandered to the petite Miss Rowe again only to find hers staring at him. "Please feel free to chart the course as you see fit."

"Marvelous. Seeing as everything is shipshape, Captain, I think I should like to meet my crew now." The sudden twinkle in her fine eyes suggested she was mocking him and his constant naval references, and might actually possess a sense of humor, albeit one buried under a thick layer of disdain. "Where are the children?"

"Awaiting you in the drawing room, Miss Rowe." He led her to the open doorway, then paused to allow her to walk through it first. "They are excited to meet you."

"Are you sure?" She sailed past, cupping her ear to listen for them with a wry smile that hinted again that humor lurked beneath her no-nonsense exterior. "Only it is so quiet, I was beginning to wonder if you had locked them in the brig."

*Chapter*
# FIVE

❧

As he, too, found the children's uncharacteristic silence unsettling, Harry hurriedly led the way to the drawing room and was relieved to see the three of them sat as still as statues on the sofa. Exactly as they had solemnly pledged to be when he had left them there ten minutes ago.

It had taken a shilling apiece and a solemn pledge of his own to take them to Gunther's on Saturday afternoon for ice cream, with the assurance that they could order whatever they wanted unhindered, to get them to behave like civilized human beings this morning. He wasn't proud of that. Nor was he particularly proud that this wasn't the first time he had been so browbeaten by the three of them that he had succumbed to bribery. The navy would be horrified at such a show of weakness as that was certainly not how they had trained him, and his military idol Sun Tzu would be spinning in his grave, too, despite his claim that victory was only ever reserved for those willing to pay the price of it. But frankly, after the battles he'd waged since blasted Flora's departure, a couple of paltry shillings, all the ice cream in Gunther's, and Harry's pride still felt like a small price to pay for a few hours of blessed respite.

"Children—allow me to introduce Miss Rowe." As one, they stood the moment she entered the room, and thanks to the promise of unlimited ice cream, even managed to pretend to possess some manners. "She will be your governess until your parents return." Or until the half-pint savages blew her entrails out in bubbles.

In turn, he beckoned them forward in age order. "This handsome young sportsman is my nephew, Master Felix Pendleton."

Instead of merely looking him up and down as she had Harry, she proffered her hand to the boy and shook it. "I am delighted to meet you, Master Felix, and to trounce you at cricket in the near future." Then she did the unexpected again and beamed at his nephew. A smile so devastating that Harry's breath caught in his throat and refused to budge—and that wasn't good.

Especially when the last woman who had taken his breath away had knocked all the wind out of his sails before she scuttled his ship entirely.

"I should probably warn you in advance that I am a mean bowler, young man." Miss Rowe folded her arms, an action which did wonders for her figure, as she offered Felix a saucy, smug grin. "In both execution and spirit."

"I shall believe that when I see it," said Felix with a smug grin of his own. He raised his eyebrows toward his sisters. "In my experience, girls cannot bowl."

"Well, this one can." Miss Rowe tapped her chest with gusto, drawing Harry's eyes once more to her pert bosom encased in tight-fitting gray serge and giving them ideas they had no right having. Especially when she was his employee and a decent employer—an officer and a gentleman—had no right to ogle the help.

*What on earth was the matter with him?*

"I'm a fairly decent batter too but lack the dedication required to be a good fielder." Her features were so animated when she spoke. Her green eyes were so friendly but mischievous as they locked with his nephew's in convivial challenge. To his utter horror, Harry was envious of that. Envious that she obviously much preferred the boy to him. "Fielding, I will confess, is not my forte, so I am little better than mediocre. You?"

"I'm an all-rounder." Thoroughly charmed and eager to impress, Felix thumped his own chest. "The best in the family. Better even than Uncle Harry here."

"Says who?" Harry folded his own arms and summoned a feigned arrogant expression for effect. Or to impress her and win one of those devasting smiles too. He could not decide which it was and concluded it was likely best not to ponder it any further. "For if it is your mother who gave you that accolade, it was given only because my sister is still bitter at my catching her out last summer in the first innings, and not because of your superior talents, young whippersnapper." He flicked his finger with a grin to dismiss Felix before he turned to the oldest of the girls. "Marianne, come and say 'how do you do' to Miss Rowe." As he turned toward the newcomer, Harry caught her staring at him, quizzical, until she quickly masked it with a smile for his niece.

"What a pretty name!" Miss Rowe bestowed her breathtaking beam again. "Your uncle has informed me that you are a dancer, Miss Marianne."

That was all it took to make the middle sibling forget her solemn pledge to behave like a restrained and sedate young lady. Because nothing suppressed his eldest niece's penchant for showing off—not even ice cream—Marianne decided to not to walk forward like any decent, well-brought-up child would, but to pirouette toward Miss Rowe for all she was worth.

Harry gave her a look. One that said he would make her pay for this insubordination by being stingy at Gunther's if she continued, but typically, it was ignored. Being a diva to her core, Marianne then finished her impromptu performance with a theatrical flourish before she dipped into an exaggerated curtsy.

"*Enchantée*, mademoiselle Rowe." And of course, because she lived to test him, today Marianne was going to be a diva *à la française*— purely to vex him. "*Comment allez-vous?*"

"*Très bien, merci!*" The breathtaking beam stretched wider as Miss Rowe's beguiling eyes twinkled, and she clapped before she shook his niece's regally proffered hand. "And I must say *bravo*, Miss Marianne! A sublime performance and such impeccable French. What an accomplished young lady you are."

"I can sing too. Shall I demonstrate?"

As Marianne's skinny rib cage began to inflate, ready to blast out one of her awful, out-of-tune arias, Harry caught her shoulders, spun her around, and sent her back to the others with a decisive shove. "You can delight Miss Rowe another time with your unique musical stylings, young lady."

Before the diva argued, he offered little Grace his most reassuring smile, praying that the half an hour he had spent with her this morning practicing walking, rather than sprinting, was still fresh enough in her mind that she wouldn't explode forward like a whirling dervish and injure herself on the furniture again. "Last, but by no means least, may I present to you Miss Grace Pendleton, who is working hard to grow into that name." It seemed only fair to both his five-year-old niece and Miss Rowe not to set the bar too high. Miss Rowe would discover soon enough that poor Grace possessed no grace whatsoever and went everywhere at a gallop, no matter what. Never mind that the sensitive baby of the family would also burst into tears if she thought she had disappointed someone in any way. What the child lacked in decorum, she more than made up with heart.

To her credit, his niece tried her best to be sedate and used two hands to pick up the edges of her frilly little skirt before she stomped slowly and methodically forward as if every single step was a challenge, her big blue eyes flicking to his as she sought reassurance for her efforts. While the new governess wasn't looking, he winked at the child and gave her a subtle raised thumb before he hid it in his folded arms.

"How do you do, Miss Grace?" Miss Rowe knelt to shake the little and doubtless sticky hand. There had been some toffees involved in the walking practice too this morning, seeing as the task proved to be such a challenge and frustrated tears had been imminent.

"My tooth is wiggling, see?" Grace opened her mouth widely and close to Miss Rowe's face, then pushed her tongue against the tiny incisor to prove that was so. "Once it falls out, I'm going to give it to Felix for his collection. He's already got all of Marianne's and his own, and once he gets all mine, he's going to string them onto a necklace to give to Mama for Christmas. He's very good at making jewelry. Last Christmas he made her a bracelet out of beetles. They were all dead, of course, first."

It took all of Harry's strength not to allow his mouth to hang slack, because of all the sentences he had hoped little Grace would say, it certainly wasn't that one.

He was about to apologize for it when Miss Rowe smiled. "I am glad to hear it, for it strikes me that a bracelet made of live beetles would be a trifle itchy. But still fun, though. Especially in church." Then she laughed.

It was unrestrained and earthy and outrageously seductive.

Seductive enough that it thoroughly scrambled his wits, and his jaw did gape momentarily until he hoisted it up like a mainsail before she turned to him with a genuine smile. "Your nieces and nephew are quite delightful, Captain Kincaid. I believe we shall all get on famously."

"Excellent." Now that they had all conspired to lull her into a false sense of security, it seemed a prudent time for him to leave before all hell broke loose and she changed her mind. "I shall pass you to the capable hands of Mrs. Rigsby so that you can unpack and prepare before your lessons commence after luncheon, which will give you . . ." He snapped open one of his pocket watches. ". . . almost six hours to steel yourself for the ordeal before you have to sip from the cup of destruction."

"You consider *Genghis Khan* a military giant whose shoulders you want to stand on?"

He shrugged, impressed that she had recognized that misquote too and more impressed that she had the confidence to call him on it. Maybe she had some steel in her spine after all. "As you clearly like to read, too, Miss Rowe, I daresay you will agree that while he was undeniably a ruthless, bloodthirsty, and power-hungry maniac with few pleasant qualities to recommend him, old Genghis knew how to fight a battle." He hoped, for her sake, that she did too. "If you will just follow me."

As her smile melted and she sailed past him again, he hung back to give the manipulative children a wink for upholding their bargain, then stiffened.

"*Norbert!*" Simpkins's panicked voice came from afar, signaling that all hell was indeed about to break loose.

"NORBERT!" Something crashed in the vicinity of the kitchen.

"NORBERT! Those sausages are not meant for you, you scabrous bag of fleas!"

There was a scuffle. One which clearly included Mrs. Rigsby as his two most senior servants loudly wrestled for the stolen sausages, then another, bigger, crash.

If that wasn't enough to raise all of Harry's hackles as he dashed into the hallway to intercede, Simpkins resorted to salty sailor insults, a sure sign that he was at his wit's end with a situation far beyond even his meticulous control. "Get back here this second, you useless, bilge-sucking, horn-swaggling, DERANGED, SCURVY DOG!"

Clearly unfettered and in a hurry to escape, Norbert's enormous paws thundered down the hallway as he barreled toward them, the string of pilfered sausages dangling from his mouth.

He dropped them the moment he spotted Miss Rowe and sped up, eager to greet the latest human to grace his pack in his own inimitable way. Before he could warn her to take cover, Norbert launched like a racehorse jumping a gate. Time slowed as Harry lunged, too late to use his body to make any significant impact on Norbert's determined trajectory. Instead, Harry's head met the opposite wall with such a thud that he saw stars, while a blur of excited gray whizzed past him.

Norbert hit Miss Rowe with some force. Enough that Harry heard all the air exit her lungs in one big whoosh. Green eyes wide, she shrieked as she flew backward beneath the animal's immense weight. Then lay motionless and winded beneath him as the giant devil-dog licked her startled face as if his troublesome, grossly untrained canine life depended upon it.

———⊙———

*A*fter the most dubious of starts, which thanks to the pompous captain had lived up to all her lowest expectations, Georgie's first day had improved rapidly.

To be fair, the only way was up after Norbert had knocked her down so spectacularly. But after dreading crossing Captain Kincaid's threshold, then having all her worst fears about him confirmed with his regimented and soulless attempt at creating a classroom, he had redeemed himself slightly by trying to save her.

That had been noble, despite his failure.

He had been so mortified by Norbert's exuberant welcome that he had apologized profusely for a full half an hour before she had managed to convince him no real harm had been done and that he could go about his day. The same could not be said for him, though, as Captain Kincaid had crashed headlong into the wall with such force a nasty bump had erupted on his forehead. Enough of one that the butler had insisted he might be too concussed to ride his horse to Whitehall. After a short argument, which the butler won, Simpkins issued him with a cold compress to use in the carriage. Despite all the captain's protestations that the wound wasn't bad enough for all that fuss, Georgie had still witnessed him press it to his temple and wince when he finally left.

Since then, with the children mysteriously missing, she hadn't done much of anything beyond unpack, take a tour of the house, and drink tea with Mrs. Rigsby. The cook had been a wealth of information about her new employer and was such a shameless gossip that Georgie hadn't even needed to ask about him.

Now she knew that Captain Kincaid had turned thirty at Christmas. That he excelled at everything he turned his hand to and that was why he had risen in the ranks of the navy so fast. That he had gone from being a boy first class on board his first ship to captain at just five and twenty, which Mrs. Rigsby believed made him the youngest ever. That he was working at the Admiralty for the foreseeable, and had been for the last two years, because it was the quickest route to promotion and because he had a talent for getting troublesome things done fast. While that talent would also doubtless ensure the captain became the youngest admiral the navy had ever seen too—as was his destiny—it was, according to the cook, also a double-edged sword. His superiors now constantly took advantage of his good nature—which Georgie would believe he actually possessed when she saw it—because they kept him so busy he barely had time to sleep.

Mrs. Rigsby had also claimed that the captain paid decent wages, treated his staff well, and didn't bring loose women home. If he did anything with loose women outside of these walls, Mrs. Rigsby couldn't say, but she did know that he had briefly been engaged, although she was sketchy on the details because it was before he moved here and so she had no clue why he and his fiancée had split. And that he sometimes sat in the garden for hours and simply stared at the plants. That particular behavior, she had assured Georgie with a shake of her head, was a sure sign that their master had taken too much on and no longer knew which way was up.

Which all felt familiar to her too at this precise moment. She had trained to be a governess for more years than any other governess of her acquaintance, and now that she was one, she had no clue which way was up either. The grateful and well-behaved young ladies in Miss Prentice's benevolent school were a very different kettle of fish to three actual children, and she'd never had to deal with an employer before.

"Is here all right?" Eager to please, Felix had appointed himself her chief furniture mover as she rearranged their classroom. He had turned up early for the first lesson with Norbert in tow. Partly out of curiosity and a greater part, she suspected, to see what he and his sisters were letting themselves in for. Hence, he had brought the dog as support, even though he had been warned by Simpkins that Norbert had to remain in the yard during lessons. Now that all the desks and chairs had been turned around, they were trying to find a new home for the blackboard on the opposite, and far more interesting, side of the room than the uninspiring location their uncle had chosen.

"Yes. Perfect. We don't want to block the French doors and this lovely view of the garden." Or the giant dog currently snoring upside down as he basked in the afternoon sun streaming through them.

She had considered trying to make the captain's configuration work despite her rebellious need to change it on principle, but knew within minutes of unpacking her books that it would be too constricting and depressing to have her new pupils stare at nothing. Nothing except her and the ridiculously large clock marking time on the wall. A depressing view for even the most scholarly of pupils, let alone these three, who had clearly not had the most conventional education.

According to Felix, who she had been gently quizzing for the last ten minutes, the children had never had a governess before. It was their mother who had taught them all to read and write, and their father who instructed them on the sciences. The eldest Pendleton claimed he no longer had to suffer through mathematics at home because he already knew all that he needed to, so she wouldn't need to bother making him attend those lessons with his sisters. He would use that time to exercise Norbert just as he did at home. He had said all that with the unconvincing nonchalance of one who would rather pull out his own teeth than solve a mathematical problem, so Georgie suspected he struggled with numbers.

Felix also claimed to have a penchant for the Greek and Roman classics despite being only ten, most especially those that included epic battles. However, he had no time for Plato because he thought the ancient philosopher spent too much time thinking and not enough doing. Homer, however, told tales filled with derring-do, so he was all right. But his favorite book was more modern—*Ornithologica Britannica* by Marmaduke Tunstall—because it was the definitive work on English birds, exactly as the title claimed.

Young Master Felix would obviously prefer a similar book on insects of the British Isles because insects were his whole life, but as one didn't yet exist, he planned to write it before he reached his quarter century. After that age, he was going to sail the world like his favorite uncle, Harry—but not in the service of the king. Instead, he was going to circumnavigate the globe single-handed while he wrote a seven-volume encyclopedia detailing all the earth's insects in time for his thirtieth birthday. Thirty, he had explained, was the perfect age to publish your life's work before you had to settle down. When she had asked why he had settled on seven as the perfect number of volumes for such a herculean task—a deliberate nod to his love of the classics—he had stared at her as if she were daft. Then explained that he would have to sail all seven of the seas to find all the countries within them to record all their insects, so therefore each volume would encompass one voyage.

She admired that ambition and logic too much to point out that it was flawed. It wasn't her place to crush his dreams when she fundamentally believed that the role of a good teacher was to nurture them. Neither was it her place to quiz him about the current level of his sisters' educations when getting important and accurate information was always better straight from the horse's mouth than via hearsay or gossip. Unless there was no other option, of course.

"So tell me . . ." Georgie threw open the French doors to allow the fresh spring breeze to whoosh into the room and ruffle the snoring Norbert's shaggy gray fur. "What makes your uncle Harry your *favorite* uncle."

"Two things," answered Felix with all the seriousness of a ten-year-old as he held up a pair of fingers. "Firstly, he reads the best bedtime stories."

An answer that Georgie hadn't expected in a million years. "How so?"

"He does all the voices and acts out all the exciting parts." An image which did not fit with the upright, staid, regimented timekeeper she had disliked at first sight at all. But then, she was sure she had seen him wink at little Grace when she had done her best to walk with decorum this morning, and that did not fit with that image either, so perhaps her first impressions did need some tweaking. He was still eminently dislikable, obviously, but not all bad like the colonel had been.

Yet.

"And the second reason?"

"He's our *only* uncle," said the boy with a shrug, "so has to be our favorite. However, I do believe that even if I had another, I would still like Uncle Harry the best."

"Why?"

Felix gave that some thought, then shrugged again. "Because he's ultimately a good egg—that's what Mama always says when he exasperates her—" He leaned toward her conspiratorially. "But only when he forgets to be a hard-boiled one."

Georgie chuckled at that fitting analogy. Captain Kincaid was clearly cut from the same unforgiving cloth as the colonel but had been made using a slightly better-fitting pattern.

That he wasn't a complete ogre was a relief as she didn't want to have to fully hate her new, and so far, only employer during their limited time together. This appointment was an opportunity and hopefully the boost she needed to finally launch her stalled career as a governess. It would not only provide her with experience, but hopefully an excellent reference from the captain when she came to leave. With her atrocious inability to impress at an interview, Georgie needed categoric proof that she was employable to tempt another family to take a chance on her. As Miss Prentice had warned repeatedly over the last few days, if she didn't bite her tongue while in Captain Kincaid's brief employ and see it through to the duration, then she would bite it off to spite her face. Therefore, no matter what the provocation, she would bite it until it bled if necessary, because beggars really couldn't be choosers. And a hard-boiled egg was better than a rotten one. At least the rest of the captain's family were lovely.

"What sort of egg are you, Felix? Only I'll wager, from our short acquaintance, that you are more a deviled than a coddled one."

"Deviled for definite." His toothy grin suited him. "As the baby of the family, Grace is the coddled one. She's frightened of her own shadow and will cry at the slightest provocation so we have to wrap her in down to protect her."

"And Marianne?"

He rolled his eyes at the mere mention of his other sister's name. "Scrambled." Then he dropped his voice to a whisper in case the middle Pendleton heard. "She's as mad as a hatter, drives everyone to distraction, and is oblivious because she lives mostly in her own world—but don't tell her that I told you."

"My lips are sealed." Georgie pretended to button them a second before Marianne and Grace came through the door holding hands.

Poor Grace looked terrified and on the cusp of tears, exactly as her big brother had warned. Hardly a surprise when Mrs. Rigsby had told her that this was the first time the children had been left for more than an hour by their mother. Add to that the fact that London was a very different place to the quiet coastal house Felix had told her they usually lived in, and none of them had ever been to anything resembling a school. Not even a Sunday school, if the boy was to be believed, so the three much-too-large-for-Grace desks and chairs must have appeared intimidating no matter which way they faced.

So too would grilling the poor thing on her abilities with numbers and letters despite Georgie urgently needing to know them to do her job properly. As much as she hated to link anything to time when her confusing employer was so obsessed by it, pitching her classes at the wrong level was a complete waste of it. However, the three test papers she had spent several hours putting together for today had been a waste of hers. They were not used to sitting examinations, and foisting one upon them now could well do more harm than good to their fledgling relationship.

But there were more ways to test the children's educational abilities, and unlike their old-fashioned uncle, she was nothing if not open to better, less stuffy ways of doing things. "Why don't we commence our first lesson in the great outdoors?" She pointed to the surprisingly pretty and well-tended garden that the captain liked to sit in. "I read somewhere that the average garden is home to over a thousand different species of flora and fauna. I wonder what lives in this one?"

"Ants and wood lice and earwigs, for certain." Felix was already out the door and keen to go hunting for them. As he bounded off, Norbert rose from his prostrate position, stretched his ridiculously long limbs, then chased after the boy with his big tongue lolling.

"And butterflies," added Marianne, prancing after her brother down the neat lawn and flapping her arms gracefully as if she had become one, completely forgetting her terrified little sister whose bottom lip was trembling because she had no earthly idea what to do now that she had been left alone.

Georgie held her hand out, smiling. "Come on, Grace." Sensing that the child wouldn't want to be too far behind the others, the second Grace warily took it, she pulled her into a run, quietly enjoying the sound of the little girl's relieved and excited giggle as they dashed down the perfectly manicured lawn so fast that the neat hedge encompassing it blurred.

*Chapter*
## SIX

~❧~

"𝓘 do not care if the ladybird we found had five spots." Marianne slapped her brother's meddlesome fingers away from the red collage insect she was decorating with black buttons. "I want my ladybird's wings to be symmetrical."

Georgie smiled as she gently wagged her finger at the more pedantic Felix, who was adamant that his sisters record nature accurately or not at all, pleased that Marianne had just relieved her of the need to teach the pair of them symmetry. "You leave Marianne to her ladybird and concentrate on the finishing touches to your shield bug."

Not that Georgie was entirely sure what a shield bug was. But the boy had known the name of every other creepy-crawly they had spied in the garden, so she had no reason to doubt that the green, iridescent shield-shaped insect they had discovered on the hawthorn bush was indeed a hawthorn shield bug exactly as he'd claimed. That there were apparently several different species of shield bug was also news to her, but even teachers learned something new every day. It was one of the most rewarding aspects of the job.

More enlightening, however, was Felix's talent for drawing. The meticulousness of the details he was currently recording on his perfectly proportioned and cleverly colored sketch suggested he had potential as an artist. "Will you be illustrating your *Insecta Britannica* when you get around to writing it, Felix? Only I really think you should. That drawing is magnificent."

His chest swelled with pride. "Of course I shall be, Miss Rowe. I fear that *I* will have to as I do not trust anyone *else* to do it correctly." He used that as an excuse to jab Marianne with his elbow. "A less diligent illustrator might take artistic liberties and that wouldn't be scientific at all. Some people aren't interested in science or truth and prefer to indulge in pointless pastimes as they are *all show* and *no* substance."

"Substance, like science, is boring," was the unbothered middle sister's imperious retort. "Much like Felix and his pointless obsession with stupid insects." A comment that earned her a glare from her brother, and which made little Grace's eyes roll subtly as they locked with Georgie's in a Lord-give-me-strength kind of way before she selected the final chalk to complete her much more interesting picture of a bumblebee.

"Ballet isn't going to change the world, Marianne! But science is."

"The world would be a dull place indeed without ballet. Almost—but not quite—as dull as you, big brother."

That was another thing she had learned about the children this afternoon. Felix and Marianne bickered constantly, mostly about nonsense which came in a steady stream of jibes and insults, so she knew to ignore it exactly like little Grace did. Running interference would be as pointless as trying to turn back the tide. It was obvious that they had niggled one other all their lives and likely would until their dying day. No amount of her nagging would ever change that.

Over the years, when she had been invited to spend her holidays with Lottie at her family's farm, she had watched her friend spar constantly with her four brothers. It hadn't been because they didn't love one another, because they clearly did in a way that had made Georgie yearn all the more for a family of her own. More that it was the way the bond of love between them all manifested itself. "I choose to interfere only when there is blood involved," was their father's sage advice when she had initially been so shocked by all the fighting, and that sage advice seemed prudent here. Especially when, to an untrained eye, it looked as if Felix was the main antagonist when Marianne quietly did everything in her power to rub him up the wrong way first.

The ladybird's spots were a case in point, as Marianne had originally counted out five buttons until a quick glance at her brother had prompted her to grab another. She had made it six purely to vex him and, being oblivious of that, Felix had happily complied. Now, he was wound tighter than a spring at her lack of respect for the truth while she was silently enjoying his outrage.

But then girls were always much cleverer than boys at manipulating a situation to serve their own ends, and Georgie already suspected that Marianne enjoyed getting her big brother into trouble almost as much as she delighted in riling him. There had been an incident earlier when she had used all her acting skills to fall over and had loudly proclaimed that Felix had pushed her.

Georgie had ignored that, too, because Felix had quietly taunted her with a slimy snail beforehand, so he was no innocent in the proceedings either. Rather than get sucked into the futility of mediating their never-ending but harmless war, she pretended she hadn't seen or heard either indiscretion. Instead, she had distracted them by suddenly decreeing that the first Pendleton who could race to the end of the garden before the others would be the one who chose tonight's story.

Thankfully, as she had anticipated, it was their furry brother Master Norbert Pendleton who won, making the decision moot and thus avoiding another altercation or any accusations of cheating. However, it had not gone unnoticed that the pair of them had resorted to all sorts of unsportsmanlike tactics in that short, mad dash up the lawn to sabotage the other. But in the reassuring absence of any blood, she had pretended to ignore all those, too, as she cheered them on. As Shakespeare had the victor of the Battle of Agincourt, Henry IV, say, discretion was always the better part of valor.

Wise words to live by—even if they did purport to come from a military man. Especially for a governess. And especially this close to supper time.

"I cannot believe what a good job the three of you have done with these sketches." Georgie beamed at them all in turn in awe and wonder. "We must display them. Where shall we hang them?"

"What about under the clock?" Marianne turned to the empty wall behind them where the blackboard had been.

"A splendid idea. But how do we hang them up without putting pinholes in your uncle's pristine wall?" Georgie looked to Felix for the answer to include him in the decision and thus deftly avoid another bickering session between the eldest two siblings.

He pondered the problem for a moment, then grinned, all previous irritation with his sister forgotten. "If we string the pictures together, we could hang them from the clock."

"Once we've all tidied up, why don't you three do that, then we can hang up the first acquisitions for our new gallery together before supper, which is . . . ?" For the first time Georgie glanced at the imposing clock and realized that it was already five minutes to five. The tidying could wait until the children were eating. "Better still, rather than be late for Mrs. Rigsby, hurry up and find where the string lives in those boxes and we'll hang your masterpieces now."

The moment the children rose, so did Norbert, and as they pulled down box after box to riffle through them, he assisted while Felix and Marianne bickered. Or at least the dog thought he was assisting by burrowing his nose in all the contents as they jostled one another, his big tail wagging as he got completely in the way. The moment Felix's hand shot in the air in triumph, clutching the ball of string, the dog grabbed it, then, assuming it had been produced so that he could play a spirited game of ball, decided to run around in circles with it while the children chased him.

Within seconds, the ball was no more and the string was tangled around everything, including the legs of the blackboard. It wobbled ominously for a moment. Georgie managed to lunge sideways to prop it up before it fell, but not before all her new sticks of chalk flew hither and thither until they shattered on the floor. A moment later, Norbert ran straight over them and ground several nubs into powder beneath his big paws, and suddenly there were paw prints everywhere too. Enormous white smudges on the once-polished parquet that she would also now have to tidy up along with everything else.

"What the blazes has happened here?" Still clutching the blackboard, Georgie jumped at the sound of the captain's unimpressed voice. Then winced at the thoroughly appalled sight of him filling the doorway.

<hr />

*H*arry blinked at the carnage in disbelief as anger bubbled. All his carefully considered order was gone. Willfully and purposefully destroyed.

In its entirety.

The three desks and chairs no longer sat in a neat row facing

the blackboard because the blackboard had been shoved in a corner. Nothing had been written on it, apart from the blatantly ignored
schedule he had put there the night before. The desks now rested in
a haphazard arc around the periphery. To make way, no doubt, for the
huge mess on the floor which was littered with so much chalk, string,
paper, and other stuff he could only imagine the children—or their
clearly useless governess—had opened up all the boxes and tossed
the contents about like confetti.

To add insult to injury, the mad dog chose that precise moment
to deposit the remnants of what once had been a ball of string on the
toes of his boots before he sat, tail wagging and eyes expectant as
if he was waiting for Harry to throw it for him, smearing the glossy
leather of his favorite pair of hessians in a slimy coating of drool in
the process.

"My apologies, Captain." Still standing in the middle of the
mess, Miss Rowe bent to begin scraping all the detritus within arm's
reach into a pile. "We lost track of time." Her cheeks had colored in
obvious embarrassment, and he couldn't help thinking that her embarrassment was the least he was due when she should be mortified
to have been caught red-handed. Ashamed at her lack of control in
his classroom. Utterly repentant that she had clearly fallen at the first
hurdle and wasn't much of a governess at all and that he had indeed
been hoodwinked into hiring her!

"We went hunting for bugs!" Grace threw herself at him, waving
a piece of paper. "Do you like my bee, Uncle Harry? I've called him
Boris. Boris the Bee."

He gave the picture a cursory glance, conscious that his current
displeasure had nothing to do with the little girl who really wasn't
to blame for any of this anarchy. "It's very . . . nice." Except poor,
sensitive Grace shriveled at his frigid tone and took two wary steps

back, her big eyes blinking rapidly as she tried to comprehend his uncharacteristically cold response.

"We've had a splendid afternoon, Uncle Harry." Sensing his disapproval, Felix decided to defend the indefensible. "The best we've had since we've got here."

"That I can see." He had to clench his jaw to stop the furious bellow which wanted to escape. Clearly aware that Harry's temper was barely controlled, Norbert's ears drooped before he maneuvered his big body behind Felix's in the hope that it would render him invisible. "It looks as if somebody has tossed a grenade in here." He had seen shipwrecks in a better state than his morning room.

"It's only a little bit of mess, Uncle Harry." Marianne brushed it all away with a theatrical flick of her wrist. "Nothing that can't be fixed." To prove that, she set about helping Miss Rowe scoop goodness knew what off his once clean and seasoned oak floor, and with a pointed look at her two siblings, snapped them into doing exactly the same.

"Your supper is ready, children." He tried to infuse less anger into that choked, staccato sentence because he didn't want them to hate him. "You had best run along while it is still warm and before Mrs. Rigsby has a conniption that all her hard work on your behalf has been in vain." Which, in a nutshell, was precisely what Harry wanted to do. For surely this . . . pandemonium deserved nothing less than a full-blown conniption at the very least. This—*this*—willful, disrespectful, ungrateful mayhem felt like a betrayal. "Miss Rowe can fix it."

"Yes. Run along." With a sunny smile for them and a breeziness that bordered on arrogance for him, Miss Rowe took control. "It is entirely my fault we are late. We were all having far too much fun." Her eyes flicked to his defiantly as if she genuinely considered fun to be more her remit than discipline and real learning. "So be sure to give Mrs. Rigsby my apologies for your *slight* tardiness this evening." There were no apologies for him, he noted, and the dismissiveness of her tone and flagrant disregard of all his efforts to accommodate her classroom in *his* space almost sent steam shooting from his ears.

He waited until they were gone before he allowed the anger to vent and was about to give her a piece of his mind when she pre-empted him, her expression more condescending than contrite.

"I am sure, to you, this all appears as if we have wasted an entire afternoon on triviality. However, I can assure you that nothing could be further than the truth." She didn't even do him the courtesy of stopping what she was doing or acknowledging the mess that had occurred on her watch. "My first three hours with the children were *very* productive and *most* enlightening."

Harry couldn't wait to hear whatever codswallop she came up with to explain away her negligence. "Really?" Because his arms wanted to wave about in abject fury while his feet wanted to pace, he folded them and leaned against the doorframe to anchor them in place. "Do tell?"

"Well, for a start, I discovered that the children have no experience of traditional education at all."

Of course they hadn't! That was because blasted Flora was in charge of it. "You don't say?"

Miss Rowe frowned at his sarcasm. "If you already knew that, Captain, it would have been helpful to have informed me of it before today. That would have saved me from having to scrap all my plans for our first lessons and avoided me having to think on my feet."

She called this—*this vandalism*—thinking on her feet! "I suppose I should be reassured that there were some plans, albeit short-lived ones, before they descended into chaos." Harry allowed his gaze to scan the untidy room again in disgust. "Although I am intrigued to understand how you thought *this* amount of chaos was a fitting educational substitute for a valuable afternoon of reading, writing, and arithmetic. Only it doesn't appear to me that you managed much of that in the three hours you had for lessons but wasted on *fun*."

Rather than wither under his righteous indignation, she did quite the opposite. "As you are a man who appreciates quotes, Captain, my favorite comes from Confucius. Tell me and I will forget, show me and I may remember, *involve me* and I will understand."

"And your labored point is?"

She went for a smile, which flattened when he failed to do anything but frown back. "That there are better ways of learning than sitting behind a desk. I learned more in your garden about the children in a single afternoon than I ever could have in the formal confines of a classroom in a week."

When he failed to look anything but unimpressed at that convenient excuse, she sighed as if he were the one who had gotten this afternoon's shambles so spectacularly wrong, preferring to focus on collecting up the buttons instead of him as she spoke.

"Both Felix and Marianne can read at a level one would expect of children several years older. Both can spell difficult words with ease, likely because they have read, and been read to, extensively from a young age. Thanks to his love of insects and the Romans and Greeks, your nephew has an impressive grasp of Latin. Marianne prefers Marlow, Fielding, and Shakespeare to Cicero and Homer, and I suspect she knows every word of *A Midsummer Night's Dream* by heart. She can certainly recite all of Byron's *She Walks in Beauty*, in both English and in French, which I am not sure is appropriate for a girl so young. Although that's more to do with my personal reservations about Lord Byron in general than his poem, so I shall reserve my judgment because I do approve of poetry in the main."

All the buttons now collected, she rose to return them to a box without glancing his way. Harry had no idea if it was the right box, or if she even cared that there was a right box as she did not bother consulting his alphabetized list on the front of it. "Marianne also has an excellent head for figures"—she bent to unravel the clump of string wrapped around the legs of the blackboard—"which is probably why she dances so well. But then again, it is often the case that those that are musical make the best mathematicians. She knows all of her multiplication tables—and by *know*, I mean your niece can use them rather than regurgitating them simply from memory. Grace knows her two-, five-, and ten-times tables, can count to at least two hundred, can do better than simple addition, subtraction, and multiplication in her head or on her fingers; however, she struggles a little with division. But as that is always the trickiest mathematical skill to master before one hits the horrors of algebra, I am not the least bit concerned about it at this stage."

She gave up on the string and grabbed a handful of feathers instead. They briskly made their way into the same box as the buttons, proving that she had abandoned his meticulous, alphabetical list of contents with the same lack of respect as she had the location of all the new classroom furniture he had been forced to pay double for at such short notice. "Felix, on the other hand, is an expert at avoiding all mathematical problems. I am yet to discover if that is because he finds everything else more interesting or if, as I suspect, he struggles with numbers as much as little Grace seems to struggle with her letters. He draws with impressive aplomb, though." She snatched up a piece of paper and turned as she held it up. The accomplished sketch of an insect was as impressive as it was detailed. "As this *Acanthosoma haemorrhoidale*—or the common hawthorn shield bug to the rest of us who aren't as entomologically well informed as your nephew—is testament. His talent and his eye transcends what is expected from a child of ten. Young Felix is an artist to his core. Perhaps even a budding prodigy in the discipline."

"Well . . . er . . ." Where he had expected blatant cluelessness, she had given him a thorough summary of the children's educational prowess, which surprised him, as he had no idea that the theatrical Marianne was a mathematician or that Felix could draw better than most adults. Or that blasted Flora had taught them anything of any substance at all. But what surprised him more, and horrified him to *his* core, was that the waning late afternoon sunlight did delectable things to her copper hair, which fascinated him. It warmed it from within and made it shimmer as if the kiss of sunset was all it took to give it actual life, highlighting the flecks of gold, bronze, and ruby woven in her curls. Colors so vibrant against the beguiling curve of her alabaster neck and so seductive they put all of Titian's efforts to distill a redhead's hair to shame. Worse, his fingers itched to touch it, so badly Harry had to uncross his arms and clasp his hands tightly behind his back in case they did. "Um . . ."

*Good heavens above, what was the matter with him!*

He hadn't been so effortlessly beguiled by a woman since his unfaithful former fiancée taught Harry the important lesson that losing his head only ever resulted in catastrophe. He had learned it so well, or so he had thought, that his sensible, logical head hadn't once been inclined to get itself lost in all the years since. It might turn occasionally, because he was a hot-blooded man in his prime and not a monk, but even if he dallied, it still stayed firmly screwed in place. It was easy to keep it so, too, because aside from the fact that he was still nowhere near to achieving the lofty career heights he had been groomed for, he hadn't particularly liked himself when he had fancied himself head over heels in love with Elizabeth.

The blinkered and bewitched Harry who had fallen too fast

and too hard had been a blithering idiot who had completely lost interest in the navy. Convinced—or more likely bewitched—that his destiny suddenly lay elsewhere, he had messed so many things up while they were together that he hadn't only lost his first ship—he almost scuppered his entire career. Worse, he hadn't been in control of either himself or the situation during those heady few months of what turned out to be nothing more than a short-lived affair. He had abdicated all the power and control to Elizabeth for the duration, however, and lived to rue the day.

Once he had recovered from the body blow of her betrayal, regrouped, and refocused on what really mattered, he went, cap in hand, to the admiral to ask for help to resurrect his tainted career from the ashes. That hadn't been an easy time either. The old man had warned him repeatedly that he was making a huge mistake to even contemplate marriage so young. The admiral had been living proof that naval marriages didn't work and had always drilled into Harry the need to avoid such permanent entanglements until he was at least a vice admiral and the bulk of his sailing career was done. He had taken his grandson's foolish decision to fall in love as a personal slight and never ceased to remind him of his stupidity forever after.

In fairness to the admiral, once Harry's heart had mended and he was levelheaded enough to analyze everything that had transpired with Elizabeth dispassionately, he was relieved to rediscover that he was a much better officer and gentleman without all that destructive yearning and pining nonsense cluttering his life. He preferred order over chaos and always had, still had a mountain of rigging to climb in his career and so, with hindsight, also knew without a shadow of a doubt that the beguiling, charming, fickle, but oh-so-passionate Elizabeth had ultimately done him a favor when she replaced him in her bed.

Exactly as the admiral had predicted from the outset.

Elizabeth would have made his ordered life a living hell if she'd have waited that short month until he'd sailed home to marry her. Marrying her would have been a mistake he would doubtless have regretted every single blasted minute since those rose-tinted, self-destructive, lust-fogged blinkers came off. When he next risked his heart, which wouldn't be until he was at least a vice admiral, it would be his head and not his emotions which pragmatically chose his mate, and he would go in levelheaded or not at all.

However, his unwelcome, fanciful, and unpalatable reaction to Miss Rowe just now had felt dangerously similar to the way he had always reacted to Elizabeth from the very first moment he had set eyes on the fair-weather temptress. His usually focused attention had always wandered when the sun had caught her hair just so too. His nerve endings had always fizzed whenever she was near, exactly as they were currently doing so close to his useless governess. Then his body inevitably got ideas that would consume him and he would lose sight of the truth. Just as he had with Elizabeth when his foolish, misguided heart got overexcited and over-romantic. He'd overlooked all her flaws and all the overabundant warnings everyone else saw, and then catastrophically overruled every single rational thought that existed in his head.

Although he was buggered if he knew why Miss Rowe, of all women, possessed the eerily similar Elizabeth-like power over him when the two women were in no way alike. Elizabeth had been a tall, willowy blonde. A traditional beauty who knew it and never failed to use it to her advantage. All easy charm and easy grace and the single most flirtatious creature he had ever met. Whereas Miss Rowe was curvaceous and petite. Freckled and, truth be told, slightly awkward in her skin. There was also a primness about her. She was dashed pretty, of course, with those sultry, green, intelligent eyes and all that scandalously tactile copper hair—but she was the complete opposite of flirtatious. Where Elizabeth's expression always suggested "come hither," Miss Rowe's reliably radiated "get lost." She was prickly, sarcastic, disdainful, standoffish, and . . . disrespectful . . . and therefore should be nothing but unappealing.

Except she wasn't. She called to him—to all of him—and that was frankly unacceptable.

He wrenched his wayward eyeballs away and forced them to behold the carnage around him in the hope that it would reignite his anger enough that her outrageous hair, like the woman who owned it, would irritate him rather than bewitch him. It didn't, and that just rubbed salt into the still-gaping wound. "I am glad to hear the afternoon gleaned some minuscule educational benefit."

His eyes wandered to her hair again. Drank in the glorious sight of it while his imagination tried to consider what it would all look like unbound. In a sizzling contrast against her soft, smooth, ivory skin. Against his will, exactly as it had always done with the unworthy siren Elizabeth, his mind began to mentally undress her. To peel away all the layers until nothing but her lightly freckled flesh remained. It was torture, made worse by the regrettable fact that she had her back to him, so his stupid mind flatly refused to show him anything more titillating than its concocted image of her naked back. The merest flashes of skin poking through her riotous tumble of improper hair, which his suddenly uncooperative imagination decided ended too far below her sweet peach of a bottom for him to discern much of either rounded cheek—

"More importantly . . ." Her sanctimonious voice snapped him out of his terrifying reverie—*thank goodness*! Just in the nick of time because she sighed again as she placed the lid on the box before she spun to face him, forcing his rampant, possessed mind and his wayward eyeballs to quickly behave. "I got to know the children this afternoon, Captain Kincaid, and they got to know me." Her chin tilted, defiant, making her pretty green eyes sparkle in the most disconcerting fashion as they locked with his. "Furthermore, thanks to our 'splendid' afternoon, I now have a clear idea of where to start with them."

Thankfully, she gestured to the mess still to be tidied, breaking the hypnotic hold her gaze had on his, leaving him oddly shaken by the experience. Shaken and ashamed and still so hideously beguiled he could barely think straight. "So you see, while I appreciate that this all looks as if no learning has occurred here today, I can assure you that in the midst of chaos, there is always opportunity."

*Did she just quote Sun Tzu?* His mind was so cluttered that he wasn't entirely sure what she had just said. It wasn't *sorry*, though. For bewitching him. For the mess. For her lackadaisical attitude to teaching or her flagrant lack of respect for him.

That he did know without a doubt.

The gall of the woman was staggering. How dare she treat him and his property as if neither mattered? How dare she . . . get under his skin and heat it until he could barely string two cohesive thoughts together? And without even trying. It infuriated him when he thought he had conquered that unfortunate, reckless, irrational part of himself.

"I can also assure you that not all of our lessons will look like this, so there really is no need to worry." There was a flippancy to her tone now that just added insult to injury. "I am a protégé of Miss Prentice, after all, so you *can* trust me to do a good job."

His temporary and uncharacteristic lapse of gentlemanly thoughts aside, he was damned if he was going to leave it at that. Not when there was chalk and string and detritus everywhere and he could see no evidence, for all her canny insights, that the children had done any meaningful schoolwork at all.

The tail did not wag the dog.

The tail *never* wagged the dog. Not while he was around! Exactly who the blazes did this minx think she was? Half a day on the job— and half a day doing a very bad job, to boot—did not give her any right to tell him to mind his own bloody business. Because this was his business, damn it! His family! His house! And his bloody rules!

"I am pleased to hear it, however . . ." Harry was about to elaborate by outlining his expectations for tomorrow after this afternoon's debacle, but she didn't give him a chance.

"If you will excuse me, I have a great deal of planning and preparation to do before tomorrow's lessons, where I can assure you a great deal of valuable reading, writing, and arithmetic *will* take place." She sailed out the door herself—as if she owned the place—effectively dismissing him and laughing at him in the process. "But first, I must fetch a mop to *swab this deck*. Enjoy your supper, Captain. And the rest of your evening."

Then all at once, she was gone and he was left with the mess and the intoxicating waft of her perfume, which was apparently all it took to send his usually level head twisting toward the unthinkable all over again.

## Chapter
# SEVEN

೪⅊

*A*ll the theory in the world wasn't much use without the means to put it into practice effectively, and no matter how much it might chafe, Georgie desperately needed proper experience and a good reference if she was ever going to get another position as a governess. Those were two of the three cast-iron conclusions she had come to after a fitful first night in her temporary bedchamber. The third and most unpleasant one was that she had foolishly allowed Captain Kincaid's first impressions of her to be bad. Which meant that her temporary position here beneath his roof could well be cut short if she didn't do a better job of appearing to be the sort of governess he wanted. If he dismissed her, then she would be not only the only protégé who could not impress at an interview, but one of those who failed to impress on the job too.

The utter humiliation of holding those two accolades, on top of the dubious honor of being the oldest protégé to ever find gainful employment after graduating, filled her with dread. So much of it, she wouldn't feel able to show her face at Miss Prentice's school again if she made a hash of this.

Especially in her first week!

The shame would be so unbearable she would have to move to the wilds of the Pennines to avoid bumping into anyone she knew. Or the Outer Hebrides. Or better yet, remove herself to the Antipodes and live in exile for all eternity with the convicts.

She absolutely could not let that happen!

Which meant that she had to find a way to convince him that she was the right woman for the position. A task that might be easier said than done after yesterday's debacle with the dog and the string.

The expression of complete horror and disappointment etched into the captain's handsome face the second he entered her classroom had haunted her ever since. Even as she had rebelled against his pompous, authoritarian tone with all the bravado of one who had grown up under the constant and crushing disapproval of the colonel, she had been hideously embarrassed to have been found so wanting and clueless after so short an acquaintance.

And she did not doubt for a second that the captain thought her clueless because the tension in every sinew of his body announced that better than any words possibly could. Not that the words he did choose to use contradicted his blatant disgust at her methods in any way. No, indeed. Sarcasm had positively dripped off every clipped consonant as he had surveyed the untidy floor.

*I am intrigued to understand how you thought* this *amount of chaos was a fitting educational substitute for a valuable afternoon of reading, writing, and arithmetic. Only it doesn't appear to me that you managed much of that in the three hours you had for lessons but wasted on* fun.

Could he have issued a more damning indictment of her teaching abilities than that? He thought she had not only wasted time, but that *she* was a complete waste of time too.

With hindsight, destroying all the order and effort he had put into her classroom once they had come in from the garden had not been the most sensible way to convince her employer that she was a governess *par excellence.*

Instead of alienating him from the outset with her modern and collaborative approach to education, she and the children could have spent a few minutes collecting some specimens in the garden. Then drawn those insects at their desks while she gently probed them with questions. What had possessed her to dispense with the desks entirely on her first day, she still couldn't fathom, especially when the captain had been so proud of them.

Then, instead of presenting him with the calm, serene scene he patently expected to see, he had been confronted with anarchy. It hadn't been that bad, of course, because he had only seen the last, damning few minutes of her efforts. But to someone like him—someone who wore two pocket watches and was so neat and fastidious he had likely never experienced so much as a hair out of place on his own head—it must have looked like the whole world had gone to hell in a handcart.

She really should have handled that better. And she shouldn't have left him with that flippant jibe about *swabbing the deck* because that meant he had been left steaming. Was probably *still* steaming because she had avoided eating a slice of humble pie and had quoted Confucius rather than apologized for making such a mess of his morning room.

But it was done now; she couldn't change yesterday. Today, however, she was adamant he would find no fault. Today, she was going to take heed of Miss P's wise words and do whatever it took to convince the captain that her classroom was running precisely as the stickler envisioned it. Even if that meant meekly standing by and biting her tongue while he lectured her or patronized her like the colonel had daily.

Or badly quoted military leaders at her.

Somewhat ironically and with a twinkle in his eye, as if he were getting the quotes wrong on purpose.

But still. The similarities to the unyielding and pompous colonel were close enough to make her wary of trying the captain's patience with the relentless enthusiasm with which she had tried her awful stepfather's. The colonel had been stuck with her and the captain wasn't, so she really had to do a better job of doing the job he thought she should be doing.

All she had to do was earn the stickler's trust.

From the back foot.

Fast.

While suppressing the rebellious St. Joan of Arc within who was positively fighting to get out and tell him how wrong he was about everything.

*Heaven help her!*

For the umpteenth time, she checked the equipment and books neatly lined up on her desk and compared them to her notes. Today, she had planned a packed schedule, which would serve as categoric proof that she hadn't wasted a single second of the children's valuable lesson time if he decided to check on her again.

Which, of course, he would.

Men like that, who were convinced that they always knew best, that all their orders should be followed to the letter without question, would be too arrogant and pompous to think that they would not have been obeyed if she pandered a little to their ego. It certainly would have worked on the colonel if she'd been able to suppress her own outrage at him long enough to try it. His revolving succession of temporary servants were adept at keeping up the right appearances whenever he was around, and because keeping up appearances allowed them to blend into the woodwork, the fool never noticed when they weren't following his orders to the letter. Ergo, she would do the same now.

She would pander to the captain's obsession with time and use it so productively that even he would have no cause to find any fault! The navy, according to Mrs. Rigsby, was the captain's life. Therefore, it stood to reason that if she could make the problem of the children disappear, her employer's disapproving focus would return to Admiralty matters, where it belonged.

"Good morning, Miss Rowe." Even though she was expecting her new pupils to arrive, her nerves were pulled too tight not to clench at Felix's greeting. Once again, Norbert was trailing on his heels, and that wouldn't do at all when the dog had played a significant part in creating yesterday's chaos. The boy scanned the desks warily, taking in the paper, quills, and abacuses gracing each one with undisguised disappointment. "What's all that for?"

"Our first mathematics lesson. I always prefer to tackle that first thing while the mind is at its freshest." They were going to cram a lot into that first hour. Papers would be filled aplenty with sums the stickler could scrutinize at leisure. Then there would be an hour of geography, which she knew the aspiring explorer Felix would adore. Then the final hour before lunch would be something the girls would enjoy—she had planned their English lesson around one of the stories in *Grimms' Fairy Tales*. A story about a princess called Rapunzel who was locked in a high tower.

This afternoon, they would start with science, and this time they would go outside to collect a few specimens to study in class. History would follow, and they would begin learning about all the kings and queens of England, starting with Alfred the Great. The day would purposefully end with handwriting practice, so that when the captain arrived at five to five on the dot to inspect the troops, the children would have pens in their hands.

If Georgie said so herself, that final lesson was a stroke of genius. Today, Captain Kincaid would not only see the physical manifestation of what he thought good learning looked like, he would return to a tidy oasis of disciplined quiet.

Felix ran his fingertip over the nearest abacus before he flicked a bead to one side, as if dismissing it. "What will I be learning while the girls do maths?"

"Mathematics as well. There is always more to learn."

As that wasn't the answer he wanted to hear, he pouted. "But I already told you that Mama and Papa have taught me everything I need to know and I'm hardly going to need anything more complex when I am going to be an entomologist." The nonchalance returned as he made his way to the globe and set it spinning. "I've been studying more important things, like surviving alone in the wild. I've even built my own treehouse, which Norbert and I camp in overnight all the time and which I doubt many other boys of ten are clever enough to do. I can light a fire without a tinderbox and cook a meal on it. I bet Uncle Harry cannot even do that." His skinny chest puffed with pride. "Those are the sorts of skills an exploring entomologist needs all alone in a strange land. You do remember that I am going to sail around the world and record every insect on the planet, don't you?"

"Of course, I remember." Georgie nodded, ensuring her smile was encouraging and not in any way patronizing. "And after seeing how well you drew them yesterday, I have no doubt that *Insectum Mundus* will be Professor Felix Pendleton's magnum opus. One that academics will refer to for centuries to come." The boy's chest puffed some more at her compliment. "But it is going to be a jolly difficult thing to write if you cannot sail the seven seas single-handed, as you plan to, because you will never be able to do that without understanding complex mathematics." She gestured for him to sit, ignoring the outraged confusion that skittered across his features as he did so with reluctance.

"Navigation, for example, requires some very complex calculations." She really didn't have a clue what navigating required, so she guessed in as convincing a manner as she could with all the bravado of an expert on the subject. "If you get the angles and the sums wrong, you could end up anywhere. Get the wind speed wrong and you could crash your vessel into the rocks because you did not leave enough time to slow it down. Not to mention, as I am sure your uncle will concur if we ask his expert naval opinion, the dangers of not calculating your provisions correctly, or worse, distributing the weight of them incorrectly belowdecks. The consequences for the good ship, Felix, could be catastrophic. There will be no seven volumes on insects if you starve to death or die of thirst on your voyage. Nor will the world ever get to read your life's work if your vessel has sunk to the bottom of the sea with you still in it."

"But . . ."

Fortunately, the timely arrival of Marianne and Grace with Polly, the young scullery maid who had been commandeered to act as the children's nanny in the mornings and at bedtime, prevented further argument.

"Good morning, girls. Please take your seats." Georgie ushered them into the room while the maid hovered in the doorway. She didn't appear to be much older than Felix herself. Fourteen, perhaps. Fifteen at a push. Too young to cope with the three boisterous Pendletons, that was for certain. The poor thing already looked as though she had been run ragged by the effort it had taken to shepherd them all into their clothes and down to the dining room.

"The children have had their breakfast and the captain told me to remind you that their luncheon will be served promptly at one and their supper on the dot of five." To her credit, Polly looked as uncomfortable issuing that reminder as Georgie was galled to hear it, and wrung her hands, pained. "If there's nothing else you need me to do, Miss Rowe, Mrs. Rigsby needs me in the kitchen."

"If you would just take Norbert to the kitchen with you, Mr. Simpkins will know where to put him until the children finish their lessons." At least she hoped Simpkins did. She hadn't asked him. Had barely conversed with him at all, truth be told, because he regarded her with almost as much bewilderment and disapproval as the captain did.

"Norbert won't have that." Felix jumped out of his seat to plead the dog's case while stroking his floppy ears. "He *has* to stay with me. I saved his life, nursed him back from starvation, and gave him a home, so we have an unbreakable bond. Norbert needs to be by my side else he'll misbehave again."

"That's true," said Marianne, nodding as Norbert buried his nose in his young master's thigh. "Ever since the first day he found him half drowned on the beach, Norbert is hopelessly devoted to Felix. Trying to separate them will not end well."

As if she agreed, or was too terrified of Norbert to try, Polly was already backing out of the door. Before she bolted down the hallway, Georgie took hold of the dog's collar. "After Norbert misbehaved in here yesterday and almost destroyed my classroom, Norbert can enjoy his morning nap in peace while we do our lessons, and he and Felix will be reunited at luncheon. Isn't that right, Norbert?" She addressed the dog in a soothing, coercive voice as she tried to lure him toward Polly and the door, but sensing shenanigans and his immediate eviction, he planted his big paws beside his young master and refused to budge.

"See." Felix folded his arms, smug. "I told you he wouldn't have it. Dogs are the loyalest animals in the entire universe. They have always been a man's best friend, but when you save a dog's life, he will never abandon you." As a reward for that loyalty, Felix bent to stroke his best friend's ears while he stared back at Georgie, defiant. "Never."

She would not fall at the first hurdle because of a dog!

If brute force wasn't going to work, and his master wasn't going to help, there was always bribery. "I am sure Mrs. Rigsby has a nice treat for you in the kitchen, doesn't she, boy? A little bit of sausage perhaps?" Norbert's ears pricked up at just the mention of the word *sausage*. "Would you like a sausage?" He tilted his shaggy head in canine indecision as he looked from Felix to her, and she knew he was wavering. "Would Norbert like a lovely sausage?" Georgie sauntered to the door herself.

The dog almost stood.

Almost.

The powerful muscles in his back legs quivered as he hovered somewhere in between a sit and a stand. But then he glanced at Felix again for approval, and when the boy offered no encouragement beyond a stern glare, returned his shaggy bottom to the floor with a thud.

"No, Norbert!" She marched back to him and tried to be commanding, pulling herself to her full but pathetic height and staring him dead in the eye. "You need to go to the kitchen."

Norbert responded by turning his head away and pretending he could neither see nor hear her.

"Felix—take him to the kitchen now!" Georgie wagged her stern teacher finger and gave him her special patented schoolmistress's stare. A stare so deadly it had brought more than one errant pupil at Miss P's school to tears when they had dared to test her. Fortunately, it did not let her down today despite Felix's unbreakable bond with his dog and, after several defiant seconds during which both Marianne and Grace gave him a stern look too, the eldest Pendleton withered on the vine.

"Yes, Miss Rowe." The boy even bowed his head in shame as his sisters exhaled in relief. "Come on, Norbert. Let's go get you a sausage in the kitchen."

Where *sausage* had been the magic word mere moments ago, *kitchen* now had the opposite effect, and Norbert went from sitting to collapsing in a heap on the parquet. As Felix tugged on his collar, the dog went rigid, using his immense weight to glue himself to the floor. "No, Norbert!" The boy yanked the collar and the dog barely slid an inch. "You have to go to the kitchen!"

Georgie and Marianne rushed to help maneuver the beast out, and between the three of them, they managed to drag him another foot toward the door. Little Grace then joined in, pushing ineffectually from the rear, and while they all grunted from exertion, all Polly the scullery maid did was blink at them.

"Some help would be appreciated, Polly," Georgie said through gritted teeth, and after yet another blinking pause, the girl entered the fray.

Finally, they had some purchase on the prostrate Norbert and managed to shift him another two feet before his carcass went from inflexible to floppy. It made no scientific sense, defying all the laws of gravity, but for some reason a floppy Norbert was now quadruple the weight of a stiffened Norbert, and no matter what the five of them tried, the lax muscles had rendered him immovable. Almost as if he were now part of the very fabric of the floor itself and there forever.

"Oh, for goodness' sake!" Like a petulant child, Georgie stamped her foot, furious that she had been bested by a dog on only her second day when he had been partly responsible for thoroughly ruining her first. As she racked her brains for an alternative means of moving him, she glanced at the looming clock and realized, with a start, that she had already wasted fifteen minutes of valuable lesson time. Any more and she would be woefully behind her new schedule, the blank sheets of paper atop the children's desks would not be covered in reams of sums, and the lack of evidence of a rigorous and traditional mathematics lesson would hardly impress the captain when he came to inspect her later.

If the dog refused to compromise, someone had to.

"Norbert can stay for this morning." She consoled herself that it was only a temporary surrender while she regrouped. "But he will not be allowed into this room this afternoon under any circumstances." She would barricade the door with her own body if necessary because when the captain returned at the end of the day, there would be no dog to spoil her tidy, disciplined oasis of quiet. This time she would pass muster.

She would pass it with flying colors!

On that she was resolute.

# EIGHT

◈

*H*arry could hear Norbert's plaintive howling the second he turned onto Hanover Square a little before five. It was so loud he didn't need Lady Flatman to flag him down to inform him of it, yet she did anyway.

"He hasn't stopped for three hours, Captain Kincaid. *Three. Whole.* HOURS!" His most disagreeable neighbor clasped her hands beneath her ample bosom as she glared at him while he dismounted so he could be admonished on her level. "It is wholly unacceptable, sir, to expect the other residents in the square to be forced to listen to that commotion while you are off gallivanting."

There was no point in clarifying that trying to get the bloody useless layabouts on the bloody *Boadicea* to finally finish boarding the deck so the rest of the urgent work on it could commence was not gallivanting. And the less said about the new and urgent situation with supplies in Portsmouth, the better. Lady Flatman wouldn't care if a ship full of sailors set off across the Atlantic with nowhere near enough food to keep them alive until they arrived in Nova Scotia. She wasn't a fan of men in general. Something she had made more than plain, repeatedly, ever since he inherited the house. They were all libertines, chancers, and despoilers as far as she was concerned, and nothing would shake her of that rigid opinion. But she had taken an instant dislike to him the day he had moved in simply because he had the affrontery to be not only a man, but an unmarried one, to boot. For apparently, bachelors were all in league with the devil and his very presence was enough to turn the genteel tranquility of this tiny corner of Mayfair into Hades.

"You are quite right, Lady Flatman. I will do my utmost to ensure that it does not happen again."

He knew that was a promise he couldn't keep, but he made it anyway. It had been a long day already, and Harry had only left the Admiralty for an hour so that he could check on his equally useless layabout governess. Incessantly wondering about her today had been more of a distraction than he needed, and she had invaded his concentration too many times in the worst possible way. Thanks to her, and blasted Flora's blasted children, there was a mountain of work he still had to attend to when he returned. So tall it would be a bloody miracle if he saw his bed before midnight again tonight. If he wasn't careful, at this rate, he would keel over from exhaustion before the month was out. A man in his prime wasn't meant to survive on five paltry hours of sleep a night. When he was admiral of the fleet, he would issue a directive insisting that all sailors should get at least eight as standard. They'd be more efficient as a result, so that was hardly an indulgence.

"That dog is a menace, Captain Kincaid. A *menace*!" He nodded because he couldn't argue with that—and because there was little point in doing anything but nodding. When Lady Flatman wanted to tear him off a strip, there was nothing to be done except take it on the chin, look contrite, and settle in for the duration. "My poor maids have still not been able to eradicate the stain of his mishap from my doorstep." She pointed to it and Harry dutifully glanced that way.

"I apologize again for that . . . um . . . mishap. Sincerely." The white stone looked spotless as far as he was concerned, and by his own admission he had higher standards than most, so he would have noticed any hint of a stain, but he composed his expression to one of penitent solemnity anyway. Then tried to maintain it without wincing as Norbert let rip again with a cry so tragic one would think he was in the midst of having his tail sawn off with a blunt blade.

"If that incessant howling wasn't enough outrage for your unfortunate neighbors to have to endure, you also seem determined to bring the entire neighborhood into *disrepute* too."

There was something about the way she said that with such a scandalized shudder that made him think that he was missing some vital piece of information. "Has Norbert done worse than howl today, Lady Flatman?" Because if Simpkins had fed him chicken again, or worse, let him near a pie man, Harry would not be responsible for his actions. Just in case, he scanned the pavement for the foul evidence until Lady Flatman jabbed him in the arm with her finger.

Hard.

"I am not talking about your disgusting dog." She was bristling now, her face contorted in a scowl so fierce it would curdle milk. "For it is you that I find more *disgusting*!"

"Me?" Harry looked around again, although Lord only knew what for. "What have I done?" Apart from go to the Admiralty before the cock crowed, work until he was cross-eyed on nonsense not of his making, and return home exhausted. His day had been so full, he hadn't even had time for any luncheon. He was pretty certain a man in his prime wasn't meant to survive on two hasty slices of

toast in the small hours any more than he could with just five hours
of sleep. Thanks to tiredness and hunger, he could barely spell his
own name.

For one futile moment, he hoped that he was hallucinating this
entire conversation until Lady Flatman prodded him again.

"Have you no *shame*, Captain? I know that morals are lax in the
navy and that a sailor has a girl in every port—" She dropped her
voice to a hissed whisper. "But moving your *fancy woman* into your
house, here in the genteel environs of Hanover Square, while decent
families reside all around you, is beyond the pale!"

"I can assure you that I do not have a fancy woman, Lady Flatman!" The very chance would be a fine thing when he barely had the
time nowadays to sleep in his bed, let alone have some recreation in
it beforehand.

"I saw her!" His pious neighbor looked at him down her crooked
nose as if he were the steaming mess Norbert had left on her doorstep.
She pointed to the severe slate gray bun on top of her head. "Red hair
and . . ." She flapped her hand in the vicinity of her bosoms, which
sat significantly lower than the pert pair owned by the flame-haired
vixen she was complaining about. "Let's just say she looks the sort
who would tempt."

Harry didn't know whether to laugh, cry, or be affronted by the
suggestion. He picked affronted purely because he thought it was
the one his neighbor would find more acceptable. He figured it was
better that she witness his outrage than to acknowledge his woeful
lack of any whiff of a fancy woman or to admit that, for all her faults,
there was no denying that his new governess was exactly the sort who
tempted—damn her. The hair and bosoms alone were enough to turn
his head. Add in the finer-than-fine green eyes, the tart, sultry mouth,
and all that alabaster skin, and she was practically a siren. Thank

goodness she had an objectionable personality and was atrocious at her job, as every idiot knew that sailors and sirens did not mix—as his last disastrous dalliance with a siren was testament. Elizabeth, Lord bless her treacherous soul, had quite put him off sirens for life.

"Miss Rowe is not my fancy woman, Lady Flatman, and I resent the implication both on her behalf and mine!" Sometimes a man had to stand up and be counted rather than nod—even if that meant locking horns futilely with the perennially outraged Lady bloody Flatman! "Miss Rowe is the governess I have hired to look after my nieces and nephew in my sister's absence!" In case that wasn't rebuttal enough, he felt compelled to elaborate. "And she is not just any old governess, Lady Flatman, she is one of the best. From Miss Prentice's School for Young Ladies, no less, hired at immense cost because she was trained as one of the *crème de la crème* and with a string of impeccable references to prove it!"

None of which he had seen, nor would he believe after the shambles he had witnessed in her classroom yesterday, but still!

"So the shame is on you, Lady Flatman, for casting such egregious aspersions on her fine character and, I feel aggrieved to add, on mine!" It felt good to expel some of his pent-up anger at his objectionable and holier-than-thou neighbor. Pointless, of course, in the grand scheme of things, as it would only make the woman hate him more, but cathartic. It also couldn't hurt to vocalize his vehement denial of any attraction he might harbor for the flame-haired, Confucius-quoting temptress, because he absolutely would not succumb to it.

Only an idiot stuck his hand in the fire twice.

"Shame. On. *YOU!*" He gathered up his horse's reins and looked down his own nose in disgust as he stomped off toward his own front door while fresh but righteous anger bubbled in his gut.

*Fancy woman!*

As if he had any free hours left in his week to enjoy one! The last time he had spent time alone with a woman in the altogether had been . . .

He searched his mind.

Well . . . he almost had a passionate affair with a lusty Scottish widow when he had visited the Glasgow shipyard last autumn.

Or at least he assumed it would have been a passionate affair if it had got that far. The clandestine kiss he had enjoyed with her in an alcove at the Officers' Ball had certainly felt promising until a crisis involving a shortfall of rigging had called him back to London. Which meant . . .

*Good grief!*

Could things really be more depressing? Was it really last summer that he had last taken a tumble between a willing woman's sheets? That was almost a year! Or had it been last spring—in which case, it was over a year, and somehow, that depressed him further.

And more importantly, surely it wasn't natural for a man in his prime to go without that for so long? No wonder his mood was so low and he had lost all the spring in his step. He had been blaming being overloaded with work at the Admiralty for his unsettling dissatisfaction with his life when his lack of a very different sort of *satisfaction* undoubtedly had a hand in it! It probably explained why he had experienced such a visceral and inappropriate jolt of lust for his useless governess yesterday too.

Instantly, his melancholy was replaced by relief, because it wasn't natural!

It wasn't natural at all—thank goodness! But it was easily fixed.

Which also meant that Miss Rowe wasn't special in any way at all. Harry did not need to worry about having his head turned again by a dangerous siren because history was not about to repeat itself. His overwhelming reaction to her yesterday hadn't been so much her as the fact that she was *female*.

A man in his prime wasn't designed to go without for so long and despite all of Flora's constant nagging that at thirty it was long past time that he stopped sowing his wild bachelor oats, got back in the saddle, and found himself a wife, she had a point. While he was a good decade away from being a high enough rank to consider marriage, the real problem was that since his promotion to the Admiralty, he had woefully neglected sowing any wild bachelor oats at all!

His field of oats was barren!

He had some serious catching up to do.

But where the blazes was he supposed to find the time when the blasted Admiralty and the bloody *Boadicea* currently took all of it?

He pondered that new worry while the groom relieved him of his horse and Simpkins relieved him of his coat, then banished it to add it to his list of things to do. Right now, he had a bigger problem to contend with. He jerked his head toward her classroom. "Dare I ask how today went, Simpkins?"

As his butler's expression was taut thanks to all the howling and goodness knew what else, Harry braced himself to hear the worst.

"That blasted mutt will be the death of me!" He used a dusting rag to punctuate each word, clearly at his wit's end as he was still wearing his brown polishing apron, which he would never usually be seen dead in to open the door. "He's been caterwauling outside the kitchen door nonstop for hours now!"

As Harry really couldn't do anything to solve the problem that was Norbert, he ignored that. "How did our new governess cope with her first full day with the hellions?"

"They haven't killed her. Or at least they hadn't when I last saw her at luncheon. She could very well be dead by now, of course. I certainly wish I was." With that optimistic report, Simpkins marched off, muttering old sea dog obscenities about Norbert as he disappeared back to his polishing.

Alone, Harry allowed himself a few seconds of calm before he steeled himself to enter the lion's den and behold the havoc that been wreaked today. Despite knowing it had to be done, and the inevitable carnage he knew he would be confronted with aside, after his peculiar reaction to her yesterday, he would feel much happier avoiding Miss Rowe today. And forever for that matter too.

He considered knocking on the classroom door, and was about to, when the door opened and there she was.

"Good afternoon, Captain." She stepped to one side and ushered him in with a regal sweep of her arm. "The children will not be long—they are just finishing their penmanship practice."

Which miraculously—unless he actually was hallucinating thanks to his lack of food, sleep, and oat sowing—indeed they were.

To his great surprise, all three of Flora's hellions were not only seated behind their desks, which he noted still defiantly faced the opposite direction to his clock, they at least all had pens in their grubby hands. They were also using them in the way pens were made to be used.

More shocking was that the rest of the classroom was as neat as a pin. Instead of the chaos he had expected, there was glorious order. Almost as if she had done the impossible and completely conquered the children's rebellious, uncivilized natures in just one day.

He would have been seriously impressed if she had also looked as neat as her classroom. Instead, Miss Rowe was undeniably frayed around the edges. Wisps of her pretty copper hair shot out like sparks from her head and the rest of her hairstyle was lopsided. Although bizarrely, and much to his chagrin, it suited her. However, there was also a tightness around her fine eyes, and her plump mouth was a trifle pinched. He also could not help noticing a tear in her rumpled dark skirt that revealed two inches of the frothy white petticoat beneath it. While his woman-starved, overworked, and sleep-deprived mind did not need the further distraction of a glimpse of her underwear, all the clues were there to suggest she was a woman who had been through an ordeal. One who was clinging to the façade of effortless control and serenity by her fingernails.

Even so, Harry was still, begrudgingly, impressed.

He hadn't managed coming anywhere close to serenity with the three lovable reprobates in the five days since they had arrived. Yet here they all were. Quiet, seated, and working. That was a bloody miracle of biblical proportions. As confounding and unimaginable as feeding five thousand with just five loaves and fishes.

He wanted to ask her how she had done it.

Take her hand and shake it.

But instead, he gave her a half smile of approval because something about the angelic scene before him seemed too inconceivable to be fully believed and raised his suspicious hackles.

Maybe even galled.

He was big enough to admit this ungracious, distrusting jealousy likely stemmed from the overwhelming feelings of inadequacy which suddenly swamped him because what she had achieved, in next to no time, was truly beyond him.

"Have you all had a productive day?" For some inexplicable reason, he was rocking on his heels, and because he had no earthly idea what to do with his hands, had clasped them behind his back like his grandfather the admiral used to do when he was inspecting the fleet.

And maybe it was his imagination, but even Miss Rowe seemed to be standing to attention as if he were.

Which was progress indeed too!

"We have, Captain. Just look at their work."

Shyly, Grace held up hers to show him lines and lines of smudged squiggles. "I have been learning to join my *S*'s." Thankful for that explanation as it gave him a clue what to look for, he smiled.

"That I can see, poppet." He couldn't. "Well done."

As the other two were now staring at him expecting similar praise, Harry took a few seconds to appreciate their work too. Felix wrote like the impatient boy he was. The hastily scratched prose and accompanying blots looked as if a nest of his beloved spiders had scurried through the ink and scrambled across the page. But Felix had written something at least, so he would be grateful for small mercies.

Marianne's handwriting was exactly like her: all bold, artful, sloping strokes which reminded him a great deal of her mother's handwriting. Flora's letters were always a thing of beauty—to behold, at least—while the chaotic but chatty contents of them often made his hair stand on end.

The last one had described, in alarming detail, her short but eventful "adventure" with glassblowing. Although how she could find humor in setting her frock on fire and having to be sluiced with an emergency bucket of water before her hair went up in flames too was anybody's guess. But that summed up his mad sister in a nutshell. Life was just one big lark for Flora. Any day, he expected to receive a cheery letter from the land of the pharaohs describing at length how she had been kidnapped by bandits while on a solo climb up the pyramids, or an essay on how she had accidentally found herself swimming with piranhas when the leaky boat she had decided to take rowing down the Nile, without oars, capsized.

His sister was as reckless as she was irresponsible—so was it any wonder her offspring were quite so . . . wild?

"Splendid work, everyone." In his peripheral vision, he saw Miss Rowe's stiff posture slump slightly in relief. The speed at which she corrected it once again suggested that something about the serene scene before him was off. Almost as if it had been choreographed. "Apart from handwriting, what else have you learned today?" Out of the corner of his suspicious eye, his new governess stiffened and that confirmed it.

"Well, we learned about this king who couldn't cook," said Grace with such excitement she almost fell off her chair, "but despite that he was still great."

"We studied Alfred the Great in our history lesson." Miss Rowe made a big show of glancing at the clock, doubtless as a ploy to get rid of him. "I am sure the children would be delighted to tell you all about him over supper." With just a tilt of her delectable body and an authoritarian clap of her hands, she dismissed him and her class at the same time. "Clear away now, everyone. You do not want to be late for Mrs. Rigsby's delicious repast tonight as I hear that treacle pudding is on the menu."

Then with a flick of just her finger, she directed them to place the papers on her desk and the books they had been using onto the bookshelf Harry had almost given himself a hernia over by dragging it into the room. The shelves now sported labels according to the subject and appeared to be filled with books that he had no hand in buying.

As the tidying took seconds, they were all chivvied out of the classroom en masse and he found himself spirited toward the dining room as little Grace dragged him by the hand, doubly suspicious as to why she was in such a hurry to see him gone.

It was on the tip of his tongue to ask but Grace squeezed his hand to command his attention instead. "We were very good today, Uncle Harry."

"I am very pleased to hear it." He beamed down at his youngest niece, still marveling at the astonishing transformation of the three destructive and feral miscreants at such impressive speed regardless of his niggling suspicions as to how.

Perhaps he should be chastising himself for ever doubting Miss Rowe's abilities? He wasn't convinced, but he was supremely grateful that he at least still had a governess and that, on the surface at least, things were going better than expected. He would keep his beady eye on her until she had convinced him. After all, as Sun Tzu quite rightly said, it was always prudent to keep your friends close and your enemies closer. Whichever Miss Rowe was would soon reveal itself.

"I am very proud of you all."

And he was.

So proud he ruffled Felix's hair, as he had fully expected the boy to be the first to lead the rebellion today. His nephew had a stubborn streak a mile wide and, like blasted Flora, had an allergy to being kept inside. "After all these years of barbarousness, who knew you had such restraint and dedication in you?" Harry hadn't, but suddenly, everything in his garden was rosy again now that calmness had been, at least temporarily, restored to his house.

He wasn't really beguiled by Miss Rowe, simply in dire need of a woman's touch. Miss Rowe could both teach and discipline children exactly as Miss Prentice had promised and Flora's little savages could behave! How bloody marvelous was all that?

All he had to do was find the time to eat, sleep, and sow some of those well-needed and well-earned wild oats, and his garden wouldn't just be rosy—it would be in full bloom.

That warm, reassured, and relieved feeling lasted all of five seconds until Marianne ruined it.

"Of course we did you proud, Uncle Harry." She whispered this out of the side of her mouth so that Miss Rowe could not hear. "Only a blithering idiot would ruin the chance of unlimited ice cream at Gunther's before Saturday and not even Felix is that stupid."

*T*f I were to measure it in fractions, he is nine-tenths dislikable. He is a staid, stiff, pompous fuddy-duddy who has archaic ideas about the education of children and a tendency to lean toward the draconian in its execution."

Georgie was still smarting about the way Captain Kincaid had criticized her that first afternoon despite him holding his counsel in the three days since. However, it was as plain as the perfectly straight nose on his disapproving face every evening at precisely five minutes to five that he was biting his tongue about her methods as hard as she was biting hers about his. Where, devil take him, he somehow managed to emerge from nine hours working at the Admiralty and a brisk horse ride home across the city without a single hair out of place while she always resembled a woman who had been dragged through a hedge backward.

Thankfully, there were no lessons to worry about on Saturday or Sunday, so this morning she had taken the children, the dog, and Felix's cricket bat to St. James's Park. They all had a thoroughly lovely

time whacking the ball around while Norbert assisted with the fielding, then spent the remaining hour catching tadpoles in a glass jar so
they could study them properly before they released them back into
the pond.

All without any threat of scrutiny or silent judgment from her
impeccable stickler of an employer.

She had only been in his employ for half a week and already
dreaded those brief, daily visits to her classroom more than anything.
His intense brown gaze was always everywhere as he asked questions
about everything the children had learned. Georgie knew he would
scrutinize all their written work for the day, too, given half a chance,
and not just the pages she allowed him to see. Although why she felt
compelled to hide the rest was a mystery, as almost all the children's
written work was perfectly fine. If one ignored Felix's woeful lack of
any formal mathematics work—which he had a talent for avoiding
until she tricked him into learning some covert sums outside during
their breaks—he at least made a stab at everything else. And while
his sloppy handwriting might leave a lot to be desired, the boy had
a clever and mature way with the written word. Marianne loved to
write irrespective of whether that was numbers or letters, and little
Grace was doing perfectly fine, too, especially when one considered
she was only five.

But when the captain's annoyingly symmetrical dark brows furrowed every afternoon as he scanned each sheet of paper left on the
children's desks alongside whatever else she had left oh-so-casually
lying around on hers, she panicked. Especially when he always made
a point of querying why she had chosen to, again, waste at least one
to two valuable hours of learning in the garden in the middle of every
day where conveniently, no written work was ever done. She was already running out of ways to explain that, in her professional opinion,

not all learning had to be written down and that, in fact, the best learning often stuck in the brain when no writing was done at all.

Those brief visits unsettled her so much, she was on constant tenterhooks ever since. Especially as the daily handwriting lesson was really the only one in which the children fully behaved themselves how he expected them to. Marianne had a big hand in that. A bigger and more persuasive hand than the exiled Norbert's constant howling throughout every afternoon did to distract them all. For some reason, and despite the withering power of Georgie's trusty schoolmistress's stare, Marianne's was just as potent. Whenever the other two siblings began to lose focus, she gave them a warning look that somehow held the power to bring even Felix up short.

As much as it had come in useful in the last few days, the unspoken message in Marianne's eyes and the way Felix especially seemed to physically suppress himself while under the glare of it bothered her. Georgie could not quite put her finger on why, but the feeling that they all knew something which she didn't refused to go away, and that unsettled her almost as much as the captain's daily inspections did.

"And the other tenth?" Typically, Portia asked the most important question and the only one Georgie couldn't yet answer. Three and a half days in and she still couldn't quite work Captain Kincaid out at all. In so many ways, he reminded her of the colonel and yet in so many more ways, he didn't.

"Hard to say." She stared at the Saturday afternoon rowing boats bobbing on the Serpentine while she tried to find the right way to explain her conundrum. "The children plainly adore him. So does the dog, although goodness knows why as the captain seems to have even less patience with Norbert than he does with me—and that is saying something." It was as clear as the suspicion shimmering in the stickler's stormy, dark eyes that he was unimpressed with everything about Georgie. Even her carrot-colored hair vexed him. She knew that for a fact because his gaze would often flick to the top of her head as if he couldn't quite believe hair could be such an awful color either.

"Is he cruel to him?"

"No!" It was a vehement response because she would not have been able to stay employed by a man who was cruel to an innocent animal. "He moans about Norbert but . . ." She huffed because the truth only made the captain more likable. "He never fails to stroke his ears when the dog comes to him, and when he thinks nobody is looking, he even allows Norbert to lick his face while he kisses his nose." She had almost choked when she had spied that from her hiding place on the landing last night when the captain had arrived home late.

"Well, that is always a good sign." Lottie threw the last crumbs of the bread she had brought with her at the swans waiting for it at the water's edge. Thanks to their different work commitments, that there were three of them all in the same place at the same time was almost unheard of nowadays. The only friend missing on their little jaunt through Hyde Park this sunny Saturday afternoon off was Kitty, who was traveling with her latest employers around the south coast. "Children and animals are always the best gauge of a person's character."

Lottie dusted the last crumbs from her hands with an unladylike slap, then threaded her arms through Georgia's and Portia's as the three of them set off around the Serpentine back toward Mayfair. "Dogs especially are stingy with their affections if they sense anything untoward. One of our most docile farm dogs took such a dislike to the oil seller, we had to shut her in the stables whenever the man turned up. We could not fathom why. But then it came to light that the oil seller was a wanted criminal. A murderer, no less! A man who had swindled an old lady in the next county and then throttled her when she threatened to report him to the authorities. But the dog knew that the scoundrel wasn't a decent man the second she met him. Because dogs *know* such things. They are always a better judge of character than us humans."

"Maybe." Georgie refused to believe that the dim-witted Norbert was a better judge of character than she was. "Except he is such a stickler. For everything, but most particularly time. Do you know he even wears two pocket watches! And constantly refers to both. What sort of a person does that?" She had certainly never witnessed the like.

"One who cannot afford to be late. Or one who is so important his time is stretched to the limit. Neither make him a bad man." Lottie's reasonable, rational, and cheerful acceptance of the captain's most peculiar quirk irritated Georgie. "Perhaps if we buy Kitty two, she might actually remember to use one of them and will thus keep this new post longer than she managed the last. Just five days to get dismissed is a staggering record—even for her."

It was, but Georgie had only been working for the captain for four days and could not shake the worry that despite the neat and tidy classroom and well-behaved children he saw every afternoon at five minutes to five sharp, he still did not trust her as far as he could throw her. Nor did he particularly seem to like her either. He most definitely did not rate her abilities as a governess, else he wouldn't keep checking up on her. Which meant that all her hard work to change his initial poor opinion of her had failed. All in all, she was unnerved—by the apparent precariousness of her situation and more so by the man.

Something peculiar happened to her skin whenever he was close by. It heated and prickled and tingled and did not seem to fit her bones properly. It was so overwhelming, she could not get him out of her classroom fast enough—which at least meant that the children were never late for supper.

"An obsession with the clock is an objectionable quality, to be sure, but I'll wager that isn't the main thing about your captain that grates." Portia's good opinion was never easily won. She was a cynic at heart—usually too cynical, in Georgie's humble opinion—but in this instance, it was welcome.

"It isn't. He has an annoying tendency to quote military leaders, even the unworthy ones." Friday it had been Napoleon, after she had reassured him that all was well, so he really did not need to keep disrupting his busy day to inspect hers when he could ask Simpkins or Mrs. Rigsby to do it in his stead. He had shrugged. Then suppressed a smile as he said, "If you want a thing done well, do it yourself." And for once, the wretch even quoted Old Boney verbatim too. "He is also interfering and obviously arrogant enough to assume that his interference is necessary."

"All men think they know best, that hardly makes your captain unique. It does guarantee that he is vexatious, however." As a sister to a house full of brothers, Lottie had the most experience with the breed. "Is he also patronizing and condescending?"

"He is absolutely both of those things too. And so disapproving he puts me on edge." She had also never been so aware of her own body in her life as she was when his was nearby. "He was engaged once—apparently—though it came to naught, and one cannot but wonder if that was because he is so intractable that he made the poor woman run a mile." For how exactly could any woman measure up to the high standards he both set and expected?

How did any mere mortal?

"He's a nitpicker. A man who seems to expect the entire universe to bend to his will. He's too serious and far too full of his own importance."

"Again, all traits that simply make him male." Lottie brushed it all aside. "Throw in some gravitas in society and a healthy bank balance and you could be describing every gentleman of the *ton*."

Except he wasn't like every other gentleman of the *ton*. Most of those mere mortal aristocrats spent their days balancing their ledgers and their evenings at their clubs and hadn't accomplished any of what Captain Kincaid had. They hadn't risen through the ranks at lightning speed on nothing but their own merit. Nor did they single-handedly keep the entire Royal Navy afloat, which, if Mrs. Rigsby or Simpkins were to be believed, he did.

"You will get used to it." Portia squeezed her arm. "And you will rise above it and put your duty first as Miss Prentice taught you to because, frankly, you desperately need the money and the reference he will write after you have earned every penny."

"But I am not convinced my duty is to him when surely it should be to the children I have been tasked with educating?"

She was coming to despise the regimented nature of her lessons inside and resented that she had to keep a close eye on the clock to avoid spending more time outside than he would allow her to get away with. Her inner Joan of Arc had always flexed against unreasonable rules and boundaries, and she had bitten her tongue so much since Wednesday, it was a wonder she had any tongue left. Her classroom already felt less like her domain and more like a prison thanks to him and, like the children and Norbert, she wanted to be outside. What better place to teach them about the world than being surrounded by it? Especially when outside, they always got so much done! The Pendleton brood weren't used to a classroom. Felix and Grace, especially, found the confines of one stifling. Every time she was released from her seat, that little girl had accumulated so much unspent energy, she practically exploded and ran into something or fell over something. The poor thing was covered in bruises. "Shouldn't their needs come first?"

Now it was Lottie's turn to squeeze her arm. "That is the tightrope we have to walk, Georgie darling. The trick is to make it appear as if your duty is to the captain on the surface, while doing what you think best for the children behind his back. Once he stops watching you like a hawk, I have no doubt that you will work out how to do that, for what you lack in diplomacy, you make up for with tenacity. In the meantime, rather than resent his interference, try to see it in a positive light." If Portia was the cynical friend, Lottie was the eternal optimist. "He clearly cares enough about his nieces and nephew that he feels the need to reassure himself that they are being properly looked after."

"You can choose to see it that way. I choose to call a stiff and pompous nitpicker a stiff and pompous nitpicker." Yet even that apt description did not seem to properly fit the man. "Although, once in a while the captain does seem . . ." How to describe a feeling—an instinct even—that wasn't fully formed. "Almost human."

Portia laughed at that pathetic attempt to distill her conflicted emotions into words. "As opposed to what?"

Georgie shrugged, amused herself by her own inarticulateness despite the inordinate amount of time she had dedicated to pondering Captain Harry Kincaid so far. "A soldier. A sailor. An officer. A stiff and unyielding military being who expects everything to be just so and believes all his orders are so profound that they should be followed to the letter." Because he was so much like the colonel in so many ways, it made no sense to her that he really wasn't like her horrid stepfather at all. Apart from being as unhealthily obsessed with his career as the colonel had been, of course.

"That simply makes him *an employer.*" Portia offered her a pitying smile. "This is still your first position, Georgie, and—"

"There is no need to rub it in!" Even amongst her best friends, her own shocking failure at securing a post after so many attempts was humiliating. "I can assure you, that was not for want of trying."

"I did not mean it as a dig," said Portia, unoffended, "merely an observation. You have come to this all bright-eyed and bushy-tailed, enthused with lofty plans and even loftier expectations of what your role as a governess entails. Whereas those of us who have suffered employment for a while now have had all that wistful enthusiasm ground down. Mostly by the crushing realization that in the real world, we are not considered rational, independent, useful, and talented women at all, but mere *employees.* Paid to do a job, but instantly forgettable after we have worn ourselves out to do it well. And easily replaceable if we fail to measure up to our taskmaster's expectations."

Her politically radical friend curled her lip in disgust at the word *taskmaster.* "I am afraid nothing about that will change until the right to vote is extended to the minions as well as the masters. Until that necessary revolution happens, do what I do. Think of the Four *D*'s and force yourself act in the manner that we have been trained to, even if doing so gets on your last nerve and makes you hate yourself."

"Duty, decorum, diligence, and discretion at all times," parroted Georgie and Lottie in their usual parody of Miss Prentice's lecturing tone before they wiggled their eyebrows simultaneously. Because, since they had been girls, they had promised themselves that after a life of service and good behavior, when they were all wizened spinsters expected to shrivel and die quietly, they had plans to do the opposite. To pool their resources and buy a cottage somewhere, then

spend their dotages doing absolutely everything in their power to purposefully and outrageously ignore all four of Miss P's hallowed tenets
until the last one of them turned up their toes. It might be cold comfort
for the husband she would never get to marry or the family she would
never get the chance to make—but at least it was something to look
forward to even if it wasn't what her heart wanted.

"Exactly! And if that fails to stop you railing at the heavens at
the cruel injustices of life, console yourself that as a governess, you
come significantly higher in the servants' pecking order and get paid
more than a poor, abused scullery maid while trying to ignore that
because of the *inferiorities* of your sex"—Portia paused to scowl
again at what she considered the most flagrant of those injustices—
"and your inability to wear breeches in public, you will never achieve
the superior status or salary of a butler or a gamekeeper."

"I've worn breeches in public," said Lottie with a grin, "and can
confirm it is very liberating. In fact . . ." She dropped her voice to a
giggled whisper. "I am wearing them now." When they both gaped,
appalled, at her, her grin turned smug. "I often put them on instead
of a petticoat. It makes running after *my* pompous employer's awful
children so much easier and one never knows when a clandestine
opportunity to ride something from his lordship's fine stable arises.
If the family all disappear in the carriage, for instance, on an impromptu trip to Gunther's, I need to be prepared."

"You do know that he will dismiss you on the spot if he ever
catches you." Portia rolled her eyes in despair. "Exactly like Lord
Rochford did when his neighbor tipped him off that you kept riding
his stallion."

"That horse was put on this earth to run like the wind." Lottie
waved that caution away as if it was no matter. "Not trot along sedately
under the weight of his fat backside. And please do not give me *that*

look, Portia Kendall, as obviously I have learned from my mistakes and now avidly avoid riding in Hyde Park like the plague, no matter how early the hour. Nowadays all I do here is stroll around sedately like a proper governess should and, if the whim strikes, I sometimes feed the ducks." Their incorrigible friend wiggled her brows. "On the subject of feeding and impromptu trips to Gunther's, I am starving, so who fancies an ice cream?"

With nothing better to do, the three of them hurried out of the park and along Charles Street until they joined the queue of people waiting patiently outside the shop at the corner of Berkeley Square.

A queue that, thanks to the clement, sunny weather, stretched so long it almost curved into Bruton Lane.

"If they have run out of violet ice before we get to the front of this ridiculous line, I shan't be responsible for my actions." Lottie stood on tiptoes to see if she could spy the counter through the window. "The lemon is a poor substitute."

Being taller than both of them, Portia also raised herself to get a better look. "Rest easy. There is an entire barrel full of violet. Enough for everyone here—not that I shall be having any, because today's cakes look too divine. There is a raspberry confection that has my name on it."

Also preferring cake to ice cream, and too short to see anything but the man in front's armpit, Georgie had to wait until the queue shuffled several paces forward before she was finally able to crane her neck high enough to get a look at the display for herself. Then instantly froze at the sight of her employer sitting at a table directly in front of it.

Laughing.

*Laughing!*

Who knew that he could? Or that it would suit him so much when all she ever saw him do was frown.

At least to her.

"Oh my goodness!" Of all the people to collide with on her day off, it was the one she wished to see the least. Especially since he was the picture of dashing, sartorial elegance in his perfectly tailored forest-green coat whereas the stiff breeze that had whipped across the Serpentine had played havoc with her coiffure. To such an extent that not even the twenty pins she had used to secure it had held it in place properly. Doubtless her head looked as if a bright orange firework had exploded beneath the brim of her bonnet. "We need to go!"

Her first instinct was to run, and she would have if Lottie hadn't dragged her back by the sleeve.

"Not before I get my violet ice!" Then, noticing Georgie's panicked expression, Lottie kept hold of it. "Is everything all right? Only you look as though you've seen a ghost."

"He's not so much a ghost as Captain Kincaid!" Doing her best to hide behind Portia, and with her back turned to the window, she subtly gestured his way. Too subtly, apparently, as both Lottie and Portia were now both craning their necks trying to make him out.

"Is he the one with the crinkly gray hair and the straining coat?" Portia's curious gaze was too close to the window. "For if he is, I must concur that he *does* look like an old curmudgeon."

"Not him. The captain is the dark-haired fellow. Seated beside the potted palm." She would have added the tall, commanding, outrageously good-looking one with the dazzling smile but kept that description to herself in case her friends decided to tease her about it.

"There are four potted palms and several dark-haired gentlemen." Lottie's face was also now so close to the window her breath was misting it. Georgie yanked her back.

"Could you try acting with a bit more discretion!" Despite the wall and several rows of busy tables beyond it, it still felt appropriate to drop her voice to a whispered hiss. "You are a protégé, after all."

"Could you try to be a bit more specific, then!" Lottie did a very poor job of acting nonchalant as she continued to search for him. "There must be close to a hundred people in there and at least twenty of them are gentlemen with dark hair."

Realizing that she would not be allowed to escape until her friends had seen the dratted captain for themselves, Georgie did a quick, surreptitious scan behind and blinked in shock when she finally noticed Felix, Marianne, and Grace sat with him. Had they just arrived? Or had she been so overwhelmed by the sight of him they had been rendered invisible? "He is the one directly in front and to the left of the counter. The one sitting alone with the three children."

There was a long pause until Lottie broke it.

"*That* is Captain Kincaid?"

She nodded.

"*That* is your uptight, pompous, staid fuddy-duddy?"

She nodded again, scrunching her eyelids in mortification. "Oh, this is just too awful! I really cannot go in there. I wouldn't know the first thing to say to him outside of work."

"He really doesn't look like a fuddy-duddy," said Portia as she eyed him with open curiosity. "Or a stickler or a self-important nit-picker for that matter either."

"Looks can be deceiving." Just because he was suddenly smiling at the children did not mean he wasn't an arrogant, insufferable pedant the rest of the time.

"On the subject of looks," Lottie said, nudging her. "You failed to mention that Captain Kincaid looked so . . . *splendid*. Or that he is a prime physical specimen of manhood or that he is filled with so much obvious *vim* and *vigor*. Or that he fills his coats so magnificently." She wiggled her brows. "I wish my employer were so easy on the eye. I would forgive all his pomposity if he were as tall, dark, and handsome as yours is. In fact, I'd be happy to swap places with you, Georgie, if you find him too difficult to work for."

"So would I." Portia was practically ogling him through the window now. "If one is doomed for the foreseeable to be a minion, it would certainly make the injustice of it easier to bear if I were his."

"Now there's an idea . . . I know it goes against absolutely everything that Miss P taught us, but if I were you . . ." Lottie sighed dreamily. "I'd forget he was my employer and I'd use my wiles on him. A man like that needs thorough kissing, marrying, and skipping off into the sunset with, as I should imagine it would be heavenly to wake up next to him in the morning." As a farmer's daughter, Lottie had always been the earthiest of them when it came to such things and often said things that shocked. But while that outrageous proposition was shocking enough, the next words were worse. "Although I sincerely doubt the night with him would be a chore either."

While Georgie's mouth gaped, Portia merely agreed, a wicked glimmer in her eye as she ogled the captain some more. "Oh, that wouldn't be a chore at all. Especially the kissing part. He has the look of a man who would do it well." Her friend chewed on her bottom lip as if she could taste his on it.

"Oh, indeed he does," agreed Lottie with another sigh. "Very well."

Georgie nudged them both to stop them gawking, oddly jealous that her friends were so tempted by the captain when they knew precisely what they were sighing about. Both had been thoroughly kissed at least thrice apiece by different gentlemen and had both been very candid about the experiences. In fact, after a particularly brief but passionate fusing of lips with one of her old employer's groomsmen last autumn, Lottie had declared a tie between the right sort of kiss and galloping across a field as the most invigorating and pleasurable experience a woman could have, and that spoke volumes.

It also threw up a great many questions now that she felt forced to contemplate the captain's lips herself. Enough that Georgie, who nobody had thus far ever wanted to steal a kiss from, briefly pondered what being kissed by him must be like until she checked herself. "I cannot believe what I am hearing! Nor that apparently you are both prepared to overlook every bad thing I have told you about him based purely on the breadth of his shoulders and the look of his mouth! Some friends you are!"

Portia exhaled in an uncharacteristically wistful fashion. "He does have excellent shoulders and a mouth to die for. I'd let him have me."

"Me too," said Lottie with a shameless leer at the captain again. "It's one thing to have to meet your maker without ever having a ring on your finger, but it would be a travesty to do so in a package marked UNOPENED, too, and he is . . ."

"Agreed." Portia nodded with a wicked smile. "A marvelous memory to recall on one's deathbed."

That was the last straw, and Georgie forgot to whisper. "Are you both so shallow that all it takes is a handsome face to seduce you?"

"It's not *just* his mouth or his face. Or even his shoulders, although those are incentive enough." An unrepentant Lottie turned to stare again, and when that earned her a jab in the arm, shrugged. "If one ignores his many attractive physical attributes, he also seems to have a nice way with the children."

"He is their uncle! Their only uncle—so he has to be nice to them."

"Do you see any other lone uncles in there, or even fathers for that matter, laughing over a mountain of ice cream with three children?" Lottie's eyes wandered back to Captain Kincaid in blatant appreciation. "Did *you* not hear what I told you about the perceptiveness of children and animals? If the dog loves him and those children plainly worship the ground he walks on, then he cannot be all bad, Georgie. It's simply not possible."

"Maybe he's been such a stickler toward you because he genuinely does care deeply about their welfare exactly as Lottie said. Have you considered that?" Clearly, Portia was now so enamored of his good looks that she had clean forgotten that she was a cynic who rarely gave anyone the benefit of the doubt until they had proved themselves worthy with deeds and not words. Instead, she smiled soppily as she gestured his way, needing neither deeds nor words when apparently, shoulders were quite enough. "And that is why they adore him so."

Of course they adored him! He was a man who excelled at everything, after all, so of course he would also excel at being an uncle too! The overachieving wretch.

"Anyone can bribe a child for an hour or so with ice cream." Although for some reason, he seemed to have bought the children the entire shop. "Stuffing them full of dessert does not make him redeemable. In fact, it suggests quite the opposite. That he is so irredeemable that the only way he can make them like him is to bribe them with treats." Even as she said it, Georgie didn't fully believe it. The children had loved him before the presence of ice cream. The way they spoke of him and the frequency in which he appeared in their conversations were proof that, for all his many, many, *many* faults, there was something intrinsically decent about him, even if she had no firsthand experience of it.

Felix had called him a good egg, when he forgot to be hardboiled, and there was no sign of that hardness today. The egg who sat inside Gunther's this afternoon was as soft as soft could be.

Against her will, she was compelled to glance at him again, and managed to catch him gently wiping little Grace's ice cream–covered chin with his napkin, watching him smile as he did so and his besotted niece smile back.

Drat him.

Portia was right. He adored those children too.

And a soft-boiled Captain Kincaid was not a version of him she ever wanted to be forced to contemplate.

## Chapter
# TEN

❧

*H*arry shook the worst of the water from his hair before he used his key to open the front door. He never expected poor Simpkins to wait up for him past eleven, and at almost two in the morning, his trusty retainer would have been in bed for hours. He had left the lamp burning low in the hallway though, and, as was customary when his master ran out of hours in the day at the Admiralty to do what they expected of him, he had left a fresh candle lying on the side to light his way to bed. Or to the kitchen where another solitary supper of bread, cheese, and cold cuts would be awaiting him.

Sadly, it was a routine which had become all too familiar in the last two years. The more supposedly impossible things he managed to get done, the more convoluted complications the top brass sent his way to test him. All problems that apparently nobody else in His Majesty's entire navy had the wherewithal to solve, and he resented it. They were relentless. The work, never-ending. Tonight, worn down and worn out and so sick and tired of the constant battles he had to fight on the navy's behalf, Harry felt as though he were drowning in it all, which was ironic as the rain outside was so torrential, it was a wonder he hadn't drowned on the miserable, lonely ride home.

That the sudden storm had materialized out of nowhere exactly three minutes after he had set off seemed indicative of his current bad luck, where everything that possibly could go wrong did. The bloody *Boadicea*, the constant stream of problems sent his way by the Admiralty, Flora's unexpected trip to Egypt, the unwelcome responsibility of the children. Mad Norbert. His troubling governess and his more troubling and unwelcome reaction to her, and now he could also add the collective merchants of Portsmouth into the mix. The latter had ensured that the lazier Sunday he had promised himself and willed his life away all week for was ruined before it had even started. All things completely out of his control, all conspiring together to take advantage and to put what felt like the weight of the world on his shoulders.

Being soaked to the skin with a good inch of water squishing inside his boots seemed like the least of his worries and a fitting end to one of the worst weeks of his life. To make his utter misery complete, if he couldn't sort out the Portsmouth problem from his desk in Whitehall fast enough, he had orders to go there with all haste to fix it at the source because, clearly, the Admiralty thought he hadn't suffered enough.

Not having the energy to eat, or even to shrug out of his sodden coat, he used the lamp to light his candle and squished wearily up the stairs. He let his coat fall in a heap on his bedchamber floor, tossed his soaking waistcoat and ruined cravat on top of it, then sat on his mattress to summon the last of his strength to toe off his boots. While he did so he wondered what, precisely, he was suffering all the Admiralty's nonsense for when none of it seemed to bring him any joy.

He was in the process of peeling off his cold, damp shirt when the shadows dancing in the dim room were obliterated by a shard of lightning that was immediately followed by clap of thunder which boomed so loud and so close to his house that the window rattled.

A split second later, there was a bloodcurdling scream.

One which made him sprint out of the door and up the stairs to the floor above in a blind panic and start Norbert howling as if his life—or someone else's—depended on it.

An equally stunned Felix met him head-on as he reached the landing, his faithful hound in tow. "It's Grace! She's terrified of thunder!"

As Harry could now hear her crying hysterically, he did not doubt his nephew's assessment for a moment. "It's all right, poppet." He burst into the girls' bedchamber as another flash of lightning briefly banished the darkness, and his little niece screamed again. The sight of her pale, petrified face as she hugged her knees to her chest tore at his heart and made him want to slay dragons.

"It's just a storm, sweetheart." She cowered at the answering thunder, looking so small in the middle of the big bed, so afraid, her hands covering her ears before he could scoop her into his arms. "Shhhhh . . . I've got you. It's just a storm. It won't hurt you."

As more lightning followed, she clung to him, her heart hammering so hard it beat like a drum against his ribs. Trying to help, Norbert pressed his forehead into the small of her back, sandwiching her tight between them while he growled at the next rumble of thunder as if that alone would make it stop.

It did nothing to calm his terrified niece, who was now screaming at the top of her lungs.

Harry carried her toward the landing, reasoning that the dimmed lamplight would be more comforting than the jarring flashes of bright light which were now coming thick and fast as the storm raged directly overheard. The moment he stepped into it, he almost bumped into Miss Rowe.

"What's happened?" Wild-eyed and even wilder-haired, she hadn't bothered grabbing a shawl or a robe in her haste to get to them. Two small bare feet poked out beneath the hem of her voluminous nightdress, which wasn't fastened by the ribbons at the neck so hung slightly askew, exposing more of her creamy left shoulder than he was comfortable seeing.

"Grace is afraid of the thunder," said Felix as he stroked his baby sister's arm.

"And Marianne?" Miss Rowe's panicked gaze darted hither and thither. "Is Marianne all right?"

Realizing that he hadn't seen her at all, Harry twisted to look for the missing child in the bedchamber, and when he saw no sign of her, began to panic too. More lightning illuminated the big, empty bed, showing him nothing but the tangled covers Grace had left behind.

As his youngest niece screeched some more and clawed at his neck, dread settled in his stomach. "I don't know where she is!"

If she had run off somewhere scared, too, and hurt herself, he'd never forgive himself.

"She's sleeping, not missing." Matter-of-fact, Felix stomped back into the bedchamber. "Mama always says that a hundred pipers could march right over Marianne's belly and they wouldn't wake her. The only way to wake her up most mornings is to drag her out of bed by her feet." As both he and Miss Rowe blinked in disbelief that anyone could possibly sleep through this, the boy yanked the blankets back to reveal her. Marianne was indeed curled up, oblivious of the commotion going on around her.

"Well, at least someone is sleeping," said Miss Rowe as she reached up to stroke the still-crying Grace's back as Harry carried her out onto the landing again. Once there, she turned to Felix. "I take it that a dedicated man of science such as yourself is not scared of thunder."

"Of course not. It is simply weather." Like the wisest of old sages, the boy then added, "Even a thousand years ago, Aristotle knew that thunder is merely the sound of the wind smashing against the rain clouds."

"Then back to bed with you, young man, and take your dog with you." To Harry's complete surprise, she then turned to him. "I'll take her if you like. You've had a long day."

Harry did like.

Because he had had a long day, was still sopping wet, dead on his feet, and had to be up with the lark again, and frankly, had no idea how to deal with a terrified child in the middle of the night. His stomach was in knots and he was way out of his depth. "If you don't mind . . ." He tried to peel his niece from his body, but another rumble of thunder made her grip him tighter.

"Don't leave me either, Uncle Harry." At that wretched plea, he knew that he could not abandon the little girl, no matter how much he was out floundering. "Please."

"I won't, poppet."

He glanced at Miss Rowe again and shrugged at the sympathy he saw in her expression. "You go. I'll stay with her till the storm passes."

"If you're sure?"

"There is no point us both being awake."

"Papa always gives me some warm milk when I'm frightened." Two small arms wound their way tightly around Harry's neck, sealing his fate. "If I am *really* frightened, like I am now, he melts some chocolate into it and lets me sit on his lap while I drink it." Even scared witless, Grace was still the arch manipulator. "Some chocolate would make me feel like I am safely back at home with them." And by implication, not here with him, where she apparently didn't.

Harry had no clue if the miniature Machiavelli burrowed against him had said that on purpose to multiply his guilt, or if she meant it. Either way, the knife twisted further and the substantial weight on his shoulders seemed to double in size.

"Then say good night to Miss Rowe and let's go get some."

His niece's voice was small. "Good night, Miss Rowe. I'm sorry for waking you."

"No apology is necessary. We all get scared sometimes." She cupped the girl's cheek, smiling, sending a waft of the floral soap she favored toward Harry's nostrils to torment him almost as much as her still-exposed skin. "Good night, Grace. I think you are right—some chocolate in your warm milk would definitely do the trick. It always sends me off to sleep." She flicked her gaze toward the attic, clearly in two minds about leaving him. "Should I wake Mrs. Rigsby so that she can make it?"

"Only if you are in a hurry to die, Miss Rowe." Like Marianne, his cook could sleep through cannon fire. "Not even Simpkins is that brave, and he was at Trafalgar." Because Harry's woman-starved eyes wanted to drift to her exposed shoulder again while his addled mind wanted to wander down that dangerously rutted road it had no place wandering, he inclined his head instead. "Good night. Sleep tight."

At least one of them would.

Even if some miracle occurred and Grace settled quickly, the sultry, seductive image of all that untamed, wild red hair and an askew nightdress was going to be a bloody difficult one to shift. At least until he finally got around to sowing some oats elsewhere.

⸻⸻

*G*eorgie returned to her bedchamber, stared mournfully at the inviting, toasty bed awaiting her, and sighed.

It didn't matter that Captain Kincaid was still nine-tenths dislikable; she couldn't leave him to it.

She wouldn't leave her worst enemy to a screaming child in the middle of the night and be able to sleep tight, let alone one who was thoroughly soaked from the raging storm himself.

But trust him to suit being soaked when anyone else would resemble a drowned rat. Yet Captain Kincaid had managed to be somehow more handsome damp and disheveled. He also smelled divine slicked in rain, the moisture on his skin fresh and earthy. The thin linen shirt he was wearing was so wet it was practically translucent as it stuck, in the most intriguing manner, to the muscles in his arms and back.

Obviously, she had tried not to notice those things and had failed miserably.

She blamed Lottie and Portia for making her see him like an attractive man. There was no denying that his body was as perfect beneath his sodden clothes as his handsome face was poking above them. If she were shallow like Portia and Lottie, Georgie had to concede that it was the sort of body to make a woman go all aquiver.

She sighed again, annoyed with herself for that flagrantly dishonest excuse, as parts of her were, if not completely, all aquiver. The rest were dangerously close. Her pulse, which had ratcheted to a gallop thanks to the sudden screaming that had wrenched her from the deepest depths of sleep, was still cantering thanks to the sight of the captain's splendid, water-sluiced torso.

Who knew that wetness rendered a man more attractive?

Or that a wet, half-dressed, and disheveled Captain Kincaid was somehow two-thirds more handsome than an impeccably attired and dry one?

Worse, to her utter shame, Georgie was not only hovering on the cusp of all aquiver, she was also irrationally—and uncharitably—annoyed that the frightened little girl in his arms had prevented her from properly ogling his perfect chest too. Mortified that her racing mind was suddenly filled with questions about it. The most burning of which was whether that chest was as smooth, rugged, and bare as one of the marble statues of the ancient gods in the British Museum, or if it was dusted with hair? She didn't particularly have a preference—she just wanted to know.

Desperately.

Which all pointed to her being as shallow as Portia and Lottie, and perhaps more so, because they had no reason to dislike him, and she disliked him intensely.

Although less so since yesterday.

It was difficult to loathe and despise a man who took children for ice cream and laughed alongside them while they ate it.

Now she had tonight's conflicting evidence to add to that. Though his room was downstairs, he must have dropped everything and sprinted to get to Grace before Georgie, whose room was on the same floor, scant feet away. Yet he had still beaten her to it.

He was also clearly wet, cold, and dog-tired—and yet he had acquiesced to his niece's pleas without a moment's complaint or reluctance. Then charitably sent Georgie back to bed when she sincerely doubted that there were many men, and mere uncles to boot, who would eschew a night of slumber for a child. Especially when their governess, who he was paying handsomely to look after those children for him, stood before him ready, willing, and expecting to step into the breach.

The colonel wouldn't have behaved like the captain just had in a million years. He would have had no sympathy for a child's tears. In fact, he would have responded to them with explosive outrage that his rest had been disturbed, no matter what the cause of the distress. Exactly as he had done whenever she had been upset while her mother was alive—when her dear mama had borne the brunt of his anger. Quietly and without complaint but still without bending to that tyrant's will wherever her daughter's well-being or happiness was concerned.

Which, of course, never ended well for poor Mama.

Not that her mother had ever complained about her dire lot in life nor ever mentioned his cruelty. To her, the sacrifices she had made were worth it because it kept a roof over Georgie's head and food in her belly. Georgie had been her mother's everything and had told her so every single day. Oh, how she missed that!

Instinctively, her fingers went to her mother's locket where it rested on her collarbone, and she tried to will all those bad memories away. Despite the horrid life she had with a husband nobody could love, her mother had been all sunshine and light regardless of the unpalatable choices widowhood and then poverty had forced her to make. She had always been so much more than Georgie's protector and her champion. Mama had, first and foremost, been her friend, and it was all those happy memories that deserved to be celebrated, not tarnished because of that vile man, now that she was gone.

Except tonight, the thunderstorm lashing the house and little Grace's fear reminded her too much of the only occasion when she had forgotten to cry quietly into her pillow in the terrifying first days after her mother had died. That night, the colonel had threatened to beat Georgie within an inch of her life if she didn't stop sniffling, not cuddled her close and offered to melt chocolate into her milk like the captain just had. And with nothing but love and concern swirling in his eyes for the frightened little girl left in his charge.

Clearly, she was going to have to reevaluate her original fraction and lower his disagreeableness to seven-tenths based on tonight's noble and heroic performance alone. Six and a half if she factored in Gunther's yesterday too.

Drat him.

With a more irritated sigh, she grabbed her robe, and in so doing, caught a glimpse of herself in the mirror.

Her uncooperative hair had, of course, escaped the tight plait she had entrapped it in at bedtime and was a riotous, orange mess shooting from her scalp. If that wasn't bad enough, she'd clearly been having one of her infamous unrestrained fidgeting dreams before she was rudely awoken, because her nightgown was undone and was twisted in a manner that, frankly, wasn't decent. Scandalized by her own reflection, she yanked the dangling sleeve back onto her shoulder and huffed as she tied the neck ribbons tight.

Good heavens above! What a shocking state to have been seen in.

Especially by such a perfect physical specimen as him!

As soon as her robe was on and the belt knotted tight, she slid her feet into her slippers and then twisted her horrid hair into a knot which she secured with at least twenty pins in case it had any notion of showing her up in front of him again. One final glance in the mirror reassured her that her disappointing reflection was at least proper before she ventured downstairs.

Everywhere was dark except for the soft glow emanating from the kitchen, and the only sounds beyond the elements still raging outside were the deep, reassuring tones of the captain's voice.

". . . the Vikings believed the thunder was caused by the wheels of Thor's mighty chariot hitting the mountaintops, and the lightning was the sparks from his hammer."

That he was also telling his niece a story to alleviate her fears did peculiar things to Georgie's heart. Because that was how things should be. How a real man—a surrogate father—should treat a child.

"Is Thor a carpenter, Uncle Harry?"

"Absolutely not. He was the Viking god of war." He chuckled as a saucepan clattered against the range. "He wasn't out in his chariot fixing things, poppet, as he was more about destruction than repair. Thor had quite the temper on him, apparently, and liked to take his bad moods out on everyone else. Hence all the noise up above us."

Georgie hovered outside the door and was in two minds as to whether she should interrupt such a private and tender family moment at all when she heard him rummaging to no avail. "There is no rhyme or reason to this pantry, Grace. The flour is next to the butter and the jam is next to the tea. There are random spices all over the place and Lord only knows where Mrs. Rigsby hides the chocolate— but it's not near the coffee, which is where I would put it. Nor the tea because tea is a drink that so obviously needs to reside beside the eggs. Her logic is baffling."

"Not everything needs to be alphabetical." Georgie couldn't help but smile as she sailed in, and then almost choked on her own tongue as he emerged from the pantry with his niece hugging his leg and a wry smile on his face. Not that she noticed the curve of his mouth straightaway. Or little Grace clutching him as if her life depended upon it. Her eyes were too busy noticing the unmistakable shadow of dark hair beneath the soggy front of his shirt. Hair that dusted his pectoral muscles in the most intriguing way, then arrowed down his abdomen—although she couldn't be certain of that as the thin, damp linen was too loose around his middle and refused to cling there while she investigated.

"Why don't I put you out of your misery and take over?" Off-kilter, Georgie gestured to a chair well away from the stove so that she wouldn't have to look at him all damp and disconcerting while she prepared the chocolate. Especially as her nipples had decided to pucker in sympathy with his when hers weren't even wet or cold, so had absolutely no excuse for misbehaving so outrageously. Thank goodness for the heavy robe tightly knotted, else they'd have publicly disgraced her worse than her horrid hair and askew nightgown already had. "You sit down with Grace."

"That's very kind of you." Acting more awkward than she had ever seen him, he picked the little girl up. Whether that was to offer the scared child some comfort or to protect his modesty from her suddenly hungry gaze, she had no clue, but was grateful for it all the same. "And probably just as well, as I'd have only burned the milk anyway and then incurred Mrs. Rigsby's wrath. Despite this being *my* kitchen, I am not allowed in here upon threat of death."

"Good for Mrs. Rigsby! Perhaps I should do the same to keep you out of my classroom?" A glib, impertinent comment which slipped out before Georgie thought better of it. She blamed the see-through shirt.

Amusement laced his tone. "Are you threatening mutiny, Miss Rowe?"

"There is only so much daily scrutiny and complete lack of faith in my abilities that I can take." Aware that she would likely rub him the wrong way again if she continued challenging him, Georgie had some stern words with her inner St. Joan while she fetched the jug of milk and supplies from the pantry. "But I shall make you trust me. On that I am resolute. I am tenacious when I put my mind to something, Captain. Relentless even, and I shall prove to you that I am an excellent governess—mark my words."

"I do not doubt that for a second, Miss Rowe." Although, rather tellingly, despite her calling him out on it, he made no attempt to inform her that he either trusted her or that his inspections would soon stop. Instead, as more thunder rumbled, he settled himself on the chair with Grace on his lap and carried on telling his frightened niece all the ancient theories of its causes in an ironic but soothing voice while she made the drinks.

Even with her back to him as she stirred the pot, something about his tone as he waxed lyrical sent unwelcome tingles down Georgie's spine. She could not ascertain whether that was the ever-deepening velvety whisper that melted his normally clipped consonants in the most sinful way, or the gentle cadence of his phrasing. Or perhaps it was the strange intimacy of the kitchen. Or the strange intimacy of being almost alone with a man. Whichever it was, it played havoc with her nerve endings. Nerves which were still not fully over the new, and scandalous, knowledge that the front of his upper torso draped in damp linen was as impressive as the back of it was.

Keeping her eyeballs on the milk pan when they were determined to wander back did nothing to make her relax either. Nor did measured and even breathing, or reciting the entire alphabet both forward and backward in her mind. By the time the wretched milk began to steam, she was wound tighter than a spring and was so aware of his presence and the strange thrum of her body that it took every ounce of strength she possessed to pour the chocolate into cups without sloshing it everywhere.

"Here we—" She spun around, clutching two steaming mugs, only to be met with the thoroughly disarming sight of the captain cradling a sleeping child as if she were the most precious thing in the world. Smiling at Georgie as if they were in this together—like a family. Coping with the trials and tribulations of parenthood together.

Simultaneously, the pull of intense longing made both her heart and her womb ache for all they had long ago resigned themselves to never having. Yet while that felt alien and frightening—it also felt right. Inconceivably right. Yet so wrong that the sheer folly of that mad, errant, out-of-the-blue, futile fantasy was staggering.

But appealing.

*Oh, so appealing . . .*

Appealing enough that her body was seriously urging Georgie to use her nonexistent wiles on him exactly as Lottie had so outrageously suggested. Yesterday it had been inconceivable, but tonight . . .

Thankfully, he put a finger to his lips to shush her, so she was spared spewing out the garbled nonsense which hovered on hers. Then he pointed to the window, smiling, and she almost sighed aloud at the intoxicating sight.

"The storm has passed."

Georgie had been so preoccupied with a barrage of odd emotions and the strange sensations going on within that she hadn't noticed, but nodded as if she had and managed to choke out, "This chocolate is wasted, then." She hoped her breathiness passed as a convincing whisper in deference to the sleeping Grace rather than from the odd flutterings going on in her throat and her loins.

"It's not wasted. We can take it back up to bed with us." Although he hadn't meant it at all how her ears decided to hear it, that sentence set Georgie's imagination alight. Images of him lying on her bed, half dressed in a translucent, damp shirt, looking all rumpled and sinful and smiling in her tangled sheets as they welcomed the morning together skittered through her mind. Then whizzed down all her nerve endings, reawakening her shameless nipples again before they fizzed in the most unnerving way between her legs.

*Good heavens above! What was all that about?*

"Y-yes." *Marvelous!* Now she genuinely was so all aquiver she was actually stuttering. Her and him? A pompous military man like the colonel? Ridiculous. *Ridiculous.* Inconceivable. *And yet . . .* "What a good idea."

"One that will hopefully settle us both back to sleep." He tossed that over his sublimely perfect left shoulder as he left the kitchen, oblivious that his whisper drizzled over her skin like warm honey and rendered her so ripe for the picking that she barely knew herself at all. "Not that I've actually been to sleep yet—but I live in constant hope."

"Y-yes." Gracious, but she was pathetic! Shallow, stuttering, and positively swooning, and all thanks to a damp shirt and a deep voice. "Sleep would be good." Not that she held out much hope that even the steaming chocolate would be enough to soothe her currently addled, racing thoughts or smooth her outrageously improper nipples into submission. Both were wasted on him.

*Surely?*

But the idea had already lodged itself deep in her psyche like a weed that wanted to grow, and Georgie had no choice but to follow him up the staircase with the chocolate. No choice but to notice the way the muscles in his arms and back flexed beneath the clinging linen as he carried his precious cargo. No choice but to drink in the sight of his firm backside and thighs encased in tight buckskin as his long legs climbed the stairs. No respite from the affectionate new feelings that assaulted her. Made her question and made her want.

In sheer hell, she watched him gently tuck the sleeping child into bed, and then, when Georgie assumed that he could not possibly fluster her any more than he had already, his fingers brushed hers as she handed him a mug.

Brushed, then lingered, and she felt it everywhere.

From the tips of those tingling fingers to her toes. From her suddenly eager lips to more outrageous places.

In her heart and in her soul, and that felt right too.

"I'm sorry but . . . might have to go away for a few days." Was his fingertip intentionally caressing hers? "Portsmouth . . . navy business."

Georgie nodded, too aware of his touch to form any words fast enough. "Y-your family will be well looked after in your absence. You *can* trust me."

He nodded too as he stared deep into her eyes, his own as wary and indecisive as she suspected hers were, and that was all it took to make her body want with more ferocity than it had ever wanted anything before. And her heart swell with . . .

He suddenly snatched both the cup and his fingers away in one abrupt but fluid motion, blinking as he stared, making her wonder if that simple touch had as profound an effect on his person as it had on hers.

Which, of course, was likely the most ridiculous notion she had ever had!

"Thank you for your assistance tonight, Miss Rowe." Without the shield of the child to hide behind, he was immediately back to being all stiff and awkward again. He could barely meet her eyes. Could barely hold himself still. Could barely contain his obvious desire to be well rid of her. Which all rather suggested that her touch repelled him far more than it attracted, and that made her feel both stupid and inadequate to have reacted so differently. "And thank you for the chocolate." He inclined his head as if they were two distant acquaintances passing on the street rather than two half-dressed people alone on his landing who had just behaved like a married couple. "Good night."

"Good night, Captain."

She bobbed a stiff curtsy and turned, forcing her feet not to bolt to her bedchamber as they wanted while still moving toward it at pace.

She did not want to turn around and yet could sense him watching her, because the heat of his gaze seemed to burn through her nightdress as it followed her. In case she was imagining it, she turned, and their eyes locked.

Only briefly because he curtly inclined his head again before he spun away. But still . . . that intense look had felt poignant. Significant.

Seductive.

Thoroughly confused and totally overwhelmed, Georgie leaned her back against the door the second she closed it. She hugged her own mug to her rapidly beating, totally befuddled heart while clutching her mother's locket for strength as she listened to his retreating footsteps return down the stairs to his own bed.

Wondering how on earth it was possible that the stiff, authoritarian, annoyingly perfect but pompous military stickler whom she loved to hate had somehow managed to go from being nine-tenths disagreeable to at least three-quarters agreeable in the space of just one day.

*Chapter*
# ELEVEN

$\sim$

his morning we are going to work on fractions—one of my absolute favorite mathematical topics." As Georgie had been making headway with their daily routine, she saw no reason to change the children's schedule for their second week, even with the captain gone. Getting the mathematics done first thing got it out of the way and with Felix's combative attitude toward it, felt prudent.

Once that chore was done, they would move to something all the children enjoyed—history. Made all the better by the fact that they had reached William the Conqueror in their chronology of notable kings and queens of England, and that tyrant was a fun one to teach. There was blood and guts and gore galore from the beginning of the fellow's reign to the end. And then there were all the oppressive castles he built. Who didn't want to learn about castles? Or sieges and rebellions?

And perhaps, simply to prove the point to the captain that chaining the children to their desks for hours on end every day wasn't the best way to encourage them to learn, she would teach the history outside. Set them all free of this classroom for an hour or more despite knowing that he wouldn't be happy about it. If, by his own admission, Mrs. Rigsby did not have to suffer his interference in her kitchen because she had put her foot down, then surely Georgie could do the same? Especially as he was currently miles away in Portsmouth. She only had till August, after all, to prove all her untested theories about education correct. She had certainly waited long enough for the opportunity, so it seemed a shame to waste it. Especially if the captain's bark was worse than his bite, as she was increasingly convinced that it was, beneath all his regimented pomposity.

The easily waylaid part of her certainly wanted that to be the case, as he had rather occupied her thoughts since Sunday night's thunderstorm. So much that it had taken over an hour to plan this one lesson alone. It didn't help that she'd been having vivid dreams involving a dimly lit but homely kitchen, damp clothes drying before the fire while she warmed the naked captain up in the most improper way. Dreams that felt so real she had awoken breathless and flustered this morning. That was most unlike her. She blamed that scandalous wet shirt, his deep, silken whispers, and the potent finger brush, as clearly those three things combined in such quick succession had done wonders to scramble her wits.

And everyone knew that the night played tricks on the mind, especially when Lottie's improper suggestion about Georgie using her wiles had also been so fresh in it. She had also never been so intimately alone with a man, so was it any wonder her tangled thoughts had run together and had given her imagination nonsensical romantic ideas since?

It really all had little to do with him.

When Georgie allowed a man to properly scramble her wits, she was resolute that it would not be a nitpicking and pompous military man.

No, indeed! She'd had enough of those to last a lifetime.

Two lifetimes!

Although why she was compelled to keep pondering it at all was a mystery.

It wasn't as if a handsome, wealthy, eligible, ambitious officer of the crown would even think to look at a lowly, stumpy, orange-haired temporary governess as anything but what she was.

Thank goodness.

And there she went again, thinking of him when she was supposed to be teaching the children maths. "Can anyone tell me what a fraction is?"

"Urgh." Felix displayed his disapproval by lolling back in his chair. "Who cares."

Georgie smiled as she rolled her eyes at Marianne, expecting his sister to roll hers right back as had quickly become their habit whenever Felix complained about doing any sums. Except she didn't. Marianne huffed too.

"For once I agree with Felix. It is too nice a day to waste on dreary fractions. I think we should put on a play instead."

"Yes! Let's!" Little Grace bounced in her seat so fast she almost fell off it. "Can I play a princess?"

"No." Marianne did not even bat an eye. "I am always the princess because I can sing and dance like one, but you can be a fairy."

"Urgh." Felix again, sliding down the chair. "I think I'd prefer fractions."

"That is just as well because fractions are what we are doing." Georgie handed out the diagrams of circles that she had prepared, all with a dot to mark the center. Then she gestured at the two separate blocks of fractions written on the board. Grace would work on the top to find the half, then the quarters. Marianne and Felix would do the same but would continue to measure out the eighths and the sixteenths. Once that was done, the eldest two would use their diagrams to learn to add the fractions together while the youngest used hers to find and shade in three quarters.

"A fraction is what we call a segment or part of a whole—"

"Urgh!" Felix's head hit the desk this time. "I really can't be bothered with mathematics again. It really is a pointless waste of my time." Assuming that she couldn't see, his feet nudged the already sleeping Norbert beneath his desk to encourage the dog to distract him. Delighted, the big dog jumped up, stretched, and began to furiously wag his tail as he waited to see what fun his manipulative young master had in store.

Wise to that trick, Georgie retrieved a chunk of carrot from her desk and called his name, wiggling it. As he loved carrots almost as much as sausages, the dog instantly headed her way, then sat obediently at her feet as he awaited it. "Good boy, Norbert . . . now lie down." She pointed to the floor beside her desk and he collapsed there, his big brown eyes transfixed on the drawer where he now knew the carrots lived in case another chunk was forthcoming.

"If you look at the diagrams on your desks and imagine that the circles are apple pies that need to be sliced ready for a tea party—"

"I don't feel well." Looking in the finest of fettles, Marianne suddenly stood. "May I be excused so that I can go and lie down?"

"No." Georgie folded her arms to reiterate how unconvinced she was. "Sit back down and stop wasting everyone's time." Then, because all three of them were behaving oddly, she shook her head. "What on earth is the matter with you all today? I've never seen you all so distracted so early in the day."

"I am going to be sick." Rather than comply with Georgie's instruction, the girl folded her arms too, but across her stomach, then feigned a few fairly convincing gagging motions to add credence to her lie. "The room is spinning." That was where the performance failed, as Marianne was overacting now for all she was worth. "I might even faint too if I don't lie down soon, Miss Rowe." The subsequent swaying would have been comical if Georgie hadn't been so irritated by the blatant attempt at sabotage. She was almost as irritated by that as she was by her unpalatable, imagined, intimate, and amorous nocturnal surrender to the captain—of all people.

*Drat that damp shirt!*

"Some fresh air would help." Felix bounded to the French doors, and with no whiff of any additional carrot to keep him where he was, Norbert bounced beside him as the boy wrestled with the lock. The second it opened, his theatrical sister collapsed in a graceful heap on the floor, and believing it—or in cahoots with it—Grace flew out of her seat to fuss over her.

"Oh, for goodness' sake!" Georgie's fists made their way to her hips as she gave them all her best schoolmistress's stare. "Do you all think that I was born yesterday?" As Felix already had one foot out of the door and Norbert was prancing about on the terrace in readiness, she marched toward them and yanked the doors closed with the dog on the other side of them. "Go sit down this second, Felix." Her pointed finger brooked no argument, but still he dragged his feet as he belligerently did as he was told. "And you can get up, too, Marianne. I am well aware that you are playacting and I am not the least bit impressed by it."

Marianne remained prostrate, her eyes too tightly clenched to be in an actual faint, testing Georgie's mettle. Grace, however, started to waver under her steely teacher's glare and shook her sister to encourage compliance. When her sibling refused to wake, she glanced up at her with a trembling bottom lip. "I think she might be dead, Miss Rowe." Within a split second, tears spilled over the little girl's cheeks, and the moment they did, Felix used it to his advantage.

"Marianne is definitely dead." He wrapped a brotherly arm

around his weeping baby sister's shoulders. "It's just us now, Grace. Just you and me. No more Marianne. No Mama. No Papa. Even Uncle Harry has deserted us. We are all alone now."

That was too much for the sensitive five-year-old to bear and, clearly believing it, the little sniffs turned into full-blown cries as her whole world fell apart. Beyond the glass of the French doors, the now-exiled Norbert followed suit and howled in sympathy for all he was worth.

With her lesson plan now unraveling faster than the sensible bun she had pinned her horrid hair in, it was Georgie's turn to huff as she gathered Grace into her arms. "Marianne is not dead, darling. Your brother and sister are playing a cruel joke, is all." While Marianne still did her level best to resemble a corpse on the floor, she turned her most evil eye to Felix. "A very cruel and callous joke indeed, and they should both be heartily ashamed of themselves for upsetting you so." A crime that could not go unpunished, so she sighed again. This time for herself.

As much as she preferred to spare the rod, Miss P had instilled in her the need to ensure that punishments were fair, fitting, and had to be followed through if you wanted to be taken seriously. Empty threats or deferring the power to their uncle when he returned, or their parents, weakened her stature in both the short term and most especially in the long. Seeing as the two eldest were already testing her authority today, she had to stand firm now or she might as well wave the white flag of surrender and give up all hope of ever being an effectual governess to these three until August. "As penance, they have both lost all playtime privileges for the rest of the day, which means that during the morning break and after luncheon, neither of them will be allowed outside."

Felix's sharp intake of breath told her that he considered that a fate worse than death, whereas Marianne remained unmoved, determined to remain as tragically dead as Pyramus in act five of her beloved *A Midsummer Night's Dream.*

"Furthermore, should Marianne refuse to be resurrected from the grave in the next ten seconds, then she will also go to bed tonight without any supper for playing such a cruel trick on Grace." The girl stiffened slightly but still refused to budge. "One . . . two . . . three . . ." Georgie's expression was purposefully deadpan, her tone simultaneously clipped but calm. "Four . . . five . . ."

Felix nudged his sister with his foot. "I think she means it, Marianne."

"Six . . . seven . . . eight . . ."

"*Marianne!*" Felix kicked her this time. "Stop!"

"Nine . . ."

With a Sleeping Beauty–type yawn, the middle Pendleton stretched as if she had been indeed in the deepest of slumbers and cracked open one eye. "Did I pass out?"

Clearly, it was going to be a very long and arduous day.

"Get back in your seat, both of you, and pick up your pens." Dispassionately, she walked to the door, still carrying the hiccuping Grace, and let Norbert back in. Thankfully, his howling stopped immediately, but sensing the suppressed anger held inside her, rather than bounding in, tail wagging, his scruffy tail hung limp. So did his ears as he edged in, as quiet as a mouse, before he collapsed, contrite, beneath Felix's desk, staring at Georgie intently over his crossed paws in case she decided to give him a telling off too.

"As I previously stated, a fraction is a smaller portion of a whole . . ."

*G*eorgie had higher hopes for a better Tuesday after the miserable Monday. After the fake faint in the first lesson, and despite the punishments she had been forced to dole out, the rest of that day had gone rapidly downhill, necessitating both Marianne and Felix to go to bed without supper. Even little Grace lost all her playtime privileges after she decided to run in a rapid circle around the classroom and then accidentally crashed into the wall. They had all clearly made the collective decision to do as little work as possible and to test her boundaries—and test them they had.

But Tuesday was as challenging as Monday had been and the less said about the shambles that had been Wednesday, the better. Now, everyone in the classroom was as miserable as sin—including Georgie. Even Norbert's plaintive but lackluster howling from the back of the house where he had been banished had lost all hope, as if he didn't expect this miserable existence they were all trapped in together to get any better. The only consolation was that the captain wasn't around to inspect the shambles. But as the days stretched since she had last seen him on the landing, the threat of the next inspection when he returned while she was now fighting a war with the children was keeping her up at night. Almost as much as the memory of him in that dratted wet shirt.

This wasn't the sort of teacher she had always wanted to be, and these dry, uninspiring, desk-bound lessons resembled nothing that she had ever wanted to teach. The children certainly had no enthusiasm for the silent book learning she had been forced to implement to get them to realize that poor behavior would not be rewarded. The written work they had produced in the last three days was at best substandard, at worst nonexistent, and they hadn't been able to do anything even remotely fun at all as a result. The only positive was that they were halfway through Thursday and, so far, she hadn't had to lock horns with anyone nor hand out any serious reprimands. Instead, the three Pendletons sat dejected, pens in one hand and depressed chins in the other, willing the interminable day to end.

"Pens down, everybody." Someone had to break the tense monotony, and it stood to reason that someone was her.

Praying that she could salvage things before the die was cast for all eternity and without the classroom reverting to anarchy again, she smiled at them all for the first time since Felix's initial rebellion. "I think we can all agree that, so far, this week has been a thoroughly awful affair." Warily, both Felix and Marianne nodded.

"If it is any consolation, this . . ." Georgie gestured to the comprehension questions she had written on the board concerning the dry text they had been studying because the excitement of *Grimms' Fairy Tales* had proved too distracting. "Is not how I envisaged teaching the three of you the usually joyous subject of English literature. I had planned to do things that were a bit more fun and intended for us to turn 'Hansel and Gretel' into a play that we could perform for Simpkins and Mrs. Rigsby . . ." Marianne's eyes lit up at that. "But couldn't because, unfortunately, the three uncooperative Pendletons who have been sitting in this classroom since Monday are not the same three that I taught last week. We did have more fun last week, didn't we?"

The eldest two nodded again warily while Grace did not know how to respond, so simply shuffled in her seat.

"So what changed?" It was a perfectly reasonable question and one Georgie had pondered incessantly herself—almost as much as she had pondered her peculiar overreaction to the captain. "Why were you able to focus and behave last week and not this week?"

An odd look passed between the eldest two, which both quickly quashed to a shrug.

"Come on now, you are obviously very intelligent children who were, while boisterous, still a delight to teach right up until the end of Friday, and perfectly lovely company on Saturday morning and all day Sunday when we had no lessons. Yet this week you have been . . . well, frankly . . . a nightmare. Belligerent, lazy, defiant, disruptive, and so disengaged that every single day has felt like three weeks since, and I think we'd all much prefer to pull out our own teeth than be stuck here together like this in perpetuity."

Another odd look passed between Felix and Marianne. One that confirmed there was something else afoot than them merely testing her patience.

"Well, I suppose if we cannot have a frank and open conversation about the problem to see how we can all collectively fix it, things shall just have to stay as they are then until your parents return to rescue you from the endless torture of silent book learning . . ." She turned to wipe the blackboard with a duster, then picked up her chalk. "Back to our dull English comprehension . . ."

"We don't have any incentive to behave," said Marianne, sounding like the most spoiled child who ever lived. "And we are not used to this way of learning." She gestured around. "We do not have a classroom at home, and I so miss home."

"An incentive?" She sympathized with the whole classroom argument as this change to their usual routine probably did feel constricting and alien, and she empathized that they were homesick because she missed being at Miss P's. Being here in this lovely but strange house with all these new people was too reminiscent of her nomadic, rootless childhood to feel comfortable. The loss, albeit temporarily, of the reassuring security of the only home she had known since the age of sixteen was most disconcerting, made more so because she was simultaneously missing the daily presence of an irritating,

wholly unsuitable man she did not want to be missing. But still—
Georgie had never heard the like.

"Something to make behaving worth our while," clarified Marianne, as if her solution was a magical wand.

"As in a gift or payment of some sort?"

"Yes, precisely, as that is what we are used to," said Felix, nodding
as if his sister's explanation for their shoddy behavior was perfectly
reasonable. "Uncle Harry forgot to promise us anything to behave this
week, so perhaps, as we haven't seen him, if you did . . ."

"I see." Although she didn't—unless . . . "Why would you expect a material incentive from either me or your uncle to do anything?"

"Because Uncle Harry *always* promises something whenever we
come to visit." This also came from Felix. "*Always.*"

"Right . . ." And because things were beginning to fall into
place, she pulled a thoughtful face as if contemplating the merits of
a similar arrangement with them. While she heartily approved of the
odd reward here and there for consistent hard work or doing something truly exceptional, she also knew that rewarding the mundane
was a slippery slope. "What sorts of incentives work best for Uncle
Harry to ensure he gets the best out of you?" She smiled rather than
frowned because she wanted to prize more information out of them.

"Well, last week it was ice cream," said Marianne, unaware that
she had just opened Pandora's box. "As much as we could eat at Gunther's if we behaved for you all week and didn't immediately frighten
you away—but usually it's a sixpence or a shilling if it's just to get us
to behave for an afternoon."

Clearly there was a sliding scale to the bartering system, and
they were used to their palms being greased.

"Or some sweets," added Grace shyly. "Toffees are my favorite."

The last was added hopefully as if she believed Georgie might immediately go out and buy her some for simply mentioning it. "But Felix and Marianne prefer licorice."

"Do they indeed?" Suddenly all the silent, cryptic looks between the siblings last week made sense. As did their forced compliance. For three children who were not at all used to traditional schooling, they had certainly settled into it fast enough. She should have known that that was too good to be true, when every class of well-behaved pupils at Miss P's had always tested her boundaries first. Proper respect always came at a cost, after all. "Out of interest, how long has he been *incentivizing* you?"

"Always," said Marianne. "He's always liked to buy us things."

"We used to get some splendid things when he came back from a long voyage. He brought me back a spear from Africa once." Felix's face lit up at the memory as if that dangerous piece of inappropriateness was the best gift he had ever received in his life. "Mama has locked it away though—until I grow up. In case I accidentally kill something with it." His furrowed brows suggested he thought that a grave injustice.

"He once bought me ballet shoes from the Bolshoi." Marianne's expression was dreamy. "I loved those shoes."

"So much they fell apart," added Felix with a curled lip of disapproval. "She pirouetted everywhere for six whole months. It was very annoying."

"I love my dolls' house." Grace was eager to share the captain's largesse too. "Uncle Harry fetched it all the way from Amsterdam. I would have brought it with me here, but it's too big to travel."

"Don't forget all the puppets and the theater." Marianne again, with a grin at her brother. "We each get a new puppet for every birthday and Christmas. I got a ballerina marionette last Christmas, Grace got a pony that makes clippety-cloppety noises when it moves, and Felix got a spider."

"It even has hair," said Grace with a shudder, "so Mama has expressly forbidden him from chasing me with it, as he knows that I don't like them."

"What lucky children you are. It sounds as though your uncle has thoroughly spoiled you all for years." And good gracious, that new knowledge did further unwelcome things to Georgie's heart. A heart she was determined to keep hardened against him but which still seemed rebelliously determined to quicken for the dratted man instead.

Felix nodded. "Mama always says that it makes Uncle Harry happy to buy us things. She said it was his way of making up for spending so much time far away across the sea and being too busy to come home to visit us in Devon."

And they had clearly continued to use that generosity against him.

What clever and enterprising little rascals they truly were—and what a well-intentioned but blithering idiot the captain had been. He had the gall to question her untraditional approach to child rearing when his superior "rigor" basically involved out-and-out bribery! If Captain Kincaid had been home now, she'd have marched to his study and given him a piece of her mind for such misguided but flagrant stupidity.

Did the captain not know that if you gave children an inch, they took a mile, and that they would ruthlessly exploit any chink they saw in the armor? Those things did not make these children bad because they were *children* and that was precisely what children did if they did not know where the boundaries lay. But as an adult, and apparently as a great leader of men, Captain Kincaid should have known better.

Instead, thanks to a combination of guilt and most likely exaspera-tion, he had effectively surrendered all the control he had over these tarnished but resourceful little cherubs because they now ruled his roost.

But not on her watch.

"And do you usually receive similar incentives from your parents to do all the things that you should?"

While the two eldest shared another telling look to gauge how to answer that leading and potentially damning question, Grace shook her head emphatically, and they both winced. "No—of course not! Just Uncle Harry."

"Interesting . . ." Georgie gave them all a conspiratorial smile before she stared directly at Felix. "Why *just* Uncle Harry?"

"Because he likes things to be just so and gets all . . ." He looked to Marianne for the right word to explain it.

"Twitchy."

"Yes . . . twitchy when they aren't."

The plot thickened—but still she smiled as if she wasn't abso-lutely horrified by the manipulative skulduggery she was hearing, even though she was strangely comforted by the sublime new knowl-edge that even the impeccably, effortlessly perfect captain possessed an Achilles heel. "So, let me guess, you all work together to ensure that he gets as twitchy as possible whenever you visit to reap the rewards?"

"Not always." Felix shrugged. "Sometimes we make him twitchy without actually trying to."

"But still reap the rewards regardless, I'll wager."

As Felix grinned, Georgie rested her bottom on her desk and folded her arms, allowing her smile to slide from her expression and be replaced by a look of utter disappointment. "Do your parents know that you've basically been conspiring against, and then shamelessly blackmailing your poor uncle for years by misbehaving unless he pays you what is tantamount to a bribe?"

The silence was deafening, but she let it stretch until all three of them hung their heads in shame.

"Am I to assume then, that you intended that he hear all about your misbehavior this week from me, or Simpkins, or Mrs. Rigsby, or Polly, so that he would feel obliged to incentivize you a bit more?" Marianne stared at her hands and Felix chewed his bottom lip guiltily while little Grace's started to quiver. "Are you proud of being so underhanded to a man who so obviously adores you?"

Three bent dark heads shook in unison. But because Miss P had taught her that it was always best to allow the wrongdoers time to contemplate their actions, Georgie waited some more until one of them panicked and broke ranks. Interestingly, the one who broke first was Marianne, but she did so in a way that attempted to mitigate the consequences rather than face them.

"You are right, Miss Rowe. We've been bad. Very bad and we are heartily ashamed of ourselves."

Felix nodded too with mock solemnity. "You should absolutely send us all to bed without any supper again tonight as punishment because we deserve it—and then we can all draw a line under it." He also clearly feared any potential repercussions from the other adults in the family more than he did from Georgie.

In solidarity with her brother, Marianne wrung her hands, contrite. "We won't misbehave for you again, Miss Rowe, will we?" The other two nodded. Much too readily. "We have learned our lesson."

For a split second that she wasn't proud of, Georgie considered accepting the children's sworn compliance. It would certainly make her life easier. It would also ensure that the captain would have no cause to dismiss her between now and August, and thus end her concerns about not getting a decent reference at the end of her tenure. However, she dismissed that self-serving thought as fast as it entered her mind, as it was morally wrong. She might not particularly like—correction—particularly *want* to like or be attracted to her clearly two-faced stickler-for-the-rules employer, but she would not make a bargain with the devil simply because it made her life easier.

What sort of a governess would she be if she willingly allowed these children to learn the lesson that misbehaving and manipulation was acceptable? That taking advantage of the two-faced stickler's big heart was something they should continue? It went against everything she fundamentally believed about justice and fairness, and her entire educational ethos.

"I am afraid that, unlike your poor uncle, I cannot be blackmailed and will not be incentivizing your good behavior under any circumstances. At least not with material rewards. I am also, frankly, shocked and disappointed that you think such duplicity is acceptable and suspect your mother and father would be too." They all hung their heads at the mention of their parents, confirming that the way they behaved at home was clearly very different to the way they behaved here. "However . . ." She would throw them one bone, as they were children and this situation wasn't entirely their fault. "I also do not think that it is my place to punish you for all the wrongs that you have plainly done to your poor uncle, nor do I think that a punishment from me will right them."

Felix exhaled with relief first. "Then you won't tell him?"

She also refused to make any promises that she couldn't keep. "I prefer to believe that you will all be decent enough to do the right thing and tell him yourself the next time you see him, as I think you all owe him a huge apology. Don't you?" When they responded with only dejected silence, she pushed them again. "Well, don't you?"

"Yes, Miss Rowe," said Felix and Marianne in unison while Grace's bottom lip trembled again.

"Is he going to punish us?"

Georgie sincerely doubted it in any way near what he should because he was a soft-boiled egg through and through with these tiny terrors, but she shrugged and let them think they were in some jeopardy. "He should, because you have all treated him very ill in the face of his generosity and kindness toward you over the years. A man who goes out of his way to purchase spears and ballet shoes and dolls' houses and puppets—the absolute most perfect gifts for the three of you—does not deserve to be blackmailed."

She would leave that final thought to marinate in their consciences until he reappeared. By which time she had high hopes they would feel so wretched about it, their confessions and their apologies would be heartfelt and she wouldn't have to force them out of them.

"But that is between you and he. In the meantime, I think we can all agree that your atrocious behavior of the last few days cannot continue. So, I propose we declare a truce." As three pairs of ears pricked up, she clarified with a wag of her finger. "A truce and not a bargain, and I know that you are all too clever to know that there is a distinct difference between those two things."

Georgie smiled then and unfolded her arms. "The terms of the truce are simple. If you all make the effort to behave as well as I know that you can, from this moment forth, I shall return to teaching the sorts of lessons we all enjoyed last week." Like Mrs. Rigsby had, it was time Georgie put her foot down. "I am not suggesting that *all* of those lessons will be fun, of course, because I am your teacher and sometimes I will need to test you to check that you understand things. And sometimes you will have to learn things that you do not particularly want to, or find difficult or boring, because they are important things that all children need to learn. But I will always do my best to make those lessons as engaging as I can, so long as you try your best to be engaged." There was also a distinct difference between *will* and *try*.

"You'll notice that all I expect is for you to *try* your best. I do not expect you to be little angels all of the time, for none of us are perfect." Not even Captain Kincaid, although that splendid revelation shouldn't buoy her in quite the way it had, nor make him two-fifths more likable than he already was. She offered them her most benevolent smile. "Do you agree to the terms for our armistice?"

Three dark heads nodded as one.

"Then what say you we get out of this stuffy classroom, fetch Norbert, and practice our reading in the garden?"

❧

*A*fter an interminable week and a half of long hours at the Admiralty interspersed with a miserable stint in Portsmouth sorting out all the merchants there, Harry decided to do something he hadn't done in a long time.

He left Whitehall early.

He was sick and tired of fighting fires that were not of his making, and sicker still of constantly pondering Miss Rowe when he did not want to be. After their oddly charged moment on his landing ten days ago, the vixen had infested his mind and inserted herself so deep beneath his dermis that her essence had haunted him ever since. To combat that, he had taken to avoiding her wherever possible, which of course she had taken as carte blanche to revert to doing everything her way again.

According to the irritating but ever-vigilant Lady Flatman next door, she and the children now spent at least half of their day outdoors in his garden or at the park, leaving the ordered classroom he had made for her mostly redundant. Not that it resembled his ordered classroom any longer. Incrementally, by stealth and sheer bloody-mindedness, she had changed the damn room entirely—and for the better. The neat line of desks seemed to float around to wherever she fancied on the periphery of the room, and the polished parquet in the center was now covered with the big, round rug he had fetched back from one of his travels that had languished in one of his empty bedrooms ever since. It had been wasted there, he now realized, as the vibrant pattern and all the colors of nature, which had first drawn him to it in that bustling souk several years ago, seemed to have been tailor-made to sit beneath these French doors, swathed in the late morning sunlight.

The big clock was now surrounded by his nieces' and nephew's artwork. Little Grace's barely formed, overbright childish daubs sat beside Marianne's whimsical, fairy-tale view of the world. Pastel, romanticized drawings of castles and princesses, fire-breathing dragons, and knights of yore which made him smile despite him currently having little to smile about.

And despite the lack of traditional rigor or rules, and despite all the kite flying, tadpole collecting, cricket playing, and laughing his governess encouraged on a daily basis, his nieces and nephews were thriving. They adored Miss Rowe. Talked incessantly of her. Most galling of all was that they behaved for Miss Rowe because she could control them with the mere quirk of an eyebrow. If he happened to be around to see it, she would then quirk that eyebrow at him, the message in it clear. *I told you I was an excellent governess.* And he liked that about her. Liked her spirit and her cheek and the inherent rebelliousness which made her instinctively challenge his original expectations rather than fall into step behind them.

It made him like the rest of her too, damn it, and that wasn't helping matters at all. Not when his unwelcome and incomprehensible attraction to the contrary minx had to stop.

What the hell had he been thinking to caress her fingers like he

had? To gaze so longingly into her eyes? To have almost—almost—
tugged her closer because he had been sorely tempted to taste her.
To want more from her than he damn well should be wanting when he
had so many more important things to do?

Getting waylaid by a woman—again—after he had spent the
last two years doing whatever it took to expedite and elevate his career after a woman had almost scuppered it was sheer madness. Especially when he was so close to climbing the next rung up the ladder
that he could smell it.

Harry wasn't daft. He knew that his name was on everyone's lips
at the Admiralty. The top brass, they now eyed him with undisguised
interest. He was the heir apparent, to what he still did not know, but
he was owed something big after all the outstanding work he had put in
there at their express behest. Everyone knew that. To risk all that now
simply because he had felt so empty inside—and because something
about his prickly governess called to him on a visceral level—was the
dictionary definition of lunacy.

A man in his prime—one on the cusp of his next big promotion—
shouldn't be feeling as empty as a pauper's purse or so angry at himself
that he wanted to punch a wall.

He should feel proud of his achievements. Invigorated. Impatient. Excited for the fresh challenges awaiting him in his career—
not flat and worn down and so uninspired by the navy he could barely
drag himself out of bed in the mornings.

Thankfully, this afternoon, as he had been staring, lost, into
space, Harry had had an epiphany.

His current dissatisfaction with his life was all his fault!

Thanks to his own ambitions, he had allowed himself to be lured
to the Admiralty. Then he had allowed himself to be swamped with
so many of their problems, Harry had taken on far more than he

could chew and lost himself in the process. He had said yes when he should have said no. He had negotiated when he should have laid down the law, and he had neglected his own wants, needs, and, bizarrely, the furtherment of his own career because he had been too overworked to see to those things. He had, in short, hoisted himself by his own petard.

That had to be why he felt so uninspired, and that had to be why, when his exhausted mind had clearly been at its most addled, he had that odd moment on the landing with Miss Rowe.

Well, no more! Now that he had identified the problem, he would fix it, because fixing things was what he did best. He was going to keep Miss Rowe at arm's length, stop fantasizing about the prickly minx, and prioritize himself for a change. Reclaim his life, insist on his next overdue promotion, and find joy in his career again. He was also going to enjoy being a bachelor and sow some wild oats with determined abandon as a matter of urgency. Tonight, in fact! That would rid his mind of his most beguiling and befuddling employee once and for all.

Before the sun set, he was going to clean himself up, take himself out, and find himself a willing woman he could have a mad, passionate, but dispassionate fling with. Or a mad passionate night with. Or even a mad, passionate interlude in a conservatory with! Whichever opportunity presented itself first, he was going to grab it with both hands and thereby slake all his pent-up lust and hopefully banish all his unsettling emptiness as well. Kill two wretched birds with one stone. Three, if it also freed him of the incessant pondering of Miss Rowe's contrasting pale skin and flame hair. Of her compact but tempting figure and her seductive eyes, or her tart mouth for that matter too. Because, frankly, he never wanted to have to contemplate the vixen's lips ever again. Her lips, like the rest of Miss Rowe, were absolutely not on his bloody extensive list of things he had *to do*.

A surprised Simpkins met him at the front door. "You are home early?" Then he frowned, alarmed. "Has something happened?"

"Of course not. I am simply home a little earlier than usual"—by about eight hours!—"so that I can get ready for Admiral and Lady Nugent's ball tonight." Where he fully intended to cross his new number one priority off his list—those oats. "So I shall need a bath run immediately."

"You . . . are going to a ball?" Simpkins struggled to hide his surprise, as Harry burned most of the invitations he got nowadays because he never had time for them, and if he did, he was always too tired to bother. "Very good, sir."

"I shall need you to dust off my dress uniform for the occasion."

Simpkins looked even more surprised by that request. "Are you sure, sir? Only it's unseasonably warm for May and I'll need to polish all the buttons before its fit to be seen. They've not been done in a while."

"Then polish them until they shine while I'm in the bath, Simpkins." He rubbed his chin and decided it was far too stubbly to be considered gentlemanly—especially when entertaining a woman. If he found a willing one tonight, he was jolly well going to give her carte blanche to have her wicked way with him this very evening, so it made sense to look his absolute best and be politely smooth at the same time. No woman wanted whisker burns. "And lay out all my shaving things too."

Clearly peeved by that, his retainer scowled. "But you only had new evening clothes made for town last month, sir, and they've not yet been worn. A rather splendid set of evening clothes they are, too, which are pressed and ready and nowhere near as hot as your dress . . ."

"As Admiral Nugent was the man who dragged me to the Admiralty to prove my mettle, I must impress him." And thereby make a start on priority number two—claiming his next promotion.

"You can impress him just as well in your evening clothes as you can in a uniform, and nobody wears their uniform here in town anyway and—" Harry stayed him with a raised palm because they were both men of the world, and the new no-nonsense Harry had already wasted enough time justifying himself when he was supposed to be resolute. "I am going to be wearing my uniform because I am due some *shore leave*, Simpkins."

They both knew what *shore leave* was a euphemism for. Just as they both knew that, for some inexplicable reason, while it either irritated or intimidated the non-military men, there wasn't a lady alive who did not prefer a man in uniform to one without one. His impressive but somewhat uncomfortable gold–trimmed navy captain's coat had always attracted women like flies. In fact, it hadn't once let him down in all the years he had worn it. Neither had the lieutenant's coat he had swapped for it. Never one for propriety, Flora had always joked that Harry's navy uniform was like catnip and no woman was safe from him when he wore it, so he was praying it still worked. A roll around a different woman's mattress felt like the only way he was going to ever get his imagination to stop conjuring inappropriate images of Miss Rowe in his mind while he laid on his.

"Ah . . ." said Simpkins with a tap to his nose. "Yes, of course, sir. And if I might be so bold, I am glad to hear it. I was trying to find a subtle way to suggest that a bit of *shore leave* was long overdue. In fact, can't remember the last time that you . . ." Needing neither the cringeworthy lecture nor the reminder, Harry stayed him with another hand in stark warning. Simpkins winked, unrepentant, as he backed away. "I'll have those buttons so shiny all the ladies will be able to see their swooning faces in them. You'll look so resplendent you'll have no trouble attracting—"

"Just go, will you!"

"Yes, sir!" A grinning Simpkins disappeared out the doorway, then immediately reappeared in it with placating hands. "I know that I'm probably talking out of turn, but it occurs to me that if some *shore leave* is in the cards, then might I be so bold as to suggest that I lay out the newer breeches . . ." They also both knew that the newer breeches were a polite euphemism for the bigger breeches Simpkins had had made behind Harry's back because, as much as he wanted to deny it, he wasn't quite as lithe onshore as he had been out at sea. The lack of weevils in the biscuits and Mrs. Rigsby's excellent cooking had added two inches to his waistline in the last two years that no amount of exercise seemed to shift. He kept himself fit and his belly was still as flat as a pancake, so he was determined to convince himself that those extra inches were the muscle which was meant to be there without the skimpy ship rations. But still—they galled. "They'll be less . . . constricting when you're . . . *dancing*, Captain."

As much as the suggestion mortified him, for so many reasons that he was sorely tempted to blush when they both knew what *dancing* was a euphemism for, his faithful manservant made a valid point.

On their last outing, his old dress breeches cut him in places that breeches shouldn't cut and, as a result, had distracted him all evening. He hadn't purposefully gone on *shore leave* that night, but if he had, those breeches would have ruined it, as he'd spent the entire evening willing them not to keep creeping up his backside and had ended up leaving early. He'd be a much better and more charming flirt if he was comfortable, so he gave the crude wretch a curt nod before he spun away and sprinted up the stairs.

The newer breeches would also be much easier for a willing woman to strip him out of before the long-overdue *dancing* commenced, which was, if all went to plan, the only reason he intended to wear them. Whatever it took, he had to banish his dangerous but growing obsession with Miss Rowe from his mind once and for all.

# THIRTEEN

৫৬৶৶

*I*nstantly floppy at the threat of a bath, Norbert glued himself to the entrance of the yard and refused to budge. Wise to his methods, Georgie simply attached some rope to his collar to tie him fast to the gate while the children went off to fetch the buckets and soap.

"It is your own stupid fault." She was immune to his big, soulful, outraged brown eyes too. "I warned you not to swim in the Serpentine again, but you went and did it anyway." There was no way she was allowing him inside when he was covered in mud, pond weed, and algae. Especially after the unfortunate incident with the fox excrement last week that Simpkins, quite rightly, still wasn't fully over. The defiant dog had purposefully gone swimming through the most stagnant part of the lake to cover himself in algae, just as he had found what the fox had left and then gleefully rolled in it.

"Dogs like to hide their scent," said Lottie as she helped Georgie drag the huge hound toward the gate post. At a loose end since her sudden dismissal from her last position, her friend had accompanied

Georgie and the children to the park so that she could spill her most recent tale of woe to someone guaranteed to be sympathetic. "Just in case a predator is around."

"There aren't any predators here in Mayfair."

"Animal ones, at least." Lottie shuddered as she looped Norbert's lead several times around the gatepost. "Sadly, there are all too many human ones, as I have recently learned to my cost."

"You'll soon find another job, Lottie. You always do." With the dog secured and unable to escape, she gave her friend a comforting hug despite not being the least bit surprised Lottie had once again been caught red-handed riding a horse from her employer's stable. That she had been discovered by the employer's octopus-armed libertine of a son was unfortunate, especially as he had tried to blackmail her into keeping her secret in return for certain *favors*. "Console yourself that at least you were wearing your breeches and sturdy riding boots when Lord Chadwell's son made those unseemly advances toward you, as he won't be in any position to importune another innocent employee for some considerable time." Thanks to a house full of brothers, her friend had known precisely where to aim her knee to dampen the randy lord's ardor. And, apparently, dampen it Lottie had, so thoroughly that the physician had to be called. "The hunter became the hunted."

"There is that," said her friend, grinning as she strode to the pump and made short work of filling a bucket while Norbert cowered at the prospect of an imminent dousing. Then whimpered.

"This wouldn't be necessary if you'd have stayed on the grass like I asked, you daft dog." Georgie tickled his ears. "If you are going to continue to live under the captain's roof, you are going to have to buck your ideas up, young man, as nobody wants to live with a stinky dog, even if he is as delightfully mad as you are." For all his faults, she had quickly grown to love Norbert. His constant, usually snoring presence, was soothing. Like a roaring fire on a cold night, there was something homely about a faithful hound by your side, and Norbert had taken to hovering around hers as soon as the children went to bed and keeping her company until she did.

There was, much to her surprise, also now something homely about Captain Kincaid's fine house too. Enough that she felt almost as settled there as she had at Miss P's, and in practically no time at all. The stickler might insist it was shipshape at all times, but he had furnished his house more with comfort in mind than for appearance's sake and had filled it with so many unusual and intriguing souvenirs from his travels that it was a unique and interesting place to live. It was also a fascinating window into the stickler's soul and one that again made him incrementally more likable. Vibrant rugs from Persia ensured the hardwood floors weren't drafty and he had used all the silks he had collected from Asia to inject subtle pops of color into every room.

There was also a permanence about the place which she approved of. This was his home and not a transient billet like the succession of soulless places the colonel had dragged her to live in. The captain owned all four walls and all the furniture within them, whereas the colonel had only ever rented furnished places because he preferred to travel light. For her unsentimental and frigid stepfather, too many belongings, like too many emotions, simply got in the way. Already, Georgie knew that she would miss this welcoming enclave in Hanover Square when she would have to leave it. Almost as much as she would miss the boisterous Pendletons and their algae-covered mutt and, much to her continued chagrin, the confusing and often atypical military man who owned the house. Oddly, here already felt like home, although she was pragmatic enough to accept that it was likely only one of many temporary homes in her future. But such was a governess's lot, irrespective of how much Georgie secretly yearned for just one home. All of her own.

"Mrs. Rigsby told us to use the scrubbing brush," announced the returning Felix, holding it aloft. "Just in case."

Norbert took one look at it and balked, then tried to wiggle his head out of his collar so that he could escape. In case he managed it and wreaked havoc indoors, Georgie grabbed it. When that did not give her enough purchase to keep the dog still, she had no choice but to fling her leg astride his filthy fur to hold him steady.

She grabbed the bar of soap from little Grace's outstretched hand and gestured to Marianne to let loose the first bucket Lottie had filled, gritting her teeth to brace herself for the cold and the inevitable battle ahead.

With a bit too much relish, Marianne sloshed the contents over the pair of them. As the icy water hit Georgie's stomach, she yelped, and so did Norbert.

Except when he yelped, something jumped out of his mouth.

Something green and slimy and so unexpected that both girls began to scream.

"It's a frog!" shouted Felix quite unnecessarily as Norbert bucked beneath her to try and capture the poor thing again. "Norbert brought a frog home!"

"So he did," said Lottie, grinning, instantly more fascinated by the croaking amphibian in the yard than she was any help holding Norbert back. "And a big one at that."

Relieved to be free, the frog hopped as far away from the dog and the screaming girls as he could while Georgie held on for dear life. It bounced across the yard at lightning speed, jumped up the front step to the kitchen, and then disappeared inside.

"Well, don't just stand there! Catch it!" As Georgie issued that instruction, Mrs. Rigsby and Polly started screaming in the kitchen just as Norbert dropped to the ground, dragging her with him. She clung to him for as long as she could, but his fur was too wet and her fingers were too slippery as the dog wiggled and twisted beneath her for all he was worth. Then he was gone, leaving her sitting in a puddle of water and pond weed and goodness knew what else, still clutching his collar.

By the time she scrambled up and followed all the others inside, the kitchen was pandemonium. Simpkins had joined the fray and was chasing the hopping frog toward the pantry with a mixing bowl in his hand. As she was made of sterner stuff, Lottie seemed determined to catch the slimy interloper with her bare hands as she edged closer, while Felix was hanging off Norbert as if his life depended on it, doing his best to keep his dog from following the frog to the pantry and failing miserably. Marianne, Grace, Polly the maid, and Mrs. Rigsby were all hysterical now—Mrs. Rigsby screeching from atop the kitchen table—while the remains of what looked like supper lay scattered across the kitchen.

With a battle cry, Simpkins suddenly lunged with his bowl, and to everyone's surprise, actually caught the frog beneath it. Or at least beneath it for as long as it took for the pottery vessel to break as it impacted on the flagstones. While the now prostrate Simpkins began to curse, the poor frog made another break for freedom. He hopped past Lottie's grasping hands and back out of the pantry—straight into Norbert's open jaws again.

Eyes bulging and mouth swollen as if he were holding a delicate egg, the dog evaded everyone and shot out of the kitchen in a blur. Grabbing a saucepan, Georgie dashed after him.

Thankfully, out of habit, Norbert had fled to the classroom first at the furthest end of the hall, as he knew she tended to leave the French doors open. However, as the classroom door was firmly closed, there was no clear exit to the garden, so he had inadvertently trapped himself in a dead end.

As the others fanned out behind her, cutting off his escape, all now armed with various vessels from the kitchen, the dog crouched, his big tail wagging while he plotted his next move.

"NO!" Georgie advanced with purpose, her schoolmistress's finger pointed like a sword. "Put that poor frog down!"

His tail wagged some more as he bounced from side to side like a boxer in the ring, clearly seeing all this as one big, marvelous game. To taunt them, he allowed his jaws to open enough that they could all see the kidnapped but still hale and hearty frog jumping around behind his teeth.

"Put it down! NOW!"

"There's no escape, you scabrous bag of fleas!" Beside her, Simpkins snapped open a tablecloth and held it up like a matador, ready to trap the dog in it if he had to. "Open your mouth or I'll break your blasted jaws!"

"Be a good dog, Norbert." Felix pushed himself to the fore and tried to use reason in case Simpkins carried out that threat. "Let the frog go and I'll get you a sausage."

As always, his ears pricked up at the word *sausage* and, sensing an opportunity, Mrs. Rigsby pretended to rummage in her apron to convince the dog that she had one. Norbert's attention wavered for a split second, but that was all it took for Simpkins to smother him in the tablecloth as he and Lottie tried to wrestle him to the ground. However, instead of disorientating him or stopping him as it was supposed to, it did neither, and Norbert was off again like a shot. Only this time, draped in linen like a ghostly apparition as he barged a hole through Marianne and Grace, knocking the littlest Pendleton onto her bottom in the process.

He had shed the fabric by the foot of the stairs and so galloped up them unhindered, pausing on the landing only long enough to coquettishly check that everyone was still chasing him before he was off again.

Georgie watched him disappear into a bedchamber and plunged after him, only to skid to a stop by the unexpected sight of the wide-eyed, soap-covered, and spluttering Captain Kincaid shooting upright from what she assumed must have been his reclined position in his bathtub.

If she had thought he suited a damp shirt, he suited his birthday suit much better. At least from the waist up, which was all her suddenly hypnotized eyeballs were capable of looking at. His arms were quite magnificent. The muscles cording them were utterly perfect. His shoulders were a thing of beauty, and his chest . . .

Good heavens above, but that marvelous expanse of wondrousness very nearly had her sighing aloud.

"What the blazes!" Too surprised by the sudden intrusion of the entire household, an openly ogling Lottie, and the dog now flying toward his bed to give any consideration at all to his modesty, the captain waved his razor in the air. "Not my dress uniform!" That was when Georgie realized she was gaping at him, practically drooling like Norbert did at the wares hung in the butcher's window, and hoisted her jaw back up. "Not tonight! Somebody stop him!"

Plaintive, panicked words which spurred Simpkins to lunge for it as if his life depended on it. He managed to hit the mattress and cover the captain's smart navy-and-gold brocade coat with his body before the filthy Norbert landed on it.

No sooner did his paws hit the well-sprung bed than the dog immediately burped out the frog. It wasted no time hopping from the pillow to the captain's magnificent naked shoulder; then, as he screamed in shock and before the laughing Lottie could grab it, it dove headfirst into the safety of his bathwater.

*Chapter*
# FOURTEEN

❧⚘❧

𝐵 y the time he had finally captured the frog that Norbert had smuggled into the house, cleared all the sniggering spectators out of his bedchamber, and stuffed his body into the damned too-tight breeches because the newer ones were now covered in muddy paw prints, the ball was in full swing when Harry arrived.

It hadn't been the best start to his planned night of oat sowing, but at least it had gone some way toward alleviating some of his tiredness. His heart hadn't stopped racing since the dog's rude interruption and, thanks to all the pumping blood coursing through his body, he had a bit of a spring in his step. A spring that would come in handy for a ball and, with any luck, the other delights which might follow it. Especially as, and despite his shock at the interruption, his stupid heart had leapt at its first sight of Miss Rowe earlier, and that absolutely had to stop.

As if it was meant to be, he collided with a familiar and very fine feminine face straightaway. "Why hello, Captain Kincaid. Don't you look dashing this evening? So dashing I'd have saved the first waltz for you if you had bothered arriving before it was done." The notorious widow gave him an unmistakably come-hither look over the top of her fan.

"There is still the second to look forward to, Mrs. Templeton." For some peculiar reason, flirting felt awkward, probably because he was out of practice, so he persevered because she was exactly what he needed. "Or the last."

She held out the wrist, where her dance card dangled in invitation. "Or we could cause a scandal and you could have both—but only if you find me some champagne first."

"It would be my pleasure." Harry held out his arm and she threaded hers through it proprietorially as he led her to the refreshment table.

She undressed him with her eyes as they clinked glasses, and then she paraded him around her similarly brazen friends for the next half an hour, still clinging to him like a limpet. Her fingers constantly explored his bicep in a manner which let him know that she was fair game and quite content to be caught.

He wanted to be relieved that already, more than dancing seemed assured. He also desperately wanted to feel some enthusiasm for the attractive and uncomplicated woman on his arm, as she was precisely what he had come here for—but instead he remained unmoved. He tried to convince himself that, too, was down to his lack of practice and not a genuine lack of interest and that he would warm up as the night wore on. But even as she twirled too close when the waltz began and plastered herself against him as they danced around the floor, nothing kindled in his too-tight breeches.

By the time the dance ended, Harry was again making fresh excuses for his apathy. Excuses that blamed his breeches for constricting him exactly as Simpkins had warned and which made it even more imperative that Mrs. Templeton should dispense with them at her earliest possible convenience.

Except, he wasn't that keen. Or keen at all for that matter. Really did not want to be here. Should probably go home . . . He stared longingly at the door and tried to think of the politest excuse to extricate himself from the willing woman still clinging to him.

"Captain Kincaid." One of the footmen tapped him on the shoulder, ruining his plan to escape the ballroom completely. "Admiral Nugent needs an urgent word with you."

Moments later, he was shown into Nugent's smoke-filled study. The discarded glasses all around the abandoned stubs of expensive cigars suggested another meeting had just taken place, and with men who were much more important than Harry was. He shook the admiral's hand, then gingerly lowered his constricted backside into the chair opposite. Trying hard not to read anything into a sudden invitation from a man who, if all the naval gossip was to be believed, was next in line for admiral of the fleet.

"You did a damned good job sorting out that mess in Portsmouth, Kincaid. A bloody fine job. Well done."

"Thank you, sir." In keeping with the new, no-nonsense, single-minded Harry who was going to look after himself for a change, he decided to take the compliment rather than brush it away as he normally did.

"Those blighters had us over a barrel there for a while until you sorted them out."

"It turned out those merchants just needed a firm hand on the tiller to correct their course." And issue a stark reminder that if they wanted to renegotiate the terms of the contracts before the contracts were up, then the navy might as well put all those contracts back out to tender.

"Calling their bluff like that was a flash of genius."

It had been a flash of sheer, unadulterated frustration, but Harry smiled at that compliment too and did brush it away in case he came across as too cocky while he waited for the admiral to tip his hand. "It was hardly genius when the opportunity to defeat the enemy is always provided by the enemy himself. If those greedy merchants had read Sun Tzu, they would have realized that they had overplayed their hand long before they forced mine."

"You fought fire with fire, Kincaid, and I admire that. Sometimes a line has to be drawn in the sand." As that sentiment wholly supported all the conclusions Harry had recently come to himself, he nodded. "And it seems that you are the man required to draw it." He decided to absolutely take that resonating compliment too.

"I'm of the firm opinion that if you give some people too much rope, they'll hang you with it." Harry crossed one leg over the other and did his best to look like a man who was completely in control of all aspects of his life. Albeit one who had stupidly forgotten that his damned breeches were too tight for comfortable leg crossing before he had crossed them but was now stuck with the consequences. The sort of man that Nugent might believe was worthy of a well-earned promotion he'd dangled like a carrot for two long years without him having to ask for it. More importantly, the sort who would stand up for himself and refuse if the Admiralty was about to shaft him with more work when he already had too much to cope with. "I prefer to keep the line taut."

Nugent steepled his fingers and nodded. "That is precisely why I'm sending you to Plymouth." A part of Harry died inside at the mention of that wretched place before another part died when he gave him the reason. "I want you to work your unique magic on the *Boadicea*. It needs to be seaworthy by early July if it's to lead the fleet out on the first of August."

"With the greatest respect, Admiral, getting that ship seaworthy by July would take more than magic—it is so far behind schedule that it would take a miracle. I am not the man for that job." If the Admiralty had already sucked most of the joy out of his soul, blasted Plymouth and the bloody *Boadicea* would shrivel it to a crisp. He had come to hate that wretched ship almost as much as he had always loathed the place it was being built in. In fact, he hated it so much, that when he became admiral of the fleet, he was going to have the bloody thing scrapped just because he could!

"I've done all that I can with that ship. The work-shy layabouts at the Plymouth Dockyard need a bigger gun than a mere captain to light a fire beneath their arses. They need a man with more brocade on his coat." He gestured to the gold rope aiguillette draped over Nugent's right shoulder. "Besides, I was only drafted to help with the *Boadicea* when I could—and I have tried my best—but the truth is, it is hard to be effective when I am already spread too thin to give such a mammoth task all the time it deserves. What with all the procurement contracts I oversee . . . and . . . all the additional projects and responsibilities I've been saddled with of late." In his panic, excuses—ungrateful sounding excuses to the man who had given him the opportunity to impress at the Admiralty—spilled from his mouth. The speed at which they did so made the next in line to be the admiral of the fleet frown.

"Have you been to Plymouth to give them what for?"

"Well . . . um . . . no, sir. There hasn't been the time . . . and I already have too much on my plate keeping all the shipyards and boats stocked with what they need and—"

"Not anymore you don't. You are relieved of all that nonsense. From this day forth, your only responsibility is getting that ship out on maneuvers by August." He passed Harry's folded and sealed orders across the table. "You are expected at Plymouth on the first of June. There will be an office and a substantial staff awaiting you at dock when you arrive, and I shall make sure that everyone there knows that I have delegated all responsibility to you. You will speak for me and anyone who doesn't do exactly what you tell them to will have me to contend with."

The doors to a different sort of hellish prison seemed to slam shut around him. "But sir, I also currently have the additional responsibilities my sis—" Again he was cut off.

"You are wasted on procurements, Kincaid. A sailor of your caliber shouldn't be concerning himself with the price of flour or whether there is enough lantern oil in a warehouse. He should be the one in command and not the navy's lackey. You only have that one blemish on your record, after all." The one blemish nobody would allow him to bloody well forget about—Elizabeth. "And you are not daft enough to make that sort of mistake twice."

Which was the only good thing to come out of his failed engagement.

He had been in the first flush of love, or more likely lust, when the news had come that he had finally earned a ship of his own. He was to take command of it upon his return from his short, final voyage as a lieutenant and he had been thrilled by the promotion. Just not as thrilled as he was to have found the supposed woman of his dreams.

Sailing away from Elizabeth after their spur-of-the-moment betrothal had been the hardest thing he had ever done. He had only done it after his grandfather had intervened and had ordered Harry's commanding officer to refuse his request to take some urgent leave for a hasty wedding and honeymoon before he took on his first helm as a captain. The admiral had been so furious with Harry for behaving like a love-consumed lunatic, he had threatened to have his own grandson court-martialed if he disobeyed and locked in the brig for two months for desertion and insubordination. A sentence which would have scuppered all his wedding plans for far longer, so he had no choice but to comply.

Yet with hindsight, it had all been for the best. If he hadn't reluctantly sailed away that day, her fickle gaze wouldn't have wandered to pastures new, and their union would have crashed on the rocks later when he would have been bound to the treacherous wench for all eternity. Stuck with the biggest mistake of his life and regretting it daily. Exactly as his grandfather had predicted.

Worse, he hadn't just lost Elizabeth during his short absence either, he had lost the promised ship, too, after word of his planned stupidity made its way to the wrong ear and it was decreed that he wasn't ready for the responsibility of a helm yet after all.

"You were young and stupid but took your medicine like a man." Nugent gave him one of those pitying looks that he had come to loathe. "Then excelled when we finally did promote you to captain, so we don't need to dredge all that nonsense up again." Although he just had, and Harry's toes were curling inside his boots because the navy worked hard to remind him of his stupidity at every juncture. "Your grandfather, God rest him, raised you for better and bigger things and your time at the Admiralty was only ever intended to grease those wheels, so to speak. But now they are greased and it's time you reaped the rewards of your efforts outside of it."

While Harry couldn't really argue with that, he still did. "I believe I could do better and bigger things at the Admiralty . . ."

"You've outgrown the Admiralty as I knew you would. We all did." Nugent smiled. "I've had them throw a lot at you, I know, but when I promised your grandfather before he died that I would continue your training and keep pushing you higher, I also told him that I needed to test your mettle. I needed to be sure you actually were all of what he hoped you would become. But seeing as you've passed every test with flying colors . . ." He chuckled at his own pun and another part of Harry withered inside. "And even though there are a great many in this service who will still say that I am mad to entrust you with so much responsibility when you are barely out of leading strings, I've been watching you closely for the last two years and my decision is made. The *Boadicea* is yours. To get seaworthy and . . ." He paused for dramatic effect. "To command once it is."

Admiral Nugent held out his hand, beaming. "Congratulations, Captain—I do not know of another sailor who deserves a one-hundred-and-twenty-gun first-rate ship of the line more than you do." He pumped Harry's hand vigorously. "You are every bit the fine sailor your grandfather was and more. I suspect this ship is but the first of many great things in your future."

As "thank you, sir" seemed the only appropriate response, Harry tried to say it with some enthusiasm while Nugent reached for two fresh glasses on the sideboard and poured them both a brandy.

"Now, obviously you know that there are never any hard and fast promises in the Royal Navy, but in another year or so, once you've proved yourself capable of handling my flagship . . ." He pressed the drink into Harry's suddenly limp and sweaty hand. "I'll probably delegate command of a small flotilla along with it when I'm not aboard. Make you *Commodore* Kincaid. How does that sound? See if we can't push you up to vice admiral within five years." Nugent did not wait for his answer, as he clearly thought he already knew it.

Harry had stupidly once thought the same, yet suddenly didn't. Instead, all he could think of was a tightening rope and could not tell whether that was because his was about to run out or it was forming a noose for his neck. "Cheers."

"Cheers."

But as Harry raised his toast, instead of feeling proud of this unheard-of rapid promotion and excited for the fresh challenges the navy was offering, all he felt was numb.

# FIFTEEN

❧

eorgie had been in an odd mood all evening. Unsettled and distracted. While she knew that a great deal of that was as a result of the unexpected but enlightening sight of the captain in his bath, she also felt bad for what had happened. She hadn't seen him since the frog had sought refuge in his bathwater and Felix and Marianne rolled around the floor, hysterical, as if the whole debacle was the funniest thing they had ever seen.

She knew an apology was in order.

"What time will Captain Kincaid be back?" If the memory of his naked torso was destined to make sleep impossible, she might as well wait up until he got home to get it over and done with. "I need to speak to him."

"Those fancy balls tend to go on way past midnight," said Mrs. Rigsby, stirring her customary pot of bedtime cocoa for all the servants to enjoy before they turned in for the night. "So I don't suppose he'll be home till one."

"He won't be back till morning," said Simpkins over the top of his newspaper. Then, with a saucy wink, added, "He's on *shore leave* tonight, Georgie, for the first time in forever, so he might not even turn up till the afternoon if he's lucky."

"How can he be on shore leave when he hasn't gone away to sea?"

At Georgie's baffled response and the butler's subsequent chuckle, Mrs. Rigsby gave him a clip around the ear and a glare so potent it made Simpkins laugh all the harder behind his well-thumbed copy of the *London Gazette*. "He's . . . um . . . indisposed, Georgie, that's what Simpkins means." The cook's cheeks reddened as she tried to answer and then reddened some more at Georgie's still-baffled face. "Doing the sort of things that sailors are *infamous* for doing when they get to port."

"Oh," said Georgie, none the wiser until Simpkins threw his head back and roared at her naivety and Mrs. Rigsby's entire face blushed scarlet and suddenly it all made sense. "*Oh!* Well . . ." Her own cheeks burned hot, but not as hot as the instant flash of outrage and jealousy. "I suppose I shall have to speak to him tomorrow, then." Although how she was supposed to look him in the eye when she'd likely spend the rest of tonight picturing him entwined with a horrid, light-skirted but doubtless stunning temptress, she did not know.

Blushing herself, Georgie raced out of the kitchen and slammed straight into the captain's chest. Instinctively, her flattened palms braced against that solid wall of maleness and felt those intriguing muscles over his ribcage. Felt the heat emanating from his skin even through his clothes. Even felt the drum of his heartbeat beneath, which seemed to speed up and race at the same unnerving canter as hers did.

She risked glancing up and lost herself in his stormy gaze. She was so entranced, she would have likely remained staring doltishly into his dark eyes for all eternity but, to her utter horror, he held her out at arm's length with a startled frown. Then every bit of her pale and insipid redhead's skin instantly combusted, and she burned so pink she knew that she would put a beetroot to shame. "My apologies, Captain Kincaid. I wasn't expecting you to be here . . . um . . . so early."

"I wasn't expecting to be here myself either, but alas, here I am." He attempted a smile, which quickly wavered as his eyes drifted to her horrid hair, and then gave up to address Simpkins over her shoulder as if she wasn't there anymore. Which was just as well because it gave Georgie a well-needed moment to return her scrambled wits to some order. "Sorry to disturb you at the end of your day, Simpkins, but I'm afraid I need a quick word . . . in my study."

Everything from the tone of that statement to its delivery suggested that the quick word wasn't going to be good. The way he stalked off afterward confirmed it.

"Of course." With an odd glance at Mrs. Rigsby, Simpkins followed his master down the hallway, leaving a still-blushing Georgie all alone with Mrs. Rigsby and a maelstrom of improper thoughts and sensations that did nothing to calm her racing heart.

"It appears his *shore leave* was either curtailed or canceled." And she wasn't entirely sure what she felt about that beyond relieved. "*Poor* Captain Kincaid."

"Poor Captain Kincaid, indeed." Oblivious to her sarcasm, and thankfully Georgie's seething but irrational jealousy, Mrs. Rigsby stared down the empty hallway, thoughtful. "Did he just seem off to you?"

"As he's always off with me, it's hard to tell." Although she sincerely doubted his paramour shared that problem. He wouldn't be off with her. He'd be *on*. "I am naught but a disappointment to that man." By the disgusted expression on his face as he had peeled her off him, he would certainly never be caught dead even contemplating some shore leave with her. Not that she wanted that, of course.

Not rationally, at least. Because why on earth would she harbor romantic thoughts for a man like the colonel?

Except the captain wasn't like the colonel in the slightest. He might be a bit stiff and pompous and a dreadful stickler, but he was also kind and charming, noble and so handsome he made her all aquiver, so irrationally, she had started to harbor them anyway. Pathetic, shallow fool that she was.

"By off, I mean . . . bothered." The cook removed the steaming cocoa from the range and poured some into three cups. "Not himself. Upset, even."

As Georgie took the proffered cup, annoyed at herself for her ridiculous reaction and futile attraction, she shrugged. "Again, as I have a habit of upsetting him, I really couldn't say." Except she also sensed he wasn't himself for some reason—and that bothered her. "He always seems to carry the weight of the world on his shoulders, but they did look a bit more . . . burdened perhaps than usual, yes." Had she become so enamored of the man—or his dratted shoulders—that she now misguidedly thought that she could read him too? What fanciful nonsense was that?

A lost cause, that was what. Because she was clearly an idiot. The biggest, daftest, and most masochistic ninny to ever live if she was seriously harboring a tender for him! *Captain* Kincaid. A man who wore a uniform! A man who lived for his uniform! And a man who hated her horrid hair so much he could barely stand to look at it for longer than he had to!

Georgie was so staggered by her own stupidity it was a wonder she wasn't currently spitting actual feathers! While she completely understood why he disliked her hair, because nobody could dislike it more than she did, he didn't have to be quite so obvious about it. That was just plain rude. And he liked to go on *shore leave* with a seductress who likely had compliant and elegant hair of an acceptable and attractive shade. And that was all crowned by the inescapable and inexcusable fact that the wretch wore a uniform and she could tolerate that least of all!

"He's not usually so easily unsettled." Mrs. Rigsby sipped her cocoa. "I wonder what's happened?"

"Nothing good, that's for certain." How Georgie knew that when she barely knew him, she wasn't sure, but it set her on edge regardless. A very different sort of edge than the news of his *shore leave* had.

Whatever it was, it obviously put Mrs. Rigsby on edge, too, as she was uncharacteristically quiet while they both waited for Simpkins to return. When he did, though, he was smiling. "The captain has been promoted and it's a hefty one, to boot. They've given him a flagship, although it's still being built, and they've also dangled the commodore's carrot, so he'll shortly be receiving all the bells and whistles that go with that lofty rank. I'm chuffed for him." Simpkins grabbed his mug of cocoa and toasted the air with it. "He deserves it."

"Oh, thank goodness!" Mrs. Rigsby clutched her ample bosom, laughing. "His return was so subdued I was sure he had received bad news!"

"Thankfully, it was the exact opposite." Simpkins's smile stretched even wider. "He's just a bit overwhelmed by it, that's all. He's also got a lot to do before he leaves, so I dare say he doesn't know quite where to start with it yet either."

"He's leaving?" Against her better judgment, Georgie found little to celebrate in that. "Why, when the ship isn't even finished?"

"Somebody has to oversee the finishing of it and who better than the man who will take the helm?" Simpkins settled into his chair to drink his beverage. "He has to report to Plymouth next week."

"For how long?"

"For the foreseeable. He might venture back to town on the odd occasion while he recruits the right crew, as he'll need a good eight hundred of the best sailors, but he's been stationed to the Plymouth dock until August when the *Boadicea* has got to be finished. Who knows where they'll send him after? That all depends on where the worst trouble is."

"What do you mean by trouble?" The more Georgie heard, the more her horrid, unappealing orange hair stood on end.

"Well, war, obviously," said Simpkins, as if she were daft. "A first-rate ship has over a hundred guns for only one reason, Georgie, and that's to blow the enemy out of the water."

"Oh dear." Images of the tragic death of Nelson skittered through her mind. "That isn't good."

"It isn't good." Simpkins beamed. "It's bloody marvelous! They only entrust those that are first-rate with a first-rate ship of the line. Warships are cumbersome and temperamental brutes who need a steady hand and a quick mind to keep them afloat. But the captain has both those things in spades, so he'll do fine. Especially with the right crew behind him, and I'll be one of them. He asked me to be his sailing master again. I'll reenlist as soon as we get to Plymouth." Simpkins sighed with satisfaction as he sipped his cocoa. "It'll be good to get back out to sea. I've missed it."

"But not so good to always be sailing toward trouble, Mr. Simpkins." Georgie's vivid imagination had decided to abandon all its scandalous musings of her as the captain's willing distraction in favor of more macabre prophecies of potential doom. "You could both be killed."

He shrugged at Georgie's comment. "Such is a sailor's life. Sailing toward trouble is what we do, and we all have to die of something. At least the hot kiss of a musket ball or the punch from a cannon is a quick and clean way to go." He shrugged those grisly ends off as if he was completely at peace with the risks. "And we'd likely have our names chiseled in perpetuity onto a monument somewhere, so that will be nice too."

"Nice?" Were all military men this mad? "But what about the children?" If the threat of death wasn't enough to make the captain think twice about going, then maybe reminding him of his responsibilities on land might. "They were entrusted into his care by his sister! Surely he can't just abandon them at the drop of a hat?" Especially if sailing away from them involved him being blown to smithereens!

"Of course he can. This is the biggest promotion of his career and his sister will understand that. Not that he needs her understanding when she didn't even have the decency to ask him if she could leave the blighters here. And they've still got you, haven't they?" Simpkins seemed shocked by her outrage. "It's not as if the little buggers are his."

As that cavalier response only served to annoy her, and because she was suddenly so unsettled by the bombshell that had just been dropped on her from on high, Georgie decided to try and reason with the captain instead.

As she stalked to his study, irrationally more furious at him for getting promoted than she was with his shore leave she didn't hold out much hope he would listen. Military men only ever put themselves first, last, and always—even if that also meant they got themselves killed in the process. However, she had to say something. When something was wrong, it was wrong, and not saying so was wrong too. Him going—leaving—now felt wrong. So wrong someone had to fight against it.

She went to hammer on his half-open door, ready to give him what for, but paused when she saw him staring out of his window at the night. His posture told her that while Simpkins was celebrating his master's elevation, the master wasn't. She had never seen anyone look quite as lost as the captain did at this precise moment and, once again against her better judgment, she instantly pitied him.

"Might I have a word, Captain?"

He spun around at her question and forced a weak smile. "Of course." He swept a reluctant hand toward the chair in front of his desk. Then slowly lowered himself into his own seat with a wince as he stared briefly at her awful hair again. As much as her inner Joan of Arc had plenty to say, now that she knew he was troubled, she would start gently. Try to be a diplomat for once, despite it not being her forte.

"I hear congratulations are in order—*Commodore*." She had never seen him in uniform before and was unprepared for how good he looked in it. He wore it well. Or perhaps, in this moment, he *bore* it well, although she had no clue why she thought that beyond the fact that it seemed to be one of the things currently weighing him down. "That is quite an impressive leap, even for someone like you, who is no stranger to early promotions."

He waved that compliment away, his brow furrowed. "I am not a commodore yet, Miss Rowe, but yes, I suppose it is quite a leap to be given a ship of such gravitas so early in one's career." His Adam's apple bobbed as he swallowed—hard—and his expression became so grave he looked ten years older than the version of himself she had witnessed sitting in his bathwater not four hours ago.

"I hear things will be quite rushed if you are to get to Plymouth by next week."

"Yes." Perhaps she was imagining it, but his eyes were more bothered than thrilled. "There is a lot to organize." Out of habit, his fingers fiddled with one of the pocket watches strung across his pale cream, brass-buttoned waistcoat, as if that would help slow time in the interim. "I am yet to know how to find enough hours in the next thirty-six hours to do it all."

"Just a day and a half? So soon?"

He shrugged. Even that seemed to take all his effort. "The interminable journey to Plymouth alone takes a week." His shoulders slumped some more. "Plymouth has never been the easiest of places to get to. By land, at least." He forced his frown into blandness again, unconsciously touching the other pocket watch and formalizing his posture as if he were suddenly eager to be rid of her to get on with things. "But you wanted a word?" His eyes fixed on the pile of letters on his desk rather than look at her, and he quickly selected one to slice open and read. An unconscious, or perhaps entirely conscious, gesture designed to let her know that the contents of his missive were more important than anything she might have to say. Yet while that made her inner St. Joan bristle, it set alarm bells ringing in that peculiar, intuitive part of her that was convinced it saw into his soul. Something was very wrong here, but she did not know what.

"I wanted two, actually." He might want to speed this conversation up, but she needed to do the opposite if she was going to convince him to reconsider leaving straightaway as that niggling voice in her head told her she needed to.

"Firstly, I wanted to apologize for the unfortunate incident with the frog earlier. Had I known Norbert had brought a friend home from the park, I never would have allowed him near the house. Had I also known that you were home, I never would have interrupted your bath as I did, and then inadvertently dragged in the whole household behind me. At the very least, I should have knocked before I attempted to relieve Norbert of his contraband."

He waved that away. "What? And deny everyone such splendid entertainment?" His eyes danced briefly as if he also saw the funny side of the debacle. "That young lady you brought in with you could barely contain her delight at my predicament. I believe she even snorted at one point."

Her friend had done more than snort. Lottie had snorted, ogled, and then waxed lyrical for ten minutes after the incident on what a truly fine specimen of manhood the captain was. Then, in front of Mrs. Rigsby, her incorrigible friend had reiterated her opinion that Georgie should absolutely use her wiles on him at her earliest possible convenience before somebody else pipped her to the post! "I absolutely must apologize for Lottie. She grew up in a houseful of men and struggles with ladylike behavior."

"If anyone should apologize for earlier, Miss Rowe, it is that mad dog. Although I suspect he is also entirely unrepentant for either the havoc he wreaked with the frog or the mud he smeared over all my bedsheets." He forgot to suppress his half smile momentarily, and her silly heart sighed. "How is said frog?"

"Delighted to be back in the Serpentine where he belongs. Felix and I took him *without* Norbert, who was less than delighted to be left behind."

"His howling suggested as much." That amused him too, she could tell, but he pushed it away fast. No sooner had his smile melted than his eyes returned to a missive on his desk, suddenly looking again every inch the single-minded military man who had more important things to do with his time than waste it on a conversation with a governess. "However, I daresay the dog would not have had the chance to kidnap the poor frog in the first place if you hadn't gone back to wasting almost every hour of the children's valuable lesson time outside again when you have a perfectly serviceable and well-stocked classroom here in the house."

"Wasn't it Wellington who said being born in a stable does not make one a horse?"

"And what has that to do with frogs and your aversion to classrooms, Miss Rowe?"

"That your particular area of expertise is commanding men to do precisely what the navy expects of them and mine is to encourage children to learn in the best possible way. Therefore, I fear that we shall have to agree to disagree on the benefits of confining education to the classroom."

"If you know enough Wellington to be able to quote him, then you will also know that discipline is the soul of an army—" Now he wasn't simply misquoting, he was ill-quoting too.

"I am surprised a proud English militarian who fought in the War of 1812 against America would stoop to quoting George Washington to prove a point."

He went to counter, then frowned. "Are you sure that was Washington?"

"Sure enough to wager a hundred guineas on it, Captain, as he also said that military arrangements and movements, in consequence, like the mechanism of a *clock*, will be *imperfect* and *disordered* by the want of a part." Georgie could not help reaching across the table and flicking one of his two pocket watches as she practically sung that. "And that always reminds me of you."

What had possessed her to say that? Do that? And with a wry smile on her face that let him know that she thought his obsession with time was funny.

"Right, then . . ." He glanced down at his still-swaying watch,

unimpressed, obviously back to being the hard-boiled Captain Kincaid who was easier to dislike than the soft-boiled one she had made
hot chocolate for ten days ago, because his whole demeanor was formal again. Her fault. She had insulted a clock and that was clearly
a cardinal sin. "What was the second thing you wished to discuss?"
He then clicked open one of his dratted watches to let her know that
she'd already had all her allotted time, and that forced Georgie to
give her wayward tongue a warning.

*Be diplomatic!*

"I wanted to talk to you about the children." His eyes narrowed,
expecting the worst. "They need you and it isn't fair for you to leave
them."

She thought he was going to tell her off for her impertinence as
she fully expected—but he didn't. He held her gaze for several moments, irritated, before his shoulders slumped again.

"It isn't fair." He sighed as he nodded his agreement, surprising
her yet again that he occasionally possessed the ability to be reasonable and . . . human.

"Can't you postpone leaving for just a few weeks? At least give
them a bit more time with their favorite uncle, while they are already
missing their parents so much, before you abandon them. They *are*
your responsibility, after all." Of its own accord, her schoolmistress's
finger began to wag. "Entrusted to you specifically by your sister, and
such disruption in their young lives again so soon after—"

He caught her finger mid-wag. "Before you lecture me on *my*
responsibilities—which I can assure you I need no reminders of—"
There was anger swirling in those dark eyes now. Anger and guilt
and, she could have sworn, briefly a hint of despair in them too,
although she couldn't be sure when his skin was touching hers and
hers seemed to have come alive as a result. As that was most distract-

ing indeed, she tugged her finger from his grasp and clasped it on her lap. "I had already decided I would drag the children along with me to Plymouth rather than simply *abandon them.*"

"What?" She hadn't expected him to say that.

"I shall task Polly with packing all their things tomorrow, so they are ready to leave with the lark the following morning as I must be in Plymouth by the first." He fiddled with the paper on his desk again rather than look at her in a way that made her wonder if he was about to inform her that her services were no longer required. Tasking Polly with the packing certainly suggested that. As the lack of "us" did in the telling "leave with the lark" comment, which did not in any way seem to include her. "As inconvenient as taking them with me is, it feels like the most prudent thing to do as it will be impossible to watch over them as I have *specifically* been entrusted otherwise."

"How selfish!" That retort exploded angry enough that even the captain was taken aback.

So much for diplomacy and tact!

But in her defense, his affronted and patronizing tone had brought St. Joan to the fore, and once she was out, she was out. As, it seemed, was Georgie—at least as far as this temporary position was concerned. Which all rather made the need for diplomacy moot anyway. "And how irresponsible!" The renegade finger wagged again. "You cannot *drag* them all the way to Plymouth!"

His dark brows furrowed in the same arrogant manner as the colonel's always had when one of his *superior* decisions was questioned. "Whyever not? When not a moment ago you argued that my abandoning them again was too disruptive and wasn't fair, so how is taking them with me worse?"

"Because forcing children to up sticks and move to a strange place simply at the whim of the navy will be even more disruptive and unsettling for the poor dears when they have only just settled here!" That was a travesty that Georgie—and not St. Joan—felt passionate about. "As one who was constantly dragged around at the whim of the army until I was sixteen, I know that whatever barracks you incarcerate them in will not help them thrive." That, she had bitter experience of. "Children are considered a nuisance to the military, Captain Kincaid. They are expected to stay shut indoors and be kept well out of everyone's way." Her schoolmistress's finger wagged wildly now, and because she was incensed and apparently had nothing to lose, she let it do so with impunity.

"They endure unrelenting boredom, make no friends, have no respite from the regimented monotony and it crushes their spirits until there is nothing left of them to crush! Such a life, no matter how short, leaves scars, and those children . . ." The wagging stopped when Joan of Arc's righteous finger suddenly pointed to the ceiling above, where those children were currently sleeping in blissful innocence of the travesty about to be inflicted upon them. "Your nieces and nephew—who adore you for some inexplicable reason—deserve better!"

For a moment, he appeared more amused by her outburst than outraged before he masked that with more matter-of-fact blandness. "Which is precisely why I am taking them *home*, Miss Rowe. My sister's house in Cawsand is seven miles as the crow flies from the Plymouth Dockyard. I shall be staying with them there."

Then, rather than enjoy her shocked expression as much as he seemed to want to, he returned his attention to the papers on his desk. After he frowned some more, he huffed but still did not look up.

"Despite my continued reservations about your somewhat untraditional methods of educating my sister's feral children outside rather than in the classroom where they belong, or your incessantly and unnecessary wagging finger—" He glared at it because it was still poised, forcing her to lower it in contrition. "—the children seem to like you—though heaven only knows why—so I was going to ask you if you would like to come with us?"

There was the faintest glimmer of amusement and mischief in his dark eyes as he stared levelly. "Help mitigate against all that *disruption* that you are so incensed about that prevents the little monsters from *thriving* until my flighty sister returns. But if the thought of upping sticks and being dragged to Devon at the Royal Navy's whim for just a month doesn't appeal, I quite understand. You signed on expecting Mayfair, not the distant hell of Plymouth, and as I am about to breach the terms of our original contract, I shall of course pay you until the end of it if you choose to jump ship early. Kindly let me know your decision in the morning, Miss Rowe, and we shall go from there."

He picked up his quill and offered her a dismissive nod. "I bid you and your finger good night."

## Chapter
# SIXTEEN

❧

*N*orbert can wait the five minutes it will take me to settle your very unsettled sisters in the room. Little Grace is dead on her feet and Marianne cannot help being a bad traveler. She hasn't chosen to feel queasy and you should be more sympathetic." In his peripheral vision, Harry watched Miss Rowe wag a finger at the whining Felix while he sorted out his horse. "And I do not care that you think that being ten gives you the right to do as you please without the need for any adult fussing. You are not wandering off alone in this strange place and that is that."

A whole week on, filled with futile soul-searching, and he still had no earthly idea what had made him invite her along too. Especially when his promotion and imminent departure to Plymouth had been the perfect excuse to get rid of her.

Harry had been determined to do just that the night she came to his study after the unfortunate incident with the frog. Thanks to the mountain he had to climb with the *Boadicea*, and his mounting and terrifying attraction to the siren, he had already decided it made the most sense to banish the distraction of her once and for all. A quick, clean, and ruthless cut that he had known would hurt initially because he had allowed himself to get too attached to her but which, like lancing a boil, would make him feel much better in the long run. Then, with his focus all channeled on just the one troublesome ship rather than being spread too thin here, there, and everywhere, he could exorcise the strange but debilitating dissatisfaction which had gripped him for months, and he could find some joy in his promotion.

He had intended to thank Miss Rowe for her efforts to date, pay her a handsome severance, then never have to see or think or go to war with himself about her ever again.

That had been his plan right up until she had lectured him on responsibilities, and then some masochistic devil inside of him, the part that enjoyed her fiery, rebellious temperament too much, had suddenly invited her along. An invitation he had regretted constantly in the seven days since he had made it—yet despite that, and despite all his lofty promises to himself that he would rescind it well before they hit Plymouth, he hadn't yet found the strength to do it. Instead, he had been such a belligerent and self-centered lion with a thorn in its paw that all the children were now actively avoiding him too.

"But Miss Rowe—Norbert's legs are crossed in desperation, and I've stayed at this inn at least a thousand times!" The very bored and crochety Felix was pouting at his freedoms being curtailed by what he saw as the unreasonable selfishness of his sisters. "And I've walked Norbert in those woods alone at least a hundred! Besides, I shan't be alone, as I shall be with Norbert and Mama always lets me!"

"Do I look like your mother?" The siren circled a finger around her lovely face with a smile that only made it lovelier. "And do I have your mother's express written permission to allow you to go off unchaperoned?" She patted her clothing to hunt for the imaginary missive. "Because you are not leaving my sight without it, young man, so you might as well stop arguing." She ruffled Felix's hair affectionately with another breathtaking smile that only made Harry want her more. "You know that I am a thousand times more stubborn than you are, so you also know arguing with me is pointless once my mind is made up. If Norbert is *that* desperate, he can use that patch of grass over there while you both wait for me."

"But the woods here are a haven for rhinoceros beetles and the rare pearl-bordered fritillary butterfly!"

"Which we shall go hunting for *together* just as soon as I have settled your sisters."

"But Miss Rowe, it will be dark soon!" Felix stamped his foot, and instead of telling him off for his petulance, she cupped his cheek in sympathy.

"In which case, we shall get up as the sun rises and go hunting for them extra early so you shan't miss them. I should imagine those woods will be buzzing with life at dawn and you, me, and Norbert will have it all to ourselves."

Credit where credit was due, the vixen had the patience of a saint with those children and had miraculously managed to conquer them into their somewhat chaotic version of submission all week. Six days of incessant travel and hours and hours cramped in his carriage with the little savages and that bloody enormous dog and she still managed to smile at them each evening when they finally arrived at an inn.

He didn't have a clue where she found the resilience, but he was beyond grateful that at least one of them had it. The closer they got to Plymouth, the harder it became to keep going, and despite the massive promotion awaiting him there, he had a sneaking suspicion that the only reason he followed the damned coach in the first place was because Miss Rowe was in it. Something about her presence gave him the strength to put one foot in front of the other each day—which he was grateful for—but also kept him awake at night in the worst possible way. The very definition of a double-edged sword and one he hoped he wouldn't end up falling on.

"Uncle Harry will grant me permission to walk Norbert alone, won't you, Uncle Harry?" Felix shot him a pleading look. "I won't go far, I promise."

"Don't drag me into this. If Miss Rowe says that you cannot walk Norbert without a chaperone, then you absolutely cannot."

"But it isn't fair!"

"Neither is your incessant whining, nephew, so desist."

There wasn't a hope in hell he was going to undermine the governess. Not when she was doing a much better job of managing the three little Machiavellis than he ever had. Unbelievably, she'd even taught the little scoundrels some lessons on the journey which had, miraculously, gone some way toward keeping them entertained. Harry knew that for a fact because his wayward eyes frequently wandered to her inside that carriage. And, even as he castigated his continued lack of willpower each time he caught himself watching her, just a glance in her direction was enough to lift his bleak mood for a while.

As Felix stamped his foot and pouted some more, Georgie smiled her thanks at Harry for his lackluster intervention and, as it always did when she bestowed a rare smile his way, something peculiar happened in the vicinity of his heart.

Heaven help him.

Harry heaved his saddle from his horse and carried it into the stable himself rather than hand it over to the waiting ostler as an excuse to escape Miss Rowe and her unwelcome allure.

Then, even though he was as dead on his feet himself after nine hours of riding, he decided to brush the horse down himself too, rather than follow her into the inn and pine futilely some more. Yet still, to his chagrin, he pined anyway.

Then there was blasted Plymouth!

They would be there tomorrow, so that level of dread was high. He had barely set a foot there since Elizabeth. Although his loathing of the place had started before she had turned him into a pitiable laughingstock. Before her, he only ever returned if the admiral ordered it or whatever ship he was on sailed there. Since his grandfather and parents had passed, Flora only ever managed to get him to come nowadays after so much incessant nagging that he ran out of excuses. It was so much simpler to allow Flora to believe that his broken heart made it difficult to return when the truth was that Plymouth, and most especially Cawsand, always reminded him too much of all the chaos he had been so relieved to escape for the navy. But those awful memories were still there waiting for him now. Those and the whole heap of fresh, chaotic hell that would come from readying the bloody *Boadicea*.

Lord, how he loathed blasted Plymouth!

"Felix!" Of course only Miss Rowe's voice could snap him out of his self-pitying reverie. "Felix, where *are* you?" She was outside in the stable yard and heading his way. He knew that because his nerves danced at the proximity. "Is Felix in here with you?"

With great reluctance, he paused in his brushing to answer so that he could shutter all the need in his eyes before he looked at her. "No." Braced, he turned and tried to appear like a concerned uncle rather than a drowning man who desperately wanted to cling to something that looked alarmingly like her. "The last I saw of him was in the yard a few minutes ago. Sulking."

She got a pretty wrinkle on her nose whenever she was perturbed that begged to be smoothed with a kiss. "If that boy has disobeyed my express instructions and taken that dog out alone, I shall not be responsible for my actions!"

She disappeared back into the yard again to call for the boy, only to return after a few minutes, looking worried. "I'd go out hunting for him but there are woods in every direction, so I have no clue which way the wretch has gone."

"It's only been a quarter of an hour so he can't have gone far, and he's tired and Norbert is bound to be starving, so I doubt they'll be gone long." As this, however, seemed to be one of those irritating situations that he, as a diligent uncle, could not ignore, even when drowning in a pit of irrational despair, Harry tossed down the brush to follow her back outside. "You go this way and I'll go that." He pointed to the two areas of woodland on either side of the road. "Norbert will need a tree to do his business against, as heaven forbid that useless mutt ever lift his leg without one, and he's been cooped up in a carriage for three hours so he's bound to need the nearest."

They immediately parted ways, which suited Harry just fine. The less time he spent in Miss Rowe's intoxicating presence, the better. He spent twenty minutes searching in his allotted woods, which turned out to be more a small copse than a forest, and then returned to the inn, convinced he would see the contrite scamp already there with Miss Rowe and a flea in his ear. But she wasn't there either.

He checked inside, and when nobody had seen hide nor hair of either of them, nabbed Simpkins to help. As they arrived in the stable yard, a rather panicked Miss Rowe returned.

"Any sign?"

Harry shook his head. "I've searched every inch of that little wood and there is no sign."

"I ventured as far into the other one as I dared." She pointed to it. "I went at least a half a mile in, but it is too vast for one person to search effectively and it's too dense and uneven around the river to maneuver with ease."

"There's a river?" That complicated matters, and not in a good way.

She nodded gravely. "Not a big one, but its lively enough to be of concern."

With his own panic rising now that the sun was setting, Harry tried to think. "If he's got himself lost, we need to find him before it gets dark." Out here, in the middle of nowhere, they both knew it would be like searching for a needle in a haystack. "I dread to think how he'll cope out in the wilderness alone all night."

"I am sure the wretch will cope far better than those who have to hunt for him will." Miss Rowe was justifiably angry. "As he apparently camps out overnight at home all the time with his dog."

"He does?" That was news to Harry.

"He can even light a fire, or so he claims. So as long as he hasn't hurt himself and has the common sense to stay where he is and await rescue, Norbert will look after the rest. That dog would give his life for your troublesome nephew. Felix saved his, after all."

"He did?" There seemed to be huge swaths of his nephew's recent life that Harry had somehow missed because he had been too busy with work to notice, and that added another layer of guilt to the heavy pack on his shoulder. "How?"

"Young Master Felix apparently found that scabrous bag of fleas half-starved and washed up on the beach like a drowned rat a couple of months ago." Even Simpkins, who had no particular fondness for either the children or their dog, seemed to know more about Harry's kith and kin than he now did, and that brought him up short. They might all be as mad as hatters and as irritating as an itchy rash, but his family were everything to him. Or had been before the Admiralty had clearly taken over his life. Suddenly, he simultaneously resented and felt ashamed at that intrusion. It also went straight to the top of his list of problems to fix. "So close to death that he had to find a couple of fishermen to help carry the wretched beast home, where he hand-fed him and nursed him back to health." His trusty right-hand slapped him on the back in manly reassurance. "Georgie is right." Oh, she was Georgie to him, now was she? And how pathetic was Harry for being jealous at that too? "Norbert won't let anything bad happen to Felix. I daresay if something had, he'd have come right back here to fetch us. That dog might well be a crazed menace, but he's got a compass inside his head that would rival any sailor's."

When Georgie and Harry simultaneously turned to him, quizzical, to explain how he knew that bizarre tidbit, he shrugged. "I'll admit I might have tried to lose him in Hyde Park during one particularly trying walk and the bugger still beat me home."

"Well, that's something." Not much, but enough to give Harry hope that all was not lost. "Even if it means we are putting all our trust in blasted Norbert."

Rather than run around like headless chickens after a second search in the larger woods again proved fruitless, Harry organized a proper search party as soon as they regrouped at the inn.

Thankfully, as the London-to-Exeter post had overnighted here too, there were a couple of extra men to add to the motley group who gathered in the stable yard with lanterns. After a short and heated battle, which Harry lost, Miss Rowe refused to wait at the inn and insisted on joining the search. As the only woman, and as he was— ironically—the only man he trusted with her safety, he then had to insist that she stay close to him for the duration.

Split into two groups, and with the reluctant and put-upon inn-keeper and his ostlers in Harry's, they headed toward the river that formed a natural barrier. One he hoped that even the reckless Felix wouldn't have attempted to cross.

But as the minutes stretched to an hour and there was still no sign of Felix, the darkness cloaked them. Then when the heavens decided to open to soak them, making every step more treacherous, it became clear that Harry's sensible and thorough plan was in jeopardy because the stench of mutiny was in the air.

*Chapter*
# SEVENTEEN

❦

*L*et's turn back and search again at dawn when we can actually see something." The innkeeper refused to budge and addressed his staff rather than Captain Kincaid, who had already gone farther ahead after he had tried and failed to reason with the man. "We're on a wild goose chase tonight, lads, as I knew we would be." He glared at Georgie while jerking his thumb at the captain, letting her know in no uncertain terms, yet again, that he thought that this was all their fault. "I told him this would be futile before we set off and you heard him just now—he still refuses to listen."

"That's because he's right!" The captain might have given up all hope of getting the innkeeper to help, but she hadn't, and they had more chance of finding Felix with more eyes looking for him than fewer. "We can't stop now! The poor boy must be terrified, and we've come this far. We have to meet with the other group as planned or they will think that we are lost too—and it would be criminal to do that to them." Especially when she could not disagree that all of this was all her fault. As one rebel understood another, Georgie never should have let Felix out of her sight. Not when he had been so determined to be.

"Not my problem." The innkeeper raised his meaty hand rudely near her face. "And what's criminal, miss, is that nobody would be lost if you and that idiot up ahead had kept a closer eye on your charges!" Again, an undeniable fact she could not disagree with. "Hopefully the boy has more sense than either of you do! If he's got any at all he'll have found some shelter and will stay there till morning, when we actually stand a chance of finding him."

"But—" The meaty palm came up so swift again, it almost hit her nose.

"It's late. It's pitch-black and this is a wild goose chase. So if I say we're done for the night, we're done. You and his nibs over there can battle on if you're daft enough to do things his way and still think that the other group are daft enough to have not turned back already, but he ain't the boss of me and neither are you." He spun around and started walking away. "Come on, boys!"

The two ostlers began to follow. She grabbed the arm of the second and most sympathetic to try and stop him, but the young man shook it off. "I'm afraid he *is* the boss of me, miss, so I've got to listen to him . . . sorry." And off he went too.

"Captain—wait!" Georgie shouted, and when he didn't stop, likely because he was still furious at her for not properly supervising his nephew too, she picked up her sodden, mud-filled skirts to dash after him. "The others have turned back."

He grunted but didn't slow.

"If you are quick, you might be able to reason with them some more. He knows the lay of this land better than we do and we need as much help as we can get if we are going to find Felix."

The captain still did not bother stopping. "You can only reason with a person who wants to be reasoned with, Miss Rowe, and our friendly innkeeper doesn't." Unperturbed at the desertion, he continued onward, then paused to watch the ostlers' lanterns disappear. "But it is late, it is dark, and you are soaked to the skin, so you should return to the inn with them before you catch your death of cold."

"What, and leave you to get lost too?"

She saw his eyes roll in the lamplight before he hoisted it aloft to point at the stars. "I'm a sailor, Miss Rowe, so I read the night sky as well as I read a map. I can assure you that I won't get lost, so go. In fact, I insist. I'll move quicker without you. This is no place for a woman. Especially such a . . ." He flapped his hand in the general vicinity of her body. ". . . compact one."

He couldn't have called her a hindrance more plainly if he had tried, and while he was probably right because his legs were much longer and not weighed down by layers of skirts that caught on everything, his dismissive lack of faith in her abilities incensed St. Joan within.

"You can insist until you are blue in the face. I am not giving up. I shall continue to search for Felix alone, if need be." She pushed past him to continue onward and immediately caught her skirt on a branch.

"Somehow, I knew you would say that." He bent to yank the fabric free.

"If you knew it, you should have saved your breath, Captain." To prove that she wasn't a liability, Georgie sped up and knotted the sides of her skirts as she did so to stop them dragging, cursing herself for not wearing breeches beneath them as her friend Lottie always did. "Being female or compact will not slow me down, I promise."

"Though Miss Rowe may be but little, she is fierce," muttered the captain, misquoting Shakespeare for once rather than another pompous military man.

"She is indeed." He clearly meant it sarcastically, but Georgie knew it was true. She might have lost Felix, but she was going to find him—or die trying. "And just like the woman the Bard described, when I am angry, I am both keen and shrewd—and I *am* angry."

"So am I." He allowed her to have the lead for all of two minutes before he streaked past. "I am going to strangle bloody Felix if we find him alive." She could hear the fear in his tone, the *if* in that sentence shrieking volumes.

"You can choke the last breath from his neck after I've given it a good wringing first—*when* we find him, Captain. It was me he disobeyed, after all, so surely I have earned that pleasure first?"

"How about we toss a coin for the honor if we find the little rascal?"

"*When* we find him, Captain."

He managed a half smile as he nodded. "*When* we find him."

For the next fifteen minutes, neither spoke other than to call Felix's name into the void. Neither did either of them mention what was also becoming obvious—that as the riverbank got steeper, the rushing water in the gully beneath sounded faster and significantly angrier than it had before.

Distracted by intrusive thoughts of doom while castigating herself for not predicting Felix's rebellion, Georgie slipped on a slimy piece of exposed rock beneath her boot. Before she hit the hard, rocky ground and did herself serious mischief, she flung herself into the cradle of a crooked tree trunk, but still managed to wind herself in the process.

Rather than alert the captain that she was down and incur yet another lecture about this being no place for a compact woman, she took a moment to recover while he continued to shout for his nephew ahead.

"FELIX!" The rushing water swallowed much of his effort. "FE-LIX, WHERE ARE YOU!"

In case he turned to see her collapsed in a heap, Georgie joined in, hoping he would assume that she had fallen behind again on purpose. "FELIX!" She cupped her hands around her mouth to amplify her shouts. "NORBERT!"

Something wafted on the midnight breeze. The cry of an owl? A fox?

She strained her ears, doing her best to block out the camouflaging noises from the water and the captain's shouts farther ahead, and heard the noise again.

Could it be a human's cry?

A child's?

She strained some more.

No! It was a howl! It was faint and distant, but unless a pack of wolves had survived their extinction in England and had lived secretly and undisturbed for hundreds of years, then it had to be Norbert.

"Norbert!" She hauled herself out of the tangled arms of the dead tree to scan the area, and when the dog answered with another bloodcurdling howl of distress, she knew she could not possibly be mistaken. "Captain! Come back!"

Captain Kincaid burst out of the shadows ahead, barely illuminated by his lamplight in the dregs of the moonlight, and she beckoned him closer. "Listen!"

Georgie cupped one hand around her ear to show him which direction the faint howling was coming from, and his expression changed when he eventually heard it too.

He ran toward the sound like a man possessed, grabbing her hand as he rushed past, and together they dashed as close to the edge of the slippery, steep riverbank as they dared.

While they both bellowed down it, the light from the lanterns caught two pinpricks of ghostly green which seemed to flicker behind the shadowy leaves of a bush. They danced closer and closer and suddenly the entire bush collapsed beneath the weight of Norbert's huge paws as he galloped toward them, barking.

The dog stopped directly below them, dancing on the spot, barking for all he was worth as his shaggy head stared downriver, as if begging them to clamber down the bank and follow him.

The captain wasted no time complying, but as he skidded downward on the wet rocks, he held up his hand to stop her following. "Wait there!"

"Oh, for goodness—" Then he held up both palms in surrender.

"I am not suggesting that you cannot climb—but this bank is too steep and too wet and if Felix is hurt I am going to need your help to get him back up it!" Then he sped off after the dog until his retreating lantern was sucked into blackness.

In two minds as to whether she should do as instructed or rebel, Georgie began to pace, stopping abruptly when she heard Simpkins's party calling from up ahead.

"OVER HERE!" She waved her arms in the air to attract their attention. "HELP!"

What happened next all seemed to unfurl in a blur.

As the cavalry arrived, so too did the barking Norbert, and within moments the silhouette of the captain reappeared down below. His lantern was gone but as she raised hers to light his way back, there was no mistaking he was carrying a child.

Simpkins and one of the other men scrambled down the bank, and within moments, a pale, shivering, and sobbing Felix was passed from man to man back up the bank and into her waiting arms.

"I slipped," he muttered as he buried his face in her neck and sobbed for all he was worth. "And I've hurt my leg."

"We'll fix it." She cuddled the boy close and rocked him like a baby while it took all the men, including Simpkins, who still loudly proclaimed hatred of the scabrous bag of fleas, to get Norbert back up to the top of the bank. As soon as his paws hit *terra firma*, he flung himself at Felix and licked the distressed boy's face. Then he licked Georgie's, and then, as the captain tried to heave his belly over the edge of the slippery bank, he thoroughly licked his face too.

## Chapter
# EIGHTEEN

༄

"Thank the Lord it's just a sprain. Only Felix could get himself lost and injured chasing a butterfly." The captain returned to his sleeping nephew's bedside after seeing the physician out. He smiled as he whispered, his relief at his nephew's safe return so palpable she could feel it.

That it was just a sprain did little to make her feel better about it and, she reasoned, nor should she. In the last two hours, the what-ifs had consumed her. Georgie knew the blame lay with her. If she hadn't left him sulking in the stable yard, Felix wouldn't have stormed off and wouldn't have gone on to fall down the riverbank where he could have, very easily, been more seriously injured.

"I never ever thought I'd ever hear myself say this in a million years—but thank the Lord for Norbert too." The devoted dog and undisputed hero of the hour had flatly refused to leave his injured master to sleep in the stable—much to the turncoat innkeeper's complete disgust—and was currently stretched out and snoring next to him on the bed. He twitched and gave a little sniffle as Captain Kincaid stroked his ear. "I owe him a year's worth of sausages for saving the day. Flora would have murdered me if her precious son had come to any serious harm while under my care. Of course, she might still murder me for losing him in the first place." He chuckled at that. "Flora is like a lioness when it comes to her cubs."

"She won't. You were the hero of the hour."

He refused to take that compliment and shook his head. "Even in daylight I doubt we'd have spotted him in that deep ravine without Norbert's guidance. If Felix had fallen a couple of inches either way, the river would have taken him. Something, or someone, was certainly looking out for my troublesome nephew tonight. He's a very lucky boy indeed."

A couple inches either way from death! New and sobering information which only made Georgie feel worse.

"It is me that Flora should murder. I'm the one who lost him." The guilt of that was so unbearable Georgie could barely stand to be in the same room as herself. "The innkeeper was right—*I* am the *someone* who should have been looking out for him!"

"This really isn't your fault, no matter what that idiot innkeeper said." He placed a comforting hand on her elbow, which Georgie vehemently shook off. In this precise moment, she deserved neither his misplaced kindness nor his comfort.

"Felix had been delegated to my care and I should have known that he would wander off and I should have insisted he accompany me inside. All the signs were there. Miss Prentice trained me better than that." Every time she looked at the boy's many bruises and grazes, it was all she could do not to burst into wretched tears of recrimination.

She had hovered on the cusp for a good hour now and that showed no signs of abating. In fact, the more time she had to think of all the horrors that could have happened, especially now that she knew poor

Felix had been but a scant couple of inches from certain death, the closer those tears came.

The captain's smile was much too forgiving. "Miss Prentice teaches her protégés how to read minds?" His hand grazed her arm again before he clamped it behind his back. "Had I known you possessed that skill, I'd have paid you treble and worked harder to censor my thoughts."

In case she blubbed in front of him, which was suddenly a very real possibility, she surged to her feet and fled to the door. "I shall go check on the girls and then rest assured, I shan't let Felix out of my sight again till morning."

That was the very least she could do before the captain inevitably dismissed her in the unforgiving cold light of day, as he had every right to. Before he did, she realized that the only decent thing to do was fall on her sword, so she paused at the door without turning around, as she did not trust herself not to disgrace herself while she did it.

"Obviously, as I have let both you and the children down with my lackadaisical neglect, I shall tender my immediate resignation." That broke her heart too as she adored the children and, as much as she had tried to fight against it, she was coming to adore him. After tonight, the captain had risen to at least nine-tenths likable and possibly even nine and a half. He had been relentless in his quest to first find Felix, then to get him home safely, and then to get him the best medical care. He had ridden to fetch the local physician himself and brought him back at record speed, then stood over him while he examined the boy and bandaged his swollen ankle. He had even paid the man a ludicrous amount of money to then tend to Norbert's cuts and grazes too, reminding her of what Lottie had said about how much you could tell about people from the way they treated animals.

"But obviously I will stay as long as it takes you to find a suitable replacement."

Georgie practically ran to the sleeping girls' bedchamber, where she took a few moments to compose herself. Then, only when she was certain she had her emotions completely in check, did she leave to relieve their uncle.

Except the captain wasn't still sitting with Felix as she had expected. He was standing on the narrow landing of the inn and obviously waiting for her with more concern in his eyes than she deserved.

"There is absolutely no way that I am going to accept your resignation when this really isn't your fault, Miss Rowe." As if he knew that she was blaming herself and feeling utterly wretched as a consequence, he smiled. "I cannot imagine why you could possibly think that it is when I heard you give Felix very clear and precise instructions to stay put and not wander off alone. Then I reiterated those instructions, and he still willfully chose to ignore them."

"Because he is the child, Captain Kincaid, and children are unpredictable beings at the best of times. I am being paid handsomely to know that and anticipate it." The dratted tears pressed against her eyes again and she wrestled them back.

His fingers brushed her cheek, and it took all her strength not to lean into his big hand and weep. "You could not have stated plainer that you expected him to stay put unless you had nailed my rebellious nephew's feet to the floor."

She swiped that away. "Stop being kind, Captain. I deserve to feel awful. He was my responsibility but thanks to me, F-Felix could h-have . . ." Before she could stop them, the floodgates opened, and she felt her face scrunch into an ugly mess. Mortified, she covered it with her hands. "H-he c-could h-h-h-have . . . d-d-d-died!"

Through a crack in her fingers, she could see his eyes widened with fear at the prospect of a blubbering woman collapsing in a wailing heap before him, but to his credit, he did not bolt. Nor did he reprimand her for such an unseemly display of unnecessary and self-indulgent emotion as the colonel would have. Instead, he rummaged in his muddy coat for a handkerchief before he held it out to her, and that thoughtful gesture alone only served to make her cry harder.

"There, there." When she failed to take either the handkerchief or his advice, he waved the linen square in front of her face. "Please don't cry. This isn't your fault. Boys will be boys and Felix has always been a naughty one. Might I remind you that if you hadn't heard Norbert down on that riverbank, I'd have marched right past him and Felix would still be all alone and in pain down there. You are more hero of the hour than I."

"I only heard N-Norbert because I fell over while trying to get my *c-compact* legs to keep pace with yours." Which was hardly an act of intrepid heroism. "It was more by luck than j-judgment that I happened to fall where I did."

"So?" He chuckled. "Even in the midst of chaos there is always opportunity."

"Please d-don't quote S-Sun Tzu at me t-tonight, C-Captain, as he really won't make me f-f-feel any bet-ter." Georgie was snorting now too. Like a pig.

A hysterical, short-legged, probably blotchy, orange-haired pig.

"Then I shall simply quote me then—from the heart. Thank you, Miss Rowe. For refusing to stay at the inn while we searched despite all my stupid orders to the contrary. Thank you for refusing to abandon me when everyone else did and thank you for falling over in such a timely manner, as if you hadn't, Felix would still be at the bottom of a gully." He waved the handkerchief again. "Now please stop crying. I beg of you. It's killing me."

When she still failed to grab it, because taking the handkerchief meant removing her hands from her blotchy face and allowing him to see the unattractive snorting and the hiccuping rather than just hear it, he grabbed her by both shoulders instead. Then, to her complete surprise and utter humiliation, instead of shaking her out of her hysteria as she had fully expected and doubtless deserved, he immediately gathered her into his arms, where she collapsed in a wailing heap against his chest.

*Chapter*
# NINETEEN

೧ৡৢৢ৶৴

*T*o say that she was inconsolable was the understatement of the century. He had never witnessed a woman cry so hard and so much in his life—and he had grown up with the overemotional and theatrical Flora, who could cry at the drop of a hat over nothing. "It's all right." Because it was.

And it very definitely wasn't.

As much as his heart bled for her, and as much as he was prepared to do whatever it took to get her to realize that she wasn't to blame, the last thing Harry wanted to be doing at this precise moment was holding the siren in his arms. Yet here he was, holding her tight and trying his hardest not to enjoy the way her petite but curvy body fitted so perfectly against his. "Nobody died. Nobody was seriously hurt and certainly, nobody needs to resign."

As none of his words seemed to be penetrating her guilt, he gave up trying and simply held her for as long as it took for the worst of her tears to subside. It was every bit the hellish torment he had known it would be, but it couldn't be helped. He couldn't leave her like this. It really was breaking his heart.

As the sobs finally turned to sniffles, she stiffened in the cage of his arms and lifted her head, but flatly refused to remove her hands from her face. "I'm sorry for . . . carrying on so. I am not usually one for tears."

Somehow, he knew that was the case. Just as he knew she was now hideously embarrassed to have shed any. "It's quite all right. It has been a particularly trying evening."

"It's all your fault that I cried—you were too kind."

"It's a dreadful flaw of mine." He chuckled at her reprimand, relieved that she was more her tart self again. Yet he was still reluctant to let go of her, even though holding her wasn't the least bit sensible. "You have my solemn pledge that I shall behave like a beast the next time my idiot nephew decides to disobey orders, get himself lost, and make you upset."

"Thank you." He could hear her smile, even if it was still hidden behind her hands. "I've always fared better with shouting and insults and blame." Unaware that in one sentence, she had told him something unsettling about her background which he knew he would not be able to forget, she wiggled the fingers of one hand slightly. "If I could trouble you for that handkerchief now, it would be much appreciated."

Harry released his arm only enough that he could pass it to her, then hugged her close while she blew her nose into the linen and dried her eyes. So proud, and yet still so clearly riddled with guilt, it physically pained him to witness it.

"If anyone needs to do better, going forward, it is me." It wasn't fair of him to allow her to carry the burden of guilt, and it definitely wasn't fair not to acknowledge his own. "I am the one who dragged the children on this trip. And while I did my best to convince myself that I was being an excellent uncle for putting their needs first, I am also aware that I didn't so much delegate the responsibility of looking after them to you on this arduous journey, as abdicate all *my* responsibility to them to you too."

She glanced upward, blinking, and he couldn't even bring himself to spend longer than a moment looking in her red-rimmed, tear-swollen eyes because he had had a big hand in putting those tears there. "I've forced everyone into the carriage at dawn every single day, then pushed through on the road for longer each evening than was either reasonable or necessary, and left you to entertain my charges and suffer the consequences. When I know that Grace gets fractious cooped up inside for more than two hours at a time without a decent opportunity to expel some of her boundless energy. When I know that Marianne gets sick with the constant motion of the carriage, especially after luncheon. Just as I also know that Felix needs to be outside almost as much as he needs air and water. Not only did I purposefully ignore all that, not once in the last six days have I joined you in the carriage to help. I am heartily ashamed of myself."

"But that is silly." He did not dare look at her, so rested his chin on her head instead, trying not to enjoy how well it fit there. "You hired a governess, Captain Kincaid, at great expense I might add, to take care of the children, and despite all your doubtless justifiable reservations about me, you still gave me the choice to accompany them. Please do not feel guilty for expecting me to do my job."

"Now you are being too kind, Miss Rowe, but I will not let you." If an apology was due, he might as well do it properly. That meant some honesty was required, although not complete honesty for obvious reasons, and some humbleness would not go amiss either. "When we both know that I haven't merely left you to do your job, I haven't done more than say good night to my nieces and nephews since I left them with you to go to Portsmouth, and for all their many faults and foibles, you are right, they adore me, so they do not deserve that. I am their uncle. Their only uncle, and I used to be a really good one. I still am because I adore them too and should have tried harder. Especially in Flora's absence. Yet I have gone out of my way to give three innocent children—my own flesh and blood—the cold shoulder for weeks now, and all to indulge my own pathetic and selfish desire to wallow in my own deep well of irrational, miserable self-pity."

She deserved that much honesty. "I was wallowing in it up to my neck when Felix wandered off, when I could and should, as an officer or a gentleman or an uncle or, most especially, a decent human being, have taken him to walk his dog while you dealt with his clearly distressed sisters. And for all of that, I am truly sorry." From this day forth, he was going to do better. Much better. His solemn pledge to her. To the children. To himself.

Miss Rowe had gone still in his arms, and as the silence stretched, both things gave him no choice but to look down at her to see what she thought about his confession. But where he expected irritation or judgment or, miraculously perhaps, even some forgiveness, all he saw were two furrowed ginger eyebrows, a much-too-pretty tearstained face, and the wrinkled, perturbed nose that never failed to charm him.

"Why on earth are you wallowing up to your neck in a well of self-pity, Captain Kincaid?"

"Well, I . . ." Her green eyes were stormy, concerned, and so compelling, he answered before he had the wherewithal to censor himself. "I know that I should be ecstatic about this promotion but . . . I am not and I do not know why." Any more than he knew why he couldn't seem to let go of her.

Apparently, content to remain in his arms, she gave his response some thought and then searched his eyes again as if they held the answers he could not find. "Could it be because you prefer the work you do at the Admiralty over sailing the seven seas in search of trouble?"

He shrugged, then reluctantly let his arms fall to put a sensible foot of distance between them. "My dissatisfaction began *at* the Admiralty, and I've always loved the sea but . . ." Harry threw up his hands. How to explain something he didn't understand himself? "I feel ambivalent about going back there."

"An ambivalent man doesn't look as miserable as you have this past week. You've resembled one headed toward his own execution rather than one looking forward to his next great adventure."

A perceptive comment that was likely closer to the truth than he was comfortable admitting, even to himself. "Perhaps I looked miserable because I loathe Plymouth and all its environs with every fiber of my being?" He tried to smile but couldn't when he knew Plymouth was just one of the symptoms of his current malaise and not the root cause.

"What's wrong with Plymouth and all its environs?"

"I grew up there." As much as he seemed incapable of not revealing his ludicrous and self-indulgent disquiet to the vixen this evening, he had no intentions of telling her everything. Certain uniquely Plymouth-based things, like all the bailiffs and Elizabeth and the rescinding of his first captaincy, were too private and painful and humiliating to admit aloud. "And found it . . . suffocating."

"Ah," she said as if she understood that cryptic answer entirely. "I only have to hear the dreaded words *Ipswich* or *Preston* or, heaven forbid, *Newcastle*, and a part of me dies."

"Army postings?"

She nodded. "A barracks is, in my humble opinion, the most depressing place to live if you are not a soldier. There is nothing to do but read and the reading available is deathly dull. There is only so much military strategy a compact girl can read about before she wants to burn it all."

Harry wanted to step forward and trace her ironic smile with his fingertip. Instead, he folded his arms in case he gave in to the urge. "I did wonder how you were so well informed about Sun Tzu." Just as he now wondered how much shouting and insults she had endured in those barracks—and by who.

"But, spared the dratted prison of the barracks, I am sure none of those places are truly as bad as I remember them." As if she sensed he was about to ask that deeply personal question, she pivoted the conversation back to him. "And perhaps Plymouth won't be as awful as you remember it once you see it again from an adult's perspective. Then maybe you will also find your smile again."

"And if I don't?" Because that was what was at the crux of it all.

"Then I suppose you will need to do some serious thinking, Captain, to work out exactly what it is you want before the navy sends you somewhere else that you do not want to go." There was no arguing with that simple but concise logic. "What do you think you want?" She folded her arms, too, and leaned against the wall of the dim, narrow landing, awaiting his reply.

He shrugged again as if he had no clue, which was only partially true because there was one thing he knew he wanted—even if it was the one thing he shouldn't. "I know what I am supposed to want—this promotion. More promotions." He spread his arms. "All the promotions it takes until I reach the top of the mast. That is what I was trained for."

"And what do you find yourself wanting instead?"

He wasn't sure if it was the question, or their location, or the fact that they were all alone.

If it was tiredness or despair or the constant yearning which he couldn't conquer.

He wasn't sure if it was the honesty, or her concern, or her smile, or the fact that she had only just left his arms and they missed her. Or the way the lamplight set fire to the copper in her hair, or the way her smile was like a balm to his soul.

He knew without a doubt that it was madness.

The most assured path to his own self-destruction. That he should say good night and put as much distance between them as was possible for the short time she would be in Plymouth with him. However, the masochistic devil inside of him had apparently taken control of his mouth, so he answered her question in the only way he could in this intimate and charged moment.

With the truth.

"You."

---

*G*eorgie knew that the captain was going to kiss her well before he did, because he didn't pounce or grab or even gather her close first. Instead, he slowly dipped his head, then paused scant inches from her face to give her ample opportunity to say no.

In truth, and she did not know why she knew it, his eyes were begging her to do so as he hesitated. Then hesitated some more. Their faces so close that she knew he was holding his breath just as she was holding hers.

She also knew that he would respect that no if she found the strength to utter it. Would immediately step back and apologize and then would probably never ever try to kiss her again. Which, in that precise moment, felt like a tragedy. Especially when the air crackled around them and being kissed by him, right this second, seemed like the only thing she wanted to do.

So instead of shaking her head, she tilted it upward. Instead of running away and then locking her bedchamber door, as any sensible governess would do when their employer wanted more from her than the job she was paid to do, Georgie stood on tiptoes to close the distance. Then, so eager to experience her first kiss with a man she was beyond eager to be kissing, sighed when she pressed her mouth to his.

What followed was a revelation. One that absolutely made all of Lottie's claims about the right sort of kiss correct.

Captain Kincaid's started gentle, but she still felt it everywhere. His lips whispered over hers as if she were something decadent and luxurious he was in no hurry to rush. When he finally touched her, that was reverently too. He used the tips of his fingers to trace her cheek, which awakened all her senses and every single nerve ending.

He smelled like the fresh, crisp, earthy night air of the woods.

Tasted like home.

Like fate.

Like sin.

Perfection.

Ready for more, Georgie stepped closer, tugging him by the lapels in an invitation to continue, but for a moment, he hesitated again. Then, on a surrendering sigh, snaked his arms around her waist as he deepened the kiss while she welcomed every new sensation. Her entire body simultaneously floating and so ripe with wanting that it felt like the most natural thing in the world to let it.

When her hands begged to go exploring, she took them on a bold journey beneath his coat. Over his chest. His shoulders. Down the wide and solid plain of his back. When his went exploring in return, she heard her own moans of appreciation, barely recognizing herself as she welcomed his caresses.

Because she had never been like this.

Never imagined she could be. Not when Miss Georgina Rowe

was the sensible but uninspiring sort. The unsentimental, unromantic, not-easily-impressed sort. The sort who had long resigned herself to the life of passionless servitude and spinsterhood she had been trained for and wanted to be grateful for. Yet here she was, transformed into a passionate woman who craved seduction.

Thanks to his talented mouth, her level head no longer ruled supreme. Instead, it was her body that controlled every inch. Nothing existed beyond her new needs and this potent kiss she wanted to last forever.

Except it didn't, because he suddenly wrenched his mouth away.

Stared at her wide-eyed. Panicked and uncertain as though he wanted to run far away—yet he seemed incapable of letting her go.

His breath sawed in and out. His heart raced beneath her fingertips. And his eyes—his mesmerizing dark-brown eyes—were heated with desire. "This is madness."

Georgie nodded as she held on tight—because it was. Glorious, unfettered, and addictive madness that she didn't want to stop.

His arms loosened. Unlocked themselves from behind her back. Found their way to her hips instead while he tried to calm his breathing. She was sure he was going to step well away until his gaze dropped to her lips and he scrunched his eyes closed, but before they did, she saw the war in them. All the desire.

All the need.

All for her.

*Her!*

That really was the maddest thing of all. That this intoxicating man, who could have his pick of women, currently wanted her.

He swallowed. Hard. And when his eyes opened, his heated gaze latched immediately onto her mouth and he growled in frustration as he tugged her hips back to his. So close that she was left in no doubt of his desire for her as it throbbed hot and hard against her belly through all the layers of their clothes. His mouth found hers again, then feasted. As if he wanted to gorge on her now rather than take his time. Every hot, fevered, and gloriously intimate kiss sent all those fizzing champagne bubbles within her tummy ricocheting everywhere until she was drunk on him.

At some point, her back found the wall and her leg wrapped itself around his hips to anchor him. By then, she was witless and practically boneless and so desperate to have him inside her that all propriety had flown out of the window. Shamelessly in pursuit of her own pleasure and so caught up in the kiss that nothing else mattered. As he began to hike up her skirts, she wrestled with the falls of his breeches. Both in such a hurry to finish what they had started that Grace's cry brought them both up short.

Still panting with unslaked lust, they were both barely decent when the little girl emerged from her bedchamber rubbing her eyes, oblivious of the passionate, carnal insanity she had just interrupted.

"I had another nightmare, Miss Rowe." Then she held out her little hand. "Will you sleep with me in my bed again tonight?"

*Chapter*
# TWENTY

Harry had thought that the pit of despair he had been wallowing in could not possibly get any deeper, but he was wrong. Not only had he crossed the respectable line between employer and employee, he'd exacerbated his ill-timed and unwelcome yearning for the siren.

Who knew that a simple kiss could enthrall him so? Ruin him so spectacularly that he knew no other would ever match it?

The darndest thing was that Miss Rowe's initial kiss had been so clumsy, it shouldn't have affected him so spectacularly. But that had been the start of his undoing. Then the clever minx had learned so fast she had made him unfurl like a sail.

She was such a passionate little thing. There had been nothing coy about her when she was aroused, and he had been left in no doubt that she had been last night. The soft, encouraging moans and greedy sighs as she sought her own pleasure had stoked the flames of his desire until they had positively burned. He'd lifted her hips to his and pressed his hard cock against her, for pity's sake, and instead of being scandalized by that outrageous liberty, she had wound her shapely leg around his waist and ground her womanly hips against it.

Her nipples had been so puckered with need he had felt them all the way through his clothes, tempting him. When he had given in to that temptation and had filled his hands with her pert, perfect breasts, she had moaned and writhed and bucked her hips some more and, heaven help him, he had been seconds from having her. Worse, he could not shake the seductive knowledge that she would have let him.

How, exactly, was he supposed to cope with all that new and torturous knowledge today? Tomorrow? Next week?

Until blasted Flora decided to come home to save him from himself and the dangerous siren who consumed him?

His intense physical attraction to her aside, there was no denying now that something about her called to his heart as well as his body. The clues had been there before last night. In truth, they had been there from their very first meeting, when he hadn't been able to take his eyes off her. Amongst all that spontaneous attraction had been something less definable beyond a sense of serendipity. He'd felt it like a jolt the second her lips touched his. That sense of rightness, like a bolt sliding into place, which he was pretty certain he had never experienced before—which was worrying.

Now he was left not only wanting to know what it would be like to possess all of her in the carnal sense—but to know all of her too. What she thought. Her hopes and dreams and . . . essence, he supposed. He also had the overwhelming urge to woo her. To charm her and court her. To make her his in every possible way, and that was . . . terrifying. Not only because this was the absolute wrong time to enter into such madness, but because he knew in his heart that if he ventured down that treacherous path again, that there would be no coming back. The previous siren in his life had not been in this flame-haired vixen's league. Miss Rowe was Salome and Delilah and Helen of Troy all rolled into that compact, passionate, and indomitable womanly package. An intoxicating and addictive enchantress. One oozing spirit, determination, and uniqueness. She was very definitely the sort of woman a man couldn't sail away from—when he very much had to. The sort he would foolishly sacrifice a career for.

All control for.

Himself for.

The exact sort, if he was stupid enough, that he would allow history to repeat itself for, so he had no choice but to end things between them before it was too late, and certainly before they arrived in blasted Plymouth.

He could hardly dismiss her. In her own irrepressible way, she had done everything so right, the children not only loved her—they behaved! However, there was no denying his life in Plymouth would certainly be less painful if she was safely two hundred and fifty miles away from him. And as tempting as it was to say to hell with it all and just have her the once and be done with it—as men had been prone to do for time immemorial when they had an itch to scratch—Harry already knew once with her wouldn't be enough. She was the sort who lured a man willingly onto the treacherous rocks of forever.

"Good morning, all." Harry took a deep breath and strode into the stable yard. He hoped his façade of breezy calm was more convincing than it felt because his besotted heart thudded at the sight of her in the same plain gray traveling dress he had thoroughly ravished her in last night, giving his still-rampant body ideas.

She stiffened at his voice and was blushing profusely by the time she turned around. Although to her credit, even though you could probably fry an egg on one of her overheated cheeks, she was also doing her very best to appear unbothered by the inescapable and inexcusable fact that only a few hours ago, her oh-so-sensitive breasts had been filling his greedy palms. While his insistent erection had been twitching against her tummy.

"Is everyone well after all the . . . um . . . unnecessariness of last night?" It was probably best to lay his cards on the table straightaway, even if he was looking directly at the subdued Felix as he said it.

"I'm sorry, Uncle Harry." His nephew stared at his feet. "I'm sorry for wandering off and I'm sorry for not listening. But most of all I am sorry for all the trouble I caused."

"Miss Rowe has already issued her punishment for Felix's disobedience," said a gleeful Marianne as she pirouetted toward him. "He has to go to bed straight after supper every night for a week and is not allowed to step a foot outside without an adult for a month. Simpkins says that if Felix had been in the navy, he'd have been given at least twelve strokes of the cane while bent over a cannon. But as he hasn't got either a cannon or a cane handy, he is going to make him polish everyone's boots for a week instead."

His eldest niece caught his hand and stared up at him, expectant. "We are all curious what your punishment will be? Grace and I think that you should burn his cricket bat as he wasn't a particularly good brother last night when we were both under the weather. Instead, he put his needs first and that's unbelievably selfish." Out of the mouths of babes! As Harry had also put his needs first last night.

"Well . . . um . . ." How the blazes was he supposed to think of a fitting punishment for his nephew when he still had no earthly clue how to tell Miss Rowe that last night had been a huge mistake? Probably the greatest of his life, and after the epic one called Elizabeth, that was saying something. "I . . . um . . . haven't decided yet. I should . . . um . . . probably consult with your governess first to see what she thinks is appropriate." He looked to her properly for the first time and felt his own earlobes fill with blood, although thanks to the inordinate amount of the stuff still flooding his groin, he hoped they weren't red enough to notice. "Shall we . . . um . . . discuss last night now?" He gestured to the other side of the stable yard where they would have some privacy. "Simpkins can load the children and Norbert into the coach, can't you Simpkins?"

From his comfortable seat next to the driver, Simpkins scowled. "If I must."

"You must." He offered her an approximation of a smile which felt more like a grimace. "Shall we?"

"If I must." She grimaced back, cringing with mortification, but she followed him across the yard, dragging her feet and making him hope that she had had as many reservations about their incendiary kiss as he had. In unspoken and tacit agreement, they walked beyond the stable yard until they were completely out of sight or earshot of anyone, her looking at her hands as if her life depended upon it and him looking every which way but at her.

"Well, this is awkward." It was a feeble way to break the ice, but someone had to. "But . . . um . . . I suppose I should apologize for . . . um . . ." How many *ums* could one grown man manage in a minute? "Well . . . um . . ." Harry was dying. Dying on his feet with his stupid ears burning and couldn't seem to string a sentence together.

"What I mean is . . . um . . ." He knew that he was wincing. There was a pain between his eyebrows because the furrow there was so deep. "I think we can both agree that last night was a dreadful mistake."

Finally, her eyes snapped to his. They looked incensed and . . . yet still hurt. "A *dreadful* mistake, to be sure."

Was that vehemence or sarcasm? If it was the former and she

bitterly regretted last night, then that swift denial hurt him, although he was in no position to be wounded by her echoing his lie. If it was sarcasm and he had hurt her, maybe that suggested that she hadn't thought it was a mistake at all until he opened his mouth and put his big, booted foot in it. In which case, maybe . . . "Well . . . um . . . perhaps that is too harsh a . . . um . . . maybe it wasn't so much a mistake as . . . um . . ."

So much for his iron reserve to resist the allure of her if he was already wavering at the first hurdle and the masochistic devil inside him was angling for a compromise! When any compromise beyond complete resistance would likely ruin his life! "By *dreadful mistake* I mean that it shouldn't have happened and, in all likelihood would never have happened in a million years if . . . um . . . circumstances hadn't been so fraught, and you and I hadn't been . . . um . . . thrust together all alone in the thick of it."

She looked down at her hands again, nodding. "Of course, it wouldn't."

As he sensed only partial agreement in that proud affirmation, and as he could hardly admit to her that his poor heart had already been broken once and he feared that he would never recover if he gave it to her, he clung to that handy excuse with his fingernails, embellishing it for all he was worth.

"Let's face it, we were both tired—exhausted, in fact—had spent most of the night worried sick and expecting the worst. Both of us were riddled with misplaced guilt too and clearly shaken by the ordeal. Inconsolable in places . . . and in dire need of some . . . comfort." He flapped his hand at her, like the worst sort of coward passing over all blame, as if it had been entirely her fault that he had enjoyed the feel of her in his arms so much, or that his willpower had evaporated along with his wits.

"Was it any wonder emotions were running high, and we mistook our understandable mutual relief at Felix's safe return for . . . um . . . m-more?" Marvelous. Now he was stuttering too. "And that . . . um . . . the . . . um . . . comfort we offered to one another got . . . um . . . out of hand."

"All the stress affected our heads." She was nodding like a woodpecker, fixated on the strings of her reticule she was twisting in her busy fingers, rather than allow him to see if the message in her eyes matched her words. Which was probably just as well, as, for all his assertions otherwise, only a blindfold would disguise all the yearning in his. If hers yearned too, then he just did not possess the strength now to resist the pull of her. "And we lost them."

"It meant nothing." He forced a smile past that lie to choke out another. "Nothing beyond two overemotional people letting off some steam in the heat of a *very* trying moment."

"Of course it meant nothing!" She was smiling, too, as she finally lifted her head. It was every bit as brittle and unconvincing as his own and so, of course, made his stupid heart soar because it gave him hope. "I am *so* relieved that you said that." She blew out a breath as if she were. "Otherwise, things between us going forward would have been very awkward indeed."

Something told him that she was lying through her teeth, too, but he did not have the strength to call her on it because he absolutely did not have the strength to even begin to consider how he would cope if he indulged his heart's burning desire. "Which is exactly why I wanted us to clear the air this morning. Put all that . . . um . . . silliness . . ." He flapped his stupid hand again, hating himself as well as that errant appendage. "Behind us."

Hers began to flap in unison. "Forget it ever happened."

"Exactly." As he wanted to fiddle nervously with one of his watch chains, he clamped his hands behind his back and rocked on his heels like his curmudgeonly grandfather used to whenever something displeased him.

"That is much appreciated, Captain Kincaid."

He waved that away while the masochistic devil inside him screamed that a woman who had ground her hips against his cock while she had moaned into his mouth had surely earned the right to call him Harry? That she should simply be Georgie too because he now knew the exact shape and weight of each of her breasts!

"Let us never speak of it again, Captain."

"Speak of what, Miss Rowe?" He tried his best to look like a man whose memory had been erased entirely and not one who still remembered how she had melted as his thumbs had teased her nipples. Nipples he had pondered long and uncomfortably hard all night as he had wondered if they would be as pale as her skin or as pink as her lips. How they would feel in his mouth as his tongue tasted them and she moaned his Christian name over and over again until . . .

*Bloody hell, Plymouth was now doomed to be the most horrendous punishment he had ever suffered!*

# TWENTY-ONE

❧

*N*ot just a mistake, but a *dreadful* mistake!

Georgie had never witnessed a face filled with more horror and remorse than the captain's had this morning, and the sting of those damning words still hurt. Probably because, as her wanton body had continued to want his, she had spent most of the night weaving ludicrous romantic fantasies about what would happen next.

Whimsical, improbable nonsense that ultimately involved them skipping off hand in hand toward the horizon rather than him sailing away toward one, gleefully alone. No doubt wearing his commodore's uniform better than any man had a right to, his course set upward to bigger, greater things.

She did not know what galled more—that he had made her feel so pathetic and worthless, or that she had not only allowed it, she had welcomed it! Stupid, gullible, and needy idiot that she was! Her bruised heart ached so much she kept catching herself rubbing it.

"We're almost home!" Squeezed beside her in the cramped carriage, Marianne still managed to find the space to bounce in her seat as she pointed out of the window. "That is Kingsand and Cawsand is just behind it!"

They had been following a picturesque coastal road for the last hour. The beauty of the scenery and ocean was completely lost on Georgie thanks to the captain's blithe callousness. But even in her subdued and humiliated state, the vision of twin villages nestled amongst the steep, rocky hills that framed the wide blue bay was breathtaking. So pretty that, like her charges, she, too, pressed her nose against the window as the carriage jerked upward and into cottage-flanked lanes so narrow, there was barely room for the carriage at all.

Halfway up the hill, it veered from the main road to take a rutted mud lane through a field. There was a single house at the end of it, and by the way the children were grinning, the quaint, quirky, asymmetrical building surrounded by a wild-looking cottage garden was clearly home. It was a pretty vista, which was swiftly spoiled by the sight of Captain Kincaid galloping on ahead, and while principle and pride dictated that she should immediately turn away, her wounded gaze followed him all the way to the house.

The same gray-haired man who had relieved him of his horse after he had hauled the captain in for a manly embrace opened the carriage door as it came to a stop on the gravel driveaway.

"Well, if it isn't my three favorite heathens!" He grinned at the children as he lifted each out while Norbert danced circles around his legs. "And you must be their new governess." Kind eyes twinkled in a weathered face. She estimated him to be at least seventy but no less robust for it as he seemed as sprightly as he did friendly. "I cannot tell you how much I pity you for that dubious honor, Miss Rowe." He held out a large, work-roughened hand to help her down, and it was filled with strength. "I'm Tom." His broad West Country accent had a musical lilt that matched his cheery character. "For my sins, I am

Flora's jack-of-all-trades here at Guillemot House. I do everything from tending the garden to mending the constantly leaking roof to pretending to be the butler if they are having company that expects to be impressed."

He swept an arm toward the front door to usher her inside. "Welcome, miss. I'll apologize for my wife in advance, as she has no boundaries."

As if that was her cue, an older woman appeared on the rose-covered porch and within seconds, her apron was immediately dripping with effusive children. She hugged all three, loudly proclaiming how much she had missed them in an accent that matched her husband's exactly, then used the long wooden spoon in her hand to direct them all to the kitchen. "Don't think I haven't counted every bun and every biscuit, you gannets! You'll eat the savory first or I'll toss all those cakes on the fire!"

As the thunder of smaller feet fled toward the food, her laughing eyes gave Georgie an unapologetic and thorough appraisal. "I'll confess when I heard Harry was bringing along a governess, I pictured a pinched and sour-faced old hag and not such a young and pretty thing as you." To Georgie's complete surprise, she was then enveloped in a hug. "I'm Ada. Head cook and bottle washer. Font of all local knowledge because I'm an outrageous gossip which I'll make no apology for." Straightaway, Georgie decided she liked Lady Pendleton's servants very much. "But where are my manners! You'll be wanting some tea and some sustenance after such a long journey!"

The captain was nowhere to be seen, but the children were already seated at the long kitchen table when Georgie was pushed into the chair beside Marianne. Felix had his mouth stuffed full despite his clean, empty plate. As he reached for another icing-smeared bun, Ada's spoon swooped down in warning.

"It's always bread before buns in this house, them's the rules, no matter how differently they do things in London." Then, without skipping a beat, the force of nature that was the head cook and bottle washer slammed her trusty spoon down, grabbed a knife, and began to carve thick slices of ham. She piled it on everyone's plate while Tom hacked the enormous loaf of bread into pieces with the same finesse as one would chop a log for the fire. As he thrust them around, he practically threw one at Georgie as he sat opposite.

"There you go, Miss Rowe."

"Miss Rowe?" Ada seemed appalled by that formality, especially as she had taken a seat at the table. "We don't do airs and graces here in Devon. What's your given name, child?"

"It's Georgie," said Georgie, finding this convivial and communal approach to eating rather charming. She had never seen a table where the servants mixed with those they served before now, and while she had heard that occasionally governesses were invited to eat with the family, she had never been invited to break bread with the captain. Not even on the long journey here. "And I'm not really one for airs and graces either."

"Can we call you Georgie too?" Marianne openly fed the begging Norbert a slice of her ham beneath the table.

"Absolutely not!" Ada answered for her, wielding her spoon across the tabletop again, clearly more annoyed at the question than the dog being fed from the girl's plate. "You rascals need to learn your place and you don't get to call anyone other than family by their given names till you're old enough to get married. Them's the rules." The spoon suddenly went limp as she grinned at a new arrival. "Well, don't you look well, Simpkins! I'm glad to see that fancy London housekeeper is keeping you well fed."

"But her food is not as good as yours, Ada. Nobody's is." A rare compliment from Simpkins, which made the older woman preen. Georgie slathered some butter on her bread and almost sighed aloud as she took a bite, but her pleasure was interrupted.

"Do you have family, Georgie?" Ada smiled, unaware she had just hit a raw nerve.

"Not anymore. My mother passed when I was ten." Georgie flatly refused to include the colonel in that as he had never been like family. For all she knew, he could be dead and buried and, frankly, good riddance.

"Oh, you poor dear." Ada reached across the table to squeeze her hand. "It must have been hard to be orphaned so young." It had, but it was not something she was prepared to talk about at this table. "How on earth do you cope with being all alone in the world?"

"My three best friends are as good as sisters and I have Miss Prentice, of course, who took me into her school, gave me a home, and mentored me to be a governess. That is a family of sorts." She took another bite, hoping the topic would be dropped, then almost spat it out when the nosy Ada pried deeper. "What took your mother?"

"Smallpox." After it had spread around the barracks like wildfire.

"And your father?" Good heavens, but Ada was relentless.

"A carriage accident, I believe, although it happened while I was still a baby, so I have no memory of it and Mama did not like to speak of it." As this was all getting more personal than she was comfortable with after such a short acquaintance, Georgie deflected. "How long have you and Tom been here at Guillemot House?"

Ada had no problem talking of her past. "I started as a maid of all work for Flora's parents at fourteen and Tom came a year or so later to work in the garden."

"You met here?"

The housekeeper smiled with affection at her husband. "We met here, fell in love here, got shackled here, and raised our five children here."

"Which certainly feels like forever," said Tom with a roll of his eyes, which earned him a thwap of admonishment from the wooden spoon. It did nothing to stop him. "Forty-five years is a terrible sentence when there is no hope of a pardon."

"How romantic." Even after all these years, it was plain the couple were still in love.

"Indeed it is, as I daresay not many find their soulmate at fifteen." Ada began to slather a slice of bread with butter with a wistful smile. "But because we started young—"

"Too bloody young!" interrupted Tom, purely to make everyone laugh. "She took advantage of my lack of sense and then she took advantage of me!"

His wife carried on as if he wasn't winking inappropriately at Simpkins. "—we're already up to eleven grandchildren with another expected any day."

Georgie had just popped a third, much bigger, chunk in her mouth to chew when Ada surged to her feet, her spoon once again raised at the ready as she bellowed toward the hallway. "Where do you think you are going when luncheon is on the table?"

It was Captain Kincaid who answered. "I'm sorry, but I have to report to my ship straightaway, Ada."

"Not until tomorrow, you don't, so sit your backside down at this table, young man, and eat first." Ada's eyes had narrowed as she sighted him down her spoon. "Don't make me come fetch you." The spoon turned slowly to point to the chair next to Georgie's—which was, horrifically, the only empty seat left. "I've not seen hide nor hair of you for a year, so you'll spare me a few minutes before you hurry to escape us again!"

Marianne nudged Georgie, then whispered, "This house makes Uncle Harry twitchier than we do." Another new piece of information she wished she did not find intriguing.

"But Ada—"

"Don't *but Ada* me, you scallywag!" She shook the spoon rather than her head. "Sit, Harry, or I'll be forced to drag you by the ear like I used to!" She rolled her eyes at Georgie's mortified expression, assuming that she had paused with a mouth full of bread because she was shocked to hear anyone speak to the master with such disrespect. "I changed his stinky bottom as a baby and he's felt the sting of this spoon more times than anyone else in this house ever has, and all of them well deserved, so he knows better than to disobey me."

Those smiling eyes flicked back to the captain and they brooked no argument. "Sit! Tell me all you've been up to. And don't think you can skip over any detail you included in one of your monthly letters, young man." He wrote a servant letters every month? Now that was another intriguing detail about the wretch that Georgie wished didn't charm her. "As I'll be wanting to hear all from your mouth just as I always do because I've got a million questions."

"Just as she always does," added Tom with an unsubtle wink to everyone while Georgie sensed the captain approaching the table. Then willed the floor to swallow her up before she was forced to sit next to the wretch.

"Five minutes," he said while scraping the chair out with the same thwarted belligerence of Felix after he'd been refused permission to walk his dog at the inn. "Then I really do have to go."

Satisfied, Ada sat and served him a giant wedge of a meat pie, the enticing aromas of rich, softly stewed beef and gravy filling the kitchen. But not quite filling it enough that Georgie's stupid, wayward nostrils didn't inhale the spicy essence of the captain's cologne as he reluctantly slid into the chair next to hers.

It made no difference that he had ensured that there was a respectable gap of several inches between them. Her pathetically needy body blossomed with awareness regardless.

*Chapter*
# TWENTY-TWO

❦

Harry had sat beside Miss Rowe during luncheon for twenty interminable minutes and she hadn't so much as glanced his way for one second of them. Instead, she'd behaved as if he didn't exist at all. While he undoubtedly deserved her frostiness and definitely needed her indifference if he was going to resist his inconvenient yearning for her, he could not bear the thought he had hurt her feelings. He had been so absorbed with guilt, he hadn't given the bloody *Boadicea* a single thought during the short forty-minute sail from Cawsand to Plymouth.

But with the entrance to the Royal Navy Dockyard looming, he needed to push all his regrets to one side. Easier said than done after he had overheard her telling Ada some of her troubled family history before he had tried to sneak out. Now he hadn't just been a cad to an innocent governess in his employ—which was unconscionable enough—but he now knew that the strong-willed and seemingly indomitable itch he couldn't scratch was all alone in the world, bar the few friends she had made at Miss Prentice's School for Young Ladies.

That she had been rendered fatherless while still in the crib and motherless under such dreadful circumstances while about the same age as Marianne. His family had always driven him to distraction, but he could not imagine how lonely his life would be without them. Blasted Flora might well be the bane of his life, but she had always been a shoulder to cry on when fate had been cruel and vice versa. Through the best of times and the worst of times, they had always had each other.

To have no one must be horrendous. Isolating and frightening. It certainly explained why Miss Rowe was such a feisty character. She had had to face everything life threw at her alone, and that took grit.

Still, it must have been terrifying for a little girl to witness her mother deteriorate with illness. Smallpox was such a dreadful way to go. He'd borne witness to an outbreak here in Plymouth, years ago, that swept the dockyard and had killed so many so indiscriminately and so quickly it beggared belief. It had been horrendous to watch as a powerless adult from the periphery, so he shuddered to think what it must have been like for a child in the thick of it. Especially a child imprisoned in the depressing family quarters in a barracks where stiff upper lips were expected and everyone would have been too busy soldiering to help her get through that traumatic ordeal. With her father already long gone . . .

In which case, why had she been dragged from barracks to barracks until the age of sixteen?

There was another story there and one, no doubt, judging from her speed at changing the subject at luncheon, that wasn't a nice one either. She had hinted as much last night before he had hauled her into his arms and kissed her.

*I only have to hear the dreaded words* Ipswich *or* Preston *or, heaven forbid,* Newcastle, *and a part of me dies.*

Why the blazes had an orphan traveled from barracks to barracks until she turned sixteen? And more importantly, what had happened to her there to give her such bad memories? He hated the thought of someone else upsetting her almost as much as he hated himself for it. He needed to apologize. Set the record straight. Try to find a way to tell her that it wasn't her fault he could not presently indulge his heart when . . .

"It's good to be back on the water." Simpkins encroached on his reverie. He waved at the heavily armed guards on the harbor wall and then pointed to Harry's uniform, which was all they needed to see to allow them to sail straight past.

Harry had decided to don the full pomp and ceremony of his dress uniform, complete with the blessedly roomier and freshly cleaned newer breeches, to intimidate the lazy layabouts on the bloody *Boadicea*. He had also put it on to remind himself of who he was and to refocus his mind on what he had been sent here to do. Except he was still unable to focus on anything, currently, but her.

"I'll bet you're excited to see your ship and to get her shipshape, Captain?"

"Very." A complete lie. Dread now joined all the guilt and confusion he was feeling. It settled like lead in his stomach. "I fear there will be a lot to do but, as one of the greats said, Alexander, I think, there is nothing impossible to him who is prepared to try."

Harry sincerely hoped that was the case, at least where the *Boadicea* was concerned. Just as he had everything crossed that this unwelcome, and suddenly torturous, stint in Plymouth would reinvigorate his enthusiasm for his naval career. He was being given a brand-spanking-new flagship, after all, and that was a momentous honor. One few of his contemporaries would ever experience. He should be happy about it.

Surely?

"That's the spirit, Captain!" Simpkins quickly gathered the small sail on the creaky boat the Kincaid family had used to cross the Sound for at least forty years. For reasons best known to herself, blasted Flora had had it painted bright red and yellow and dotted the sails with childish daisies. Therefore, despite its diminutive size, the little boat stood out against the dark, sensible colors of the navy fleet—much like the beguiling Miss Rowe did in a crowd—drawing every eye to its inauspicious arrival.

With the perfect timing of a seasoned sailor that negated any need for Harry to lift a finger from the canary yellow rudder, his right-hand was up and ready to toss the line to the waiting man on the dock. "Captain Kincaid reporting for duty on the HMS *Boadicea*." An instruction that had the shore team hopping and saluting as if he were visiting royalty, no doubt thanks to Admiral Nugent, who would have warned them to expect hellfire to rain down on whoever stood in Harry's way.

With his embarrassing boat tethered, Harry saluted back, then waved away all offers of an escort to take him first to his new office and then his ship. He knew this place like the back of his hand thanks to regular visits here throughout his boyhood with his grandfather. He also needed a few silent minutes to bury all his tumultuous emotions before he had to be the no-nonsense Royal Navy fixer that was Captain Henry Augustus Kincaid.

Plymouth Dockyard was its usual noisy flurry of seemingly chaotic business, which wasn't actually chaotic at all when you understood its necessary rhythm. Along the quay, an endless plethora of naval vessels of all shapes and sizes were tied tight to the giant iron bollards while being either loaded for a voyage or unloaded after one. Their many naked masts resembled reeds swaying gently against the horizon. Tall, spindly cranes whose size belied their strength—much like Miss Rowe—swung enormous loads wrapped in tarpaulin or rope, giant parcels of supplies holding everything from spare rigging to the sailors' rum rations.

As he watched the familiar scene, Harry realized that after just a week, he did not miss his procurement job at the Admiralty at all. If anything, he was relieved to be done with that logistical nightmare. He wouldn't do that job again if they paid him quadruple. A welcome realization which buoyed him slightly.

Maybe some distance from that suffocating role was all he had needed to be able to see the wood for the trees? He had been so busy in Whitehall that he never had the time to allow his true feelings for that thankless promotion to properly manifest. Yet now, he could see why he had been so dissatisfied with it all with crystal clarity. It had been a means to an end and not what he wanted to do. Which all rather suggested that this massive change of direction in his career was for the best too. That epiphany gave him renewed hope that he would find the enthusiasm for his career that had been sorely missing this last year as well and . . .

"There she is, Captain!" Simpkins was beside himself with joy as he pointed out the *Boadicea* between the piers at the very front of the building yard. "Blimey, she's a beauty! Look at the size of her!"

If a person's first reaction was the most honest one, then Harry's wasn't half as effusive as Simpkins's. Yes, there was no denying that the *Boadicea* was indeed a handsome vessel—even swaddled in scaffold and with workmen's cradles filled with paint pots dangling from her rail. She was also impressive; enough to take his breath away. At least fifty cannons already poked out of the gunports of the triple decks on the starboard side. Three chunky masts stabbed the sky above, naked and still awaiting their sails. So vast that she dwarfed all the other ships around her and so regal she demanded everyone's respect. Yet as he craned his neck upward to take it all in, Harry still did not feel that surge of pride he had expected as her captain, nor any sense of connection to the vessel at all, for that matter. Only irritation that it existed and a sense of . . . flatness.

His boot had barely touched the gangplank than he was piped aboard with all the misplaced ceremonial formality that only His Majesty's Royal Navy could properly pull off at a moment's notice.

Word had clearly already made it to the few men on board that the new captain had turned up early to surprise them, as the shipwrights still working on the bow were doing their best impressions of busy men on a mission. That it was barely two on a Thursday afternoon and he could only count five of the supposed fifty workers also explained why the bloody *Boadicea* was so far behind schedule. Whoever was in charge was very lax indeed. While he made a mental note to find out who their useless supervisor was and have him replaced quick sharp, the motley crew of just three sailors up on the main deck had started to gather, ready to be inspected.

A very tall, very thin, very young lieutenant met him and saluted with all the stiffness of one who wanted to make the very best first impression. "Captain Kincaid, I am Lieutenant Ashley Gregson." The clipped, aristocratic accent was a dead giveaway that Gregson was either some titled gent's heir or his spare. "It's an honor to be serving under you, sir." Although he was at least six and twenty—by which age Harry had already taken his first command—Gregson appeared too wet behind the ears to be given such a position of authority on a ship this big. However, as Harry had been an early bloomer too, he decided not to judge a book by its cover and to give the lad a chance, as he knew how it felt to be judged unfairly for the unforgivable crime of youthfulness. "Stand at ease, Gregson. When did you get here?"

"Yesterday, sir," said the lieutenant, not standing any easier. "I was transferred from the *Kingfisher*." A big enough boat that suggested young Gregson might well know his poop deck from his mizzenmast after all. Although by the assessing expression on Simpkins's face, his right-hand was unconvinced. But such was the usual wariness between the commissioned sailors and the enlisted. The navy, in their narrow-minded wisdom, refused to promote fine mariners like Simpkins, who had clawed their way up the hard way, into the officer class. That was still reserved for gentlemen only, irrespective of how competent the gentlemen actually were at sea—and so many weren't. It would be one of the first archaic things Harry abolished if he ever became admiral of the fleet.

He decided not to overthink why he had put an *if* in that casual thought in case it meant something significant, when up until now it had always been a definitive *when I am admiral of the fleet*. It was just a random thought, after all, on the back of a busy and fraught week; there was no need for his mind to single that random one out and imbue it with unnecessary gravitas. Although it did anyway.

"Then seeing as you have a day's head start on us, why don't you give us the tour, Lieutenant?"

❧

"Your supper is stone cold," said Ada unapologetically as she waved her wooden spoon at Harry seven hours later. "In this house, supper is served at seven on the dot and always has been in the fifty years I've worked here. Them's the rules, Harry, and a man who wears two watches should do a better job of arriving on time."

"Sorry, Ada." He did his best impression of a man contrite. It came easily tonight because he was contrite. Despite trying his hardest to focus all day on the bloody *Boadicea* and its myriad problems that he needed to fix in just a month, his mind had wandered too frequently back to Miss Rowe and how he had upset her instead. "At least I am back in time for the children's bedtime." Although judging by the silence in the house beyond this kitchen, he might be too late for that too. "Where are they?"

"Gone for their baths." The spoon jabbed at the ceiling. "If you shake a leg, you might see them before Georgie tucks them in for the night." Clearly everyone on the planet had the right to call the siren by her given name except him, and that galled, even though he knew he needed that formal barrier between them. "Where's Simpkins?" She tilted to look behind him with an expression that said she knew full well why his right-hand wasn't there. "Don't tell me. He's gone for a jar at the Ship tavern."

There was no point denying it. Cawsand was small and the community as thick as thieves. "As he's ceased being my butler, his evenings are now his own—but he did say he was only going for the one."

"Well, when he finally gets home after the five or six that he's really gone for, let him know that his food is cold too." She gave him a light thwack on his arm with her spoon. "You'll both be home by seven tomorrow, young man, or I'll make you wear your dinner like a hat."

"Yes, Ada." Harry had known her too many years not to believe she meant it. "I really am sorry." That was bound to be his easiest apology tonight. He still didn't quite know how to tackle the next one and decided he would play it by ear when the time came.

And talking of time . . .

He checked one of his pocket watches for Ada's benefit. "I'd best shake a leg, as you said, to catch the children." After which, he needed to have a more difficult conversation with their governess than this morning's. Except this one would be based on truth and not the pathetic and handy lies he had unintentionally hurt her with.

Harry took the stairs two at a time in his haste to get to her and get it over with, then paused in the half-open doorway to watch her in action.

She was curled up on the bed with Grace, reading the children a story. Her vibrant hair was gloriously unruly after a day herding his nieces and nephew and had long escaped its pins. Norbert had made a pillow of her feet and was snoring upside down and spread-eagled across the bottom of the mattress while Felix was listening intently from his cross-legged position on the rug. Marianne was lounging on her belly next to him, her chin propped in her hands.

As Miss Rowe read something about a pumpkin at midnight and a woman running away from a handsome prince who was left bereft with just her shoe, both Harry's nieces inhaled. "How is he ever going to find her again?" asked Grace, so engrossed in the tale she thought it was true.

"He's not," replied Felix, matter-of-fact. "She's a maid and he's a prince and they move in very different circles. He'd be marrying below himself and princes don't do that in real life."

"If there's no happy ending then I do not wish to hear the rest!" Marianne yanked off the paper crown she was wearing, and before she threw it in disgust, Harry could not resist intervening.

"I am sure it will end happily if you give your poor governess some peace and quiet to finish the story."

Miss Rowe jumped at that, took one look at him, and blushed. Then she snapped the book closed at the same time as she surged to her feet. "You shall have to wait until tomorrow night to see how it ends. I shall leave you all to say your good nights to your uncle."

She could not even bring herself to look at him as she scurried past. Proof, if proof were needed, she now thoroughly hated him, although whether that was as a result of him taking gross advantage of her person last night or thanks to his clumsy, cowardly words of this morning, he had no clue. The masochistic little devil within was rooting for the latter, as that was the only option which could be fixed to end happily for them like the prince and the pumpkin lady—and to hell with the navy. That devil wanted him to ignore all the sound and pressing reasons that made her and him impossible, simply to have an excuse to kiss her again. Preferably as soon as possible.

As there was no way of apologizing with the children present, he let her go. But she had barely gone ten feet when there was a commotion downstairs that stopped her in her tracks and brought him and the children up short.

"In the absence of her ladyship, then her blasted brother can compensate me!" Harry chilled at the unfamiliar voice coming from the front porch. The word *compensate* dragged him instantly back to his childhood, when all the debt collectors had queued angrily at their door. It also awoke Norbert, who began to bark before he flew off the bed to join the fray in the hall.

"Now see here!" Tom was equally incensed downstairs at the aggressive tone of the interloper. "You've no right to come barging here at this late hour when you know the master and mistress won't be home for months!"

"I want paying, Tom, and I damn well want paying tonight!"

"Then you can come back and state your case politely to Harry during daylight hours, like a decent person!" By the sounds of wood being wrestled, Tom was attempting to shut the door on the interloper while holding back mad Norbert, and neither the debt collector nor the dog would have it. "There is nobody to receive you here tonight!"

"Oh yes there is! I saw her bloody brother with me own eyes not ten minutes ago, riding home across the field in his fancy uniform! So he will see me now! I'm sick of being fobbed off by you and Ada when I'm owed!"

"You've got no proof that any money actually *is* owed!"

"Got no proof!" The stranger's voice rose several octaves, and so did Norbert's barking. "What's this if it's not proof! I'm not going until I get my money!"

As the children's eyes had widened at the drama unfolding downstairs, and as Harry remembered only too well how frightening it was for a child to have to listen to a bailiff's threats while powerless to do anything to stop them taking what they wanted, he rushed to the stairwell. If it spared them that same anxiety, then he would pay his sister's debt whether there was proof she owed it or not. And despite bloody fuming at his blasted sister for racking up debt and ignoring it. Why the hell hadn't Flora learned the same awful lessons from their financially incompetent parents as he had? Especially when she had been as terrified of it all as he had been back then. To put her own children through the same torment because she was a flighty disaster who couldn't run a bath was beyond the pale!

He slowed before he took the stairs, as he was determined to keep the calm upper hand, no matter how chaotic the situation sounded. His sister might be up to her eyeballs in debt, but thanks to all the admiral's hoarded money and Harry's talent for investing it, he was as solvent as could be.

"What seems to be the problem, sir?" He would be polite and accommodating for the sake of the children, who were already quite scared enough, and he would make this go away no matter how much it cost. But when she came back, by Jove, Flora was getting both barrels!

At Harry's approach, the interloper pointed at him with a quaking finger and raised his other fist high in the air. From it, dangling by the scruff of his neck, was a gangly puppy. "Look what your bloody dog did to mine!"

He recognized the man as a local farmer rather than a debt collector, and it did not take a genius to work out that the long-limbed and scruffy pup he was holding was the fruit of Norbert's loins. The thing was Norbert all over, only in miniature. He had the same long snout, the same shaggy gray fur, and the same big brown eyes.

"People hereabouts pay good money for one of my sheepdogs and this cuckoo in the nest is eating me out of house and home!" The man took a pace forward and jabbed his pointed finger again. "I warned your bloody nephew to keep his dog away from my bitch, and I warned your sister too, but did they listen? Now I have to suffer the consequences. This dog would be worth a guinea if it had been born a collie like its mother and the rest of the litter, but nobody in their right mind is going to pay a farthing for a sheep dog who looks like this! You owe me a guinea, sir, for this runt, and at least five shillings for all the food he's eaten since Bessie birthed him."

A sum that didn't add up at all. "So to be clear, Norbert impregnated Bessie, your sheep dog?"

"Yes."

"Who then went on to have a litter of pups numbering . . . ?" He paused to allow the disgruntled farmer to fill in the blank.

"Seven!"

"And the other six?"

"Came out perfect."

"And . . . it's just this one you require compensation for and not the whole litter?" Clearly the farmer was as thick as two short planks if he thought that those other six hadn't been tainted by their enormous father's unruly lineage. They would all have a touch of Norbert about them, no matter how much they currently favored their mother. It might not be visible now, but it would be, and then God help their new and unsuspecting owners, as they would be in for a ride. Then would doubtless want their money back.

The farmer held out his hand. "One guinea and six shillings, if you please. I shan't be leaving without it." He planted his feet and glared. First at Harry and then at the giant, randy, barking Norbert beside him.

*Chapter*
# TWENTY-THREE

⨳

he captain turned to fetch the money and, spying them all watching from the stairs, smiled at his niece as cool as a cucumber, as if nothing untoward was the matter at all. "Kindly fetch one guinea and six shillings from my bedchamber, Marianne."

She did as he asked and there was a long, awkward silence from everyone except the still-barking Norbert while they all waited for her to return with it. The captain checked the amount, then patted Marianne on the head as if she were the cleverest child on earth to have counted it right the first time, and with another breezy smile, he then counted the coins into the man's outstretched hand. Purposefully slow to vex him while Ada, who had joined them from the kitchen, gripped her spoon as if she fully intended to use it if the intruder dared speak again.

As the last coin was transferred, he folded the farmer's fingers over them and did not let go. "Can we agree now that the full debt has been paid?" Georgie could not quite fathom what he did, but something about his demeanor had changed. He was taller, somehow. More arrogant and completely in control. So hard-boiled and imposing, she barely recognized him.

"It has, sir."

"And can we also agree that coming to a house at nightfall, raising merry hell, and scaring my nieces and nephew at bedtime is both rude and unnecessary when we could have had a polite conversation first thing—like decent men? We are neighbors, after all."

"Well . . . er . . ." Flummoxed at being pulled up and more flummoxed that the captain's hand still held his fist like a vise. "I . . . er . . ."

"I shall take that as a yes." The captain's smile was icy. Menacing, even. "Kindly apologize to them all for causing such an abhorrent scene."

The farmer blinked and stuttered out an apology as if he had just been told off by his father. "My apologies, Miss Marianne, Miss Grace, and Master Felix." Then, sensing the weight of the captain's disapproval, he turned to the servants. "And my apologies to you too, Tom. Ada."

"Splendid." Looking every inch the fearsome commodore of a Royal Navy flagship, he finally let go of the man's hand and with a fake smile said, "Now disappear before I set our dog on you."

The man practically broke into a run in his haste to leave, the offending puppy still dangling from his fist as he went. Georgie was on the cusp of running after him to rescue the poor thing when the captain spoke again.

"What are you going to do with the pup?"

Emboldened by the few feet of distance and disgruntled at his thorough dressing-down, the farmer was all belligerence again. "This runt ain't good for nothing but drowning!" An answer that instantly made little Grace burst into horrified tears and the faces pale on her shocked siblings. As if he, too, understood English, Norbert began to howl at that unfair death sentence, and she watched the captain's shoulders slump.

"Give him here."

The farmer dropped the puppy on the ground and stalked off, leaving the poor, terrified thing in a collapsed heap on the gravel. He was there barely a second before the captain scooped him up and cradled him to his chest. Then tried to subtly calm the thing by rubbing its ears while he stalked back, doing his best to look like a man thoroughly put-upon.

Much to Georgie's chagrin, that kind gesture went some way toward redeeming him when she had promised herself after the whole mortifying *dreadful mistake* incident this morning that she would loathe him with a fiery passion for all eternity. Hell hath no fury, after all, and she felt rightly scorned as well as thoroughly humiliated. But he had just saved an innocent puppy, so she supposed that rendered all bets off—at least temporarily.

"It appears, children, that you now have a second dog." He gently held the puppy out, then instantly cradled it close again when Ada's omnipotent spoon slashed in the air.

"That's not how it goes, Harry. A dog has to choose its own master. Them's the rules."

"Aye, she's right," said her husband as if the captain had just broken one of the Ten Commandments. "The poor thing will never be a happy hound otherwise."

"Like Norbert chose me," added Felix as if he too knew that there were laws about dog ownership, or vice versa, that the rest of the world was unaware of. "And you did save his life, Uncle Harry, just like I saved Norbert's, so I think that dog is already yours."

"Felix makes a valid point," said Tom again, pointing toward the shaking puppy, who had buried his shaggy head beneath the captain's smart navy coat. "He clearly likes you."

"I daresay, to his eyes, any human would be an improvement after that awful farmer threatened to drown him. That does not make him mine. So why don't we all settle this once and for all by getting this scruffy little mutt to choose which one of the three of you he likes best?" The captain snapped his fingers as he carried the puppy into the drawing room and then ordered the children to line up six feet apart.

With Norbert glued to his hip and staring up at his offspring, not quite knowing what to make of it, he turned the baby dog around to face him. "Apparently, troublesome son of Norbert"—with a perturbed look, he lifted the puppy higher to briefly check that he was indeed a male before proceeding—"these deranged people have decreed that you must choose your master or the delicate balance of the universe will be forever disrupted. You therefore have three fine choices and I'm afraid I am not one of them." Then he turned him toward the children and wandered past each, allowing the puppy a few seconds apiece to sniff them. Norbert followed before he returned to the center of the room. "Now go choose who you belong to so we can all go to bed."

He put the puppy down and it looked up at him, uncertain for a moment before his sire decided to lick him within an inch of his little life. That essential canine washing ritual done, Norbert backed away as if he, too, knew that his son needed to choose the human who would be his.

Grace, who had been struggling to contain her excitement since the puppy arrived, immediately began to call him to her. "Come to me, boy!"

"No! Come to me!" Marianne, who was appalled at that flagrant cheating, bent and patted her knees, only to be shoved out of the way by Felix.

"Come on, boy! Come to me! I'll fetch you a sausage if you do."

Then, almost in unison, both his sisters rallied against him.

"That's not fair! You have a dog!" Then they looked to their uncle and to Georgie, pleading them to take their side as much jostling and more promising of sausages went on.

"Stop it, all of you! You are frightening him!" Georgie pointed to where the poor puppy had retreated into the gap between the captain's boots. Then, because the little thing looked thoroughly overwhelmed, she postponed the decision before things got too out of hand. "The puppy can choose his new master in his own sweet time when he is more settled and you three have calmed down!"

Three similar bottom lips all protruded at once and then stuck out some more with her next directive. "Go to bed, the lot of you, and leave him in peace."

"But Miss Rowe!" Felix stamped his foot. "We love puppies."

"Cuthbert will still be here tomorrow. But right now, he is scared stiff, has just been separated from his mother for the first time in his very short life, and has been deposited in a strange house by an angry man who wanted to drown him. That is enough trauma for a little one to cope with in one evening, so control yourselves!" Three dark heads bowed in shame. "Bed. Now." She pointed to the stairs.

"But Uncle Harry!" Marianne, in her true manipulative fashion, sought to undermine that instruction. "If we are good and quiet, we could help make him feel at home."

"I think that is Norbert's job." An answer which none of the children could argue with now that Norbert was licking the puppy again between the captain's boots. "He'll look after *Cuthbert* tonight." He flicked his amused gaze Georgie's way at her presumptuous choice of the dog's name. "Do as Miss Rowe says, or I shall keep the puppy for myself and refuse to let you ever play with him." He pointed to the stairs too and parroted her words. "Bed. Now."

He seemed surprised when the children did exactly as he commanded but covered it quickly when he caught her watching. "It appears we have a second potentially mad dog, because one wasn't bad enough." His smile was uncertain. "I hope he is every bit as deranged and impossible as Norbert is. That will teach my sister to leave her horrid children in my care."

"That was a very nice thing that you just did." Credit where credit was due. "The children wouldn't have slept a wink tonight if you hadn't taken Cuthbert in." As that seemed like the opportune moment to bid a hasty retreat herself, and because he had saved a puppy's life and that made him significantly less hateable than he had been an hour ago, Georgie spun on her heel to follow the children rather than be all alone with him. "But I'd best go check that they have indeed gone to bed as requested."

She was about to climb the stairs when she realized he had followed. "Why Cuthbert?"

She turned and, at the sight of the puppy back in his arms having its ears tickled again, felt her resolve to despise him waver further. "As the name Norbert suits Norbert so well, and as he is the son of Norbert, Cuthbert seemed to fit." She shrugged, more awkward than she had ever felt before. "But please feel free to change it. He is your dog, after all."

"He absolutely isn't and . . ." Suddenly he looked more awkward than she had ever seen him before. "Can we talk?"

"It's late and it's been a long day . . ."

"Please . . . Georgie." The sound of her name on his lips did odd things to her insides. "I feel awful about this morning and I need to say some things to make that right. I certainly cannot say them with Ada listening." His dark eyes uncertain, he used the puppy to gesture to the huge crack in the kitchen door, where the head cook and bottle washer indeed hovered. "Just give me five minutes or I shan't sleep a wink either."

"Well, I . . ."

"Just five minutes." With one hand, he unclipped a pocket watch from his waistcoat and held it out. "You can time me."

"Five minutes." She took the proffered watch. It felt warm, like him. "Then I really do need to go and see to the children."

On leaden feet, she followed him back to the drawing room and cringed as he closed the door, willing the floor to open up and swallow her to spare her another repeat of this morning's hideousness. As she had too much pride to let him see how humiliated she was, she perched her bottom on the edge of a comfortable chair near the fireplace and forced herself to look at him and not at her hands. She ensured the watch face was visible to remind him he had only five minutes.

As she had hoped, his gaze drifted to it. "If it is any consolation, if nosy Ada gives us five minutes before she finds an excuse to barge in, it will be a miracle." He took the chair nearest and tried to put Cuthbert on the floor, but allowed the puppy to nestle in his lap the second he began to cry. He took a few moments to make a fuss of him as a myriad of uncertain emotions skittered across his much-too-handsome features, and then sighed as he lifted his eyes to hers.

"I am so sorry about this morning." Before she could flick that away, he reached out and caught her hand. Her stupid flesh rejoiced at the contact. "Please let me finish, Georgie. I almost have a garbled speech worked out and I am determined to be honest with you, even though doing so will likely make things even more awkward between us."

"I am not sure that is possible." Because his hand on hers felt too good, she extracted it and folded it in her lap in case it trembled and gave away her nervousness.

"I panicked." He huffed out a breath, steeling himself. "I'd been tossing and turning all night, trying to figure out the best way to say that that kiss could never happen again, and with no justifiable excuse except the unpalatable truth, I lied. I blamed heightened emotions and the fraught situation for behaving as I did and that wasn't fair. It was a coward's way out and you deserve better than that."

"I deserve the *unpalatable* truth?" Georgie swallowed past the lump in her throat and tried not to look hurt. "What makes it so unpalatable?"

He immediately winced and looked as if he too wanted to bolt, and she braced herself for the reasons which she knew would be truer than him losing his head. She was a penniless governess, for a start, and he was a man of means and standing. Perhaps the fictional and lowly Cinderella might be able to snare herself a prince, but such nonsense only happened in fairy tales. That inescapable difference in their stations aside, unlike the stunningly beautiful Cinderella, she was hardly the catch of the day to begin with. She was short and sturdy, and he hadn't been able to disguise how much he hated her horrid orange hair since the first moment they had collided at Miss P's. He was staring at it again now with a pained expression, and only her stubborn, rebellious pride kept her from covering it and agreeing that she completely understood his aversion.

"How to put this without sounding . . . selfish?" He raked a hand through his thick and neat dark hair and winced some more. "You see . . . um . . . the thing is . . ."

"Oh, for goodness' sake! Spit it out, Captain, and put us both out of our wretched misery!" She hadn't realized she had surged to her feet until she saw him blinking up at her.

"All right . . ." He swallowed, then shrugged. "I am about to fulfill the next stage of my dream—*my destiny*—and you are a distraction that I absolutely cannot afford. I know what I am like when I am head over heels in love with a woman and, frankly, that is a complete besotted mess." His unexpected words tumbled out fast, as if they were as much of a surprise to him as they were her. "I cannot think of anything but what my heart desires. Become slapdash and lackadaisical with all my naval duties and . . ."

"I'm sorry?" Suddenly winded and unstable, Georgie groped for the chair behind her and collapsed back in it. Surely he hadn't really just mentioned love and her in the same sentence?

He looked both terrified and utterly disarming at the same time. "I'm a sailor, Georgie, and you are . . . a siren." He swept his gaze up and down her body, then squeezed his eyes closed as if she were indeed temptation incarnate. "And as much as I yearn for you to be mine, everyone knows sailors and sirens do not mix."

She had no words.

What on earth was she supposed to say to that? It was simultaneously the most wonderful compliment she had ever received and the most ridiculous thing she had ever heard.

The seconds ticked past, and realizing that she had stopped breathing, she let the air out of her lungs in one loud whoosh. "Perhaps you need spectacles, Captain, if you think this—" She flapped her hands at her horrid orange hair, which was well on the way to resembling the full bird's nest it always did by sundown despite the thirty pins she had poked in it not two hours ago to keep it in place. "—is what a siren looks like."

"I think we can dispense with the *Captain*, don't you?" He choked out a laugh. "You have had your hands all over me, madam, and I have certainly had my hands all over you. We both know that we were moments from making mad, passionate love last night, so I think we are long past the need for formalities . . . Georgie." Then, apparently surprising them both, he reached out and reverently twirled a finger in one of the curls that now framed her face. "And this is precisely what a siren looks like. I've seen Botticelli's *Venus* with my own eyes and she is plain compared to you."

For the second time in as many minutes, she was rendered speechless. For so many reasons.

The unvarnished reminder of how intimate they had been.

Being told that she was as good as beautiful for the first time in her life.

Because the finger in her hair had moved to caress her cheek and that alone awoke every improper nerve ending in her newly wanton body.

"While I cannot pretend anymore that I don't want you, Georgie, I wanted you to know why I cannot have you." He yanked his hand away and fisted it in his lap. "If I had you, I wouldn't be able to find the focus to get my ship finished and I certainly couldn't sail away from you—and I have to. Being shackled to a sailor is a miserable and lonely existence, and one that practically guarantees a failed marriage, and that wouldn't be fair to you either. I can count on one hand the number of my legions of married comrades who aren't miserable, as absence doesn't make the heart grow fonder. More often than not, it turns hearts cold."

And he seemed devastated by that fact. "You would end up lonely and resentful of my career and I am nothing without the navy. It is who I am. I wish it wasn't, but . . ."

They both jumped as the door flew open with such force it slammed into the wall. "I made us all some cocoa." Ada shamelessly breezed in, carrying a tray, and then sat herself beside Georgie with a grin as an apologetic Tom skulked in behind, carrying a cake. "Now, what are we talking about?"

# TWENTY-FOUR

᪡

*H*arry woke with a start when Cuthbert licked his nose.

He lifted the warm bundle of fur from his chest and deposited him back on the mattress where he had been forced to allow the puppy to sleep. "Yours is very definitely not the face I want to be waking up to."

Thanks to Cuthbert's talent for hogging the bed, and despite confession supposedly being good for the soul, Harry had still slept fitfully. It was impossible not to think of Georgie when she was mere yards away in her own bed, and he still wasn't convinced that he had done the right thing in telling her how attracted he was to her. There hadn't been any time to gauge her reaction to his revelation after Ada had interrupted their little tête-à-tête. Once Ada started asking questions, there was no stopping her, and before he knew it, it was bedtime.

He had tried to leave the puppy downstairs to sleep, of course, because he was a man who had to sail away and really couldn't own a dog. He had even made a comfortable bed for the thing in the sitting room, but Cuthbert was having none of it. He also flatly refused to sleep in with Norbert. Something Harry found out an hour after he had gone to bed at the same moment he learned Norbert knew how to open doors. One minute he had been staring up at the ceiling, yearning to snuggle up with Georgie, and the next, when his door knob turned and he sat bolt upright praying that it was her, it had been the giant, shaggy hound who had stomped in with the gangly Cuthbert dangling from his jaws, clearly irritated that his own slumber had been disturbed. He deposited his needy son on Harry's mattress, then promptly left. He even managed to pull the bedchamber door firmly shut to ensure that his spawn did not escape to bother him further.

As the puppy had instantly curled up into a ball and closed his eyes as soon as it burrowed against him, Harry felt mean trying to evict him and had reluctantly let him stay.

"Do not get used to this, dog." Suddenly annoyed at everything, he wagged his finger at Cuthbert as he padded to his washstand and sloshed cold water into the bowl. "You've had a whole night to settle in and today you need to choose one of the children to glue yourself to forevermore."

The animal tilted his head as he watched Harry sluice his upper body in the cold water and soap, clearly fascinated at the strange ritual, then half jumped, half fell off the bed to come sit by his feet, staring up entranced while he shaved.

"It is an important day today." Why he was compelled to make conversation with a dog was beyond him, but he went with it. It was an important day and it wouldn't hurt to reaffirm all that he had to do in it. "I've got to sail to blasted Plymouth while the cocks are still crowing, I've got to meet with the supervisor of the useless layabouts on the bloody *Boadicea* and then I've probably got to dismiss him and find a replacement. Then somehow, in around five blasted weeks, I've got to get that ship in a fit state to sail, so wish me luck."

The list of things that still needed to be done was longer than both Harry's arms put together. It wouldn't be so bad if they were small and niggly tasks but some—like fitting the copious numbers of bunks that would be needed for the seven hundred and fifty men who would need to sleep on them—were massive jobs. Massive problems, too, if all the rope and hammocks hadn't yet been ordered! "Then I've got to learn how to sail the damn thing while also teaching the crew how to, so that will be fun. A lot can go wrong on a one-hundred-twenty gunner, so I can't say that I'm looking forward to July." It wasn't just the training maneuvers he was dreading. He was dreading August too as that would also signal the return of Flora and the departure of Georgie and that was something he did not want to have to contemplate regardless of his need to resist her. Somehow, life currently felt better with her near. A problem which would, hopefully, resolve itself once he found his naval feet and enthusiasm for sailing again.

"But as Nelson said, duty is the purpose of an officer and all private considerations, no matter how painful, must give way to that. Or words to that effect, Cuthbert, so I don't have any other choice." Harry sighed in resignation and must have sounded so miserable that the puppy gave him a soulful, sympathetic stare before he licked his toes.

"You're a good dog, Cuthbert—but don't tell anyone I said so." In case that gave Cuthbert false hope, he felt obligated to clarify. "But don't get any ideas of staying with me because His Majesty's navy might well tolerate a cat on board a ship—but a giant, mad, future Norbert they will not." He bent to tickle the dog's ears as he toweled the last of the soap from his face, and that was when he saw his dress breeches. Or to be more precise, what was left of his dress breeches!

Something had tugged them from the chair he had laid them on and ripped them to shreds. Tiny pieces of what had once been the left leg of the supremely comfortable *newer* breeches Simpkins had had made behind his back were now scattered across his bedchamber floor like confetti on a trail that led back to the bed. Another long but ragged ivory strip, which may or may not have once been part of the waistband, lay atop the patchwork eiderdown where he had allowed the puppy to sleep.

"Cuthbert! What have you done!" Harry picked up what was left of the only pair of dress breeches he possessed that did not strangle his wedding vegetables and then shook the rags at the puppy, incensed. "I take everything I just said back! You are a bad dog, Cuthbert!" And today—the most important day in his career so far—was already a bad day, and it hadn't even started.

———◈———

It was safe to say that Georgie hadn't had the best first official full day as the children's governess in Cawsand. The change of location and the weeklong break in their routine meant that they had completely forgotten most of it. Worse, she was so distracted by the captain's confession last night that she was an atrocious and short-tempered teacher. So disorganized, overemotional, and preoccupied, it was as if she had never taught a lesson in her life.

She had tried teaching them outside to begin with, and when that proved near impossible, she had tried to teach them inside. Then, run ragged and so confused by it all, she had decided to write the entire day off and had reasoned some fresh air and some vigorous exercise on the beach was the answer. For the children to let off some well-needed steam and to give herself some space to try to organize all her jumbled thoughts and emotions into something resembling order.

He thought her attractive.

A siren.

The sort of woman he could never sail away from if he allowed himself to fall head over heels in love with her.

Her!

And yet he was still going to sail away.

Because for all his pretty words, he wouldn't allow it because his military career was, and always would be, his one true love and she couldn't compete.

She knew that she should really be relieved by that, as being shackled to a military man was her worst nightmare and not something she would ever do after her miserable and nomadic childhood and the way her mother had suffered. But instead, she was upset. Disappointed. In him. In herself. At irony, for tempting her with the most unsuitable man possible. At fate for its impeccably awful timing. That all those things irritated because if she couldn't be relieved at her lucky escape, then at the very least, she should be angry at him for falling so short of what she deserved.

Except—

He had been trying to be noble. He had been trying to do what he thought was best, for her as well as him. She had seen that as plain as day in his dark, stormy eyes when he had acknowledged that being shackled to a sailor was a miserable existence. Just as she had witnessed the war going on in them because he wanted her but was too much the officer and a gentleman to just have her the once—even if she'd undoubtedly let him.

What a stark difference that was from Lottie's recent experience with an employer. Her friend had had to physically defend herself from that ignoble libertine's unwelcome advances and had been dismissed as a result. Both Portia and Kitty had similar experiences, and the flagrant abuse of female employees was so widespread that

Miss P taught classes on it to try to keep her protégés protected. She supposed she should be grateful that the captain—Harry—was cut from a different cloth. Despite all the inevitable new awkwardness his honesty had created, she still felt safe under his roof and she still had her job. She had to focus on those positives and put all the rest to one side.

For the sake of her sanity and her foolish heart.

Why couldn't they have met a year ago, six months ago, before he had been offered a promotion he could not refuse? Then, if what he had claimed was right, he'd have become so besotted with her that he would have become lax in his duties and wouldn't have got this wretched promotion at all. Wouldn't that have been wonderful? Even if he stayed with the navy but worked at the Admiralty, that would have worked. His charming house in Hanover Square was a long way from a soulless barracks, and she would have loved the opportunity to make a life there with him. A stupid and fanciful notion which the part of her that had always hankered for hearth and home, love and family, already mourned disproportionately when it had never really been in the cards.

But now, when her temporary position here ended as she had always known it would, she would leave with a hole in her heart and a bittersweet memory of a great love that might have been. All combined with the worry that he could be anywhere in the world, sailing directly into the worst trouble on his flagship. Trouble he might not sail back from.

"I caught a crab!" Grace ran toward her, holding her bucket aloft. "Isn't he beautiful?" She tried to stop just shy of Georgie, but still ended up crashing into her.

She smiled at the bounty and tried to look impressed despite the dull black crab being smaller than her palm. "He is indeed." To make the girl smile, Georgie took the bucket and showed the contents to Cuthbert, who hadn't yet made his mind up about either the sand or the children, so hadn't left her side since they had arrived at the beach an hour ago. "Isn't he lovely?" The puppy gave it a tentative sniff and backed away as soon as one of the crab's pincers snapped out of the water. "Now go return him to the rock pool you found him in, in case his mother is missing him."

As Grace dutifully did as she was asked, Georgie tried to count her blessings. At least she had a job—her first, thank goodness! And with a decent employer, to boot, with the prospect of good references. She also had the soothing sounds of the ocean and the sun on her face. Two things she had never really experienced before. They might have all had a fractious day, but the children were happy now too. The girls were exploring the shallow rock pools that hugged the granite framing this tiny beach, while the limping Felix and Norbert paddled in the gentle waves rippling up the sand. The setting was idyllic, even if some of the circumstances left a lot to be desired.

"Uncle Harry!"

Felix suddenly began waving at a dot of a sailboat in the distance. He was soon joined by the others at the shoreline, and they all waved at his impending arrival while Georgie tried to quell her quickened heart. It had been inevitable that they would have to collide at some point after last night's inconceivable conversation, yet she still had no earthly idea how she was supposed to behave around him now.

As the sloop came closer, it was clear he was alone. His impressive naval regalia did not fit with the jolly yellow-and-red-striped boat at all, and yet somehow, the incongruity seemed to suit the man. Suited his contrasting personality which at one extreme was the staid stickler who got things done, and the other, the generous, thoroughly soft-boiled egg who didn't take himself too seriously. He certainly did not look less manly on the scarlet sloop, even with the big hand-painted daisies blooming on the sails.

He waved at the children as he maneuvered the vessel to the sea wall and secured it to one of the rings, and by the time that was all done, they had all hurried across the sand to greet him.

He swung each child in the air, then petted Norbert before he looked her way. Even with a hundred yards of distance, the potency when their gazes locked was so tangible it made her heart ache. Beside her, even Cuthbert seemed to sense the change in the atmosphere, and for the first time in an hour, ventured a few feet from Georgie. His little tail wagged as the captain hoisted Grace to sit upon his shoulders before he made his way across the beach toward Georgie.

"Not in the classroom again, I see." His smile was winsome, as, she suspected, was hers.

"There is no classroom at Guillemot House, thank the Lord, so your customary complaint is moot." Were they now supposed to behave as if nothing seismic had shifted between them? "How was your first official day as the captain of a half-finished flagship?"

Thanks to all of Ada's incessant prying last night, she now knew that the Admiralty had given him a veritable mountain to climb in a near-impossible time frame, and the strain of that showed on his face. There were slight shadows under his eyes and his whole body sagged with over-burdened weariness.

He lowered Grace to the ground and sent her and her siblings back to the rock pools to play before he answered. "As awful and trying as I expected it to be. I had to dismiss the shipwright in charge along with six of his most troublesome laborers."

"Why?"

He gingerly seated himself on the sand, close enough for them to have a polite conversation, but not so close that they could accidentally touch. Cuthbert instantly arranged himself between his legs so that he could gaze up adoringly while his already favorite human idly stroked his fur.

"Because it became apparent he had purposefully sabotaged the build. The navy pays them all a day rate rather than a job rate, so to maximize their earnings, once the shell of the bloody *Boadicea* was finished and all the work went inside and conveniently out of sight, those lazy layabouts were only working four hours a day. If that." Although he didn't look particularly surprised by that outrage. "I've also had to put the naval officer who supposedly oversees all of them on a charge, as he's little better than a drunkard marking time until he can claim his pension. He's so disinterested in the bloody *Boadicea*, he couldn't even be bothered to get his flabby backside out of his chair to come and visit me on my first day. I had to go find him. In a disgrace of an office that stunk of rum."

Clearly, they were going to behave as if nothing seismic had happened at all—but at least they were conversing as friends, for once, rather than an employer and an employee who never quite knew on which level to talk to one another. Apt, she supposed, to scrap those formalities when they had, as he'd quite rightly pointed out, been seconds away from making mad, passionate love.

"But on the one positive note, it does appear that somebody, somewhere, has had some forethought and has ordered most of the equipment the ship needs to make it seaworthy, so that is one less headache. Until we can find a suitably experienced and reliable master shipwright to supervise the rest of the build, Simpkins has stepped into the breach. I left him reading the riot act to the remaining laborers, who are now in no doubt that he expects their day to start at eight sharp and to finish nine hours later. Five minutes shy either way and he's warned them their pay will be docked by half a day. Hence, I am here alone as he's decided to spend tonight on the bloody *Boadicea* to make sure they all arrive on time."

"The bloody *Boadicea*?"

He winced. "My apologies for the coarse language. It has been one of those days."

"My ears aren't that tender and that wasn't my point. It was more that you've unconsciously said it three times. Is that really what you think of your ship?"

"As that ship has been the bane of my life for the last few months, I suppose calling it that has become habit." He pulled a face, unaware that he had called it "that ship" rather than "my ship"—which was interesting. "It is difficult to think positively about something which has been nothing but trouble."

"Then, I suppose, at least we will all know when things have improved, as you'll have dropped the instinctive 'bloody' before the *Boadicea*, Captain."

"From your lips to God's ears, Georgie." He stared out at the ocean for several moments, frowning. "Is it so hard for you to call me Harry?" When his gaze turned back to hers, all the longing was there again. "Only last night, when I confessed my deepest, darkest secret, I never did get to hear what you thought about it."

What did he expect her to say to that, exactly, when he had already nipped in the bud any deeper relationship between them in favor of his "bloody" ship? "At this stage, I daresay that doesn't really matter."

"It matters to me." He raked a hand through his hair, staring out to sea again, his expression bleak. "But I suppose you are right . . . Under the circumstances, it is probably a topic best avoided." His accepting smile did not touch his eyes. "How was your day?"

"As awful and trying as I expected it to be." She had intended the mirroring of his words to sound ironic, not wistful. "The children and I are still finding our routine here in Cawsand. They are used to doing things here a certain way and we have fallen out about it repeatedly today."

"Ah . . ." he said, gazing at them. "My sympathies. My sister is not one for rules and routines and this place"—he threw his palms out to encompass the village as well as the beach—"has always been synonymous with chaos. At least to my mind."

"Is that why it makes you twitchy?"

He laughed at that. "Twitchy? Now there is an interesting adjective, but apt, I suppose." Unconsciously, he flexed his fingers and arms as if releasing the tension from them. "My parents, alas, had more in common with Flora's approach to life than mine." As if he had shocked himself by admitting that aloud, he was quick to counter. "They were not bad people, of course. Far from it, in fact. But lived their entire lives without restraint, or often much sense of responsibility, and that can have its challenges."

A fascinating window into the way he was. "How so?"

"They lived from moment to moment, often in the moment, and gave little or no thought to tomorrow. Or to money. As a result, they had no contingency plans for things like bills and the many calamities that the lack of those things tends to create."

"But you did." It wasn't a question because she knew enough about him to know that Captain Henry Kincaid liked everything to be just so. If his childhood had lacked any order, it made sense that he would value it disproportionately.

He rearranged his long legs with a sigh. "One of us had to, or everything would have gone to complete rack and ruin. Thankfully, the admiral—"

"The admiral?"

"My grandfather—Admiral Gaunt—plucked me from all the chaos early on and gifted me with the unforgiving structure of the navy, which much better suited my character. The salary also gave me the ability to repair some of the holes in the family finances, which helped me sleep better at night."

Even more fascinating! "Why did you call him the admiral and not Grandfather?" Georgie had a funny feeling they suddenly had something fundamental in common.

"Good question." He shook his head, flummoxed, as if he had never considered the reasons before. "Everyone called him the admiral, but bizarrely, that title suited him. He was . . ."

"A rigid, strict, unyielding and unsentimental militarian?"

He chuckled. "I suppose so. How did you know?"

"Because my stepfather—the colonel—was exactly the same."

"Ah—you had a stepfather. That explains the mystery of why you moved from barracks to—"

"Uncle Harry!" Grace flew across the sand like a gale. Hot on her heels was Marianne and bringing up the rear at a much slower and uneven pace, thanks to his recent gamble with death, came Felix. All three were grinning.

"When can we go to the tea shop in Plymouth again?" Grace hung off his sleeve like a limpet. "You always take us there whenever you are home and you haven't been home in such a long time, we've all forgotten the last time!"

The other two nodded.

"It has been forever," said Felix.

"Longer than that," added Marianne.

"And you haven't taken us anywhere or bought us anything since the last time we went to Gunther's and that was *ages* ago. And don't say that you have to work." The youngest Pendleton pouted. "Because you always have to work and we are your own flesh and blood and we adore you."

"Well . . . I am sure we can squeeze a trip in." The captain—Harry—was instantly all guilt. "I have a meeting at the Barbican on Monday, so I suppose . . ."

That was when Georgie realized the children had lied to her. They hadn't confessed to their uncle about all their blackmail as they had promised faithfully to do almost two whole weeks ago. They had instead taken advantage of the time he had spent at the Admiralty and the suddenness of this trip to Devon to quietly forget about it.

As Grace was currently twisting their obviously guilt-ridden uncle around her manipulative little finger, she directed her focus toward the elder two, who were egging the youngest on with excited claps.

She folded her arms and quirked one unimpressed brow and waited for them to feel the weight of her glare. It was the more intuitive Marianne who noticed first and, with a nudge, brought her brother up short. At least they had the good sense to look contrite and both ceased clapping to stare at their feet. "I believe the children would prefer to have a private but urgent word with you before you make any hard-and-fast plans about a trip to the tea shop on Monday. Isn't that right, children?"

She took a moment to pin each with her most fearsome schoolmistress's stare, enjoying how each child withered beneath it. Even Grace, who had initiated this latest blackmail attempt as naturally as she took in air, shriveled with chagrin.

"Yes, Miss Rowe," muttered three bowed heads in unison.

"Words probably best had this evening, I'll wager." After all, there was no time like the present and she did not trust them to do it now unless they were forced into it. "But first, go collect all your things from the beach."

"No!" Felix's eyes widened in panic. "You promised us we could play here until six and it's . . ." He helped himself to one of Harry's pocket watches to stare at the dial. ". . . only a quarter to." He turned the watch to face her. "*Please* can't we have the last fifteen minutes of fun? We have been cooped up in a carriage all week!" And now he was trying to manipulate her!

Before she could give him a stern piece of her mind, his frankly clueless but well-intentioned uncle answered. "Go—enjoy the sea some more." That was all the reprieve the little rascals needed, and they dashed off, eager to avoid telling him the truth for just a little bit longer.

He waited until they were out of earshot before he turned to her, quizzical. "Firstly, how do you get them to behave with just a raised eyebrow? And secondly, what do they need an urgent word with me about?"

"Well firstly, it comes with practice and a lot of essential ground-work, and secondly . . ." Georgie folded her arms with a huff. She did not want to break her promise to the children, but as they had broken their promise to her and he had asked, she felt she had no choice. "I know all about the unlimited ice cream at Gunther's the other week to get them to behave for me. Just as I know about all the shillings and tuppences and toys you shower them with as bribes to do what they should. I also know that, as a result, those little rascals have been fleecing you for years."

"They have?"

"Of course they have! They know precisely how to make you twitchy—"

"That is the second time you have called me twitchy in as many minutes!" His face was half amusement, half astonishment.

"Perhaps Marianne's adjective isn't the correct one to properly describe how uncomfortable and irritable you become when things are a little less than calm. But you should know that they often purposefully misbehave or do whatever they can to make you feel guilty, and then they continue to do it until you surrender to their will."

"No . . ." He adored them so much he didn't want to believe it.

"Yes! They tried the same shallow tactics on me after you left for Portsmouth, which obviously did not wash at all, and that's how I prized the truth out of them. Why else do you think I interceded when Grace twisted your arm back there? Why I suggested, in the strongest possible terms, that they have a talk with you as soon as was possible and why all three of them are presently so determined to make this visit to the beach last as long as it possibly can? They are all in cahoots and have all been blackmailing you into rewarding them for misbehaving!"

He shook his head, chuckling. "They are just being children and I am a much too worldly wise adult to be daft enough to fall for . . ." She knew the precise moment he realized she was telling the truth because his mouth went from open and stunned to shut and flattened in an instant. "Why, the little—"

"But please do not tell them that I told you, as the little devils deserve all the pain of confessing it cold. They all swore a solemn pledge to me over a week ago that they would come clean, and they didn't."

"They *have* been fleecing me. Why didn't I see it sooner? I've only known the little Machiavellis all their lives." He seemed both stunned and impressed by their industry.

"You're their uncle and not a parent or a teacher. It's a very different role. It is also lovely that you want to spoil them, but now that they are in your care, you really do need to learn how to control them without paying them, or you will turn them into monsters. That will take a bit of groundwork on your part, but as Nelson rightly said, first gain the victory, then make the best use of it that you can."

"*You* are quoting Nelson at *me* now?" He seemed more amused by that than the children's skulduggery.

"My labored point is, the time has come for a line to be drawn in the sand and, I am afraid, it is yours to draw."

"Well . . . I . . ." He blinked at her, looking far more handsome than a befuddled man had a right to. "Do you suggest that I punish them when they tell me?"

That he had asked her expert opinion warmed her. That he seemed horrified at the prospect of punishing the three shameless blackmailers warmed her more. Without thinking, she reached out and squeezed his hand, and then regretted it instantly when just that touch sent a ricochet of awareness everywhere and had him staring so longingly at her in return, Georgie wanted to grab him and kiss him. "You are well within your rights to."

Georgie withdrew her hand and clamped it in the other in case it went wandering again. "But, irrespective of the folly of allowing them to exploit your good nature in the first place, they still adore you. Therefore, I think your heartfelt and wounded disappointment in them would be a much better form of punishment than any punitive sort ever could. That will really bother them." Like a moth to a flame, Georgie reached for his hand again and allowed herself just the briefest touch, which had as potent an effect. "As much as it pains me to admit it, you are an excellent uncle."

"Oh, it pains you, does it?" To his credit, he seemed more amused by her candor than incensed by it.

She smiled and meant it. "But, with my schoolmistress's hat on, I would advise that a punishment is also due. As, I must remind you, is an additional one for Felix, who still has not had any sort of admonishment from you for wandering off and getting himself lost two nights ago." Was it really only two nights ago? It beggared belief that so much had changed in so short a time. "And by a punishment, I obviously do not expect you to exact any physical one. As I can assure you that those never work." Every time the colonel hadn't spared the rod with her, it stoked St. Joan's rebellious fire further.

He was visibly relieved by that. "All right, Madam Schoolmistress, I bow to your superior knowledge. What do you suggest is fitting punishment for those three scoundrels?" He glanced toward them with love. Disappointed and peeved love, but it was the correct sentiment under the circumstances.

"Hit them where it hurts."

"I thought we weren't doing violence?"

She nudged him with her elbow because his chuckle told her he was simply being pedantic. "Earlier bedtimes for all three of them for a month and some unpleasant chores around the house for the girls should do the trick. The more disgusting the better, as neither like to get their hands dirty."

"Noted. And for Felix?"

"Something mathematical. He loathes it with a burning passion and will do anything to get out of learning it, and he is so far behind his sisters in the subject he needs the extra lessons. Except don't make them look like lessons, as . . ." He placed a finger on her lips, then sighed as he pulled it away.

"I might have been an idiot—but I am not always." He gestured to the winding lane above with the tilt of his head. "Do you know your way back to the house?"

"Of course I do. Because I am not an idiot either."

"Good." He buttoned the sleeping Cuthbert into his smart uniform coat and then gingerly stood as if he was in some physical pain before he helped her up. "Leave me with them. As Drake said, I cannot command the winds and the weather—but I can at least try and wrestle back my command of my blasted sister's manipulative offspring. They will come back repentant and I will have reclaimed my dignity, or we'll all die trying."

"I'm pretty sure that was Nelson too—*Harry.*"

# TWENTY-FIVE

❧

"They have used twelve thousand yards of rope so far, Uncle Harry." Beside him on the Plymouth dockside, Felix consulted his list and, anticipating Harry's next question, poked the corner of his tongue out as he did a quick calculation. "There is another forty thousand and eight hundred yards of rigging left in the store, so there should be plenty."

"Excellent." He patted his nephew on the head, oddly enjoying having an apprentice, albeit a press-ganged one. "We should probably order ten thousand yards more, just to be safe. This is a bigger ship than the *Victory*, after all." Felix was still in a state of shock that Nelson's ship had needed thirty miles of rope. Georgie had been right. Felix loathed mathematics, so commandeering him to spend a month as his assistant had been a stroke of genius he was smugly proud of. It might have started as a punishment, but Felix was thoroughly enjoying following him around, and they were both learning from the experience. "Make a note of that, then I think we are done for the day."

Once the shipwrights left at five, hanging around the *Boadicea* was pretty pointless, and Harry was enjoying his new routine of finishing work at a regular time and eating hot meals around a table. That he always sailed back to Cawsand to find Georgie on the beach with the girls and the dogs at the end of their day, too, was another bonus. Those lazy, conversation-filled strolls back to the house had quickly become the highlight of his day and everything seemed well in the world from the moment his gaze picked up her vibrant hair and cheery wave from halfway across the Sound. Even Plymouth had some charm with her in it, and he found himself not minding some of the things which had always jarred, like being in his childhood home, which wasn't anywhere near as chaotic as he remembered it.

He said his goodbyes to Simpkins, who had now permanently moved into his cabin so he could sniff his beloved salty sea breeze with impunity, and then made his way behind the ship where he had moored the sloop. He was about to set off when he was flagged down by a young cadet.

"Here is the final guest list for Admiral Nugent's reception tomorrow." The lad handed over the sealed missive. "I need to ask if you wish for anyone else to be added before I pass it over to the chief petty officer of the mess."

Harry scanned the list, annoyed that he had completely forgotten about the formal dinner that heralded Nugent's first inspection of his flagship, and more annoyed that it necessitated him being here in Plymouth, back in his too-tight formal dress breeches which he had come to loathe, rather than spending an evening at home with Georgie in a pair that fit.

He had meant to have the local tailor knock him up a new pair, but thanks to all the work that needed doing on the bloody *Boadicea*, it had completely slipped his mind. It was too late now, and a long night of constriction beckoned.

"I cannot think of anyone . . ." The words dried in his throat when he saw Elizabeth's name three-quarters of the way down, and not just hers, but her husband's.

Splendid.

Now he wouldn't only have to suffer the blasted reception in his too-tight dress breeches, he would have to suffer her too. For the first time since the last time he had seen her, when he had practically begged on bended knee for her to leave the vice admiral she had left him for. And worse, he would have to face her alone.

Unless . . .

Would it be improper to ask Georgie to accompany him?

With a beautiful woman on his arm, he would feel less self-conscious facing that treacherous witch again. "Obviously, I will be bringing a guest." He thrust the list back at the officer. "A lady. So see that a space at the table is added."

"Do you have her name, sir?" said the man, riffling in his coat for a pencil while Felix's ears pricked up.

"Yes. Miss . . . um . . . Rowe. Miss Georgina Rowe."

Felix grinned at that. It was the sort of irritating and knowing grin that confirmed his preoccupation with Georgie had become the source of much family gossip, but at least he waited until the officer had gone before he spoke. "So Ada is right and you do fancy Miss Rowe?"

"Of course not."

"Then why else would you be taking her to your posh dinner?"

"Because it is expected for an officer to arrive with a lady, that is why, and because I can hardly take either Ada or Marianne, Miss Rowe is the only option left." Harry tried to deflect by chivvying the boy toward the gawdy, daisy-painted sail which had earned him the unfortunate whispered nickname of Captain Petals amongst the disgruntled but now hard-working shipwrights. "Let's get out of the harbor and I'll give you a go at navigating."

Felix was still grinning as he hoisted the sail a few minutes later. "Ada says that you look at Miss Rowe the same way as Norbert does a sausage."

"I do not."

"You do stare at her funny, Uncle Harry. Especially when she isn't looking and you don't think anyone else is."

He decided not to dignify that with an answer and gestured for them to change seats, reasoning that if his nephew was occupied with the rudder, he would be less inclined to make mortifyingly percep-tive comments. "You see that ship anchored over there? Aim straight for that and then once you reach it, turn hard starboard and we'll hug the coast all the way home."

The boy did and then grinned again. "Miss Rowe looks at you in much the same way, so we all think that she fancies you too." News that made Harry's heart soar.

"I think you all have too much time on your hands if you've got nothing better to do than make up nonsensical gossip to amuse your-selves. Now kindly focus on our course or I'll take the rudder back."

"You're *thirty*, Uncle Harry." He managed to imbue enough hor-ror into that number to make it sound ancient. "And Mama says that thirty is the perfect age for a man to settle down because you should have sowed all your wild oats by then."

*Huh!* The chance would be a fine thing. But he was absolutely not having a conversation about his depressingly barren field of oats with a ten-year-old. "Firstly, for a man like me with a career like mine, thirty is far too young to settle down. Forty would be more conve-nient." Although even as he said it, it depressed him that he had no choice but to eschew any chance of love for at least another decade.

"Secondly, and most importantly, escorting Miss Rowe to a formal naval dinner is in no way a proposal of marriage, young man, nor is it confirmation of yours and Ada's ridiculous theory that the pair of us fancy one another."

"If you say so, Uncle Harry." The wretch had the gall to wink. "But a fancy dinner might be a good start."

Harry ignored him to focus on the looming ship that had been anchored in the Sound all week in the narrow channel between Devil's Point and Cremyll. While it served as the perfect navigational marker for a novice sailor like Felix, as it kept the boy well away from the busy shipping lanes and the currents which this little sloop was no match for, it was odd that it was there when there were plenty of moorings in the merchant harbor a mile away. Odder still was the rowboat currently struggling to get toward it. Both the men in it were fighting the waves and making little headway while their boat seemed to be filled with supplies from the mainland.

"Ahoy!" Harry cupped his hands to shout above the stiff breeze then motioned to Felix to sail closer. "Is your vessel in distress?" That seemed the only conceivable reason that it was anchored in choppy sea rather than beside a tranquil quay.

"That depends on your definition of distress," hollered one of the rowers back.

"We're watertight and not sinking," shouted the other, waving them away.

As that answer did nothing to calm Harry's uneasy curiosity, and because something about this ship now felt off, he told Felix to keep heading for it before he shouted back, "Then allow me to give you a tow." He didn't think the fine-looking three-masted and at least three-hundred-and-fifty-ton ship looked like a pirate ship. Or even believe that there was any potential threat of pirates here in Plymouth with all of His Majesty's superior naval firepower, but something about it was odd. As one of the king's officers, he had a duty to investigate, and what better way to do that than to offer some help?

Help they gratefully accepted, so Harry tossed them a line, then swapped places with his nephew to steer his little sailboat close enough to take a peek at what was going on. "She's a fine ship." And she was. Beneath the peeling paint on her hull, he could tell she wasn't much more than a decade old.

"Aye, she is," agreed one of the men. "But sadly wasted on a useless man who cares more for the hazard tables and whoring than he does for his business."

"Don't speak out of turn." His companion shot the first man a warning glare. "He'll offload you if he hears you and then you'll have no job, you fool."

"Like I have a job now?" The loose-lipped sailor was indignant. "That drunkard hasn't paid us in four months and we've got no bloody cargo to haul, so he ain't likely to pay us for another four. Maybe more." He looked Harry up and down, taking in his well-worn day-to-day uniform with a frown. "Are the navy hiring in Plymouth? I promised myself I wouldn't go back to it, but beggars can't be choosers and I'm sick to my back teeth of bobbing around here while we wait for a miracle."

"The navy are always hiring." Harry jerked his head toward the ship. "Why do you need a miracle, lads?"

"Because the stupid sod owes so much in mooring fees to every port in England that we can't sail into one of them without getting ourselves impounded, so we're all stuck here while he"—he jerked his thumb toward the windows of the captain's cabin—"tries and fails to win back all he's lost at the local hells."

"We've run out of credit with all the local merchants too." The more belligerent sailor decided to chime in. "So we're in such dire straits, unless something changes our stars soon, that we'll all have to abandon the *Siren* and its useless captain to the Sound."

"The *Siren*?" For a moment, Harry thought he'd misheard until his saw the nameplate. "She's called the *Siren*?" An ironic and eerily prophetic name.

"Aye," said the chatty one as he secured his rowboat to the *Siren*'s stern. "Such a shame, too, as she's a grand ship. Crossed the Atlantic last in just thirty-nine days."

Harry stared at the ship, took in its sleek, modern lines, and whistled, believing it. She'd be fast and nimble despite her size. So fast, she'd leave the cumbersome bloody *Boadicea* in her wake. "Well, I hope your stars change soon, gentlemen."

As they weren't breaking any laws, it was no skin off his nose if they stayed bobbing in the Sound. But as he relinquished the rudder to Felix again, just like the siren currently waiting for him in Cawsand, this one kept him staring at her until they turned, and she disappeared behind the bay.

❧

"Is it true, Uncle Harry, that you are escorting Miss Rowe to a fancy naval reception tomorrow?" Marianne asked that with irrepressible glee while nudging Felix, just as Georgie arrived at the dinner table. "Felix says you are."

"Well . . . I . . . um . . ." His ears burned red as he looked Georgie's way, clearly embarrassed. "I was going to ask because . . . um . . . it is sort of expected that an officer escorts a lady to these excruciatingly formal affairs and I wondered if you would mind . . . um . . . stepping into the breach?"

"It's official navy business, so apparently it doesn't mean that he fancies you," goaded Felix with a loaded wink to all the others, which said they had all sensed the attraction between the pair of them. "Will you say yes, Miss Rowe?"

"Well . . . I . . . um . . ." As her entire face had combusted too, and as everyone, bar Harry, was enjoying it, she tried to act nonchalant as she snapped open her napkin. "Of course. I am always happy to step into the breach." She tried to smile without looking like a woman over the moon at the invitation. "How formal is it? Only—" She tried to make light of the odd new tension now hovering between them by flapping her hand at her clothes. "I came to Cawsand expecting to be a governess."

"Flora will have something we can make work with a substantial bit of hemming." Ada winked at her, enjoying Georgie's and Harry's discomfort immensely. "By the time I've finished with you, you'll be the belle of the ball."

The arrival of Tom, who had been gone all day, couldn't have come a moment too soon. "Oh, I see how it is. I'm a couple of minutes late and you're all content to leave me with the scraps on the table."

"Oh hush, we haven't even started yet," said his wife. "We were just discussing the fancy naval reception that Harry has just asked Georgie to attend with him tomorrow night." As subtle as a brick, she wiggled her brows suggestively. "After supper, Georgie and I are going pick out one of Flora's gowns so that she'll look *irresistible*."

"Lucky Harry." Tom sat, grinning, needing to say nothing more to let the pair of them know that he, too, was aware there was a frisson. "But speaking of Flora, she's finally sent a letter." He produced it and waved it in the air for all of two seconds before Ada snatched it.

"Finally! She has been very lax in writing!" She tore it open without reading exactly who it was addressed to and quickly scanned it.

"What does it say?" Marianne tried to grab it, but nosy Ada was too quick.

"It says that their sailing has been smooth so far and that Gibraltar was lovely." She ran a finger along the text. "And that she and your father decided to spend a few days in Rome rather than sail straight to Malta. That she's seen the Pantheon and the Colosseum and so many ancient Roman ruins she cannot begin to describe them and . . ." Ada frowned, then sighed. "But she missed her babies too much and so they have decided to scrap their plans to search for the source of the Nile, and are instead going to spend a few more days adventuring in Italy before they take the Friday sailing back to Tilbury for an extended visit to you in London."

"When was that letter dated?" Harry was frowning as if that was bad news.

"A week ago." Ada passed it to him. "She still thinks the children are at your house."

He read the letter himself, then passed it to the clamoring children, his expression disappointed, before he forced a smile. "Then, with fair seas, she's likely to arrive at Tilbury within days and most likely, once she realizes we are all here, will make it to Cawsand in another week or so." His gaze flicked to Georgie's, and the fake smile did nothing to cover the regret in his eyes. "It appears that you came all the way to Devon for just a few weeks, Georgie."

"So it does." She forced a smile too, sad beyond measure that their time was almost up. In case that sadness showed and they all realized it was mostly for Harry, she reached for the girls' hands. "We shall just have to make our last days together count then, shan't we?" She slanted him an overbright glance and swallowed hard when she saw nothing but sadness mirrored in his dark eyes. "Make it all about fun."

Harry forced a wry smile at that. "As opposed to what? Actual lessons at desks?"

"But we don't want you to leave!" Marianne nudged her brother. "Do we, Felix?"

"That is very nice of you to say, but we always knew my position here with you was only ever temporary."

"I am sure Mama would want you to stay!" Grace, bless her, was so convinced that even Ada nodded.

"I think she'd appreciate an extra pair of hands with these scallywags, so I daresay this won't have to be goodbye."

But it would still be a goodbye to him. Staying would only prolong the agony when he had to sail away in August anyway, and Georgie didn't think she could bear to be here without him. "Sadly, as tempting a prospect as that is, I am needed back at Miss Prentice's." When the children's faces fell, she tried to put her brave mask on. "But we shall obviously all write and when your uncle has some shore leave and you next visit him in London, the three of you can see me then." It would be too painful to venture back to Hanover Square or see him once they parted ways. If it wasn't a quick and clean cut, she would likely never get over what might have been. She knew that already, so in many ways this was for the best. So, so tragic—but very definitely for the best.

To avoid more speculation about them, Georgie and Harry kept up a steady stream of vibrant conversation for the rest of the meal. She waffled on about things she would do with the children in her final week, and he told tales of all the ports their parents had visited. Describing in great detail the exact height of Gibraltar and how long it had taken him to climb, and then fetching weighty tomes from the book-stuffed study so everyone could marvel at illustrations of the ruins scattered throughout Rome. He read to the children at bedtime while Ada rummaged through her mistress's wardrobe for a suitable gown. As she tried on dress after too-long dress, she could hear him along the landing, acting out the story. His deep, velvety voice was both a torment and a comfort, albeit one that she savored and consigned to memory now that she knew there were a finite number of days left to enjoy it.

By the time the housekeeper had finished with her, it was all the adults' bedtime too, so she said her good nights to Ada while Tom locked up the silent downstairs. As she opened her bedchamber door, Harry's opened opposite.

"Are you all right with that naval reception thing?" He was coatless, his cravat long gone and his waistcoat undone, the ever-present two pocket watches missing too. The informality of his attire somehow added to the peculiar intimacy of the whispered moment. "Because obviously, I appreciate it is highly improper, and if you'd rather not spend your evening listening to dry old navy lags and their bored, unhappy wives, I completely understand. I was going to ask you quietly—but of course . . . Marianne." He was anxious or nervous or both, because his usual elegant stillness had been replaced by a more animated Harry whose words were falling all over one another. "Anyway, it is honestly all right with me if you'd rather not and . . . um . . ." He raked an agitated hand through his already mussed hair, and that, too, was unusual when he rarely ever had one out of place. "I'm sorry." He threw up his palms. "For Marianne and Felix. For all the awful insinuations over dinner. For . . . well . . . for everything, I suppose." And there was the longing and sadness again. The disappointment. The resignation.

There seemed little point in making things more awkward, so she shrugged. "I've spent the last two hours being pinned and prodded, and as neither of us will ever hear the end of it from Ada otherwise, I am happy to come to that dull naval reception with you tomorrow. Will I see your ship?"

He shrugged. "Of course, if you want to."

"Of course I want to." It was technically the other woman between them, after all, and it seemed fitting to face that with the same accepting stoicism as she was their imminent goodbye. "Then I can brag, whenever your future feats of heroic derring-do are reported in the newspapers, that I had a private tour of the Royal Navy's most mighty flagship." If she kept things light, then this would be easier all around.

"Very well." Copying her breezy demeanor, he smiled. "Be waiting at the wall at seven tomorrow and I shall introduce you to the *Bane of My Life*."

"Not the bloody *Boadicea*?"

"I am practicing being a gentleman." His eyes dipped to her lips briefly before he tore them away. "Good night, Georgie."

---

*H*arry annoyed himself by checking his pocket watch for the third time. He was pretending to listen to Simpkins's list of things that needed to be done tomorrow if the finishing of the bloody *Boadicea* was going to continue at the punishing schedule he had set. Yet all he could think of was Georgie.

As it had felt too much like they were a courting couple to go fetch her himself, and he didn't want to appear anywhere near as eager as he was to spend an entire evening with her, he had dispatched Lieutenant Gregson to Cawsand to get her. To complete the illusion that he was supposed to be too busy for anything but the huge responsibility the Admiralty had placed on his shoulders, and because he was trying to keep his arse out of his too-tight dress breeches until he absolutely had to don them, he hadn't yet changed either.

Although this felt like a significant change in the timbre and direction of their relationship, it wasn't. She had been press-ganged into doing him a favor and he had a career and ship to focus on. Tonight was a fluke. And, as she had so deftly done with much more success than he had managed, he had to keep her at arm's length.

It made no difference that he had no clue if she was feeling as wretched about their imminent separation as he was. In fact, for the sake of his sanity and his career, it was probably best not to know. The temptation would be too much, and he did not trust himself to be able to resist it.

He was about to check his pocket watch again when Simpkins groaned. "There she is! Finally!" He pointed to the small naval boat picking its way through the crowded waters of the dockside. "We can go over all this tomorrow—when you are actually in the mood to listen." His right-hand man snapped closed his notebook, and he huffed. "I know I'm likely speaking out of turn, but we've been together a lot of years and . . . well, just be careful, is all. If this is scratching a mutual itch, I'll turn a blind eye. You and Georgie are adults . . ." He rolled his eyes as Harry bristled. "Just be mindful of what happened with the *Damysus*, that's all." The stark reminder of the first ship he had lost thanks to his failed romance with Elizabeth had him bristling even more. But not even his lethal glare was enough to stop Simpkins from stepping way over the line. "And be mindful that Georgie is a nice girl. It wouldn't be fair to break her heart."

As there really was nothing he could say to that except agree, Harry waved him away. "All duly noted." Just in time for Gregson to bring the boat containing her alongside.

Her hand emerged in greeting from the blanket she was fully swaddled in, so he waved back, trying not to run off his ship to go greet her properly. He still managed to get down the gangplank in time to be the one to help her up the steep stone steps, as he wanted to be the one to enjoy the feel of her hand in his, even if things couldn't go any further than that. "Welcome to His Majesty's Naval Dockyard, Plymouth." He motioned to the early evening sunshine still blazing low in the sky and then to her blanket. "Or were you expecting Norway?"

She laughed and his foolish heart was instantly lighter. "Says the man who has absolutely no idea of the horrors that my horrid hair is capable of in even the gentlest breeze." She carefully unwrapped the layers wrapped tight over her head and then smiled some more when the pretty hairstyle she revealed seemed to be intact. Only then did she discard the rest of the blanket, and his throat dried.

Good Lord, but she was beautiful! Breathtakingly so. The green silk gown was cut low, as was the fashion, but she filled that bodice spectacularly. So spectacularly Harry swore he heard every single sailor on the quay inhale along with him, then sigh the breath out. The rest of the fabric skimmed her curves as she stood, while her copper curls crackled in the sunlight.

"Allow me," said an obviously bewitched Gregson as he helped her to the steps, and when her petite legs struggled to clear the height required between the edge of the boat, the wretch almost lifted her out. His subordinate seemed most aggrieved when Harry jumped into the boat to do that himself. He sincerely hoped that nobody noticed how hard he found it to release her once his hands had spanned her trim waist, before he led her up the steps.

Her eyes were everywhere as she took in the dock, and then she blinked at the sheer size of the ship. "Is that the . . ."

"Bloody *Boadicea*?" His whisper was proprietorial and just for her because every single man was openly staring now, and he wanted them to know that she was his. At least for the purposes of tonight. "Yes, it is. As we have at least half an hour before the carriage comes to collect us, allow me to give you the tour."

He led her up the gangplank, then could not resist lifting her again over the rail, even though she undoubtedly could have managed on her own. Then, because every man on deck paused what they were doing to gaze at her with appreciation, he offered her his arm.

Again, it was as proprietorial as it was instinctive, never mind that having her on his arm felt far too good than was sensible.

She asked a hundred questions as he showed her around, to both Harry and the instantly bewitched sailors and shipwrights still on board, and made all the appropriate sounds an impressed person would make as she ran her fingers over this and that. But the charming wrinkle on her nose hinted that she wasn't completely seduced by this grand ship either, and that made him smile. Georgie's good opinion wasn't won easily and he liked that about her.

Twenty minutes, six decks, and all one hundred twenty guns later, and they were almost back where they started on the main deck, exploring the stern of the ship. "And what lies behind this impressive door?" She touched the ostentatious gilded emblem in the center of it, undoubtedly finding all the military pomp a little ridiculous.

"The captain's cabin." Without considering the appropriateness of it, he flung open the door and ushered her inside, where they were both immediately confronted by the most inappropriate thing currently on the ship.

His bed.

# TWENTY-SEVEN

𝒩 o sooner had he let go of it and the door slammed closed behind them than Georgie watched him wince. "The doors are designed to stay closed in choppy conditions and I didn't think this part of the tour through, did I?"

"Which bit?" She gestured to the mattress with a nervous laugh, where his dress uniform, including a fresh pair of drawers, was laid out. "The fact that I am suddenly in your bedchamber unchaperoned, or the fact that every single member of your crew doubtless thinks that we are already up to no good in it?"

"I'm sorry, Georgie. If we leave right this second . . ."

She laughed at that. She couldn't help it, as he looked every inch the mortified and admonished little boy. "As I am unlikely to ever see any of your crew ever again, I sincerely doubt my reputation is in any jeopardy. Not that anyone really cares about a lowly governess's reputation anyway, so I wouldn't worry." Although in this beautiful, borrowed gown and sporting Ada's rather pretty coiffure that was threaded with silk flowers, she felt more like a princess than a servant. Cinderella for just one night, so she was determined to thoroughly enjoy this uncharacteristic foray into the world of the privileged rather than watching it from the periphery. "And on that score, I assume I am *not* your employee tonight but a . . . what?"

"Obviously you are my besotted sweetheart, as I have my own reputation to protect." He grinned, then cringed, all charmingly awkward and uncertain again. "If you don't mind playing that part, that is?"

"Again, I shall remind you that as I am never going to see any of these people again, and even if I do, they will not see me because I shall have turned back into a governess by then—and therefore be invisible—so I can be whoever you want me to be. Do you have a reputation as a lady's man?" Not that she needed to ask, because he was, devil take him, precisely the sort who would attract women in droves. Both Lottie and Portia had taken leave of their senses at his attractiveness before he had given away anything of his kind heart and charming, self-effacing nature.

He laughed at her teasing tone, folding his arms cockily. "It wouldn't be gentlemanly to say. I do, however, have a reputation for always having the most beautiful woman on my arm, so at least that will remain intact."

*Had he just called her beautiful?*

*Her!*

As she was internally melting and was determined not to swoon in a puddle at his feet, she kept her tone light. "And am I besotted because we have been courting long, or am I simply the latest in a long line of besotted sweethearts? We should both be singing off the same hymn sheet if we are going to be believable."

His smile was more amused now than awkward. "Long enough to be gloriously overfamiliar, but not quite long enough for a betrothal, as that might prove difficult to explain away later."

"Are you as besotted with me as I am with you?" She hoped that sounded nonchalant rather than needy as she flicked a finger at his smart navy-and-gold coat. "Or am I one of those silly girls who is too enamored of an impressive uniform that she doesn't care overmuch what is inside it? Only I have to be honest, I might struggle to act *that* much."

"I think I can guarantee that I shall, from time to time, regard you with longing this evening." His expression was ironic, but his eyes—his dark, stormy eyes—told her that despite their intended ruse tonight, he liked what he saw. "And I probably won't be acting." Knowledge that made her a little giddy.

"Well, I . . ." The curt rap on the door startled.

"The carriage is here." Simpkins opened the door without waiting to be asked and gave Harry a murderous glare as held out his hand. "I'll entertain Georgie while you stuff yourself into your glad rags." He claimed her briskly and whisked her back out onto the deck.

"As I'm guessing you've never been to a fancy naval shindig before, use your cutlery from outside to in, only ever pass the port to the left and never across the table."

"Why?"

"Nobody really knows but they'll get very annoyed if you do it wrong. While you're passing it, whatever you do, don't let the decanter touch the tablecloth." Simpkins gave her a warning look in case she was tempted to ask why again. "When it's toasting time, never toast with an empty glass 'cause that's bad luck, and as it's Saturday, the final toast will be to wives and sweethearts, to which you should reply with '*May they never meet.*' You got all that?"

"To the left without touching the table, no empty glass, and may they never meet."

He winked at her. "And be your usual outspoken self, Georgie, and you'll do just fine."

True to his word, Simpkins kept her company until Harry emerged from his cabin resplendent in braid, his big hat set at a jaunty, rakish angle that suited him too much. "Shall we?" He waggled his arm and she took it, then felt the eyes of the entire ship follow them until they set off in the carriage.

———————

*A*dmiralty House sat atop a hill with stunning views of the Plymouth Sound. In deference to the clement June weather, the guests mingled first on the terrace rather than inside. The setting sun picked out the shimmering braid worn by the gentlemen and all the jewels dripping from their companions, making Georgie glad that Ada had nagged her into swapping her mother's unfussy locket for the borrowed but thankfully expensive-looking gems currently adorning her neck. The faux emerald necklace and matching earrings went some way toward making her feel less self-conscious amongst all this overt finery, but no less out of her depth when every other person was *Lord This* and *Lady That* and they all seemed to know one another. Georgie had been introduced to so many illustrious people, she held out little hope that she would remember more than a quarter of those names by the time they all sat down for dinner.

To his credit, her escort did his best to make her feel included, and for that she was grateful. He also tried to quietly tell her who was who and what was what in the few moments they had alone together since arriving, but the constant stream headed his way made it difficult to do anything other than smile politely. She had known that Harry was an important man within the navy but had no concept of exactly how important until she had seen him here. In his element.

Older and clearly higher-ranking men with yards more golden thread on their tunics slapped his back and pumped his hand as if he were the prodigal son. His contemporaries, to a man, all seemed both impressed and envious of his success. The *Boadicea*, especially, was mentioned in nothing but awed tones, confirming what Georgie had worked out already the second she had set eyes on that dratted ship— that being its captain was a rare and exalted honor.

"Hello, Henry."

At the feminine voice from behind, his arm stiffened beneath Georgie's fingers. Then stiffened some more when he turned to smile at the woman. It was an odd smile. A tad disingenuous mixed with a hint of discomfort.

"*Elizabeth*." There was history between him and this stunningly beautiful blonde. Troubled and, for Georgie, as he anchored her to him more firmly, oddly troubling history. "How are you?"

The blonde's smile was tinged with similar awkwardness and something that resembled regret. "I cannot complain. I am glad to be home from dreary Canada. We've been stuck there a whole year and it's just so cold." Her elegant hand flicked toward an older officer festooned with rope and braid several yards behind, and Harry stiffened some more. "Thankfully, we and the children are home again for the foreseeable. Did you know that we now have two boys?"

He shook his head. "I didn't. Congratulations."

"Yes . . . twins. They will be four in September." By the way the muscles in his arms clenched, the timing of that was also significant. As if she knew it too, the blonde looked almost . . . guilty. That didn't stop her from artfully batting her eyelashes or running her fingertips idly along the straining edge of her bodice. She was a woman who knew exactly how attractive she was to the opposite sex and used it as a weapon. "But where are our manners?" She turned her gaze to

Georgie, assessing her in that way that only women did to other rival women, over-scrutinizing her naked fingers with interest before she smiled. "Are you going to introduce us, Henry dear?"

*Henry?* If there was indeed history between these two, why on earth was this woman calling him by a name he never used himself?

"Of course . . ." Galvanized into action, his whole demeanor was as overbright as the elegant blonde's, making Georgie wonder what it was they were both overcompensating for. "Georgie, this is Lady Elizabeth Barrett-Hughes, wife of Vice Admiral Lord Francis Barrett-Hughes. Elizabeth, this is Miss Georgina Rowe. My . . . um . . ." He squeezed Georgie's arm intently, although she did not understand the message until he next spoke. "Fiancée."

"Congratulations," said Lady Elizabeth with forced gaiety as her gaze locked with Harry's. As odd emotions were swirling in both of their eyes, Georgie instantly felt excluded. Jealous, even, but she masked it with a beam of her own as she loyally embellished his lie.

"Thank you. I am still getting used to it, as it has all happened so suddenly." She did her best impression of a woman beaming at her man in adoration. "It was so spur of the moment, he has yet to give me a ring." As the woman had already clocked her hands, some explanation seemed necessary.

"Knowing Henry, it will be worth waiting for. He always did have excellent taste. Especially in jewelry." The blonde touched her earlobe to let Georgie know that Harry had purchased the delicate rubies dangling from it, and doubtless to let him know that she still wore his love tokens. "How long will you be in Plymouth?"

"I set sail in August." He rested his hand over Georgie's, still nestled in the crook of his elbow. "So we are making the most of the time we have left. We'd like to marry before then, if we can get everything organized in time. Isn't that right, my darling?"

"There is always Gretna Green." She smiled at him soppily, still too unsettled at the sublime casualness of the word *darling* to care overmuch that he hadn't meant it. "If we left tonight, we could be back in two weeks."

"You know what they say about marrying in haste." Lady Elizabeth could not resist dashing cold water on their apparent happiness, and that spoke volumes about her character. "It rarely works out well." Her blue eyes locked with Harry's as she said that, then drifted to her husband. "But then again, few military marriages ever work out well, so—"

"Elizabeth!" From a few feet away, the vice admiral crooked his finger as he positively glared at Harry. "Lady Nugent is desirous of an audience and she has been kept waiting long enough."

"Duty calls," said Lady Elizabeth with no attempt to disguise her obvious displeasure at her husband's rude summons—or perhaps of him in general. She then reached out to squeeze Harry's hand, which sent her husband's eyes narrowing. "It was good to see you again, Henry. *Really* good."

Georgie bobbed her head politely as they watched her disappear, and her tense companion exhaled.

"Am I allowed to ask what all that was about?" She gave him a loaded look of her own. "I am apparently your betrothed, after all, *Henry*."

"Thank you for not contradicting me." He gave her an embarrassed half smile. "I promised myself I would be cool, calm, and collected when I collided with her tonight. Unbothered and nonplussed, then promptly fell at the first hurdle and panicked."

"Why?"

"Because Elizabeth was once *my* fiancée. She would have been my wife now too if I hadn't had orders to sail away. By the time I returned, expecting her to still be my fiancée, she had already gone up in the world to become Lady Barrett-Hughes instead."

His gaze wandered to the beautiful blonde and lingered, and instantly Georgie hated the woman. "She didn't even have the decency to write to me about it, so as I am sure you can imagine, it came as quite a shock when my ship docked here again just six weeks after our last tearful farewell." His dark brows furrowed as he wrenched his gaze away to laugh without humor.

"Oh, Harry." She hugged his arm, feeling petty for her jealousy now. "I'm so sorry."

"Now that I come to think on it, she never returned the ring I gave her either. Even after the massive scene I caused on her new doorstep too." He huffed, shaking his head. "With hindsight, not my finest hour, and one of those moments in life you always regret and wish you had dealt with differently."

As the callous witch was watching them, Georgie took the lazy liberty of neatening one of his watch chains in a wifely manner. "If it's any consolation, you handled just now rather well. She would have never known how uncomfortable you were."

"But you did?" He slanted her a glance. "So I now have that to add to my impressive collection of cringeworthy moments that should have been handled better."

"I am hardly going to judge you for a broken heart when I was once convinced you didn't even possess such an organ."

"You were?"

"I found you nine-tenths disagreeable back then."

"And now?"

"You hover between a six and a seven, so obviously there is still plenty of room for improvement." She nudged him playfully, oddly humbled that he had entrusted her with something so intensely personal while internally jealous that he still clearly harbored some feelings for the duplicitous blonde. "But despite the glaring fact that you remain at least three-tenths insufferable, now that I know what she did to you, it goes without saying that as your loyal employee and your friend, I hate her with the fire of a thousand suns. And in that vein, I shall work doubly hard tonight to convince her that not only was her loss my gain, but that you are so over her that you are now of the opinion that she actually did you a favor with her social climbing treachery."

As he was back to watching the woman who had got away with an odd expression on his face, Georgie watched her too. She was all smiles for Lady Nugent, but they instantly melted when her husband's hand touched her elbow. "Although if it is any consolation, it is obvious that she bitterly regrets her choices now. Imagine being shackled with that pompous, old sourpuss for all eternity? Vice Admiral Barrett-Hughes doesn't look like an easy man to love."

"And I am?" Harry's eyes searched hers intently. In case he saw that she was riddled with more irrational jealousy for that woman than she already harbored for his magnificent ship, and was likely well on the way to being more than a little bit in love with him, she grinned and hoped it looked convincing.

"Cuthbert certainly thinks so and, as my dear, incorrigible friend Lottie always says, dogs are never wrong."

⁓⁖⁓

*H*ello again, Henry."

Elizabeth appeared out of nowhere in the deserted hall-way within seconds of Harry leaving Admiral Nugent and the select few invited to a back room for more port and cigars.

"Hello again, Elizabeth." He paused mid-step out of ingrained politeness despite his urgent desire to find Georgie and leave.

He hadn't had a bad night, which surprised him when he had been dreading this reception for the precise reason stood before him, and that was all down to the wonderful woman who had agreed to come with him. Georgie had made it all rather fun, especially after he and his former fiancée had originally collided, and because she was incapable of curbing her tongue or hiding her opinions, she had been an entertaining dinner companion. She had certainly charmed Nugent, who had sparred with the vixen for the duration of the meal, and laughed riotously throughout as a result. He had even slapped Harry's back heartily as he had made his excuses to escape from the port and cigars and told him that he quite understood his need for haste, as he'd be in a hurry to get back to that intriguing minx if she were his too.

Except Georgie wasn't his and that felt wrong. Almost as wrong as Elizabeth waylaying him like this. His duplicitous former fiancée always had a particular look about her when she wanted something and right now, it raised all his hackles. Whatever she was up to, it was probably best to face it head-on.

"I hope you weren't waiting for me?"

"I was, actually." She ran her bottom lip through her teeth. "I wanted to apologize for what I did to you all those years ago."

Better late than never, he supposed, even though he could never forgive her for it. "It's all water under the bridge." He brushed it aside, relieved to know that despite his absentee forgiveness, it actually was.

It was odd. He had been dreading seeing her again after so long, and dreaded his own reaction to her more. But now that both were over and done with, the experience had been cathartic. Like a lurking foe, vanquished.

Yes, he had been every bit as self-conscious as he expected to be after all the futile and pathetic begging he had done that last time in his attempts to win her back. But he was also relieved to discover that his broken heart had not only fully healed—it was indifferent. Elizabeth no longer held any part of it.

In fact, without those lust-fogged, rose-tinted lenses clouding his vision, he realized that Elizabeth had always cared too much for the superficial in life, and her shallow conversations had, if he were honest, always bored him.

Her affectations irritated too. The practiced eyelash-flapping and unsubtle bosom-caressing, which had once drawn him like a moth to a flame, were two cases in point. They were mantraps she used with calculation to control the fools who fell for them, whereas

Georgie was oblivious of her allure, and that was so much more alluring a trait.

With the brutal clarity of hindsight, he could also now see that he had been superficial and shallow back then too. Elizabeth had been an obvious trophy here in Plymouth all those years ago when he had actively been collecting them. Widely considered the most beautiful woman in this small coastal city, he had wanted her because all his peers did, and hubris was no foundation to build a forever on. And while there wasn't a hot-blooded male at this reception who didn't envy the beautiful, vivacious redhead he had brought, he wanted Georgie first and foremost because she called to his soul.

"I never should have married Francis. You and I were always . . ." She ran her fingers along his sleeve. "So much better suited. Francis was a mistake."

He had a funny feeling he knew where this was headed, but wanted the satisfaction of the confirmation and the closure it would bring. "I am sorry to hear that—but as you rightly said earlier, if you marry in haste, you get to repent at leisure."

"At least I have given him two sons, so we no longer have to pretend to like one another." Her bold fingers grazed the back of his hand this time. "That also gives me much more freedom . . ."

Good grief! She was actually going there? "Freedom to do what?" As she had always thought all men idiots—including him—he decided to play dumb. For sport. And perhaps petty revenge.

"To take a discreet lover, if I wanted." She stared up at him from beneath her lashes like the practiced, selfish flirt that she was. "I haven't felt the urge before—but now that you are back in Plymouth and your grandfather isn't around to meddle in our affairs . . ." For good measure, she slowly licked her upper lip. "My husband and your fiancée need never know."

It amused Harry that absolutely nothing stirred within his too-tight dress breeches when throughout the formal dinner he had been in complete agony. Only a part of that was caused by the damned breeches cutting into his backside. The rest was because of Georgie seated opposite who, without any effort whatsoever, made him so rampant with need that he had been ready to explode. "Thank you for that . . . um . . . kind offer—but no thanks."

He took great pleasure in extricating his hand from her grip. "I am head over heels in love with Georgie and I am afraid she is now the only woman on the planet I want." Even as he said it, he realized the truth of it. Accepted it and simultaneously regretted it. "It was nice to see you again, Elizabeth." At least in the sense that he could now consign their regrettable interlude firmly to the past, where it belonged.

———————

*G*eorgie knew he had returned to the reception room because the air seemed to shift around her, but she forced herself to continue her conversation with Lady Nugent rather than look.

"Of course we all knew that he and Lady Elizabeth were a match made in hell." It was clear the admiral's wife disliked Harry's former fiancée intensely, as she had sought Georgie out expressly to reassure her she shouldn't allow "that horrid woman's" presence to bother her. "Elizabeth was always on the lookout for opportunities to elevate her position and there was no way she was going to settle for a mere lieutenant if there was the merest sniff of anyone with more stripes on the horizon. We were all vastly relieved for Harry when she found Barrett-Hughes. They are both so self-absorbed and selfish, they are perfect for one another."

The wonderfully indiscreet older woman leaned in to whisper.

"And between the pair of them, they always give the rest of us something to gossip about. He seems to have more mistresses than most people have hot dinners and I daresay there aren't many officers present who haven't been invited to sample her charms. In fact, the last time Francis sailed away, the running joke was that there was a permanent stepladder from the pavement to her bedchamber window and she wasn't too particular who she allowed up it."

"No!" The more she heard about Lady Elizabeth, the more Georgie pitied Harry for loving her. Not that she knew for certain that he still loved her, but he had. Once. That was enough to make her loathe the witch for all eternity.

"Oh yes, my dear—it all goes on in the navy." Lady Nugent spoke behind her fan this time. "There was also an ongoing affair with one of her husband's subordinates that ended in fisticuffs on the quayside. In broad daylight and in front of the entire dockyard. Barrett-Hughes accused the man of seducing his wife, and then the officer turned the tables and accused Barrett-Hughes of seducing his wife first. They were all at it! And worse, the younger officer practically bellowed from the rooftops that the only reason he tupped the strumpet in the first place was to get revenge on her predatory husband for impregnating his wife!"

"No," said Georgie again as her neck began to tingle with awareness. "That's outrageous." Then because she couldn't resist knowing, she asked, "*Did* he impregnate her?"

"Indeed he did!" Lady Nugent threw her head back and laughed. "With another set of twins! Then, the fathers of another three sets of Plymouth Dockyard twins—because we had had a bit of an unusual spate of them—all began to question the paternity of their own offspring and then there was more fisticuffs. The Barrett-Hugheses' mutual philandering caused such a scandal, my husband had to send the pair of them to Newfoundland for a year just to stop all the wav-

ing fists and wagging tongues. Yet the arrogant fool wonders why he
hasn't been promoted in years! When to be honest, it's a miracle he
hasn't been demoted!"

Her new friend winked as she saw Harry approach. "Elizabeth
must be spitting feathers to see you on his arm now. She likes to think
she is unforgettable, and you only have to see how Captain Kincaid
looks at you to see that she has been completely forgotten."

"Did I just hear my name said in vain?" He arrived smiling and
effortlessly delicious. As usual.

"You might have done," said Lady Nugent, unrepentant, "but
listeners never hear any good of themselves and your delightful new
*fiancée* has been sworn to secrecy on the subject." She nudged Georgie. "For my sins, as the hostess, I must go mingle with the rest of
this dreary crowd, so I shall leave you with your handsome beau and
a friendly tip that the terrace is lovely when the moon is full—and
likely quite deserted at this time of night." Then she winked at him.
"Oh, what a gift it is to be young and in love. Savor every single moment you have together, as it isn't easy being a sailor's wife."

They watched her leave before he quirked one dark brow. "Are
you going to tell me what that was about?"

"Not in a million years. How were your exclusive port and cigars?"

"Stuffy."

"Would you like to go out to the terrace for some fresh air?"

"I'd rather go home—unless you wish to stay, of course?"

The prospect of sailing across the Sound with him under the stars
made her pulse quicken. It was such a romantic thing to do, even if
no romance was on the cards. "Home it is, then. Give me a second to
fetch my shawl from . . ." She gestured toward the dining room where
she had left it.

He nodded, swiftly sat to wait, and then froze as the air was
punctuated by the unmistakable sound of ripping fabric.

His eyes instantly widened with alarm. "Oh dear." He reached his hand beneath his hip and groaned. "Marvelous."

"Was that your . . . ?"

"Yes. And all the way from the waistband to the unmention-ables. I am also *so* glad that I made the stupid decision not to add to the discomfort of my too-tight dress breeches by stuffing them further with a thin layer of underwear."

"So you're . . . ?"

He nodded, but Harry being Harry, he saw the funny side. "What a treat it will be for everyone to watch me leave this fine soiree with my entire bare arse hanging out. Such a boost to my fragile ego, too, as I get to do it in front of some of my *favorite* people, because frankly, I haven't been humiliated enough." He flicked his gaze toward Lady Elizabeth, who was positively glaring at the pair of them from across the room.

"I'll get you out with your dignity intact." Georgie didn't know how yet, but she would think of something. "Give me a moment."

She half walked, half sprinted to the dining room, collected her shawl, and then returned. "How well does your coat cover it?"

He gingerly stood so that she could take a peek. "Well?"

"Um . . ." He twisted and she got a flash of enough pert buttock that it made her mouth dry. "It is perfectly decent when you keep still but I worry the moment you start to walk or encounter a breeze, the cutaway in the tails will disgrace you." She offered him a sympathetic smile. "We could tie my shawl around your waist."

He stared at the floral lace confection in disgust. "And announce to the entire room that I've got so big for my dress breeches that they actually exploded? Where's the dignity in that?"

"I could walk directly behind you and act as a shield."

"Won't that look odd?"

"Probably—but at least nobody will see your bare arse." Georgie tilted her head toward the terrace, trying not to snigger. "If we sneak out the back, Lady Nugent did say the terrace was deserted and look at the bright side . . ." Her lips began to twitch. "At least this will give you an excuse to explain away why you called off our engagement when the time comes."

"It will?"

"Absolutely. You can tell everyone I was far too clingy—and they'll believe it because they witnessed it with their own eyes."

hey set off, Harry supremely conscious of the cold draft whistling up the exposed crack in his bottom and Georgie practically plastered to his thighs. Both of them doing their best to convey
that there was absolutely nothing untoward going on at all as they
picked a tightly knit path through the crowd.

Of course, everyone stopped them. His peers wanted to congrat-
ulate him on the *Boadicea* and, because gossip always spread like
wildfire in the navy, on his recent and sudden engagement. They
were only halfway to the terrace when Admiral Nugent reappeared
and beckoned them over, and then, because his wife had only just
told him the good news, he pressed glasses of champagne into their
hands.

Before Harry could stop him, the admiral called the room to
order. "A little bird has just told me that Captain Kincaid's charming
companion has taken leave of her senses and agreed to be his wife!"
Nugent raised his glass high in the air. "Three cheers for the happy
couple! Hip hip!"

"*Hoorah!*" shouted the room in unison as Harry gripped Georgie's hand in apology.

"When is the wedding?" shouted a commodore in the crowd.

"Well . . . we . . . um . . . ?" This was all getting out of hand very quickly and he had no clue how to make it stop. "Next year. There are obviously lots of plans to make and—"

"Next year!" Lady Nugent flapped that aside. "When you are sailing away in six weeks for goodness knows how long! No, indeed. That will not do when all the wives here will happily help Georgie with the plans." Then she apparently had an epiphany. "Better still, we shall relieve her of the entire chore, isn't that right, ladies?"

That elicited squeals of agreement from every woman present, bar Elizabeth, whose lips were so pursed she looked ready to blow on a trumpet. Pettily, that was the only part of the debacle he found some enjoyment in.

"That is such a generous offer," said Georgie, gripping his hand behind his back for all she was worth while her body still protected his modesty. "But obviously I will need to consult with my own family before I accept it." Not only were they now engaged, but she had miraculously grown a family. "They would want us to do the deed in London, wouldn't they, Harry?" She jabbed him in the back, willing him to save them.

"They'd have us hanged, drawn, and quartered if we didn't."

"I actually have to head back to London next week . . ." She jabbed him again, as if he needed any reminder at all that as soon as blasted Flora returned, she'd be gone. "So I don't think it would be sensible to make any sort of plans until I . . . um . . . return." Which of course she wouldn't, and then he'd have to come up with another lie to explain why their hasty engagement had been called off.

*Good grief.*

It suddenly dawned on him that because of one ill-judged response to his first fiancée, he was soon doomed to go down in naval history as the only man to lose two fiancées within days of proposing to them! Once was unfortunate, especially when he'd been stupid enough to propose to Elizabeth, but twice suggested he was the problem. Especially as Georgie had gone down a storm here tonight. She had Nugent and his wife eating out of her dainty little hand. To prove that, Lady Nugent pouted.

"Fiddlesticks! And I was so looking forward to accompanying you to the modiste's tomorrow, Georgie. But we also have to return to London shortly, so we could just as easily go to the modiste's there. Madam Devy is the absolute best and she owes me many favors." The light of excitement reignited in her eyes. "With your mother of course."

Georgie pinched his side this time, as if to say *This is your mess, fix it.*

"Well, that isn't going to work either as my sister would murder me if I allowed Georgie to go to the modiste's without her. You all remember Flora, don't you?" Harry pulled a face at his comrades. "She can be terrifying." A couple of men in the audience nodded, as Flora had never been one to pull her punches when a sailor was foolish enough to make a pass at her. "You are going to have to postpone all plans until my sister returns from her travels and Georgie returns here to Plymouth." Before Lady Nugent asked when that was going to be, he wafted what he hoped was a firm hand. "Now if you will excuse us, I am afraid my darling fiancée needs some air, so I must escort her to the terrace."

Another stupid lie he forgot to think fully through and one that elicited a roomful of winking, whistling, and vocalized sailor-salted innuendo that he was going to have to make a groveling apology to Georgie for the moment he got her outside.

"We were actually headed for the terrace before the admiral waylaid us." Georgie shifted positions to stand almost beside him and had miraculously managed to do something to her face to make it look pale and wan. "I've been a little under the weather all day, but I think the short sail from Cawsand proved my undoing." Her stoic but wavering smile was suitably tragic. "It's ironic that I am about to marry a sailor when sailing doesn't agree with me in the slightest."

"Oh, you poor dear." Lady Nugent bustled over to take her temperature with her palm. "You do feel a little clammy. You know what they always say about seasickness. You spend the first day of it terrified that it is going to kill you and the second petrified that it isn't. Ginger helps. I'll get the kitchen to put some in some tea for you."

"There is really no need." Keen to escape before they were forced into more lies, Harry decided to be decisive. "Fresh air always works best for Georgie, doesn't it, my darling." And she really was a darling even if she wasn't his.

"It is very warm in here," said Georgie in a faraway voice as she leaned her entire weight against him and his aerated breeches as she clutched at his waist, subtly pushing him forward in case he had a mind to linger. "I am so sorry to be such a bother, Lady Nugent."

"Clear a path!" The admiral's wife dashed ahead of them, wielding her fan like a sword, and the crowd parted between them and the French doors like the Red Sea.

As soon as they were through them, and after Harry had reassured their hostess that he really did not need her assistance any longer, they walked sedately until they were out of sight of the party. Him acting like the most concerned escort and her looking as though she could faint at any moment.

"Well, that went from bad to worse rapidly, didn't it?"

She was laughing. Giggling, in fact. It was such a delicious sound that it was infectious.

"I'm sorry. I panicked, yet again, and didn't even consider the consequences." He raked a hand through his hair, realizing that he had left his hat at the reception, and huffed. "The whole world and his wife now think that we are engaged. The crew on the *Boadicea* think that I ruined you in my cabin, and next week, I've got to lie through my back teeth yet again and come up with a suitable reason to explain why you left me."

"It was the pocket watches." She flicked one and that made her giggle more. "I felt that I couldn't compete with either of them."

"That will do wonders for my shredded dignity, I am sure." He supposed the two watches were ridiculous.

"At least nobody saw your backside, so every cloud . . ." She collapsed with laughter again as she wandered behind him to inspect the damage. A combination of the sea breeze hitting his bare bottom and her lifting the back of his coat to take a look at it raised goosebumps on his flesh.

"Oh good heavens above, Harry, that really is quite some tear. No patch is going to fix that damage." She had tears of mirth in her eyes as she handed him her shawl. "If you don't cover it up, you'll be arrested for indecency before we get to the dock." Then she snorted, as if she hadn't found anything quite so funny in a very long time. "But at least the daisies on the shawl will match the ones on your boat. Few men suit a daisy, but bizarrely"—she clutched her ribs and roared some more—"you do."

"You're enjoying this, aren't you?"

She nodded as she swiped the tears away. "I cannot wait to tell Lottie. She will be very jealous she was denied the chance of seeing your naked bottom, as she could barely speak after she saw you bare-chested in the bath."

<hr/>

*H*arry had always found sailing on a gentle sea under the stars sublime, but to do it with Georgie was magical. She had rarely been on the water, and so saw everything as a wondrous adventure. She stared, entranced, as he picked out key constellations, soaking it all in while idly trailing her fingers in the waves lapping against the hull, seemingly oblivious of how utterly beautiful she looked now that the wind had freed her wild curls from their pins.

As he had since he arrived back in Plymouth, he used the stranded *Siren* to navigate, and they both waved at the trio of sailors smoking pipes on the dimly lit upper deck. "I feel sorry for them. They've run out of money. Hence they are stuck here."

As Harry turned the rudder, she grabbed the side as the little sloop bounced across a flurry of waves caused by the strong under-water current. "How does a big ship like that run out of money?"

"Pure mismanagement when any oceangoing vessel can com-mand ten pounds a tun for cargo."

"Ten pounds a tun!" Her lovely jaw dropped. "Half my yearly salary, you mean." Her nose wrinkled as she stared over her shoulder at the ship. "How many tuns can she hold?"

He glanced back at the ship himself to estimate. "A good two hundred. Maybe two-fifty. Clearly, her captain is an idiot." He mimed drinking. "Likes his rum and his gambling too much, by all ac-counts."

"If you taught me how to be a captain, I'd take his job in a heart-beat." She stared covetously for a moment. "Two thousand pounds a voyage appeals to me."

"You'd need to learn to sail first." Before he could stop it, the little devil inside him piped up. "If you'd like, I could give you your first lesson tonight."

"Really?" Her wide smile took his breath away. "I'd love that!"

He shuffled over, not caring that he was likely making a reckless mistake as she squeezed her lush body beside him, then wrapped his arm around her so he could teach her how to use the rudder without them veering wildly off course. "You see that light over there?" He pointed to the stubby lighthouse that sat on Tor Point. "Aim there until I tell you otherwise."

She did, and as she began to get a feel for the boat, he loosened his grip on it but not his hold on her. She didn't need him to—Georgie was too spirited and independent to need anyone's support—but he needed to hold her.

"It's pulling." Her nose wrinkled in concentration.

"Of course it's pulling. That's the Channel current you can feel now that we're a long way from the harbor."

"If it's this strong on a calm summer's night, I dread to think what it's like in a winter storm."

"Man marks the earth with ruin, but his control stops with the shore." He subtly sniffed her hair because her perfume mingled with the salty air was suddenly his favorite scent.

"Who was that? Nelson?" She smiled without removing her fixed gaze from the light ahead. "Drake? Atilla the Hun?"

"Byron, actually. Despite his lack of any military wisdom, those words resonate. You have to keep your wits about you on the waves, where the tide can turn on a sixpence and every raging tempest could be your last."

"Profound. And poetic. Byron too?"

"No. All me, for once. I am the son of a failed poet, after all, despite my two pocket watches. Now bring her gently starboard." He couldn't resist cuddling her closer while he redirected her, chuckling at her baffled expression. "Starboard is right, Georgie. Turn her right and aim for that low light over there. Do you see it?" He used his finger to angle her chin. "That's the seawall at Cawsand."

"We're almost home?" She sounded disappointed, as if she, like he, never wanted tonight to end. She twisted and their eyes met, and because it felt like the most natural thing in the moment, Harry didn't even hesitate before he kissed her.

She sighed against his mouth as she kissed him back. It was an unhurried, gentle, and leisurely exploration that lasted at least a minute before their boat bounced on a rogue wave and reminded them of the looming beach. Neither did they speak as their lips parted and he shifted position to lower the sail.

She shuffled over so he could man the rudder for the tricky maneuvers necessary to get them safely where they needed to be. Waited while he tied off the boat, allowed him to help her off it, and then, seeing as that one kiss clearly wasn't enough, came willingly into his arms as he tugged her closer.

Harry couldn't resist twirling his finger in her untamed hair, marveling in its texture and the way the moonlight picked out certain strands before he pressed his lips to hers.

Still, neither of them hurried. Their next kiss was as gentle as the filmy wash that lapped the sand, and somehow all the more potent as a result. He felt her desire as plainly as she doubtless felt his pressing against her belly, yet in tacit agreement, they both respected the immovable boundary of their circumstances and held their passions back. As if they both realized that this kiss, like their relationship, was a transient, temporary escape from their real lives and responsibilities.

Because it felt fitting, he linked his fingers in hers as they slowly wandered up the silent dark and winding roads toward the house. Pausing here and there for another final kiss goodbye. Another taste of what might have been, if he wasn't him and she wasn't her and fate hadn't such atrocious timing.

When they reached the gate, he kissed her again, and because they both knew it had to be the last, the timbre of it changed. Tongues and teeth and hands frantically explored all those parts they knew they weren't supposed to in the shadow of the house. He cupped her breasts, her bottom.

She cupped his—through the tear so that skin finally touched skin—and moaned as he hoisted her skirts up. Parted her legs so that he could caress her intimately. Dip his finger inside her.

So soft.

So warm.

So . . .

"Harry? That you?" Tom's frantic holler from the porch had them jumping apart seconds before they were illuminated in the soft glow of his lamp. "Thank the Lord!" Oblivious of what he had just interrupted, he hollered behind him. "They're back, Ada!"

"Oh, thank the Lord!" Ada's muffled response was typically theatrical. "Then make haste, Thomas!" He dashed back inside, plunging them into darkness again, save only for the moonlight above.

"That doesn't sound good." Georgie's breasts fell in time with her erratic breathing and she looked every inch a woman who had been thoroughly ravished. Her hair was a riot. Her lips swollen. Her dress hopelessly creased. His fingers still damp with the dew from her body. His body so consumed with desire for her, it frightened him.

"Knowing Ada, it's a storm in a teacup." They hurried toward the house while Harry tried to ignore the excruciating discomfort of his nether regions. Even with their new ventilation, and thanks entirely to his straining, rock-hard cock taking up every last bit of give, his damned breeches were now strangling him. Their feet had barely hit the front step when Tom flew out the door again and almost knocked Georgie over.

"Sorry!" He disappeared around the side of the house carrying two big bags which, if the subsequent sounds were any gauge, were tossed into a cart. "Rebecca is in labor." Then he was gone again, leaving them to follow.

Indoors, Ada was in a panic. "Thank goodness you are both home as I didn't want to have to drive myself all the way to Hessenford in the dark and leave Tom here with the children!" She shoved another bag at her husband and then began to wrestle her arms into her coat. "The young 'uns are in bed and there's plenty of food in the pantry. If all goes smoothly tonight, we'll be back tomorrow. Maybe the day after." She grabbed Tom's coat from the peg and held it up as he returned, and only then did Harry realize that he and Georgie were about to be left.

For the rest of the night.

Totally unchaperoned.

# THIRTY

࿇

*A*lone in the kitchen, silence hung like a shroud as neither of them knew quite what to say or do next.

Georgie was desperate to carry on kissing him but knew that was too dangerous after what had just happened outside. He had touched her. There. And it had felt sublime. Her body had opened for him like a flower. Blossomed beneath his fingers. Was now so aroused she could barely stand straight.

"Could this week actually get any worse?" Harry was the first to speak and he looked as terrified by this latest turn of events as she was. He sunk into a chair. "What the hell do we do now with them gone?"

"I can look after all the children's needs in Ada's abs—" Her words died at the intense heat of his stare.

"It's not *their* needs that bother me. We almost . . . again . . . and now . . ." He threw up his palms, then buried his head in his hands. "Fate seems to want to torment us when I have to sail away."

"I know."

"If we . . . succumb . . . then I'd have to marry you and how the hell would I be able to sail away then?" When his eyes lifted again, they were bleak. "I wouldn't be able to. I'm already more in love with you than is sensible . . ." The earth shifted on its axis, and her heart leapt. ". . . already dreading sailing away more than I can bear and I've already used up all the navy's benevolence thanks to the last siren who bewitched me! I lost my first ship because I couldn't sail away from blasted Elizabeth and she didn't hold a candle to you." His yearning gaze this time was molten, which was ironic because Georgie was melting, so seduced by his words she was undone.

"It took me years to earn their trust again! Years of hard work that will all be for naught if I can't bring myself to sail away on the bloody *Boadicea* shortly as they all expect me to!" His head fell forward again and he fisted his hair in frustration. "I can't turn down a blasted flagship—even if I wanted to." Which rather suggested he didn't. Wouldn't. Irrespective of all his pretty words. "It's a flagship, Georgie. There is no recovery from that. It would kill my naval career stone dead—and forever this time. Few get given that honor and the only way is up afterward." He pointed to the ceiling. "All the way to the top. Everything I have worked so hard for. With the *Boadicea* it's all there. Finally within reach." His hands dropped between his knees in despair. "I'd have to throw all that away for you."

"I do not recall asking you to!" Anger bubbled. Mostly at her stupidity for even briefly contemplating that a man in uniform might be capable of not putting his duty above all else. "I know how important the navy is to you, Harry! How important this promotion is to you." Far more important than she could ever hope to be. "Just as I know I have no desire to shackle myself to the military again!" That door swung both ways, after all. "I loathed that life with every fiber of my being, growing up! It's a miserable existence that wore down my poor mother until it killed her!" With every passing season, more of her dear mama's light had dimmed thanks to the selfish colonel and his all-encompassing army career.

"You think I have a burning desire to repeat history, Harry? To watch you sail away, to goodness knows what, never knowing where you are, what you are doing or if you are ever going to come back? All the while stuck in some port, alone, living under the navy's rules for months on end, amongst strangers where I have to start afresh? That is until they post you somewhere different and it all happens again?" A nomadic, isolating existence which echoed the transient life of a governess—but at least that was on her terms. Devoid of all the worry, resentment, and recriminations a union between them would guarantee.

Surely?

"Then I suppose asking you to wait for me is out of the question?" His gaze bored into hers. "Admiral and Lady Nugent seem to have found a way to make it work and maybe we could too?"

"To wait for what exactly, Harry? Your return? Your elevation to commodore? Vice admiral? Admiral of the fleet? Your death in battle?" She shook her head, irrationally furious at him for being who he was. For doing what he did. For reminding her of her miserable childhood on the only night she had ever felt like a princess.

For making her want all the things Miss P had trained her not to.

To dare to dream the impossible for a moment and then dash it in the next!

The moonlight caught the gold braid on his shoulder, and she had the overwhelming urge to rip it from his coat. "I'd rather die a spinster that live through that wretched purgatory again! I hate to agree with that awful Elizabeth on anything—but few military marriages are ever happy. My mother's was a nightmare from start to finish but, thanks to smallpox, she was at least able to escape that living hell a lot sooner than I did!"

He balked at her vitriol. "Then where does that leave us?" He stood to pace, agitated. "What's the solution?"

"There isn't one." She couldn't allow history to repeat itself. Wouldn't put herself or him through that torment. Even if they could be happy when they were together as the Nugents had managed to do, she would still have to spend weeks, months, maybe even years alone again waiting for him to sail home, and that would be torture when she already loved him more than was sensible to. "We occupy different worlds, Harry. You have to sail away next month as the navy expects, and I have to leave next week and let you. That is how it should be. How it was always meant to be." How it had to be. "Tonight was the fairy tale, not our reality."

"And what just happened was . . . ?"

"Yet another dreadful mistake." It hurt to say it, but there seemed little point in prolonging the agony when they had finally reached the end of the rope. "Good night, Harry."

❧

*H*e didn't immediately follow her upstairs. Georgie had been sitting on her mattress and staring into space for over half an hour when she heard the weary climb of his boots on the stairs and then the soft, resigned click as his bedchamber door closed. She hadn't expected him to argue with her because there really wasn't anything else to say. He had his life and she had hers and, in all normal circumstances, never the twain should meet. But in a strange twist of fate they had met, like ships passing in the night, and they both had to accept that that was all they could ever be. Theirs was only ever destined to be a short and transient relationship. Separated by the reassuring barriers of station, money, and duty. In a moment of madness, they had crossed that boundary, thoroughly muddied the waters, and now they were both paying for it.

Georgie supposed the ache in her heart would fade, given time, just as she supposed he likely wouldn't remember her in a year from now. Why would he, when his star was rising and his destiny was so far removed from hers it was laughable? Better to stop it all before things got out of hand—as they almost had outside in the yard. Her body still ached from that revelation and likely would all night. She would just have to ignore it.

In an attempt to do just that, she sloshed cold water from the jug into her washbowl and then wrestled with the laces of the beautiful borrowed evening gown. As the emerald silk puddled around her feet, she caught sight of herself in the mirror and sighed aloud at the state of her hair. The exhilarating sail home had completely destroyed Ada's efforts and it hung loose in a wild tangle about her shoulders. She ran impatient fingers through it to remove the last pins, then remembered how he had twirled his finger in it on the sand, bewitched as if he liked it.

And he must like it, she realized with a start, because he had called her both beautiful and a siren tonight on two separate occasions and both unprompted. Had he always liked it?

Was that why she always caught him staring at it?

Why Felix, Marianne, Tom, and Ada had all mentioned the way he looked at her. Why even Lady Nugent this evening had commented upon it, and none of them would have done that if there wasn't a single grain of truth in the accusation.

Would they?

She stared at her reflection again, trying to see herself through his eyes, and was shocked to realize that in just her stays and her shift, her hair loose and lips kiss-swollen, she no longer resembled the awkward, sturdy, freckled sixteen-year-old whose reflection had always disappointed her.

She was a woman now.

The freckles had faded over the years and gave her pale skin a healthy glow in the candlelight. She had curves. Some cleavage. Bosoms. Sensitive, needy bosoms which had enjoyed being in Harry's hands as much as he had enjoyed holding them. He had groaned when he'd cupped them over her gown in the garden and she had watched his gaze dip to them when he had first seen her this evening.

Curious suddenly about her own allure she unlaced her stays and wriggled out of her shift, and to her complete surprise, wasn't appalled by the sight of her naked body. She turned a circle to view it from all angles, taking in the hourglass shape of her figure. Tested the weight of her breasts, traced the shape of her nipples. Watched them pucker to points in the glass as her unfulfilled body wished it was his hands on her instead. Felt the tiny knot of nerves his fingers had caressed between her legs buzz with anticipation. Her womb tighten with need. Her womanhood moisten. The walls of her vagina throb.

Good heavens, but she wasn't going to get any sleep in this state!

She dipped a finger between her legs in the hope it would take the incessant ache away, then instantly withdrew it because it did not feel as intoxicating or as sensual as Harry's decadent touch.

It was in that moment that she realized that no matter how impossible their situation was, or how transient, Lottie was right.

Georgie was resigned to waving him goodbye.

Resigned to him sailing away to more naval greatness, because that was his destiny. Resigned to never seeing him again. Resigned to him forgetting her even if she knew she would never forget him. She was even resigned to meeting her maker without ever having a ring on her finger, as that was the governess's lonely destiny, but it genuinely would be a tragedy if she went to heaven in a package marked UN-OPENED too when he was mere feet away.

Perhaps still as aroused as she was.

Was she really prepared to waste that precious gift when her ripe body wanted his so very much—and might never have the opportunity to ever feel this way ever again?

# THIRTY-ONE

❧

*H*arry lay flat on his back, staring at the ceiling and stroking the snoring Cuthbert's soft ears when he heard Georgie's bed-chamber door open. His stupid heart soared and his cock hardened with renewed hope, even though he actually held out none that she was headed his way. He strained his ears to listen for her approach and almost jumped out of his skin when his door handle turned.

And then she was there. Standing in a loosely tied robe in his doorway with an odd expression on her lovely face.

He almost knocked Cuthbert to the floor in his haste to sit up. "Is everything all right?"

She nodded and closed the door. "I don't want us to waste time fighting, Harry. Not about things that make us fundamentally you and me, under circumstances neither of us can change."

"I don't want to fight either."

Her lovely face blossomed into a nervous smile and she edged closer. He could tell by the gentle movement beneath the fabric that her breasts were unbound before she stopped awkwardly. He could see the shadowy outline of her nipples through the soft linen thanks to the flickering candle on his nightstand; the flame wove its magic with the copper and gold in her hair.

"Then I wondered if you would allow me to spend the night with you?" Her fingers went to the knot in her belt and, as the air whooshed out of his lungs, she clumsily undid it. "If you still want me, that is?"

Harry didn't even have the wherewithal to choke out one of his erudite "ums." Could barely breathe. Barely blink.

Her smile was shy. "Because I know that this can go nowhere, but I still want you." With a swallow, she let the robe fall open enough to display the naked valley between her breasts and thighs. "Do you still want me?"

He nodded as his gaze hungrily raked the length of her. There was shimmering copper between her legs too, although the rest of the soft curls on her womanhood were darker. He couldn't fathom why that was the singularly most erotic thing he had seen in his life, but it was.

He sucked in more air as he'd forgotten to breathe, and her smile altered. It wasn't one of Georgie's usual smiles—although he had always found those intoxicating enough—this one was sultry. It grabbed him by the balls and mercilessly teased his shaft, rendering him so speechless, he couldn't have uttered a cohesive sentence if his very life depended upon it.

As if she knew she had him enthralled, Georgie slowly eased the robe from her shoulders and let it fall, and he was powerless to do anything but stare, transfixed. Acres of alabaster skin. Two perfect, pert breasts tipped with saucy raspberry nipples that tightened to tantalizing points beneath his captive gaze.

"Would you make love to me, Harry?" Words he had fantasized about since the first day she had upturned his life.

"I would love nothing more, Georgie, but—" She pressed a finger to his lips as she sat on the mattress beside him.

"There are no caveats, Harry. No ulterior motives. Certainly no expectations beyond me leaving on the London post before the week is out and you sailing away from me forever. I want no promises, nor need any. I want no guilt nor recrimination from you either. You are an outstanding sailor who deserves to climb to the very top of the rigging and I am a governess who has never expected marriage. But if I'm destined to die an old maid, I'd rather not be a *maid* in every sense, and I'd never forgive myself if I denied myself you tonight when I want you so very much." Her mouth whispered over his with a boldness that matched her new temptress's persona, and he knew he couldn't resist her. He kissed her back and she stayed his hungry mouth with her index finger again. "Although I would rather it was just me who leaves here on the post next week, so I hope you know how to prevent us making a child together. Employers tend to frown on such things."

He nodded as he mourned that child they would never have when a mixture of her and him toddling around their feet appealed so very much. She watched him frown, and the smallest crack in her seducer's façade showed.

"Are you sure you want me?"

"More than I've ever wanted anything." There was no point lying about it. No point trying to deny himself of things he didn't have the strength to fight.

"Then have me." She pressed her body against his and his flesh rejoiced at the contact. Because it wasn't enough, he hauled her into his lap and then lowered them both onto his bed as his mouth plundered hers. And would have continued kissing her until dawn had he not felt the weight of a pair of curious eyes staring.

He rolled to glare at Cuthbert, who was still sitting on the bed, head tilted as he stared. "You need to sleep somewhere else tonight, young man, as I have a much better proposition and do not need an audience for it."

As Georgie giggled, Harry swung his legs out of bed, picked the puppy up and marched him to the door. "Go sleep with Norbert." He deposited Cuthbert out on the landing and closed the door. As he turned, she was staring at his fully erect cock in fascination.

"Does that hurt?"

He chuckled at the question. "No . . . and yes. It aches . . . for you." He padded back to the bed and slid in beside her. "Now, where were we?"

Her lips had barely touched his when a high-pitched howl came from beyond the door. It was just like Norbert's, but childlike enough that Harry knew it would tug at Georgie's heartstrings. "Now Cuthbert's sad."

"Ignore him." He pressed a kiss to her neck. "And he'll go away." He smoothed his hand over her hip while he nibbled her ear, and straightaway, his earthy vixen softly moaned her appreciation. "It's time he selected one of the children as his master anyway, so this is the nudge he needed."

"I think he's already chosen his master."

"Hush your mouth." He silenced her with a kiss. Until Cuthbert howled again, louder, and she sat up, perturbed.

"If we leave him out there crying, he's going to wake the children and then this . . ." She flapped a hand between their bodies. "Isn't going to happen."

Harry growled, because she was right, then heaved himself from the mattress again to go scoop the irritating puppy up. "You can come back in, but you are absolutely not watching!" He wagged his finger at him. "And that's an order."

Harry snatched a blanket from the bed and made Cuthbert a nest with it in the corner, then caged Cuthbert within it using the fire screen, nightstand, and his Royal Navy traveling trunk. "Now be quiet and go to sleep." He wagged his finger again, trying to replicate Georgie's stern expression whenever she effortlessly controlled her errant charges, and miraculously, the mad, miniature wolf curled up in a ball with a huff of defeat.

Harry dashed to the bed this time and practically fell on her. "I believe I was around here . . ." He nuzzled her ear again and she stretched like a cat, smiling as she ran her fingers through his hair and down his back.

"That's nice."

"Just nice?" He traced his finger along her jaw and down her neck, then followed it with his mouth. "Not a word an overachiever like me wants to hear when I am supposed to be outstanding."

Her upper body arched as he caressed the curve of her breast, and then lazily around her nipple before he teased it with his tongue. It was gloriously sensitive, and as she always did when he touched her, she unconsciously demanded more. She branded him with a kiss so sinful, it made his body hum, and instinctively opened hers so that they were almost intimately joined, tilting her hips in invitation. When he ignored that to instead worship her other breast, she writhed beneath him in impatient frustration.

"Harry, please . . ." Her teeth nibbled at his lower lip as she reached between them to caress him. "Don't make me wait. I ache for you too." She wrapped her fingers around his erection, and it pulsed and twitched with need. "So much it hurts."

Within seconds, and just from her unschooled touch, he was on the cusp. All it would have taken was a few more moments and he would be lost and they both deserved so much more than that. She, certainly, deserved nothing but the most thorough and satisfying deflowering he was capable of, so he reluctantly shifted to slow things down. But as she moaned her disgust at being thwarted, he kissed her lips as gently as he caressed the hot, slick, delicate skin between her damp curls.

Her body was ready, willing, and so responsive it shocked them both and she cried out as he stroked the tiny bud of nerves crowning her womanhood. "Nice?" he whispered in her ear as her legs fell wantonly open.

"Outstanding," came her breathy response. "Please don't stop." So he didn't, but he could not resist watching her as she discovered pleasure. Within moments, her eyes were closed and her arms flung back into her lovely hair. Her perfect breasts jutting with each sensual arch of her back; her puckered nipples begging to be kissed. She thrashed and moaned and bucked her hips against his hand. Completely without shame or embarrassment as she embraced every new sensation with enthusiastic wonder.

As her breath became choppy, she moaned, impatient. But there was a wariness there, too, which made her fight the mounting sensations, letting him know that not only was he the first to have her body, but he was also the first to bring it to a climax. Knowledge that was both humbling and beguiling and almost enough to send him over the edge.

"Please don't stop."

"I won't, love." He laced his free hand in hers and she gripped it hard, her breath beautifully erratic, and then, on a shuddering exhale, she finally let go, and she was radiant and untamed as her body pulsed beneath his fingers.

She smiled when her eyes finally opened a good minute later and she caught him staring. "That was . . . *nice*." She tugged him by the hand upward and into her arms, then looped hers around his neck to kiss him. "But please don't stop. I can see already that your noble streak is plaguing you and you are having ludicrous ideas of being a gentleman and leaving this at that."

Harry chuckled because she was right. "There is still plenty we can do without me taking—" She swallowed that in a kiss.

"England expects every man to do his duty."

"You are going to quote Nelson at me?" Lord, he loved her and her clever mind and sharp tongue. "Here. In bed."

"Kiss me, Harry."

So he did, grinning, because Georgie just made him smile and being with her was joyous. Within moments she was sighing again, and so was he as he edged his body slowly inside hers. She tensed briefly but refused to let him stop or apologize, preferring to kiss him instead as she wrapped her legs around him to anchor him in place.

He paused when he was buried to the hilt, every muscle straining, to give her time to adjust to intrusion, but again, she would have none of it. She undulated her hips in a way that tortured, yet he still tried to keep things slow as they began to move together, even though it physically hurt to hold everything back when she felt so good. But Georgie wanted everything and told him so. "Don't stop" soon became "more," "faster," "deeper," spurring him on and eliminating all reason.

She felt like home, which was an odd sensation to have when so consumed with passion, but there it was. She was petite and dainty and he was big and solid, yet they fit together as if by design. Intimate flesh caressing intimate flesh in a dance as old as time, both simultaneously tender and tumultuous, totally, utterly, divinely in sync, as if this was meant to be.

As natural as breathing.

As necessary as air.

He lost himself in her until he lost his mind. As the walls of her body began to pulse around his, he felt his own climax claw at his groin and he barely scraped enough wits together to withdraw as she had asked. A split second later white stars shattered behind his eyes and his body exploded. He called out her name over and over like a benediction and told her that he loved her and she clung to him with teary emotion.

But though he yearned to hear it—strained to hear it—as they fell into the abyss together, he could not help noting that she never said she loved him back.

❦

*T*he distant crowing of a cockerel roused Georgie from the deepest slumber, and she sighed in contentment. After four blissful nights in Harry's bed, it no longer surprised her that he was propped on one elbow smiling down at her. Neither did it surprise her that she was naked and fully exposed to his gaze from the waist up. He adored her naked, and Georgie, scandalously, adored being naked for him.

As it had every single morning since they had been intimate, and before he left for the dockyard a little after sunrise, his heated gaze devoured the sight of her in the dawn's early light. First her messy morning hair, which didn't feel quite so horrid now that she knew he had a penchant for red. Then it dropped to her breasts, and then her sleepy nerve endings instantly awoke when he slowly tugged away the sheet to rake his stare over the rest of her.

Like Eve tempting Adam, she stretched languidly, knowing full well it only kindled his lust further and that within another minute he would be inside her, and within five—or less—he would take her to heaven again. It never took long because he played her body like a virtuoso. Fortunately, for both of them, once was never enough. Especially after she snuck into his bedchamber as soon as the house was fast asleep.

Now that Ada and Tom were back, she usually gave it an hour before she crept along the landing. Their first coupling was also fast and greedy but oh, so satisfying. The second was always more relaxed—until it all got too much to bear—but that second time was when they took their time and tortured one another. She was pretty certain that there wasn't an inch of her body he hadn't kissed, and while she had been diligent in last night's hunt, she had found nowhere new to kiss him either. So instead, she had kissed him *there* until he had come undone and he had returned the favor. It had felt decadent and naughty and she had loved every single second of it.

She loved making love to him almost as much as she loved him, but as their allotted time together ticked swiftly past, she was coming to dread every morning despite its passionate start. Each time the sun rose, it signaled that they were another day nearer to saying goodbye.

He sensed it too, although by tacit agreement neither of them had mentioned it, because frankly, what else was there to say? When he had to sail away and she had to let him.

His gaze was intense as he traced the shape of her face, as if consigning it to memory. He had done similar yesterday before he had kissed her, a myriad of emotions swirling in his dark eyes, which ran the gamut from lust to regret. Yet this morning, he was concentrating so hard searching her eyes that there seemed no sign any kiss was forthcoming.

"Is everything all right, Harry?" She ran her palm over his cheek, marveling at the raspy feel of all the dark stubble that had grown overnight, while trying to turn the mood playful. "Or did I wear you out last night after I insisted on that third time?" When she had awoken him from a deep sleep to ride him in the small hours.

Oh, how liberating and exhilarating it was to have the once-in-a-lifetime opportunity to behave so wantonly for a man who fully appreciated that hitherto-unknown aspect of herself!

He stared deep into her soul, his dark brows meeting in consternation as he traced his finger over her lips. "You need to know that if you ask me not to sail away, I won't."

"And what is that supposed to mean?"

"Exactly what it sounds like." His smile was wistful and a tad martyring before he placed a kiss on her nose. "If *you* ask me *not* to sail away, I won't."

"If you want me to give you an excuse to turn your back on the bloody *Boadicea*, I won't do it, Harry!" She pushed him away to sit, angry and hurt that he was trying to put her in that untenable position. "And it is grossly unfair for you to ask!"

"Why?" He had the gall to look surprised at her offense. "We've got just days left, Georgie, so I figured one of us had to say something to fix things, and it clearly wasn't going to be you." He looked offended, as if she should have already wept at his feet and begged him not to sail away days ago. "At least I am trying to think of a solution to our problem. Trying to find a way to make us work."

"And your solution is to ask *me* to ask *you* not to sail away?"

"I had hoped you might be pleased that I would do that because you might love me too!" He surged off the bed and stalked to where his clothes were neatly hung on the stand in the corner that formed part of Cuthbert's makeshift cage, then snatched up his breeches. As if that was his cue to get up, the puppy yawned, stretched, then bounded out to lick his master's ankles. "Clearly I was mistaken, and you actually do not care at all that I am prepared to make that sacrifice!" In a temper, he hopped as he fought both legs into the garment. "Which is good to know!"

"I do not want you to make any sacrifices!" She grabbed her own robe and shoved her arms into it. "I have been explicit about that since the very beginning of this." She waved her hand at the rumpled bed, as that seemed like the safest way to categorize what they had— they were lovers. Albeit temporarily. "I went into this affair with no expectations and no agenda and you know that!"

"And no inconvenient feelings either, apparently." He yanked on his shirt, then used his cravat to punctuate the air. "It did not go unnoticed that my one declaration of love was met with deafening silence!"

Of course it had been! This situation was difficult enough without having to bare her heart, and she wasn't fool enough to believe words uttered in the heat of passion. Especially when he had reiterated repeatedly his need to sail away and the detrimental—catastrophic— impact to his career of not doing so. She understood what the navy meant to him and accepted this was all they could have instead, and in doing, had gone into this with her eyes wide open. She had thought he understood the parameters of their brief foray into passion too. After all, he had been the one to set them and he had certainly never tried to chafe against them before today. Yesterday, for pity's sake, he had brought home all the maps and charts for the *Boadicea*'s first training maneuvers to show the children over the dining table. He would be sailing her to Calais and back in precisely twenty days with a skeleton crew and, he had proclaimed with great fervor, he didn't care if the layabout shipwrights had to work through the night before to get her ready.

Now, suddenly, this morning, he would apparently give all that up.

If *she* asked him to!

As much as St. Joan was tempted to throw the candlestick at his unreasonable, thick head, she wrestled her away and spread her palms, placating. "I don't understand why you would want to spoil our last days together with futile recriminations and arguments? Why you would want to tarnish our otherwise lovely memories? You know that I don't want to fight with you about it, Harry."

"No. Of course you don't." He snatched up his boots. "Or fight for us either!"

He was halfway to the door when she caught his arm, aiming for diplomacy while St. Joan leaked regardless. "Do you honestly think that you are being fair to expect *me* to be the one to ruin all your plans? To thwart your destiny? To scupper your career? To force you to make the *ultimate sacrifice*?" All variations of his damning words this past week, although she could tell from the rigid set of his jaw they failed to hit their mark. "Then, no doubt, to have you forever resent me for it? What sort of an *us* would we be then, Harry? Apart from miserable and trapped?"

"I have to go to work." He tugged his arm away. "You know where to find me if you can find it in your hardened heart to change your mind." He growled at her as if she had just murdered Cuthbert. "I shan't hold my breath!"

She let him go.

What else could she do when he was so determined to be unreasonable?

As she had got into the habit of doing these last few days, she made the bed in case Ada noticed that both sides of it had been slept on, then carried the subdued puppy to her own room just in time to hear the back door slam as he left the house. St. Joan wanted her to remain angry, but all she felt was sad, as this felt like the beginning of the end. Some strange compunction made her wander to her window and watch him stalk away, and that too seemed significant, as soon it would be for the last time.

It had to be after this morning.

No matter how tempted she was to beg him to stay—she had been a ball and chain around a military man's neck before and knew how toxic and destructive such resentment could be. Despite their best efforts to ignore it, it was already happening, and they were already both unhappy and failing to mask their mutual resentments. Already, it was all turning into one big, seething mess that was only destined to get worse. Especially as there was no compromise which suited them both. If she asked him not to sail away, he lost, and if she stayed with him and he didn't, she did. Therefore, surely it was better to have loved and lost than to experience love die. And it would die a lingering death once the bloom was gone and resentment drove a wedge between them.

Why couldn't he see that?

Or perhaps he did, and he'd lashed out in frustration because it was the one problem that even he, the Royal Navy's eternal fixer, could not fix.

---

*G*eorgie spent the morning flying kites on the beach with the children while Norbert and Cuthbert frolicked in the surf. As she was still technically their governess, Georgie tenuously linked the activity to some mathematics and tried to keep her smile despite the constant, dull ache in her chest.

"Come along, all of you!" Felix was making a meal out of packing up his kite, purposefully dragging his feet in the hope that he and Norbert would be left to follow behind because he was desperate for some freedom. As Harry hadn't taken him to Plymouth with him today, Felix was also put out. She could hardly tell him why his uncle had left in a huff, so the poor lad was convinced he had been cast aside just as things on the *Boadicea* were getting interesting. "If you are quick, I will buy you all a cake from the baker's—so long as you keep it a secret from Ada, of course. You know how annoyed she gets if anyone dares eat anything to spoil their lunch."

"Can I have a currant bun with icing on top?" The mention of cake was all it took to earn Felix's compliance, so she nodded. While it was tantamount to the same out-and-out bribery she had chastised Harry for, Georgie was inclined to spoil them all a little before she had to leave.

"Only if you keep it a sworn secret from your uncle too when we meet him here later."

For the first time, she was dreading Harry's homecoming, as it seemed another fight was inevitable unless he had had a complete change of heart during the day.

Somehow, she knew that wasn't likely because when Harry thought he had found the way to solve a problem, he was always relentless in the execution. The speed with which he was getting the bloody *Boadicea* shipshape was proof of that. Anyone who got in his way was ruthlessly flattened into submission, and woe betide them if they weren't. But she really didn't want to have to keep fighting with him, and he, for whatever well-intentioned but misguided reason, did. What had happened this morning had been brewing for days and they had both been stupid to think that they could ignore it.

When you played with fire, you always got burned.

They were seated on the seawall outside the bakery, finishing off their clandestine cakes when the morning post coach arrived. It had barely stopped when Norbert began to sniff the air, then bolted to run excited circles around the conveyance. Georgie dashed after him to stop him terrorizing the unsuspecting passengers with his exuberant brand of affection, and then stopped dead when a tall brunette alighted.

The woman was so similar to Harry around the eyes and in her coloring that she could only be his sister. The way Norbert threw himself at her and licked her beaming face confirmed it.

"My darlings!" Still swamped in giant dog, Lady Flora Pendleton opened her arms to the three dark-haired cannonballs rushing toward her, with happy tears running down her pretty face. "Oh, how I have missed you all!"

Behind her, a similarly beaming and distinguished gentleman caught Grace and tossed her in the air before he hugged her tight.

With a lump in her throat and feeling like a spare wheel, Georgie kept her distance from the emotional reconciliation until Lady Flora glanced her way, then tilted her head when she noticed her watching. "Hello?"

"My lady." She bobbed a curtsy. "I am Miss Georgina Rowe. The temporary governess your brother hired to help him look after the children in your absence." The word *temporary* physically hurt as she choked it out because it decisively stamped *the end* on this chapter of her life.

"I must say, you are not at all what I expected." Lady Flora's smile was warm, friendly, and curious. "When I learned my stickler of a baby brother had hired a governess, I imagined a fierce, humorless old maid with slate-gray hair and beady little spectacles." She chuckled in disbelief. "I never in a million years expected him to employ someone who looks as personable as you. Is he ill?"

"He was desperate," said Georgie, smiling back, already liking Harry's sister a great deal, "and beggars cannot be choosers." Noticing that Lord Pendleton was trying to organize their baggage with the coachman and needing something to do to prevent the tears prickling her eyes from falling, she rushed to his aid. "Why don't you leave me to sort all that out while you catch up with your offspring? I know they have a million things to tell you. We have all had quite the month."

It was certainly one that Georgie would never forget.

# THIRTY-THREE

✑

*H*ow blasted hard is it to string a hammock?" Harry was at his wit's end with all the incompetence on this bloody ship. "And what sort of useless sailors have the Admiralty saddled me with if they all struggle to tie a decent knot?" Out of the seven hundred hammocks that had been delivered to the main deck yesterday, only two hundred fifty were secured in situ below it. "We have less than a blasted week before we set sail for Calais and at this rate, we won't be bloody well ready!"

Lieutenant Gregson was wearing his semipermanent startled expression again as he tried to stutter a response. "Nobody is slacking, Captain—but there are only so many men you can have working in such a confined space together."

"I suppose that's going to be your pathetic excuse for the lack of powder and fuses on the lower gun deck too?" When Harry had expressly asked for that all to be ready today too. "I thought you were an experienced officer, Gregson? This isn't good enough!"

"Lieutenant—if you wouldn't mind giving us a moment." Like

a mother hen, Simpkins came to Gregson's rescue by marching to Harry's cabin door and ushering the startled fellow out. As the door slammed shut, his right-hand man folded his arms and glared. "If you don't want to be the first captain in naval history to have a mutiny before you've left the dock, then you might want to curb your bleedin' temper!"

"I beg your—" Before his outraged bluster became words, Simpkins began to jab the air between them with his finger.

"You are being an unreasonable pain in the arse! So unreasonable, I'm this close to telling you to shove your job where the sun don't shine and walking myself." He held his finger and thumb an inch apart. "Therefore, I strongly suggest you either take the thorn out of your paw, accept it's over, and start behaving like the sort of captain who deserves his crew's respect, or you go to bloody London to try and sort things out with that woman of yours! Whichever it is, you need to stop torturing the rest of the world because she chose to leave you! Although frankly, with the way you are behaving lately, I don't blame Georgie in the slightest!"

Simpkins slammed out and left Harry fuming that Georgie had even been mentioned when as far as he was concerned, her name was banned.

Forbidden!

Taboo!

He didn't want to talk about the treacherous siren any more than he wanted to think about her. When she'd upped and left on the afternoon post the same day as blasted Flora returned, without so much as a by-your-leave before he arrived home!

What sort of woman came apart in his arms before dawn and then abandoned him without a proper goodbye before dusk? Especially when only a few hours before, he had practically begged her to stay with him! He had dared to bare his heart, dared to be selfless and to do the unthinkable for her because he loved her so much, and she had as good as thrown it all back in his face. It was history repeating itself all over again and he was kicking himself for his galling, gullible stupidity. When he knew better than anyone that sailors and sirens did not mix!

Instinctively, his fingers reached for the letter he'd carried with him since he had found it on his nightstand. The short, sharp, dismissive missive that hadn't so much as broken his heart for the second time but bludgeoned it irretrievably to mush. Yet he couldn't bear to part with it when the damn thing deserved burning on the fire!

*Dear Harry,*

*Now that our time together has reached its natural conclusion, please forgive me for stealing away like a coward, but I hate goodbyes. I wanted to thank you for giving me the opportunity to be your governess and, more importantly, the honor of being your friend. Please try to keep yourself safe and do your best not to sail into trouble while you achieve all the well-deserved accolades and promotions and enjoy all the great adventures which have always been your destiny. For what it is worth, I already know that you will forever be my greatest adventure, and I shall always fondly remember our time together without the slightest hint of regret.*

*With love,*

*Georgie*

He must have read the damned thing at least a thousand times already, and yet it still cut him to the quick. Because he had begged her for forever and she had responded with goodbye.

In blasted impersonal writing.

The curt knock made him jump. "You've a visitor, Captain." As his cabin opened, he stuffed the letter back in his waistcoat and tried to look like a busy man studying his charts.

"Hello, Henry." How bloody typical of fate to send him the first woman who had made a fool out of him while he was still nursing the gaping wound left by the second.

"Elizabeth." Ingrained politeness made him force a smile, but it wasn't the least bit sincere. "What brings you here?" Although he suspected already that it was the challenge he presented. Elizabeth had never been good with the word *no*, and she had always measured her self-worth in the amount she was coveted. This was the third time she had turned up at his ship like a bad penny since Georgie's betrayal, despite him already giving her the shortest of shrifts twice.

"I find myself at a bit of a loose end with Francis gone to Dartmouth for a month." She took the chair opposite with a butter-would-not-melt-in-her-mouth smile. "I thought you might be lonely and in dire need of some friendly company too while your charming fiancée remains away." A stark reminder that he still hadn't found the courage to announce the termination of his fake engagement to his superiors and comrades yet.

Because announcing it was as good as admitting to himself that it really was all over between him and Georgie and, heaven help him, despite her abrupt departure and callous letter, the remnants of his bludgeoned heart refused to give up all hope. "All work and no play makes Jack a dull boy, after all, and according to my sources, you've been working on this ship all the hours God has sent this last week."

Her predatory gaze wandered to his bed. "Is it true you have even been sleeping here?"

As the very last thing he needed was her turning up here in the middle of the night, he denied it. "Of course not. Flora would kill me if I missed a family dinner. They are sacrosanct, as far as she is concerned." In truth, he had slept here for five of the last seven nights, so his blasted sister likely would kill him if he didn't go home tonight, and now that Elizabeth was on the prowl again, it probably made sense. "Which I am afraid I was just about to leave for . . . I do apologize." He stood and, as he had hoped, she did too. She even allowed him to usher her halfway to the door before she turned and blocked his path.

"Well, if you ever do want some company . . ." Her hand brushed his sleeve. Lingered. "I would still very much like for us to pick up things where we left off."

"From where you left me for another man, you mean, then married him before you had the decency to tell me?" Ingrained politeness only went so far, and her touch repelled him now.

"It's not as if I had any choice!" For the first time, her flash of anger seemed genuine.

"Don't tell me that your vice admiral blackmailed you up the aisle?" Lashing out with sarcasm felt good. "You poor thing."

But she lashed out too, whacking him with her reticule and stamping her foot. "But I was blackmailed, idiot! Your horrid grandfather made it plain that he would ruin me if I didn't marry Francis!"

"What?"

"He knew we'd had an . . . indiscretion . . ." Of course he had! "And he threatened to make it public unless I set you free."

"I don't believe you!" The admiral had made no secret that he disapproved of Harry's engagement and had done his darndest to talk him out of it, but it was inconceivable that his own flesh and blood would stoop to outright sabotage. "But then you always did have a tenuous relationship with the truth!"

"Well, he did!" Elizabeth bristled, indignant. "And if you don't believe me, ask my husband—because he had a promotion dangled as a reward for doing right by me so long as it was done fast. How else do you think a self-absorbed fool like Francis would have made vice admiral?"

As Harry couldn't argue that Barrett-Hughes was a fool, he strode to the door instead and flung it open, outraged at her lies, yet hugely unsettled by them. "We are done, Elizabeth. We were done four years ago when you married your idiot. I accepted it was all over then and you have to accept it now, so please never darken my door again."

No sooner had she stomped away across the quayside did he himself leave. He was sick and tired of this bloody ship today. Furious at Simpkins for mentioning Georgie and outraged at Elizabeth for . . . well, everything. That woman was a lying, cheating, poisonous serpent and if his grandfather had sent her packing—which he did not believe for a second—then he had likely done Harry a favor! A bloody underhanded, cruel, and hurtful favor, but still one he should probably be grateful for.

An indiscretion indeed!

He sincerely doubted that unfaithful tease had ever experienced a pair of cold sheets in her life! Before him! After him! Or, it would seem, while engaged to him!

He silently seethed for the entire journey across the Sound to Cawsand and on the uphill walk home, then slammed into the house, ready to snap at the first person who dared mention the slamming, only to be met by complete silence.

"Hello!" Why the hell was nobody here when he desperately needed to shout at someone? "Hello!"

"Harry?" His sister's voice came from her study. "Thank goodness you are finally home. Your dog's constant howling for you is enough to try the patience of a saint!"

"Cuthbert isn't my dog!" As he practically bellowed that from her doorway, her head snapped up, surprised. It surprised him, too, because Flora had been bent over a ledger, apparently totting up a row of numbers.

"I beg to differ, brother." Because of course the damned puppy had toddled over from his bed beneath her desk and already had his paws on Harry's knees while his scruffy little tail wagged so fast it blurred. "Dogs are like children. They are a responsibility that you cannot simply ignore for days on end. The poor thing has missed your sourpuss dreadfully, although heaven only knows why." She wafted an imperious finger that reminded him too much of their mother's. "Pick him up and give him some love."

"He is *not* my dog!" But even so, he picked the adoring puppy up and tickled his floppy ears. It was instantly soothing. "He only exists because you neglected your responsibility to take proper care of your blasted dog."

Flora rolled her eyes, jotted down a number in the miraculously well-ordered ledger, then laid down her quill. "So what has got your dander up today, baby brother?"

"Everything—and nothing." Like the surliest of children, he plonked his backside on her desk. "For starters, the bloody *Boadicea* is never going to be ready on time and according to Simpkins, the crew are close to mutiny because apparently it is my fault that they are all a bunch of useless, lazy idiots who cannot run a bath." Although now that Cuthbert had forced him to be calm, he was prepared to concede that he hadn't been the easiest of captains to get along with these last two weeks.

"Are you aware that whenever you mention your new ship, the word 'bloody' always precedes it?"

"*Harrumph!* Now you sound like Geo—" He stopped himself before he accidentally uttered the callous siren's name.

"*Hmmmm . . .*" Flora gave him one of her withering big-sister looks. "Now I suspect we are finally getting to the root of the matter."

"We are really not." He rolled his own eyes, praying they looked nonchalant.

"Ada said that the pair of you were sharing a bed."

"Poppycock!" As denial seemed the gentlemanly thing to do, he did so with gusto. "How the blazes would Ada know that?"

"Because Ada knows everything. Because she said that after she and Tom returned from the birth of their grandchild, you both had a satisfied and soppy glow about you that could only come from *nocturnal shenanigans*. And because, most importantly of all, she found a long, curly strand of damning red hair on your pillowcase when she changed the bed linens the day Georgie left." Flora offered him her most sympathetic smile. "Marianne also mentioned that she thought that she overheard the pair of you arguing on that day too, so it doesn't take a genius to put two and two together. What happened?"

As much as he did not want to have this conversation, Harry recognized that he probably needed to. For all her faults and her flightiness, Flora had always given good advice. "The usual story. I accidentally fell in love with a temptress who didn't love me quite as much back."

"You told her how you felt?"

"Twice." He felt his shoulders deflate. "The first time I think that she pretended not to hear it and the second . . . well, let's just say when I asked her to stay, she left."

"Oh, Harry." Flora gripped his hand. "I wish you had told me that before now. I'd have been significantly less peeved at your insufferable mood if I'd known that you'd had a heartfelt proposal of marriage refused."

"I didn't propose, exactly, but I definitely implied it."

"You implied it." She scrunched up her face as if he had done something wrong. "Dare I ask how?"

"It's private."

Flora rolled her eyes again. "By that, one can only assume that you were in bed, post *shenanigans* and . . ." She wafted her hand, expecting him to continue.

"I don't remember verbatim the exact words I used, but they were suitably heartfelt and certainly did not deserve the affronted reaction they got."

"Then obviously they were idiotically male if she ended up shouting at you about them and then hotfooted it away on the afternoon post. I only knew Georgie for an hour or so, but she did not strike me as the unreasonable sort."

"She is wholly unreasonable. Rebellious, tart-mouthed. Does everything her way."

All traits which made his blasted sister smile. "I knew I liked her. She sounds perfect for you, so it's a crying shame you ruined it all with whatever stupid, unromantic thing you said."

"Actually, if you must know, it was very romantic because I told her that if she asked me not to sail away, I wouldn't."

Instead of the poignant sigh he expected, Flora slapped her forehead. "Oh, good heavens above!"

"I also told her that I was prepared to make the ultimate sacrifice—for her."

"And she didn't fall at your feet to kiss them in gratitude?" In his hour of need, only his sister would torture him with sarcasm. "Clearly the woman is quite deranged and you are well shot of her!

For who wouldn't want to spend eternity with a burning martyr?" She shoved him unceremoniously from her desk. "Especially when you stipulated that you would only venture onto the bonfire if she *asked* you to." When it was put it like that, it didn't sound quite as romantic as he had originally intended. "And what did she say to such a conditional declaration of love?"

Was it conditional? He was pretty certain it had been selfless. "Something along the lines of it being unfair to her to be the one to scupper my entire career and thereby thwart my destiny." Harry winced as those ill-considered words finally sunk in. "I made a complete hash of it, didn't I?"

"No woman wants a husband she has had to nail to a cross before he will put a ring on her finger."

Harry tickled Cuthbert's ears while he pondered that. "Then you think I can fix it if I tell her I'd happily resign my commission for her?"

Flora shook her head. "I honestly think that you are approaching your quandary all wrong as, from where I am sitting, there are two things at play here." At his confused expression, she steepled her fingers on the desk. "The first is how you are going to convince Georgie to marry you after your spectacularly awful doomed-to-fail first proposal."

"And the second?"

"Is what you actually want to do about the navy. The emphasis is on *you* there, baby brother, as whatever that is has to come from you. It cannot be someone else's decision. Someone else's fault. It is your career and only you know if you are truly happy with the way it is going." She reached across the table to pet Cuthbert. "Does it honestly fulfill you? Feel like an adventure still?"

"You and your blasted stupid adventures! Not everything needs to be an adventure, Flora!"

"It doesn't—but not everything should feel like a chore either!" Oh, how he loathed when his reliably illogical sister spouted irrefutable logic! "Does the navy still excite you, baby brother? For that is the crux of this."

"I've got a flagship and in a year or so I'll be commodore." Why did neither thing elicit any excitement whatsoever?

"Those are the current circumstances—not the answer."

She was right. Devil take her. "The problem is, I have been so overworked at the Admiralty, I don't seem to have the energy to be enthused by my promotion. My feelings for Georgie have only exacerbated that. And, I suppose, have muddied the waters."

Flora, of course, wasn't going to let him get away with that tired and convenient explanation. "Your dissatisfaction with the navy began long before Georgie came into your life. I'm not convinced you've been happy in it for at least three years, maybe longer. In fact, and please don't bite my head off because I know you are convinced that the navy is your life, I think you fell out of love with it pretty quickly after the admiral passed. Maybe even before. Hardly a surprise, when it was *his* dream you were living." Flora pulled a face, clearly expecting an explosion, and she almost got it.

Except . . .

"Elizabeth came to visit me on the ship today, and claimed . . ." He laughed to prepare his sister for how ridiculous it was. "That the old man forced her into abandoning our engagement. Even went as far into threatening to ruin her if she didn't, and then claimed he promoted her idiot husband as a bribe to marry her instead."

Flora's eyes widened—but far too briefly to give him any comfort. "As much as I hate, loathe, and have always despised that two-faced, two-timing gorgon Elizabeth, I wouldn't have put it past him. You were pretty set on leaving the navy then, as I recall, and he *did* threaten to have you thrown in the brig if you took the shore leave you were due to get married." She frowned, thoughtful. "Then he punished you anyway by taking away your first ship."

"No—somebody else did." Harry scoffed at that. "He fought tooth and nail to get me that ship, so it makes no sense that he would threaten Elizabeth with ruination for ruining my naval career, then ruin it for me regardless."

"Mama didn't think so. She was convinced it was exactly the sort of lesson the controlling old curmudgeon would have taught you to keep you under his thumb, because he was cruel that way, but you wouldn't listen."

"Because it made no sense! The admiral always championed my career. I wouldn't have been offered a second ship the following year if he hadn't pushed for it."

"And thereby guaranteeing your indebtedness to him ever after." Her lips flattened. "What better way to control you? He was one to rule with an iron fist and didn't appreciate anyone daring to peek over the parapet to see the alternatives. Just look at how he treated our mother after she went against him to marry Papa. He withdrew her dowry and never wasted a single opportunity to remind her of her *mistake*, despite the fact that she and Papa were blissfully happy together." Just as he had constantly reminded Harry of his foolish mistake with Elizabeth. "It never made any sense that a man with all the money he eventually left you would leave his only daughter and her family to struggle with crushing debt rather than put his hand in his deep pockets to alleviate some of it—yet we both know he did that. Worse, he then exploited you by using the family's debts as a stick to beat you into submission with."

"No, he didn't."

"Didn't he? You never showed an ounce of interest in either the sea or the navy when we were growing up. You preferred cricket and creepy crawlies like Felix and had your heart set on academia like Papa, but once he had convinced you that you could earn enough to help pay the family's mounting bills, you were a convert. He black-mailed you into the navy, Harry. Took advantage of your innate need to rescue and fix things, then did all he could to mold you into his image." When he shook his head, it was her turn to scoff. "You began spouting all your plans to make admiral of the fleet at fifteen, and they weren't the lofty, ill-thought-out plans of a boy, brother. They were solid and sensible plans that only someone with a solid and se-rious knowledge of the navy could have plotted so ruthlessly. He was living vicariously through you, because the admiral never had what it took to make admiral of the fleet."

"Of course he did—and he would have been if he hadn't stayed in Plymouth to fight the war against Napoleon."

"Now I am going to call poppycock! He stayed in Plymouth be-cause he had rubbed everyone else the wrong way during his short stint at the Admiralty and was asked to leave."

"What proof do you have of that?"

"Beyond what Mama claimed, I don't," said his irritating sister before she prodded him with her finger. "Any more than I have any proof that he blackmailed Elizabeth into leaving you or took away your first ship to teach you a lesson. But it would be easy enough for you to find out with your rank, the connections, and the reputation of always finding all the answers nobody else can." She sat back and positively glared. "And while you are on that quest for the truth, I suggest you take the woman you so clearly love out of the equation to take a long hard look at yourself to decide what it is that you re-ally want out of life. As it occurs to me that it is long past time you stopped caring about what the admiral wanted and chose your next adventure based on your own dreams, for a change."

*Chapter*
# THIRTY-FOUR

❧

*G*eorgie had known the first of August was going to be hard, so had filled her day by relieving both Lottie and Miss P of most of their lessons. At least teaching this afternoon's deportment class would take her mind off Harry and whatever trouble the navy was about to send him to. She knew that there was due to be a big fanfare on the Plymouth dockside when the *Boadicea* set sail on its maiden voyage, because the details had made it into the *London Tribune*. Hardly a surprise when King George IV himself was going to be there to wave the new flagship off as it led out the fleet.

Lottie had been a brick during Georgie's many hours of need this past month and, of course, so had Miss P. But she had spared her mentor all the most scandalous details of her short but eventful employment as the Pendleton children's governess. Only Lottie knew that she had fallen head over heels with the children's uncle and spent half a week in his bed. Miss P didn't need to know that—but having her friend's shoulder to cry on had meant the world.

As Lottie had never intended to go to heaven in a package marked UNOPENED either, she hadn't judged Georgie for succumbing at all, but still understood why she had left. Out of solidarity, she only ever referred to Harry as "that blithering idiot" whenever Georgie's cheery façade slipped, which it did every single evening after all the lessons were done and when it was just the pair of them alone in their bedchamber.

"If it was meant to be, he would have come and got you," her friend had wisely said last night when the tears of resignation had flowed. "That he hasn't means that it wasn't and you were brave and courageous to call it first."

Georgie did not feel particularly brave or courageous. She was too miserable and too heartbroken to feel particularly noble about her decision, and in her most desperate moments still wondered if she was actually the blithering idiot who should have asked him to stay.

She had always craved a family and at least with Harry, she might have had a home and children of her own to love within it, even if their love was doomed to fail once his resentment began to fester. In being noble, she was now doomed to be alone forever, and while she had long been at peace with that before he had upended her life, that acceptance did not come as easily now. She mourned her lonely destiny almost as much as she mourned the loss of him, and today most of all. Because the faint glimmer of hope that he would come after her, which her foolish heart had held for more than a month, had finally been extinguished.

Harry would set sail at two and that, according to the clock on the classroom wall, was in precisely five minutes.

As she clutched her mother's locket for comfort, one of the first-years interrupted her melancholy as she stared at the school's ethos on the blackboard. "Which of the Four *D*'s is the most important?"

"*Duty*," she answered straightaway, thinking of Harry. "*Dili-*

*gence, discretion,* and *decorum* mean nothing unless the stanch commitment of duty underpins them. Although, I suspect it is the one we shall always struggle with the most, as it is often the most difficult to define properly. Especially as there are so many conflicting permutations."

"How so?" The protégé-in-waiting was the most inquisitive and questioning in the class and therefore reminded Georgie of herself.

"Because as a governess, you have both a duty to your employer and to your charges. You also have a duty to make Miss P proud and still have a duty to yourself, which often . . ."

The sudden arrival of Miss P prevented her from waxing lyrical. "There is a family in my office in urgent need of a governess." The older woman grabbed Georgie's hand and practically dragged her out of the lesson she was teaching. "*Urgent. Need.*" Excitement danced in her wily blue eyes. "I've told them I have somebody they can interview straightaway!"

"What?" Georgie wasn't anywhere near ready to contemplate another family yet. In fact, if she had her way, she would stay here at the school, licking her gaping wounds forever. "Lottie needs a job too and I am sure that she will be better suited to—"

"No, no, no! This family is perfect for you, dear. I can sense it." Miss P tugged her into the hallway, then frowned as she began to fuss with Georgie's hair, which was doubtless doing its own thing wildly—as usual. "They aren't particularly traditional, and as you aren't either, I suspect you are a match made in heaven. Serendipity, Georgina! I can feel it in my bones."

As her beloved mentor had said the same thing the last time she had been in this position, the similarities made her uneasy. "But I'm no good at interviews. I'm certainly not prepared for an interview. I haven't planned a thing to say . . ."

"I know. Isn't that marvelous?" Miss P grabbed her hand again and dragged her toward her office, but stopped just shy. "In this case, I suspect it is most prudent to allow the master of the house to do most of the talking, so please try your very best and say yes rather than argue."

"Is this the part when you tell me that it is best I remain mute and allow you to talk for me?"

Smiling, Miss P straightened Georgie's locket. "Just be yourself, dear." Then she pushed her toward the door.

"Aren't you coming with me?"

"Absolutely not. There are too many people in my office already and that big dog has already flattened me once."

"Big dog?" That was when she saw a grinning Lottie loitering just around the corner.

"There is a little one too, now, who is clearly besotted with your *blithering idiot*. But as a very wise woman once said, animals are always the best gauge of a person's character, so I'm prepared to forgive your idiot if you are, seeing as he finally appears to have come to his senses. But make him suffer a bit first. He deserves that." Sensing Georgie's trepidation, her friend opened the door, and there he was.

Handsome as sin, neat as a pin with not a hair out of place, but standing as awkwardly as she had ever seen him with a cheerfully panting Cuthbert in his arms. "Hello, Georgie."

"Hello, Harry." Despite her suddenly wobbly legs, she managed to keep upright as Norbert tried to flatten her too. "And hello, Norbert and Felix. Marianne and Grace. Hello, Lady Flora." With her tummy doing somersaults, she bobbed a shaky curtsy that was instantly waved away by Harry's beaming elder sibling. "And hello, Cuthbert." She wiggled her fingers at the little dog and his dangling tail wagged back. "Shouldn't you be leading His Majesty's fleet into the Atlantic?"

Harry shrugged. "I couldn't—after Cuthbert shredded my best pair of dress breeches and the reserve pair exploded—I had nothing to wear. It is apparently bad form to salute the monarch naked from the waist down." His dark eyes danced with mischief and something else. Something vulnerable and hopeful and utterly disarming. "It was just as well, as I was too busy to spare them the time in the end." He flicked one of his pocket watches. Except, for once, there was only one pocket watch clipped to his waistcoat. "So the Royal Navy had to give somebody else the bloody *Boadicea*."

That didn't bode well. Or did it? She was currently so over-whelmed and confused but hopeful that she didn't know which way was up. "Busy doing what?"

"Firstly, having a long, hard look at myself." He shifted Cuthbert to free one hand, which he raked through his thick, dark hair. "My blasted sister's idea and a good one, because ... um ... I discovered, after some serious soul-searching, that the navy wasn't making me happy and hadn't been for years. So then I had to go through all the rigamarole of resigning my commission, which of course the top brass weren't particularly happy about."

Bizarrely, neither was she. "I hope you didn't resign your commission for me."

"Of course I didn't." He lifted the puppy. "I did it for Cuthbert. Dogs, it turns out, are a huge responsibility which you cannot ignore for days on end. It wouldn't have been fair to him to sail away. He would have pined for me."

His heated gaze locked with hers to let her know, in no uncertain terms, that he had pined for her. "And, I realized, that after years of living somebody else's dreams, it was long past time to find some of my own so I have other responsibilities now too. New ones. Exciting ones. An adventure that has nothing to do with the Royal Navy." His eyes shimmered with excitement as he smiled. "Do you remember that bankrupt ship we passed in the Sound? The *Siren*?"

"I do—but I didn't realize that she was called the *Siren*."

"Well, as it seemed prophetic, and because at ten pounds a tun and within only one trip laden with cargo I'd earn fifty times my annual navy salary, that was too *sound* an investment not to take a punt on. So I bought it."

"You are the *Siren*'s captain now instead?"

He shook his head. "No. That would be Simpkins, as somebody needs to procure all the cargo contracts, and who better than me? I don't like to brag, but after all my years at the Admiralty, I know practically every merchant in England. Besides, Simpkins has banned me from his vessel until I can learn how to stop interfering, so I've pretty much hung up my sea legs. I still have to teach young Felix here how to navigate a ship in preparation for his epic, single-handed, insect-collecting voyage across the seven seas, of course, but when I'm not doing that, I'll mostly be here. Back in London. So I was wondering . . . um . . ."

He edged toward her, still carrying his dog. "Well . . . two things, actually. The first was if you would like to accompany me and my blasted sister's mad brood to Gunther's this afternoon, and the second was if . . . um . . . you might be inclined to take a voyage down the aisle with me sometime?"

Tears pricked her eyes at that pretty proposal, but Lottie was right. He did deserve to suffer a little. "And why would I want to do that?"

"Because Gunther's makes the best ice cream, of course." He shuffled from foot to foot. "And because I am madly, utterly, and completely in love with you and I am really hoping that you might feel similarly afflicted. If you aren't—and heaven knows I'd completely understand if you weren't after my clumsy and unfair *ask me not to sail away* outburst—then I'm hoping you will at least have enough affection for young Cuthbert here to take a punt on a lifetime's adventure with us anyway." He reached out to caress her fingers. "Only he's missed you dreadfully and a growing lad needs two parents."

Little Grace suddenly thrust herself between them. "Can Marianne and I be bridesmaids?"

"You can be the bridesmaid," said Marianne, jabbing her sister. "I shall be the maid of honor and Felix can give Miss Rowe away."

"You can both be bridesmaids." Lottie stepped forward to tug the girls away. "Because I am the maid of honor."

"And I'll be giving her away!" That came from the already weeping Miss P.

"Then what am I supposed to do?" Felix, typically, was now outraged.

"I'll need a best man if Georgie says yes." Harry smiled at his nephew and then turned it hopefully to her. "Will you nail your colors to my mast, Georgie?"

She pretended to ponder it. "I suppose you are nine-tenths lovable, even if you are still resoundingly one-tenth insufferable."

"An improvement at least from the last time you took my measure. I'm an ambitious man, as you know, so it's good to have something to strive for. As Nelson famously once said, he who ceases to be better ceases to be good."

"I am pretty sure that was Oliver Cromwell." She was laughing as the happy tears finally escaped and breathless by the time he had tugged her into his arms because his gaze was so intense, even though his expression was playful. "But despite your insufferableness and your inability to quote any military leader correctly, my colors are yours to nail where you see fit."

"Was that a yes?" asked Felix, looking totally baffled.

"I still don't see why you get to be the maid of honor," said Marianne with a peeved glance at Lottie.

"Is it time for ice cream yet?" That came from Grace as her mother shepherded them all out of the door. "Only Uncle Harry promised it an hour ago, and I am starving."

But by then, Georgie wasn't really listening because Harry was kissing her and nothing else really mattered, and he was still kissing her when the door clicked closed. Reluctantly, she prized her lips from his to find Cuthbert staring up at them. "We should probably save our passions for later, as aside from this being grossly inappropriate when we are in Miss Prentice's school and all around us are impressionable young girls, we are being unfair to the children when you promised them ice cream."

"Not according to Sun Tzu." He tugged her back and did unspeakably wonderful things to her earlobe with just his teeth that completely overruled her concerns about propriety. "Who—and I know, my darling, you will immediately correct me if I am wrong— was adamant that all is fair in love and war."

## Acknowledgments

It goes without saying that I need to thank all the usual suspects who put up with me when I write a book. My long-suffering family, my supportive and irreverent friends, my lovely editor, and my brilliant agent. I thank them in every book, so they know who they all are and what they mean to me.

But this time, I also have to thank the National Maritime Museum in Greenwich, London, who proved to be an invaluable source of information about the Royal Navy back in 1820. It was through them that I accidentally discovered the existence of the HMS *Brittania*, a 120-gun first-rate ship of the line that was built in the Plymouth Dockyard and launched in September of 1820. That majestic vessel became the inspiration for the fictional HMS *Boadicea* in this story because I basically copied every mast and sail to ensure I got it all right. However, unlike my *Boadicea*, it should be noted that the *Brittania* was built with no problems at all by the Devonport shipwrights back then. It was neither delayed nor plagued with incompetence, but as neither of those things suited my purpose, that inconvenient truth had to go.

I'd also like to thank whichever genius turned the old naval warehouses in Royal William Yard, Plymouth, into luxury apartments but left all the cranes intact, because it allowed me to stay and get a feel for the place where the hero in this story sometimes worked.

And finally, I'd like to thank the lovely people from the picturesque coastal village of Cawsand for leaving it so gloriously untouched. You made it very easy to send my characters back in time to what it would have looked like in 1820. Every single detail I used, from your stunning natural harbor, to your ridiculously narrow and steep roads and your dearly departed Ship inn, were all real. I did, however, decide not to mention how intertwined the village was with fishing back when this book was set. I hope you understand that I needed a fresh, crisp, and romantic sea breeze at sunset for my hero and heroine to succumb beneath—not the unsexy stench left by the day's catch of pilchards!

## *About the Author*

Kat Moran Photography

When **Virginia Heath** was a little girl, it took her ages to fall asleep, so she made up stories in her head to help pass the time while she was staring at the ceiling. As she got older, the stories became more complicated, sometimes taking weeks to get to the happy ending. Then one day, she decided to embrace the insomnia and start writing them down. Now her Regency rom-coms (including the Wild Warriners and Merriwell Sisters series) are published in many languages across the globe. Thirty books and three Romantic Novel of the Year Award nominations later, it still takes her forever to fall asleep.